Praise for Tom Abrahams

"Abrahams has a writing style that is intense, engaging, and thorough down to the very last detail...a story that will kidnap your attention and torture you with suspense."

– The Kindle Book Review

"Tom Abrahams' writing is sharp like the crack of a rifle, clear like a trumpet's call, never more so than on the pages of his novel Allegiance, where the stakes are as big as Texas."

– Graham Brown, *New York Times* bestselling author of
The Eden Prophecy

"With echoes of heavyweights like John Grisham, Abrahams rolls out the plot with precision and attention to detail giving us believable characters unlike so many of the other post 9/11 cookie cutter thrillers that clog the genre."

– E-Thriller.com

"If you like Robert Ludlum, Vince Flynn, Brian Haig or any of the great political thriller authors, Tom Abrahams is an author you need to discover today."

– Rabid Readers Reviews

"In a rising sea of political conspiracy novels, Abrahams' *Sedition* stands out as one of best I've read in several years."

– Steven Konkoly, bestselling author of
The Perseid Collapse and *Black Flagged*

"Packed with detail and plot, Abrahams' Sedition reminded me of some of John Le Carre's work. Maybe *Russia House* or *Tinker, Tailor, Soldier, Spy*."

– international bestselling author Marc Cameron

OTHER WORKS BY TOM ABRAHAMS

Jackson Quick Adventures

Allegiance

Allegiance Burned

Matti Harrold Novels

Sedition

To get the latest news go to

TomAbrahamsBooks.Com

HIDDEN ALLEGIANCE

TOM ABRAHAMS

A POST HILL PRESS BOOK
ISBN (paperback): 978-1-61868-886-6
ISBN (eBook): 978-1-61868-887-3

HIDDEN ALLEGIANCE
A Jackson Quick Adventure Book Three
© 2016 by Tom Abrahams
All Rights Reserved
Cover Design by Ryan Truso

This book is a work of fiction. People, places, events, and situations are the product of the author's imagination. Any resemblance to actual persons, living or dead, or historical events, is purely coincidental.

Post Hill
PRESS

Post Hill Press
275 Madison Avenue, 14th Floor
New York, NY 10016
http://posthillpress.com

For Courtney, Samantha, & Luke

You do you. No **Ragrets**. *Not a single letter.*

PROLOGUE

"Deep into that darkness peering, long I stood there, wondering, fearing, doubting, dreaming dreams no mortal ever dreamed before."
—Edgar Allen Poe

The sand squeaked underneath Liho Blogis. The sun was barely a distorted reflection on the waves crashing against the coral outcrops dotting the inlet.

Blogis was aware of the noise and made efforts to tread lightly as he moved up the beach on Oahu's North Shore, hoping the crash of the waves was enough to mask his approach.

They would never hear him coming.

He thumbed the safety on his suppressed Makarov pistol. The so-called PM was Blogis's weapon of choice. He'd retrieved it from the cold, dead hand of a Soviet police officer in 1988 and it was as much a trophy as it was an effective bloodletter. At twenty-six ounces, it was heavy in his hand by modern standards, and Blogis thought its blowback design was more accurate than pistols using a recoiling or articulated barrel.

A man's gun.

He'd surveilled the house on the inlet for three weeks, acting as a surfer, a tourist, a bum. The plastic surgery he'd undergone after having the bullet removed from his body provided ample cover from his targets.

They would not recognize his new nose, enhanced cheeks, or his longer, blond hair.

The bungalow was fifty meters up a tangled hill, covered in palms and underbrush. There was a single window lit with a lamp on the second floor. It was a hallway outside of the bedroom. He knew the targets typically arose in forty-five minutes.

Blogis, a student of many disciplines, was an amateur somnologist. Knowing the human sleep cycle was a valuable tool in his arsenal of intelligence and violence.

He knew that roughly ninety minutes after the couple fell asleep, they'd enter REM, otherwise known as Stage Five. REM was dream sleep. If he timed it right, as he had so many times before on similar missions, he'd surprise the pair at their most vulnerable: during a long period of REM right before they awoke. With their voluntary muscles momentarily paralyzed, they'd be unable to quickly respond. By the time they knew what hit them, they'd be dead.

Blogis checked his watch before glancing over his shoulder. Nobody was on the beach, but there were the silhouetted bodies of a half dozen neoprene-suited surfers straddling their boards, bobbing rhythmically, awaiting a swell just beyond the mouth of the inlet.

There were so many parallels between surfing and his chosen line of work. Both required unique skills, unmitigated patience, the love of control, and the urge to bridle powers much greater than oneself. Both required a tradecraft that was counterculture, a subset of rules and laws which were grossly misunderstood by anyone beyond the boundaries.

Blogis crouched in the palms, his feet digging into the dirt under the weight of his body, and he momentarily lost himself in the surf, eyeing a lone warrior who braved a large wave gathering momentum behind him. The surfer popped from his chest to his feet, crouched, then slipped into the brief curl of the water as it broke against the coral.

The surfer crashed against the loss of the wave's energy, and Blogis refocused on the bungalow. He checked his watch again and inhaled deeply, ready to initiate the task, when he heard a man's voice behind him.

"Howzit?" The man was smiling. "I don't mean a bodda you, Brah." He was speaking Da Kine Pidgin, Hawaiian slang.

Blogis glanced back at the bungalow's lone lit window before spinning on the balls of his feet to face the interloper. He caught the surfer glimpse the Makarov and raised his finger to his pursed lips.

"You Cock-a-roach this hana?" the surfer whispered, a smile snaking across his face, revealing a toothy grin. His right shoulder bore a large, black patterned tattoo that stretched from his neck to his bicep, sloping across the top of his chest.

"Stealing?" Blogis tilted his head, keeping the Russian handgun at his side. For the moment. "You're wondering if I am here to break in and steal things?"

"Fo'real," the surfer nodded, the smile disappearing. "I got a mo bettah way to do it."

"Do you?" Blogis looked past the local at the longboard stuck into the sand halfway to the tideline on the shore.

The surfer nodded again and Blogis gestured him up the hill, toward the back door.

The young man, who Blogis estimated was no more than eighteen or nineteen years old, started toward the stranger. He'd climbed two or three steps when Blogis stopped him with a pair of suppressed slugs; one to the center of the boy's chest, the other in the space between his thick eyebrows. That shot thumped the smile from the surfer's face and he crumpled to the sandy dirt, landing partly on a clump of silvery Hinahina.

Blogis scanned the beach and the surf. Nobody was close enough to see anything, so he returned to the mission at hand and inched quietly up a short set of wooden steps to the rear door. It was a twelve-paneled door with a simple lock that Blogis handled with ease, and then he slipped inside, quietly pulling the door closed behind him.

He was in the kitchen. The smell of pineapples and soap filled his nostrils as he got a better sense of his surroundings. Across from him was a granite counter, and to his left a washing machine. He walked to the counter and saw a half-empty twenty ounce bottle of Dr. Pepper, and a pair of cellphones plugged into an outlet, both of them blinking to indicate they were fully charged. Next to the sink, on the other side of the counter against the wall, was a wire basket full of mangos. An uncut pineapple sat next to the basket. There was a juicer, taken apart with its plastic parts flipped upside down on a stack of paper towels.

They had tried to make this a home.

How naive.

Blogis moved to his right and around the floral-patterned loveseat that separated the kitchenette from the living area. An old steamer trunk served as a coffee table between the love seat and a wall-mounted flat panel television. A laptop sat open on the trunk, its dark screen in sleep mode. He walked past the television and into a narrow hallway. At the end of the hall was the door to the lone bedroom. He stepped quietly, Makarov primed, past the lit wall sconce to his left, a window at shoulder height to his right.

Nearing the bedroom door, he heard the soft rhythm of jazz, an alto saxophone chirping a riff against the backdrop of trombones, a double bass guitar, and drums. Blogis paused at the door, listening to the refrain before gripping the handle and turning it. His left shoulder pushed into the door and it opened into the room.

Underneath a thin yellow sheet was the shirtless man on his back, left arm hanging off of the full-sized bed. Draped across him was the woman, sleeping in shorts and a loose tank top. Her long, tanned leg was wrapped around his thighs, her right hand on his chest, her face nuzzled into his neck. Her dark hair covered her face, but he knew who she was.

He slid alongside the bed, leaning over her, placing the barrel of the Makarov in the small of her back as he whispered into her ear.

"Bella," he said, trailing the gun up her back and along her spine, "it's time to get reacquainted with your daddy."

Bella winced, her eyes still closed. But she didn't move. Neither did the man next to her, the one who'd saved her life too many times to count. Blogis had timed this perfectly.

He pushed the barrel into the back of her neck and pulled the trigger.

PART ONE
IN THE BLIND

"There are no secrets that time does not reveal"
—JEAN RACINE

CHAPTER 1

Her screams, followed by the gasps of hyperventilation, wake me for the third night in a row. Neither of us is sleeping. How could we?

I wrap my arms around Bella, trying to calm her.

"Him again?" I ask, already knowing the answer.

She nods through her sobs, her chest heaving as she struggles to catch her breath. "It's always the same," she says. "I mean, little details are different, but Blogis always finds us. He's one step ahead of us."

"It's okay," I assure her. "He can't find us here."

Her sobbing softens and her breathing slows, replaced by the crashing of the Pacific waves outside.

I flip on the camping light hanging from the center of our four-person tent, squinting against the instant LED brightness that envelops the space we've called home for two weeks.

"You don't know that, Jackson," she says, rubbing the light and tears from her eyes. "He found us in Hawaii. He can find us here."

"First of all," I remind her, "we were stupid to handle Hawaii the way we did. A bank account, a rental house, frequenting local restaurants. The North Shore is not secluded enough."

"And this is?" she asks, slipping out of her sleeping bag, pulling her knees up to her chest. "Northern California is secluded enough? We're driving distance from San Francisco, Jackson!"

"We talked about this, Bella," I put my hand on her foot, rubbing her toes with my thumb. "We're off the grid. We don't have a phone;

we hiked more than six miles to get here. This is backcountry camping. There's nobody within earshot of us. We haven't seen another human being in more than a week."

She looks at me, her eyes swollen. "So are we going to stay here forever? We can't do that Jackson."

"I know, Bella. We need time to disappear, figure our next move, and go on the offensive."

"You say that, but we haven't done anything since we've been here. We sleep, we hike, we eat, we…" Her cheeks redden at the thought of what else we do.

"*You're* on the offensive as far as that's concerned." I squeeze her foot, trying to lighten the mood.

She rolls her eyes. "Whatever. My point is —"

"I know your point. We need to refocus. Liho Blogis is looking for us. We should figure out a way to find him first." I check my watch. "The sun's about to come up. Let's go for a walk, get some air."

"You're always too calm about this stuff," she sighs. "I imagine your dreams are much sweeter than mine."

I smile but say nothing. She doesn't need to know about my dreams. There's no point in rehashing the recurring nightmare that was my childhood, no purpose in telling that on the rare occasion I don't dream about my parents' deaths, I dream of hers.

"C'mon, we need the exercise and the distraction. Let's hit the beach."

Bella pulls her hair back into a ponytail, flipping a hairband from her wrist onto the back of her head. She slides on a pair of worn hiking shoes. "I'm ready."

I unzip the vented flap that serves as an entrance to our home, inviting a cool breeze into the tent, and Bella crawls past me out onto the sand. I pop her on her behind and join her on the ankle-high grass outside of the tent. My knee aches as I stretch and stand upright. I can tell it's going to rain even before I look out at the ominous vista in front of us.

Wildcat Beach sits on the southern end of Point Reyes National Seashore. For twenty bucks cash a night, we've crashed here anonymously. Parked on a bluff between the ocean and the green Wildcat Lake, our spot has afforded us time to think, plan, and, for better or worse, dream.

"It's breezy today," she remarks. "The wind doesn't usually get like this until the afternoon." Her head's turned back toward me so I can hear her. She's wearing a gray fleece pullover and what are best described as black yoga pants.

"Wanna walk down to the beach?" I ask her, nodding toward the sheer cliffs to our right.

We spend the next ten minutes carefully crabbing our way down to the wet, thick-grained sand that forms a narrow pre-high tide strip between the cliffs' edges and the water. A trail of sea foam fights the wind, failing in its efforts to stick to the sand. A spray of chilled foam spatters our faces and we grab hands.

"I love you," she says, her eyes fixed in the distance ahead of us, as though she's looking for a place where we'll truly be safe from the chaos that's followed us since we met. There's no port, though. It's just an endless cascade of tan cliffs, brushed with shades of green.

"I love you too."

"You've never told me why you chose Quick as your last name," Bella says, swinging my hand in hers. "I mean, I know you wanted to distance yourself from your parents, but..."

"It wasn't really that so much," I explain. "During my brief foray into the television news business, a news director told me that 'Jackson Ellsworth' sounded too provincial. He told me to come up with a stage name and to do it quickly."

Bella laughs. "So you went with the most obvious choice available."

"That's why I'm with you," I tease, stopping beyond the surf's reach on sand that's wet enough to feel firm and pulling her into me. "You were the most obvious choice."

"Oh, Mister Ellsworth," she says, "that's not very provincial of you." She giggles and kisses me on the lips.

"What does that even mean?"

"I don't know," Bella shakes her head and buries her face in my chest. "It sounded good." She slips her hands under my arms and around my back and water rushes around us, soaking our feet. Neither of us move, content to hold each other.

"That's cold," she says. "And this is my last clean pair of socks."

"Just turn them inside out. That's what I do."

"Your socks are so disgusting they could stand up on their own."

"They're ankle armor."

"Quick," she says.

I laugh and gaze out past the surf, which is angrier than usual. Off the coast there's a thick blanket of swollen gray clouds.

"A storm is coming," I remark, noticing that the rising sun is still hidden behind the cliffs to the east. The spotlights of sunshine that had begun to dance on the Pacific have disappeared.

The wind dies for an instant and there's the distant high-pitched hum of an outboard motor. It's spinning and grinding intermittently against air and water as the boat dunks the propellers into the rolling waves before popping up to meet the next challenge in the cold surf.

Bella stops walking, her hand dropping from mine. "Do you hear that?" She snaps her head to the west, looking for the boat.

"I hear it." It's getting closer and we're about to have company.

***

There are only three ways to get to Wildcat Beach; hiking, biking, and by boat. And I'm not even sure that boating is technically allowed.

That's why, when we fled Hawaii, we chose this spot. It's secluded, hard to get to, and there's a nearby private airport in Santa Rosa.

We left Hawaii within a few hours of getting a phone call from Liho Blogis. We'd thought he was dead, that I'd killed him in Germany. He'd survived and, somehow, found us hiding from the world on the island of Oahu.

We couldn't afford to wait for him to come knocking on our door, so we left. A cab picked us up at the airport in Santa Rosa, dropped us off at the ranger station at the Bear Valley Visitor Center, and we'd disappeared. For weeks we'd avoided anyone's radar. And right now somebody with a boat was braving dangerous conditions to land at our campground.

"Do you have your gun or that pair of binoculars we bought?" Bella asks without taking her eyes off of the horizon.

"No," I admit. "They're in the tent." I'm slipping.

She turns to look at me, her eyes searching mine. "Should we go back?"

"It could be nothing," I say, though my gut tells me it's *not* nothing.

"Or it could be something. I don't think anyone typically comes here on a boat. We should go back."

"Can you tell which direction it's coming from?"

Bella shakes her head.

I start to walk farther south, toward Alamere Falls. The falls are maybe a mile from us, but the water pouring forty feet from the cliff into the ocean below is an easy landmark from this distance.

"What are you doing?" Bella grabs my hand. "We should turn back."

"I'm not ready to do that. If we hike back to the tent, we're sitting ducks if this turns out to be anything,"

Bella lets go of my hand and folds her arms across her chest. "I get it. But not too long. I'm not up for a sprint this morning."

"Deal," I wink at her and trek parallel to the waves ebbing with the low tide. I start jogging south toward the falls, Bella keeping pace to my left. The tide is pulling out, but the crash of the waves is intensifying, the interval between them shrinking.

"Do you see anything?" Bella asks.

"Not yet," I reply. "I'm not even sure we're headed the right direction."

"Wait!" Bella says. "Over there!" She points out into the surf. "I see them."

About two hundred yards off shore is a white boat, slipping along the waves toward the shore, the outboard engine spitting against the rise and fall of the water.

From our distance, it looks as though there are two people on board, a man and a woman. The man is at the helm.

"What are they doing?" Bella asks. She's standing beside me, her hands on her hips. "I mean, there's nowhere to dock the boat."

"They'd have to raise the engine before they get too close or they'll damage it." I look past the boat and check the gloomy horizon. "They're alone. I can't tell where they came from, though. And this weather—"

"It doesn't add up," Bella cuts in. "I say we head back. There's no telling who they are. They could be working for Blogis."

"Or Sir Spencer."

"Or Sir Spencer," she agrees.

"Now that we know what we're facing, we can go prepare."

"Or leave now."

"We could do that. Let's go."

Then we hear the thunderous crash of a large wave and loud mechanical whine, followed by a scream.

Beyond the break, where the boat rode the waves just a moment ago, is its hull. The boat is upside down.

Bella's eyes widen. "The boat flipped! They're in the water!"

I don't see either of the boat's occupants. I reach back to peel off my left shoe.

Bella looks at me as though I've grown a third eye. "What are you doing?"

"I'm going in." I flip off my right shoe and then slip my jacket off, tossing it onto the beach.

"Jackson, no," she pleads. "You don't know who they are. And the ocean—"

"You're right; I don't know who they are. But I can't let them drown. They could be unconscious."

"They could be here to kill us!"

"Maybe." I cup her face in my hands and kiss her on the forehead. "But I can't let them die because of what they *might* be here to do."

Her eyebrows are knitted together, her mouth curled into a pout. "Be careful," she says. "Don't die on me."

"I'll be right back," I tell her, take a deep breath, and trounce into the icy surf.

✳✳✳

My lungs burn with each gasp, the taste of salt heavy in my mouth. My neck is pulsing from a heartbeat that is clearly protesting my decision to dive into the sixty degree water. The choppy surf is forcing me to pull against the water two or three strokes just to maintain my momentum toward the boat.

I bury my head into the water, kicking my feet rapidly against the weight of my pants, fighting the volley of cresting waves that seem endless. I sense a brief lull in the onslaught and pull up to tread water. Maybe twenty yards from me is the hull of the boat. It has turned parallel to the shoreline, the words *Arima* and *Sea Chaser* upside down, but clearly visible. The outboard engine, its propeller in the air, has stopped.

"Hello!" I call out, cupping my hands around my mouth to amplify my voice above the din of the surf. My legs are churning under the water to keep my body afloat. "Is anyone there?"

Nothing.

I kick my legs behind me and dive back into the water, swimming quickly to the capsized boat. I try breathing to the side, but too much water gets into my mouth. I revert to popping my head forward so that I can breathe and keep my eyes on the boat.

My muscles are tightening from the lactic acid building inside of them and the cold of the water. Even if I find either of the boaters, I don't know if I'll have the strength to bring them back to shore.

I stop again and tread water fifteen feet or so from the boat, peering over the rise and fall of the hull until another wave crashes around me. I duck under the water as it whitecaps on top of me.

I pull myself above the water and call out again, "Hello? Are you okay?" My muscles are tightening. I don't see or hear anyone and I'm afraid to get too close to the boat. One rogue wave could knock it on top of me and that would be it.

I spin enough to look back to the shore. It takes me a few seconds to spot Bella. She's a good thirty or forty yards south of me. The rip current is strong, and because I've been focused on the boat, I didn't keep my bearing.

I start to turn back toward the boat for one last check when something grips my left ankle and yanks me under the water. I suck in a quick gulp of air as I slip under, a pair of hands now grabbing at my thighs and tugging on my pants.

The water is too turbulent for me to see anything, but the hands are strong and keep pulling. I manage to grab one of the wrists and yank it off of me as I kick away from what has to be one of the boaters. I pull myself back above the water long enough to choke down some air before another, weaker tug, pulls me under again.

This time, I immediately kick away, swimming backwards until I surface. I wipe the saltwater from my eyes and tread in the surf. I duck under the water, this time with my eyes open, looking for the boater.

About five feet in front of me, I can make out a dark shape thrashing near the surface. I dive down, underneath the boater, and kick myself to the surface behind him. I pop back to the surface to suck in another breath and then carefully swim up behind the boater.

I get within a couple of inches and reach out, across his shoulder, grabbing him like the shoulder harness of a seatbelt. Gripping him under his left armpit, I pull him back, kicking underneath his body to lay him prone on the water's surface. He stiffens, fighting against me.

"I've got you," I spit through the surf. "Calm down, I've got you!"

He stops flailing and relaxes. It's only then I realize it's not a him.

It's the woman.

"I'm gonna swim back to shore," I say between deep, heaving, salt-laden breaths. "Relax and kick your legs if you can."

She doesn't say anything, but I can feel her legs flapping against my hip.

From my position, I'm now swimming with the current, with the waves toward the shore. My body feels numb, like I've been playing in the snow for too long. My back is to the shore, my right arm draped across the woman's chest, my left arm is doing all of the work, with the help of a weak scissors kick. The boat is now mostly under water, still doing its dance with the waves and terrific current. I can smell the gasoline and oil that must be leaking into the ocean.

"We'll be okay. Stay with me. Stay awake if you can." Her chest is thumping against my forearm, her heart working overdrive. Her feet kick a little faster for a few seconds and then weaken again.

Another surge of water pushes us forward and it seems like we're past the worst of it, but then the current changes and I'm fighting against the water again.

It's low tide and the water's moving away from the shore, taking us with it.

I can't tell how close I am to hitting the beach, or at least shallow enough water to stand and drag in the boater. I try to look over my shoulder but can't see far enough behind me to gain perspective. Way off to my left are the falls, cascading into the ocean. Though I can tell I'm moving farther away from them with each kick, I can't get a sense of whether I'm making progress toward the beach.

"We're there." I'm trying to convince the woman as much as myself.

Spitting out a mouthful of her hair, I resume the push to shore. Maybe another two or three minutes of concentrated effort will get us there.

From behind me I catch a glimpse of Bella over my left shoulder. She's standing in the water, reaching for me. She tugs on my collar and pulls me toward her, and I let my feet slip to the sandy floor beneath us. Bella pulls me into her and falls back into the water.

"Are you okay?"

"I'm okay," I sigh, still holding onto the woman. "Help me with her, please."

Bella reaches around my body, and together we trudge to the beach on either side of the woman. When we reach the shore, the three of us collapse onto the wet sand.

I roll over onto my back, the sky above me black with clouds, and let myself sink into the sand. My arms and legs feel as though they've sunk beneath the surface. The sound of the waves crashing against each other fades behind the sound of my own heartbeat.

Thump. Thump. Thump.

CHAPTER 2

"I couldn't find him." The woman's hands are grabbing at the sand, squeezing it through her fingers. "He hit his head, I think. I tried to find him."

The three of us are sitting at the spot where the cliffs meet the beach. Too tired to climb up to the relative warmth of our camp, we've spent thirty minutes shivering, trying to muster strength and learn more about who this woman is.

"We rented the boat in Bolinas at the marina. But we weren't experienced. We had trouble with the current."

"We need to get you warm now," Bella says. "All three of us should get back to the camp. I have some extra clothes for you. We can restart the fire."

"It looks like rain," I chatter through my teeth. "We should hurry."

Bella and I help the woman to her feet, and over the next half hour we wage a battle against our stiffening limbs and the steep climb back to the camp. We make it, barely, and Bella helps the woman into the tent. I wait outside, parking myself on the wooden picnic table at the edge of the camping spot.

Looking over the bluff and out onto the Pacific, I consider what I just did.

After everything I've endured over the last two years, after everyone I've killed and maimed in the name of self-preservation, I could have died trying to save the life of a stranger.

A stranger who could be here to kill me.

I shake off the thought that the woman is a threat, fruitlessly searching the waves for any sign of her companion. Another chill runs through my body and I shake involuntarily against the sea breeze.

Bella peeks her head out from the tent. "We're good. You can come in and change. I'll start the fire."

I shake my head and push myself up from the picnic table. "Sorry. I should've gotten it going."

She steps out and toward me, extending her arms and grabbing me into an embrace. "It's okay, not a big deal."

"I'm still kinda wet," I protest, my arms at my side. "You'll get —"

"I don't care," she cuts in, burying her face into my jacket. "You scared the hell out of me, Jackson."

"I'm sorry." I close my arms around her back. "I couldn't let them die, Bella. I felt like…"

"I get it," she says, looking up at me, her eyes warm and full of forgiveness. "I understand. Still…"

"I know."

"You need to get changed," she says, pulling away from me and patting my chest with her palms. "We need to figure out what we're going to do about that sunken boat and missing boater. It's not like I'm comfortable running up to the ranger station and calling all kinds of attention to ourselves. You diving in to save them really put us in a spot."

"I know."

"Did she say anything else in there?" I nod toward the tent.

Bella shakes her head. "No. I didn't want to press. She just said they were out for a joy ride, underestimated the weather, and lost a handle on things."

I step toward the tent. "Is she gonna come out here so that I can change?"

"Yes," Bella smirks. "I told her that she could stay in there until you went inside. It's a little bit warmer in there than out here."

"Then I'll help you with the fire," I tell her, and join her next to the stack of sticks and kindling we've been burning for the last few days.

I grab a handle of sticks from our dry stack and Bella strikes a match, kneels down, and touches the flame to the kindling. It smokes at first and then gradually catches.

***

"I should have thanked you earlier," the woman says. "I'm embarrassed. I mean, you saved my life. You tried to save…" she stops, her quivering lips pressed together.

"It's okay…" Bella inches closer to her and wraps an arm around her. "No thanks needed."

We're sitting around the fire, having eaten tomato soup warmed on the worn charcoal grill cemented into the ground next to the picnic table. We've been heating our food with Sterno cups, as opposed to charcoal. Sterno is a lot easier to cram into a backpack. We've got three left.

"I've been so rude. I haven't even introduced myself," the woman sniffles. "I'm Cydney…with a 'C'."

Bella offers her hand and the woman shakes it. "I'm Bella. This is Jackson."

I wave across the top of the flames. The woman waves back. "Thank you, Jackson," Cydney says. "My boyfriend, Cliff, he would have thanked you too."

I nod and shift uncomfortably on the ground. "You're welcome."

She presses her fingers against her temples. "I don't know what to do. I mean, I haven't been thinking clearly. Should I call the authorities or the Coast Guard or someone? I mean, somebody has to look for

Cliff." Her eyes search mine for the answer before turning to Bella. "Somebody has to pull that boat out of the ocean, right?"

A cold drop of rain hits my face, followed by another.

"We don't have a phone," Bella says calmly, placing a hand on Cydney's knee. "It's a six mile hike back to the ranger station. I don't think we're up to that at the moment. Get some sleep. Then we can lead you to the station."

Cydney shakes her head, turning to look at me again, hoping, maybe, that I'll side with her. "A map we had on the boat showed a Coast Guard station just south of here. Could we alert them somehow?"

"I agree with Bella," I say. "It's only eight o'clock in the morning. The visitor's center won't be open for a couple of hours. The Coast Guard won't put up a chopper in this kind of weather, and their boats won't find anything until the surf calms. Let's wait out the rain until ten o'clock. You can rest in there. I'll keep watch on the shore."

Cydney looks back at Bella and nods dejectedly. She gets up without saying anything further and slinks back to the tent, unzips the opening, and disappears inside.

"That was weird," I mumble.

"She's in shock, Jackson," Bella says. "That's not weird."

"No. It's weird that she gave up so easily. I figured that we'd have to restrain her from going for help once she warmed up and got some food. I mean, she seems nonchalant about Cliff being dead, doesn't she?"

"I dunno," Bella shrugs. "People react to trauma in different ways."

"I guess."

The rain is beating against the fire, trying to put out the struggling flames. The sky flickers for an instant and in the distance, the rumble of thunder rolls off the clouds and over the ocean. We clean up the cans of soup and the disposable bowls, and toss them into sealed trash containers. I take an unopened can of soup and put it back into the campsite's food storage locker. Bella puts out the Sterno with a cupful of water, leaving it on the grill to cool. It's an unspoken post-meal routine we've developed during our time here. We're a good team.

Her hair is still in a ponytail, though some of the strands have loosened and are wet against her cheeks. "What next?" she asks.

"What do you mean?"

She takes a step toward me and lowers her voice. "You think we're okay for a couple of hours? I mean, we really *should* be reporting what happened."

"You're right. I did create a real problem for us. We have to take her to the visitor's center. That compromises our anonymity. We were gonna leave here anyway, right? This just makes our decision for us."

"Right," she agrees. "Do you buy her story?"

"You don't?" I ask. "You're the one who thought I was being too cynical."

"You just got me thinking," she whispers. "That's all."

"I'm gonna grab my poncho and binoculars from the tent and then sit on the bluff and watch the waves. It won't be long and the tide will start pushing stuff back in to the shore."

"By *stuff* you mean Cliff?" she whispers, glancing at the tent.

I shrug. "Cliff, parts of the boat, whatever they had on board. In two hours, we'll pack up everything and start the hike. It'll take until close to noon, regardless of the weather."

Bella unzips the tent and I follow her inside, closing the flap behind me. Cydney is asleep on top of my sleeping bag. I'm crouched like a baseball catcher with little room to move.

"She's out fast," I say and Bella raises a finger to her lips, quieting me.

Four person tents are really intended for two people, or two adults and a couple of Hobbits. I couldn't imagine four grown adults in this thing.

I get onto all fours and reach across Cydney to grab my pack. I lift it, one armed, over her, yank it open, and pull out a desert camouflage colored rubberized roll that opens into a lightweight poncho. I dig deeper into the pack and find my compact binoculars. And from an inside zipper compartment, I grip a Smith & Wesson Governor. The six-shot pistol is loaded with my favorite ammunition, shotshell.

Even though I'm a natural-born deadeye with just about any weapon, the Governor is easy to hide, easy enough to carry, and powerful enough to stop someone at close distance. With the shotshell, I don't even have to be accurate. It sprays like a shotgun blast and does a lot of damage.

Bella's back is to me while she rifles through her pack. She turns and I motion to the tent's exit and blow her a kiss. She returns the favor and goes back to digging through her bag.

I'm not looking forward to sitting in the rain. I've done this to myself, so I accept it as penance.

***

The rain is light now, though still relentless. Near the horizon, there's a break in the thick blanket of clouds mirroring the rolling gray surf.

I'm perched on the edge of the bluff, about thirty yards from the tent. It's been an hour, and I've seen nothing. I have to keep blinking myself out of a trance, watching one swell after another build, crest, foam, and leach onto the wet sand.

My attention shifts to the clouds above me, drifting quickly onshore and overhead. They're thinning, stretching apart like oddly shaped balls of cotton.

Then, at the edge of the beach, still under the shallow surf, I see it. Something dark. A bag maybe, or a pouch.

It's definitely from Cydney's boat. I hop to my feet and start back to the tent. The rain's become more an annoying mist now, and I trudge through the grass and unzip the tent's flap to stick my head inside.

Cydney's still asleep, Bella's lying on her side, her back to me. I crawl into the tent and put my hand on Bella's thigh.

She gasps, grabs my hand and whips her head around, eyes wide, until she sees that it's me. "You scared me."

"Sorry," I say softly. "There's something on the beach. I'm going down to get it. You okay?"

She glances over at our guest and nods. She rolls over to face me, now laying on her other side. "What is it?"

"What's what?"

"On the beach," she rolls her eyes. "What is it on the beach?"

"I don't know. It's something black. Maybe a bag or something."

"Okay. Hurry back." She puckers her lips to feign a kiss and then closes her eyes again, laying her head on her extended arm.

I slip back out of the tent, careful to zip it up as quietly as possible. As much as I would have liked to curl up next to her and attempt sleep, there's debris to examine.

I trek through the grass, a thin spray of water exploding onto my shins from the tall wet blades. Past the grass, there's a muddy trail, which I cross until finding the narrow path down the edge of the cliff. Careful not to slip on the wet outcropping of rocks and compacted dirt, I descend slowly. About five feet from the beach, I jump down, landing in a crouch and balancing myself with the tips of my fingers.

The pistol is tucked in my waistband at the small of my back and I adjust it carefully. My eyes water against the stiff breeze carrying in the tide ashore. The surf has calmed infinitesimally since my rescue mission. It's still angry, though not as violent as it was ahead of the rain. There's a black object peeking out from under a thin line of foam floating on the surface of the water.

A few feet from it, I can tell it is a waterproof pouch. It's no more than four inches by six, and has a brass eyelet at one end with a long black cord looped through it. I kneel down and pick up the pouch. Opposite the cord, at the top of the bag, is a flap with a Ziploc type closure and a pair of white snaps. Holding the pouch, I turn back to look toward our camp. I can't see the tent from here. I shake the bag in my hand.

Open it!

I take a breath through my nose, inhaling the salty air, tasting it in the back of my throat, and pull back the snaps one at a time. I dig my fingernails in between the self-closing ridges of the Ziploc seal and pop it open. There are a couple of flat objects inside.

Reaching in with my thumb and forefinger, I pull out a laminated map. It's more of an index card with a black and white map of Point Reyes National Park. And on it there are some highlighted numbers. On the back of the laminated card is a key. The numbers correspond to campsites throughout the park.

Hadn't Cydney said they weren't planning on coming this far south in the boat?

I reach into the bag of tricks again and pull out a piece of folded paper. I open it up and read a series of handwritten numbers and letters.

N128XZ.

I stare at the numbers, as though I'll suddenly have an epiphany.

N128XZ. N128XZ. What do they...

I look back into the pouch and don't see anything, so I start my walk back to the camp.

Those numbers and letters were familiar.

The rain has stopped, and now the wind is carrying with it a damp chill. The sky above me is clearing. The sun will be out soon. I place my hand on a large rock embedded in the cliff about five feet above the beach and set my left foot into a comfortable notch from which to propel myself upward onto the tricky path when it hits me.

I know those numbers!

A wave of nausea runs through my body, pooling in my gut, and I back off the cliff.

I look into the pouch again, digging with my fingers, my hands shaking when I find one more item stuck to the inside of the bag. I pull a color photograph of two people stepping off of an airplane.

It's taken from a distance with a long-range lens but the image is unmistakable. At the bottom left corner is a date.

Two weeks ago!

On the tail of the jet is its FAA registration number.

N128XZ.

At the bottom of the steps is a tall woman with a dark complexion, dark hair pulled into a ponytail. She's shielding her face from the sun with her hand. Behind her on the steps, a large pack on his shoulders and another in his hands, is a man I recognize every time I look in the mirror.

***

The climb up the cliff is more difficult with a pistol in my right hand. I'm halfway up when someone screams.

My left foot slips against a wet rock and my body slides down a couple of feet. With my left hand, I dig into the dirt face of the cliff, catching my fingers against thick tufts of grass. Regaining my leverage, and assuring myself that I've got a good grip on the Smith & Wesson, my foot finds a spot and I'm back on track. Muscling my way step by step, I feel like I'm in a dream where I can't run fast enough, like I'm climbing in mud.

Another scream.

My hand grips the top of the cliff and I step onto the bluff. Ahead of me is the tent, which is moving like a bag of microwave popcorn. With the wind at my back, I can't hear the struggle going on inside.

"Bella!" I call out, darting to the tent, gun drawn. I'm just ten yards away. "Bella! Get out of the—"

Pop! Pop! Two gunshots and the tent grows still.

Ten feet from the tent I stop running. Frozen, I strain against the wind, listening for movement inside of the tent.

Nothing.

Resisting the urge to unzip the flap and risk getting shot, I level the gun at the tent and move around it to the left. Quietly, trying to control my breathing and prevent my heart from beating through my chest, I circle to the backside of the tent.

There's a mesh window on the tent opposite the flap. I step to the window to catch a glimpse of the interior. No dice. The window is closed, the tent fabric draped over the mesh.

Gun still in hand, I lower myself to the ground. Prone, I lie still, listening.

There's a rustling inside. A moan. I can't tell if it's Bella or Cydney.

I hop to my feet and back away from the tent, moving farther away from the cliff, and wrap both hands around the pistol. Exhaling, I brace myself.

"Bella!" I call out. "Are you okay?"

Silence.

I sidestep to my right and call again.

"Bella!"

"Jackson?" Her voice is weak, but I can hear it. "Jackson?"

I move quickly to the flap at the front of the tent and unzip it. On my knees, I pull back the flap and poke the gun through the opening.

The inside looks like a bear attacked. Our gear is strewn everywhere. Bella is on her back to the left of the tent. Her top is ripped; her hands are covering her face. Next to her, on the tent floor is her nine millimeter and a MAG flashlight. Its bright LED beam is aimed a couple of feet from her, toward the back of the tent where, crumpled on a bloody sleeping bag, is Cydney's lifeless body. I climb into the tent and slide next to Bella.

"Are you okay?" I lean down next to her, my mouth at her ear. "What happened?"

"She hit me with something," Bella splutters. "On my head. I don't know."

"Where on your head?" I gently pull her hands from her face and gently search for a wound.

"The back," she says. "Or the top." She looks at me for an instant and then squeezes her eyes shut. "I didn't know what had happened at first—I thought—maybe the tent collapsed. But then—she was on top of me. She hit my face."

I notice the swelling redness on Bella's left cheek and my hand finds the lump on the back of her head. My hand comes away clean. No blood.

"She was like an animal or something." Bella's eyes are closed, her speech slurred, disjointed. "She was. I just... I had my gun. Got it from my bag earlier." Her eyes open, tears pooling until they run out the sides, down her temples. "I killed her, didn't I?"

"You didn't have a choice, Bella."

She presses her eyes closed, the stream of tears widening for an instant.

I look past her to the body and the bag. Cydney's legs are pale, the bottoms of her feet calloused and dirty from the climb up the cliff.

I saved her and nearly cost Bella her life.

"I was sleeping," Bella whimpers. "Well, not really sleeping. But I was still out of it, in that nap twilight, you know? And out of nowhere, something slams into my head. My teeth kinda ground against each other. For a second, it felt like my jaw was broken even though she hit me on the back of my head.

"My vision was blurry and I rolled over, expecting to see the tent collapsing, and she's on top of me. Her eyes were crazy wild. She hit me again with the flashlight and punched me. She was like a monkey, flailing at me." Bella winces and swallows hard.

"You want some water?"

She shakes her head.

"Then you shot her?"

"Yes," she says. "I mean, no. I was dazed, and couldn't really process anything. She stopped for a second and that gave me time to remember my gun was right here."

"Why'd she stop?" I look back at Cydney's dirty feet.

"She mentioned the governor."

"What?" My attention whips back to Bella. "What do you mean? She stopped attacking you to talk?"

"Just for a second," Bella says. "She said something like, 'The governor says hello!' or 'The governor says hi!' or 'This is hello from the governor.' Then she reached back with that flashlight, ready to swing down again and I shot her. Twice."

My mind is swimming.

The governor. He got to me. Again. It doesn't matter where I go or how I hide. He wants me dead.

***

"We're going to be a target," Bella says, hiking a step ahead of me, her pack bouncing on her back. She turns her head halfway, her profile marred by the swelling on her cheek beneath her eye.

"What's new?" I huff. I'm slugging my pack, thumbs tucked under the shoulder straps.

"This is different," she says, slowing a step. "We left a dead body in a tent at a national park campsite. Our fingerprints are all over the place. It won't be long before somebody finds her, checks security cameras at the ranger station, and puts our pictures all over the place."

"We've been there before, Bella," I remind her. "Well," I correct myself, "*I've* been there before. I've been okay so far."

"Oh, right," she scoffs, "this is okay. We're running from place to place with no sense of normalcy. We're leaving a trail of death in our wake. I can't live like this."

"How's your head?" I ask, redirecting the conversation.

"It hurts."

"I bet."

"What are we going to do, Jackson?" She blows out a puff of air as we tread along a slight incline on the path back to civilization. "You always have a plan, right?"

"I have a plan."

"Care to share it with me?" She stops and turns to face me.

"You're frustrated right now," I observe. "You're in pain and you just killed someone with a nine millimeter at point blank range. Now is not the best time to discuss any plans."

"Really?" She snorts in disbelief, striding again to keep up with me. "*Really*, Jackson?" Maybe more irritation than disbelief.

"You're not going to like the plan." I tighten my grip around the shoulder straps and tug down, adjusting the pack on my sweat-soaked t-shirt. I check the GPS. We've got three miles to go.

"Try me."

"We need to meet with Blogis." I brace myself for her response but there's only the rhythmic crunch of our feet on the path. Maybe thirty seconds pass before Bella responds.

"Okay," she says.

I spin around, walking slowly backwards, and face her. The look on my face must convey my surprise.

She shrugs. "What? I get it."

"You do?"

"We have no other options," she says.

"How do you figure?"

"It's your plan," she laughs. "You tell me."

"We have the resources to disappear again, right? But we'd just find ourselves in a violent mess… again."

"Granted," she agrees.

"We need someone with more than just financial resources to help us," I continue, stepping over a large root snaking a bulge across the path and grabbing Bella's hand to help her across. "Blogis fits the bill."

"So does Sir Spencer. And *he* doesn't want us dead."

"True. But what good does it do us to seek the help of someone who won't kill us? We need the help of someone who would lessen the number of threats against us. You know, the enemy of my enemy…"

"… is my friend," she says. "I know."

"That leaves two choices. The governor and Liho Blogis."

"That makes the choice easy," she chuckles.

"It does. And if we can find something that Blogis wants from us, other than our lives, we can trade it for our safety."

"Didn't you try that before?"

"How do you mean?"

"You made a deal with Sir Spencer to gain your 'freedom,' so to speak," she says. "That didn't really work out for you. I mean, you met me," she looks back with a smirk. "But finding the neutrino process didn't buy you anything other than more trouble."

"You're right," I admit. "And I don't expect this to buy me a life either."

"Then why do it?" she asks, stopping to pull a stainless water bottle from the mesh pouch on the side of her pack. "If you don't think Blogis will help then what's the point?" She pries open the top of the bottle with her teeth and slurps a mouthful of water.

"He'll help."

She wipes her mouth with the back of her arm. "You're speaking in Jackson code."

"Blogis wants what Sir Spencer has. If we convince him that we can get it for him, that'll buy us some time, maybe give us some leverage."

"So what did you mean when you said it wouldn't get us our lives back?"

"That's not what I said. I said I didn't expect it to buy my life back. The point of this is to get you back into the real world. As much as I love you, I can't drag you down with me." I step toward her, lowering my voice. "This is my life now. It's been my life for two years. My past, what I did before I met you, got you killed today."

"But it didn't," she reasons. "And I —"

"Wait," I interrupt her. "You can disappear into Europe somewhere or maybe into South America. I'll always be hunted. First it was the governor, then it was Blogis. Who's next? Before long I'll have an army chasing me."

"That's ridiculo—"

"I seem to attract enemies like a cow does flies. We're going to find Blogis. We're going to help him. We're going to hurt Sir Spencer. And then you are starting over. The plan is to pay for your freedom with mine."

CHAPTER 3

"I don't like being back here," Bella says, shaking her head at the billboards and car dealerships rushing past our speeding car like an assembly line of commercial blight. "It's too risky."

"It's a necessary risk. We need his help to get to Blogis."

"I know, Jackson. You explained that on the plane. I just don't know why this can't be done long distance."

"I explained that too. He needs to feel our fear. I need him to think he's been dropped right into the middle of this. I meet him face to face and that works. A phone call or an email doesn't cut it."

"He'll only blab to Sir Spencer."

"I don't care if he does. In fact, it may be helpful if Sir Spencer thinks he knows what we're up to."

"Maybe," she sighs.

"Trust me on this, Bella. I know what I'm doing."

"I *do* trust you, Jackson." She turns back to the window. "I always do." Though she doesn't sound convinced, even her tacit complicity will do until I prove to her this will work.

Houston was my home for a short time years ago. I remembered it gleaming, a city with a half dozen skylines and infinite promise. One of those towers houses Nanergetix, the techno-energy company founded by Bella's late father and led by her until we had to jump headfirst off of the grid.

Bella cranes her neck to look at the glass and steel of her former home. There's a sadness glistening in her eyes that she can't hide. She folds her arms and presses them against her chest.

Home is no longer home for her either.

The car slows and the driver takes the exit, merging into the traffic that's building at a traffic light a hundred yards ahead.

"Sorry about the delay," he says, gesturing at the parade of brake lights ahead of us. "Can't help Houston traffic."

"No problem," I say. "We get there when we get there."

"How far is it from here?" Bella asks.

"We'll take a left," I reply. "Then a few blocks to the right."

"He's going to be surprised, isn't he?"

I chuckle. "Yeah. He won't be expecting me. In fact, the last time we talked, I gave him the distinct impression he'd never hear from me again. Not after what he did."

✳✳✳

The KCLA television studios were headquartered in an area known as The Montrose. It's as close to an Austin vibe as Houston gets: a vibrant neighborhood offering a mix of tattoo parlors, secondhand shops, and international cuisine. A lot of the older, larger homes double as offices for architects and lawyers.

"No need to wait for us," I tell the driver. "Could you just pop the trunk please so we can grab our bags?"

"Sure thing," he says. "Sure you don't need any help?"

"We're good," I hand him a hundred dollar bill. "That cover it?"

"You need change?" he asks, his eyes wide at the possibility of a large tip.

"Keep it."

I'm already out of the car when he thanks me. Bella and I meet at the trunk, each of us grabbing our large backpacks.

"You want me to get yours?" I ask, reaching for her bag.

She smiles. "That's sweet. I got it. You have more than enough heavy lifting to do." She slings the heavy bag onto her shoulder and leads me to the front of the building, leaving me to wonder if that was a back handed compliment or not a compliment at all.

The large glass frontage was etched with the News 4 logo, a modern looking number four connected to a circle surrounding it. I pull open the brushed chrome handle and follow Bella into the large, mid-century modern lobby.

With its high ceiling and stained concrete flooring, the lobby has a *Mad Men* feel to it. I half expect to see Don Draper traipse through, cigarette dripping from his lips, his pencil-skirted secretary swooning by his side with a legal pad.

Instead, it's a uniformed security guard sitting behind the wood veneer desk, a ledger and a newspaper in front of him, a bank of flat panel monitors and a phone to his side.

"May I help you?" he asks flatly, then curls his nose to sniff loudly.

I smile as broadly as my cheeks allow. "Yes. I'm here to see George Townsend."

"Is he expecting you?" He glances down at what I assume is a phone extension list and runs his fingers down to T.

"No, but he knows me."

"Does he?" The guard glances up with doubt and without moving his finger from the directory. "And how does he know you?" His eyes narrow. He glances at Bella and back at me.

"I've done some work with him in past."

"What's your name, sir?"

"Spencer Thomas."

"And your name, ma'am?"

"Bella Quick," she says, slipping her fingers through mine.

The guard, whose brass nameplate affixed to his white uniform shirt reads HARNAGE, pushes a button on the phone without taking his eyes off of me, and then pulls the receiver to cradle it between his ear and neck. He punches another series of numbers and offers a wet sniff.

"Allergies?" I ask. "I never had them until I moved to Houston."

Harnage nods and sniffs again. "Ragweed," he says. "Gets me every time. That and the oak pollen."

"The oak pollen is the worst." I don't have allergies, but everyone else in Houston does or claims to suffer from them. It's like a badge of honor or something. Asking someone about their allergies in Houston is akin to talking about the Yankees in New York City or the surf on the North Shore.

"Tell me about it," Harnage says, rolling his eyes. "It's always—" he holds up a finger with one hand and pulls the receiver to his mouth with the other. "Mr. Townsend, you have two guests in the lobby. A Mr. Spencer Thomas and a Ms. Bella Quick. Do you know them?"

George's muffled voice responds with what I imagine is a mix of recognition, confusion, and fear. Harnage nods a couple of times and then hangs up.

"He's on his way to greet you," Harnage says and clears his throat of the ragweed.

Behind us a door swings open and into the lobby walks investigative reporter George Townsend. His ashen complexion finds another shade of pallid when he realizes it's me and not Sir Spencer awaiting him.

I turn to offer my hand. "Hello, George. That was fast. Good to see you buddy."

He takes my hand with a limp grip and stammers to say hello. Bella stands next to me and crosses her arms in front of her. She's not playing the game with him.

"Jackson," he whispers, "what are you…"

"I need your help, George. And seeing as how you owe me one…"

He nods vacantly and then steps back toward the door leading from the lobby to the rest of the building. "Let's talk in the conference room," he says. "Better than out here."

Bella and I grab our bags and start to follow him into the bowels of the station. He stops and looks past us to talk to Harnage.

"Mike," he says to the guard, "I'll have them with me. They're good to go."

"Thanks, Mr. Townsend," Harnage says and pushes a button under his desk to release the lock on the door.

"This way." George holds the door for us and I notice sweat beading on his forehead when we walk past him.

***

The newsroom is a hive of activity at four-thirty in the afternoon. Bathed in the unforgiving light of overhead halogens, the cavernous space is honeycombed with a couple dozen cubicles to one side. On the other end of the newsroom is what resembles the bridge of the Starship *Enterprise*. There are six or seven wide desks, each adorned with triplets of computer monitors. The worker bees, wearing headphones, clack away at their keyboards, producing content for the two hours of news KCLA is in the midst of producing.

"The reporters' desks are over there," George points to the honeycomb. Most of the desks are empty, aside from the occasional potted pothos plant or regional Emmy statue.

"And over here," he references the command center as we walk past it, "is where all of the producers and writers sit. They edit the video at their computer terminals. That's why they have the three monitors. One is for script writing, a second for web browsing, and a third for video viewing and editing."

"It's changed since I was in the business," I mumble.

"It's still changing," George laments. "Every day it's more and more about digital content and satisfying the growing mobile audience."

"Where's the assignment desk?" I ask as we shuffle out of the newsroom and into a narrow hallway lined with a pair of doors on either side.

"We don't have one," he says, shouldering open one of the doors to the right. He walks in and a motion sensitive light flickers to life. "The producers and associate producers answer the phones. The assignment manager handles dispatch and fields story pitches from the producer pods. Interns also field calls."

"Interns?" asks Bella.

We find ourselves in a comfortable room furnished with Kandinsky imitations on the wall and a large, round wooden table. Around the table are a dozen high-backed, chrome and cream-colored leather chairs.

"They're paid," says George, offering us seats. "It's a competitive process. They're smart kids who are stupid enough to want to get into local television. I have one who works for my investigative team. She's helpful." George pulls out a chair and then sits down, leaning back and taking a deep breath.

"So how have you been, George?" Bella starts, despite never having met the intrepid reporter.

"Bella *Quick*?" he responds without answering the question. "I guess best wishes are in order. Where are you registered?" His hands are clasped, resting on his belly. His 120 thread-count shirt is straining against the expanse, revealing the exact spot of his naval. He's gained a few since I saw him last. I'm not judging him. It's merely an observation.

"That's sweet," Bella says, "but we're just trying on the name for size. Nothing official yet."

"Okay then. What do you want?" George turns to me. "Why are you here? And why did you say you were Sir Spencer?"

"I wanted to see the look on your face, first of all. Secondly, I don't go around using my real name much anymore. And third, I'm here because, as I said in the lobby, I need your help."

"Because I owe you," he says.

"Yep," Bella says.

"All right," he says, rocking back and forth in the chair, studying both of us. "I'll bite. How may I be of service?"

In an instant, he has morphed from nervous to overly confident. His attitude is surprising to me. Even though I'm visiting him out of the blue, zapping the blood from his brain and the feeling from his toes, he shouldn't be mad at me.

He's the one who betrayed *me*. After I gave him the goods to help put a governor in prison, and went to him seeking information about Liho Blogis, he turns around and pitches a tent with Sir Spencer.

"Don't have an attitude with us," Bella says. "When Jackson reached out to you for your expertise, you turned around and gave everything to Sir Spencer." She leans in to the desk. "Do you know how many times we almost died because of him?"

George stops rocking, aware of the sudden chill in the room. "Look, I'm sorry, okay? But you gotta look at it from my standpoint."

"What standpoint is that?" Bella asks, in boardroom mode now.

"I knew that you employed Jackson to look for some formula—"

"A process," she cuts in.

"Process…formula…" he waves his hands to shake her off, "whatever. What I knew was that Jackson was flying around the world to help you find something having to do with solar neutrinos. He needed information about neutrinos, he needed information about Liho Blogis, and, come to think of it, he wanted information about you too." His eyes dart from Bella's to mine. There's a sudden glint of satisfaction in his eyes, like a kid who blurts out an admission of guilt to an angry parent while simultaneously implicating an older, unsuspecting sibling.

Uh oh.

Without missing a beat, Bella shoots back, "Like I don't know that. What are you, a narc now?"

"No. I—I just—" George stammers.

"Just what? Thought you could deflect? This is about *you*, George, and what *you* did. Not about Jackson. Not about me. Get to the stuff that matters."

George shrinks into his seat, the leather squeaking against his back, his spare tire deflating. "I knew that Jackson was on a scavenger hunt. Your people were working on some fantastic use for solar neutrinos. The ingredients went missing. You wanted him to help find them. Sir Spencer was in the mix too, somehow. Jackson wanted to know what the neutrinos might be used for."

"And what did you tell him?" Bella's interrogating him like I'm not even in the room. "What did you learn about solar neutrinos, George?"

"I knew they were so-called 'ghost particles,'" he says. "They were a product of nuclear fusion and billions of them pass through the Earth every second."

"That estimate is low," Bella corrects.

"Whatever. They're tiny and they're nuclear, and they're invisible."

"What else?" Bella prods.

"There's research going on all over the planet. There was your place in South Dakota, Illinois, Canada, India, Switzerland…"

"And?"

"From what I could tell, there are a couple of possible applications for these things," George says. "The most obvious is using them for underwater communication. The other has to do with nuclear fission, maybe the detection of nuclear facilities." He leans forward on the conference table, planting his elbows shoulder-width apart.

"That it?" Bella raises a dubious eyebrow.

George shrugs. "Yeah."

Bella drops her hands onto the table, rubbing her palms back and forth on the shellacked wood, "What did Sir Spencer tell you about them?"

"What do you mean?" George's brow furrows with apparent confusion.

"You did your cursory research on neutrinos," she explains. "You told Jackson what you knew. But then Sir Spencer got involved."

"Well," George's eyes roll with his recall, "that's not really what happened."

Bella sits silently, awaiting the rest of George's confession.

"Jackson here," he nods at me with his chin, "told me that Nanergetix had come up with a way to detect nuclear reactors. He told me the pieces to that process were missing. He promised me additional details and confirmation from you, Bella Quick, if I helped him gain intelligence on Liho Blogis."

"That's not—" I try to interrupt to protect myself from this blindsiding.

"That's exactly what happened Jackson," he says. "I've got notes."

"Ohhhh," Bella mocks. "You've got notes." She waves her fingers above her head as though she's frightened by the prospect of notes.

"I do," George sits up straight in his leather seat. "And I gave him the info on Blogis."

"Where did you get that information?" I ask, knowing the answer already.

"Sir Spencer."

"Why did you go to him?" Bella asks.

"I wanted the story," George shrugs, eyeing Bella as if she's asked the most idiotic question in the history of idiotic questions. "I knew Sir Spencer had far reaching hands. And, actually, I didn't go to him. He came to me."

"If I recall," I interject, "all of the information you gave me came from Sir Spencer. No sooner Bella and I were on the run and he was on the phone with you."

His silence is agreement.

"So," I look over at Bella while talking to George, "we need you to flip the script this time."

"What do you mean?" He shakes his head.

"He made you promises about network jobs, right?" I ask.

George nods, his eyes at the floor now.

"They didn't happen, right?" I ask the second most idiotic question ever.

"No."

"So he owes you," I reason.

"Riiight," George laughs. "Sir Spencer owes nobody. You know that more than anybody."

"Reach out to him," I instruct. "Get him interested in what we're doing. Tell him we came to see you today, that you can help him again if he follows through on his unfulfilled promise. Then get back to me at the number on this card and tell me what how he reacts." I slide a business card across the table. It's blank except for the burner number scribbled in black ink.

George says exactly what I knew he would say. "What's in it for me?"

"A story," Bella says. "The whole story. When this is over, and it will be with your help, you'll get everything you didn't get after Germany happened."

George slides the card off the edge of the table to grip it. He flips it over and looks at the number. He purses his lips in contemplation, feigning true consideration of his options.

"Okay," he pretends to relent. "I'm in."

I knew he would be.

CHAPTER 4

"You never mentioned your lack of trust in me," Bella says mildly, sipping from a grande Americano from one of three Starbucks on the corner of South Shepherd Drive and West Gray Street.

Really. There are *three* of the ubiquitous coffee shops on one corner. Two of them are freestanding and one is inside a Barnes and Noble. How many coffee sirens does one corner need? The irony that Bella and I are perilously stuck between our own Scylla and Charybdis is not lost on me.

We're sitting in the back corner, both of us with our backs to the wall. We've gotten into the unfortunate habit of not letting down our collective guard, except with each other.

"It wasn't that…" I hedge before she grabs my hand.

"C'mon, Jackson," she interrupts. "Don't be coy. It's okay. I'm not upset."

"I'm not being coy. It's just that when I was unsure of you and what your endgame was, I wasn't going to tell you that I was suspicious."

"I get that."

"By the time we connected, by the time I trusted you, I didn't think it necessary to tell you of my earlier doubts."

"I get that, too." She brings her cup to her lips, sipping from the small opening on the plastic lid. "I just wondered about it. It seems like a million years ago, like a different lifetime."

"It *was* a different life. I feel like I've lived eight lives already."

"Why eight?" she asks, tilting her head.

"Because cats only get nine," I say. The burner cell vibrates against the small stainless table holding our coffee. We both look at the phone before I pick it up.

"George?"

"Not quite, Jackson," the familiar British voice intones.

"Sir Spencer," I reply without hinting at my surprise. Bella, however, almost spits out her coffee and suppresses a cough to keep it down. I hand her a napkin.

"How's your chest?" he asks, referring to gunshots wounds I sustained in Germany. I touch the larger of two scars just below my collarbone. Two centimeters to the right and I'd have bled out through the hole now covered in shiny, numb skin.

"Better, thank you."

I didn't foresee this. Every time I think I'm a step ahead, I find I'm actually behind. Not being a spy, not having had years of training in the tradecraft, I make a lot of mistakes. I assume too much. One of these days, I'll use that ninth life and take Bella down with me. However, I can't let her, or the pompous ass on the other end of the line, know what I'm thinking. I nod reassuringly to Bella, praying that she can't read my mind.

"I understand you're looking for me," Sir Spencer says.

"Yes. Where are you?"

"I'm in our nation's capital. There's never a shortage of business here. Ever been to the Hay Adams? Wonderful views of Lafayette Park and The White House."

"No. I've never been."

"So then," he says, "how may I be of service to you and young Bella Francesca?"

"Actually, I can be of service to you."

"You *are* impressive." In the background, I hear the ubiquitous sound of ice clinking against the side of a crystal tumbler. "You never cease to amaze me with your resourcefulness, your zest for life, and your inability to mince words."

"I'm flattered."

"What makes you think that you have anything I need?"

"I just do."

"Suppose that is the case," he allows. "Why do you want all of the pieces together again?"

"I just do."

"Come on now, Jackson," Sir Spencer chides. "Give a little, get a little."

Bella's trying to read my face, hoping to figure out where I'm headed with this, if I really know what I'm doing. I don't want to disappoint her. So I dive in, headfirst.

"I want to sell you the neutrino process."

Now he's the one sitting in stunned silence.

Bella mouths, "What are you doing?" I hold up my hand, pretending I'm in control.

"I was warned long ago to beware the beast Man, for he is the Devil's pawn," I say, quoting from one of my favorite films. I imagine it's lost on Sir Spencer. "Blogis wants me dead. So does the governor. I could barely handle one person trying to kill me. Now I've got two."

"At least," he mutters.

"I want my freedom. You promised it to me if I could get all of the pieces of the process together."

"And…?"

"And nothing," I snap. "I get you the process and you get me a new life."

"I'm not sure I follow your logic, Cornelius," he lectures with a keen reference to *Planet of the Apes*. Apparently he did get my reference. "You don't trust me. I've proven to be beyond a worthy adversary and more than a turncoat of a partner. I'd say you've gone bananas, to play out our cinematic metaphor."

"A deal is a deal," I shrug. "I didn't deliver the process as promised, so you had no obligation to grant me my walking papers. I don't blame you. You've got buyers. I know you do. Syria is a mess, Gaza is about to implode, Eastern Ukraine is a war zone. Between Israel's nukes, those in Russia, and ISIS's desire to destroy the western world, you might have a bidding war on your hands."

Sir Spencer gulps down a swig of whatever expensive scotch he's poured and exhales.

"Speaking of apes and their evolution," he opines, "Charles Darwin once said, *'It is not the strongest or the most intelligent who will survive but those who can best manage change.'*"

"He also said, *'A man who dares waste one hour of time has not discovered the value of life.'* So get on with it."

"Touché. How do you suggest we go about getting the process put back together?"

"Liho Blogis."

"Come again?"

"I want you to help me find Liho Blogis. He knows where the pieces are. I beat him once. I can beat him again."

"I'm not sure I agree with—"

"Find him," I snap. "And don't call me again. I'll call you." Click.

***

George probably didn't expect to see us standing in the lobby of his television station for the second time in a few hours. He was already disavowing knowledge of my phone conversation with Sir Spencer before either Bella or I had said a word, waving us off like we'd missed a field goal.

"Don't even!" Bella interrupts. She is getting good at playing the bad cop with George. "Are you *that* thick?"

"What do you mean?" George asks with feigned ignorance. Despite his seven regional Emmy wins, he is not a good actor. He checks his watch, on which I notice is a pricy Tag Heuer Link.

"Let's not talk here," I suggest. "Where's your car, George?"

"I…uh…I…"

"C'mon, George," I say just above a whisper. "Let's take a ride."

He nods at us and then trudges like an angry child to the front doors of the building. Bella and I exchange glances and follow him into the parking lot, where we find him aiming a remote at a silver Mercedes sedan.

"What happened to the Lexus SUV?"

"We crashed it, remember?"

"Oh, I blocked it out," I say. I'd momentarily forgotten that the day we met, just after I'd told him I was mixed up in some sort of political conspiracy at the prompting of my boss at the time, the Governor of Texas, and we'd been chased and t-boned by some contracted information extractors.

For most people, a violent collision with people trying to kill you would stick. It'd be at the most accessible part of the cortex, screaming to be recalled above birthdays and first dates, weddings and vacations. Not me.

For me it's among the first of a non-stop string of near-death experiences shaping my life over the course of the last couple of years. I've seen my life flash before me so many times that it doesn't even feel like my life anymore. It's the past of someone distant, a stranger, who maybe enjoyed Sundays falling asleep on the sofa listening to Jim Nantz call the Masters, or sitting poolside while flipping the pages of a great political thriller. That person could sling back a beer and jump in the mosh pit at a Linkin Park concert.

Not me. Not anymore.

I open the front passenger door for Bella, close it behind her, and hop into the back seat.

"The car still smells new," I say, whiffing that intoxicating odor everyone loves. I smell it for what it is, the off-gassing of the volatile organic compounds in the plastic and laminated foam in the cabin of his luxury German car.

"It *is* new," George glances in the rear view mirror. "When Sir Spencer's promises didn't come through, I signed a new contract here in Houston."

"Must be a nice new contract." Bella runs her hand along the dash like a model from *The Price Is Right*. She *so* doesn't like him.

"Good enough," he says, moving the car into traffic and shifting the subject. "You haven't said where we're going."

"Let's go to your place." I pat his shoulder and sit back against the black leather, sinking into it.

He flips a turn signal and slides into the right lane, just ahead of an older model Mazda. I'd expected him to protest, but maybe he knows better.

"Why did you give Sir Spencer our phone number?" Bella asks. "Why didn't you just do what Jackson asked you to do?"

"It's not that simple."

"Why is that?" Bella presses, turning her body toward George.

"It's just..." he glances at me in the rearview, tightens his grip on the steering wheel, and exhales. "I mean..."

"What's your relationship with Sir Spencer?" I ask.

George's eyebrows press together. He accelerates past a landscaping truck and trailer to our left, cranks the air conditioning a notch.

"I don't follow what you're saying, Jackson." He shakes his head. "What are you accusing me of?" He slows the car to a stop at the intersection of Allen Parkway and Shepherd. He's about to make a right into River Oaks, some of the highest priced real estate in the city.

"I'm not accusing you of anything. I'm saying that you claim Sir Spencer didn't help you out with a network job, despite his promise to do so. But the first thing you do after we visit and ask for your help is call him? I don't follow that."

George makes the right turn into River Oaks, where Allen Parkway turns into Kirby Drive. The thick umbrella of oaks that lines the streets delivers a permanent shade to the street and its wide, root-mangled sidewalks. The mansions that line Kirby to either side are at once gothic and modern. They sit majestically behind high iron fences and meticulously trimmed hedges, the numbered addresses boasted in etched granite or polished brass plates at the curbs.

This is oil money.

No matter how many times I've driven past them, it's hard not to stare and wonder what it would be like to live in one of them. They're like the distraction of a lottery ticket before the numbers are pulled.

This time, however, it's not the houses that catch my attention. It's the Mazda that was behind us when we left the television station. It too makes the turn on Kirby. It's two cars back and I'm pretty certain the driver is following us.

Bella squeezes my knee, bringing me back to the conversation inside the car. "Jackson, George was talking to you. What's wrong?"

"We're being followed. That Mazda a couple of cars back. I'm pretty sure he's a tail. Turn up here to the right, George."

"Why do you th—"

"Please!" I snap. "Just turn."

George brakes hard and takes the right, a little too quickly, burning some of the rubber off his expensive low profile tires. He winces with the squeal of it.

After another quick left, the road makes a slow looping curve to the left, back toward Kirby Drive. George slows at the intersection.

"Wait," I whisper.

"Why are you whispering?" Bella whispers louder.

"I don't know. Seems like I should."

She manages a smile in the midst of what is likely another pain of a situation for us. I love her.

"Should I go now?" George asks, his hand on the rearview mirror.

"Just another few seconds," I say. "Bella, check your side view."

"Nothing," she reports.

"All right," I nod. "George, go ahead. Guess I was just being paranoi—"

"Wait!" Bella says. "I see the Mazda."

"Holy crap!" George takes his hand off of the mirror and returns it to the wheel, where he rubs it back and forth as though he's trying to rev the throttle. "You were right."

"Go ahead and turn," I tell him and pull Bella's nine millimeter from the small of my back.

"Whoa!" George exclaims. "We're not about to open fire in River Oaks, are we?" He eases the car onto Kirby and accelerates into the traffic.

"You've got my gun?" Bella asks, wide-eyed. "What happened to yours?"

"What are you two?" George says. "Bonnie and Clyde?"

"Bonnie and Clyde were wanted by the FBI," Bella says. I shoot her a look that questions her reasoning. "Okay, bad example. Other than that and the guns, though, the comparison isn't fair, George."

"Other than that," I add, "the guns, that we both met in Texas, that we've killed, stolen, and kidnap—"

"Who'd we kidnap?" Bella snaps.

"Me," George raises his hand while checking the rearview.

"All right," she concedes. "Call me Bonnie."

"How can you be so nonchalant about this?" George revs the wheel again. I've forgotten how high-strung he can be.

"It's a coping mechanism, George." I check the back window; the Mazda is three cars behind us, one lane over.

"Whatever. What do you want me to do? Do you think it's the Pickle People?"

"I don't know." I try to get a better look at the driver. The "Pickle People" were contract workers for F. Pickle Security Consultants, a large private holding company providing off-the-books help to a variety of corporations and individuals. Based out of Dallas, it employs a large number of former CIA operatives. It makes the group of spooks who worked at Enron in the late 1990s look like Keystone Cops.

The governor has sent out teams of them, one after another, since my cooperation with authorities and George's reporting put him behind bars. I'm ninety-nine percent certain that the "boaters" Cydney and Cliff were FPSC.

They're almost always in teams of two, which is why the Mazda has me confused. I spot a driver and nobody else. Then, as traffic slows ahead of us and the Mazda rolls within twenty feet of us, I know who's tailing us.

"On second thought, George," I say, "I'm pretty sure this isn't Pickle."

"Why do you say that?" Bella asks.

"The driver's alone. Find the next side street and then park."

"Why?" George asks.

"I know who he is."

***

The last time I saw Mack Mahoney, he tried to kill me. We were in an empty medieval castle in Heidelberg, Germany. I'd just destroyed what I figured was Sir Spencer's chance at owning the complete process by which, for the first time since Leo Szilard conceived of the atomic bomb, someone could secretly destroy a nuclear arsenal.

"The Process," as we called it, was a heretofore previously unattainable recipe for firing beams of solar neutrinos at a nuclear weapon, rendering it inert. The beam could be fired from anywhere, through the Earth, and, in the wrong hands, could be a real problem.

The final parts were on a hard drive. I'd shot a hole through it. Mack got angry and put a hole through me. Sir Spencer returned the favor, for some reason, and nearly killed Mack. Both of us survived. And here we are again. Face to face.

"Losing a step, Mack?" I glance down at his prosthetic leg, aware of my discourtesy as he walks toward me. He's parked parallel to the curb behind George's Mercedes. I'm leaning against the rear of the car, the nine millimeter returned to the small of my back.

"Amputee joke, Jackson?" He stops a step short of normal conversational distance.

I purse my lips and shake my head. "Not at all. A commentary on your tailing technique."

"I wanted you to spot me," he says, licking his lips. They're devoid of color, a reminder of the slow spread of his vitiligo, a virus that robs his skin of its pigment in random patches.

"You succeeded."

"Hmmmph," he grunts. He's thinner than I remember him. His shoulders are still as broad, his forearms as thick with muscle, though he's lost some of his girth. His neck is thinner and bears the scar of a tracheotomy tube. His hair is close cropped, in keeping with his military training.

Mack glances past me and into the car. I sense Bella looking at us from behind the rear windshield. I didn't want her confronting him until I knew we'd be okay. She'd known him most of her life and there was too much emotion there.

"I'm surprised you stopped," he says. "I tried to kill you once already."

"There are security cameras everywhere," I say, without glancing at the three elevated cameras within immediate sight of our curbside location. Rich people like cameras.

"Video doesn't keep me from killing you," he says. "Security is the illusion of safety, Jackson. You know this as well as anyone."

"I also know that if you wanted me dead, you wouldn't be following me so as to be seen, right?"

He takes a step forward, offering his meat hook of a hand. I take it, firmly shake it, and look into his eyes. Both of us grip past the point of comfort.

"What *do* you want?" I ask him, still squeezing his hand, locked on his eyes. There's something missing in them, like they're dimmer than before.

"I want to help you," he says with a hint of a smile, releasing my hand.

"Help me what?"

"Get your life back."

A zillion questions zap through my mind, nearly every single one of them ending with, "Why?"

"I owe you."

My eyes still locked onto his, I rap on the trunk with my knuckles and Bella opens the front passenger door. Mack double blinks at the sight of her, his shoulders hunching forward.

"Hello, Bella."

"Mack." No hint of emotion. She's hiding it well as she slides next to me at the back of the car. George is still in the driver's seat, his hands gripped on the wheel.

"Mack was just telling me that he wants to help me get my life back," I say.

Bella looks at Mack and takes a deep breath but doesn't say anything.

Mack extends his arms toward us. "I owe Jackson. I owe you both, really. I know the last time we saw each other it didn't go well. I accused you of some things that were unfair. I was... lashing out."

Bella laughs humorlessly.

"My wife is dead, Bella," his admission stops her laughter, but doesn't elicit sympathy. "It wasn't the cancer. Her kidneys failed. All of that chemo… Anyhow," he sighs. "I was recovering and she was slipping away. It happened fast. There was no time for a donor. I wasn't a match. Even if I had been, I wasn't in any condition to give it to her.

"I told her what I'd done. I told her that I'd betrayed you, Bella. That after all of my years of service to your father, all that your family had done for us, that I'd blamed you for not doing more. I let that anger cloud my judgment. I'd allowed myself to be manipulated by Sir Spencer. She told me I was wrong. I *was* wrong."

Bella reaches for my hand, lacing her fingers between mine.

"I just…" Mack's pale lips quiver and he struggles to control them, "I promised her I would make it right."

"I don't buy it," Bella says flatly. "It's too much, Mack."

"It's a little convenient," I say. "I mean, you tried to kill me. You likened Bella to Judas, and then—"

"I know. I know. What I did was—"

"Unforgivable," Bella states.

Mack looks down at his feet and mumbles something unintelligible.

"What?" Bella snaps.

"I knew it was a fool's errand," he says louder than necessary. "I told my wife that. But she made me promise, so…" He waves his hands as if to shoo himself away and walks back to his Mazda. I almost feel sad for him.

Mack yanks open the door, slips into the driver's seat, struggling for a second to pull his leg into the cabin, and pulls the door shut behind him. He's working hard not to look at us, fumbling to get his keys in the ignition.

"How?" I call out, loud enough for him to hear me through the windshield.

He jerks his head and stares at us, measuring whether or not to answer.

I walk to the driver's side. "How?"

He lowers the window. "How what?"

"How did you plan to give me back my life?" I glance back at Bella, whose arms are folded across her chest in defiance.

"I know people, Jackson," he says earnestly. "They know people who know things."

"Stop speaking in riddles, Mack," I say. "I don't have the time or inclination—"

"Your parents were murdered," he blurts. "I mean, their deaths weren't accidental."

I've always known who was to blame for my parents' death. Me. If I hadn't taken a gun to school, they'd be alive. If I hadn't gotten caught with it, they'd have seen me graduate from high school.

If the vice principal and a couple of cops hadn't summoned them to campus, I'd never have bounced from place to place. I'd have had a lifelong home, without a doubt.

This is my truth.

CHAPTER 5

My parents were buried in a small plot near our home. I remember it in a way most adults remember their favorite Christmas morning as a child. It lives just beneath the surface, bits and pieces unexpectedly poking through.

The smell of wet, fresh cut grass is a memento of the wrinkled man on the riding lawn mower rumbling through his morning duties at the cemetery as we arrived in our limo. The sound of gravel crunching under rubber tires is a souvenir of the wheels of the first of two hearses kicking up dust ahead of us in the procession.

The cold of granite countertops, a token of my parents' headstones, carved to remind me of what I'd done and the date I did it.

I didn't cry at their funeral. I couldn't. Even when adults I barely knew squeezed my shoulders and told me that I'd be okay, or the pastor, who didn't know us at all, promised me I'd see them again in Heaven, my eyes were dry. It was too easy to swallow past the lump that never grew in my throat.

I was in shock, coping with a loss I was too young to fully understand. What I knew was that I was responsible and that I'd probably spend the rest of my life paying penance.

Both my maternal and paternal grandparents were dead and so was my mother's divorced sister. Social services sent me to live with a foster family for a couple of weeks until my cousin, my dead aunt's daughter, could drop her life for a few days and pick me up.

She'd missed the funeral, and missed most of my life. Looking back, I don't blame her. She was a young professional who didn't ask to raise an orphan. She was always kind to me, but never engaged or interested.

She had access to a small portion of the trust my parents left for me, which was enough to clothe and feed me. It wasn't enough, however, to send me to a private school, and so I was essentially remanded to an alternative school.

For two full years there, I learned the real definition of bullying. I also learned how to defend myself, how to fight like a frightened animal. I survived, but got angrier, and took it out on my cousin. I holed up in my room binge watching television before Netflix made it popular, ingesting a steady diet of music. I was non-communicative, except when I was a smart ass. She finally had enough.

With help from the alternative school, she talked a small prep school in Chatham, Virginia into taking me as a charity case. They gave me a scholarship, despite my poor academic record, and I moved. I never saw my cousin again, but I owe her for getting me into the boarding school. It changed my life.

Part of the deal was that I had to maintain a C average in my classes and be involved in extracurricular activities.

Running was always an escape for me, so I joined the cross-country team. I guess, figuratively, I'd always been running from something.

I kept my grades up, knowing this was a chance at something approaching normalcy I wouldn't get again, and did pretty well. My roommate wouldn't necessarily have agreed.

He transferred to another dorm after close to a year of coping with my violent nightmares. I slept through them. He didn't, and complained I would cry out loud and mumble odd things about my parents. He thought I was crazy.

I roomed alone for the rest of my time there. My friends were television and music. I could escape inside of them, live vicariously through the creativity of others. It was as healthy a way as I knew to cope.

It worked well enough that I got accepted into my father's alma mater, the only school to which I applied. I moved to Raleigh and a single dorm at North Carolina State University. The red-bricked urban campus wasn't as idyllic as the colleges I'd seen in the movies, but I liked it.

Every once in a while, I'd drive to a nearby gun range in Holly Springs to watch the rifle team practice. My dad had been on the team when he was there. The pops of the .177 air rifles somehow made me feel closer to him. I never picked up a gun, though. It felt like it would be a betrayal or something. Shooting was for my dad and me. It was our connection. I was good at something he loved.

I was a natural.

Funny how life happens.

Fast-forward a handful of years, a couple of conspiracies, and I don't go a day without making sure there's a round in the chamber.

Wouldn't my parents be so proud?

***

Mack's hotel room is next to the Southwest Freeway near Kirby Drive. His second-floor room overlooks the southbound lanes. I stand with my nose pressed against the glass, the cars streaming past the fog on the window. A faint whoosh of sound vibrates the cheap pane when a pair of eighteen-wheelers rumbles by.

Bella's in a chair in the corner of the room between a pull-chain floor lamp and the full-sized bed. One leg is crossed over the other, her foot bouncing up and down impatiently.

"I don't really get this, Jackson. We don't need Mack."

Mack is getting ice from the machine at the end of the hall. He's thirsty, and the warm bottled Ozarka waters on the nightstand wouldn't do without ice.

"I know we don't *need* him. But if he has information about my parents' deaths and how they relate to anything that's going on right now…" Three more semis barrel down highway 59 and the window rumbles against my forehead.

"How so?" Bella asks. "Jackson, look at me."

I push myself away from the glass and turn around. She's worried about me. I can see it in the bounce of her foot and the furrow in her forehead.

"It doesn't matter," I say. "I mean, the connection is thin, right? Even if we don't need him, we can *use* Mack." I glance over my shoulder at the door, step closer to Bella, and lower my voice. "We don't have a lot of people on our side," I remind her. "It's you and me."

"And George," she adds.

"Kinda. He's no more or less trustworthy than Mack."

"George didn't try to kill you."

"True. But we're dealing with a lot of gray here. There's really no black or white. No good guys, no bad guys. Just us and them, and a couple of people who might be a means to an end."

There's an electronic beep at the door, a click, and Mack shoulders his way into the room. "George still in the car?" he asks, toting the ice bucket to the desk next to the flat screen television on the far side of the room.

"Yeah," I reply. "He had a phone call to make."

"To whom?" Mack asks, dipping his fingers into the bucket and clawing out a couple of cubes.

"I don't know. Doesn't matter right now."

"Doesn't it?" Mack drops the cubes into a plastic cup and reaches for a bottle of water.

"You're not one to question anything right now, Mack," Bella interjects. "Just get to your point. We have more important things to do."

"Blogis and Sir Spencer go way back," he starts, pouring some of the water over the ice.

"We know this," Bella snaps, her glare darting between Mack and me. "You could have told us this on the street. You didn't need to drag us back to your hotel room."

"What you may not know is that they go way back with your family, Jackson." Ignoring Bella, Mack points the cup toward me before taking a swig.

"I know my dad worked with them. I have flashes of memories where one or both of them would come to our house. I'd blocked a lot of it out, but—"

"Not your father."

"What?"

"Your mother."

"What about her?"

"She was the connection to Sir Spencer and Blogis." Mack shrugs, as if this life-altering information is nothing more than an aside.

"I don't understand."

"Your mother was an asset of Sir Spencer's," he says. "She recruited your dad while they were in college."

"That makes no sense," I tell him, my brain scanning for refuting evidence. "She was a stay-at-home mom. She... my dad... How do you know this?"

"My job is information," he says flatly. "I'm good at my job."

I say nothing, waiting for more as he slurps down the crushed ice before he offers another piece of *information*.

"Your father was a crack shot, right? He was a marksman. Sir Spencer needed a marksman. Your mother put the two of them together."

"Let's say I believe this..." My hands are trembling; my chest is tight. "What does this have to do with their deaths?"

"They were leaving the operation," he explains. "Your mother, in some trite Hollywood-esque fashion, actually fell in love with your dad. They *both* loved *you*. They wanted out."

"So?"

"So," he swirls the empty plastic cup so that the lone ice cube spins around the bottom, "Sir Spencer didn't *want* them out. It was too risky to his operation."

"He killed them?" My hands are balled into fists, my teeth clenched. Everything I've known, the black and white, has smudged into an indigestible gray.

I thought I knew my parents' relationship with each other, with me. Now Mack is telling me it's wrong. I was wrong about them. I was wrong about...

Am I wrong about everything?

Mack pops open a small briefcase sitting next to the television. He pulls out a small object, tossing it to me. I catch it against my chest, almost dropping it. It's a thumb drive.

"The rest is there. It's from Sir Spencer's system."

"You got this from his computer?" Bella asks.

"From the cloud," Mack says. "Everything these days is in the cloud. People are so stupid about the stuff they put on there, thinking it's safe. Search hard enough in the cloud, and you'll find who shot Kennedy, where Jimmy Hoffa is buried, and why that Malaysian pilot downed his own airplane in the Pacific."

"You're not going to tell me?" I ask. Part of me wants to plug in the drive and devour the information. Part of me wants to throw it back at him and deny every last bit of what he's telling me.

Ignorance is bliss. Or in my case, it's the less mind-cranking of the two options.

"I did. You don't need me to spell it out. It's on the drive."

"So how does this help us get our lives back?" Bella asks.

"Really, Bella?" Mack laughs. "I know you're smarter than that."

"He's telling us that we *can't* get our lives back unless we end Sir Spencer's," I say.

***

I'm Dorothy in Oz, in search of some elusive wizard at the end of a yellow brick road. Along the way, picking up tagalongs offering help for their own selfish reasons.

George is the lion; he's got no courage. Mack is the Tin Man, in search of his heart. Sir Spencer is maybe the wizard. He's a faceless charlatan who hides behind his deception to maintain the illusion of power and influence.

I guess Bella is actually Dorothy. She's the one who deserves to go home, who spun into this world without realizing what was happening to her. Plus, she looks better in a blue-and-white gingham frock and red heels.

That makes me Toto: allegiant to Dorothy, wary of strangers, barking danger along the way. It'd be nice if she could click her heels and we'd be safely home.

Instead, we've trekked from Mack's hotel room to George's four-story town home off of Kirby Drive. These mid-rise stucco buildings, where four sit on the land formerly occupied by one, have become a developer's panacea inside Houston's crowded inner loop. They're not cheap, judging by the high six figure FOR SALE flyer on the front stoop of the home next to George's. I know television reporters, especially good ones, in a market the size of Houston are well compensated. Even with the diminution of technology and the ever-present journalists who report, carry a camera, and edit their own material, the top dogs make good money. They don't, however, make costly timepiece, high-end SUV, and super-expensive home types of cash.

George pushes the buttons on a keypad by his garage door, opening it electronically. It rises, revealing an empty space, save a Thule bike rack, a Cannondale racing bicycle, and a set of Ping golf clubs in a large personalized bag emblazoned KING GEORGE.

His Highness slips a key into a deadbolt above the handle on the door into the first floor of his home and invites us to follow him. He doesn't close the garage door behind us, but instead bounds up a set of stairs to the second level.

It opens into a wide expanse of a stereotypical bachelor's home. The walls are a shade darker than white, adorned with oversized Leroy Neiman prints.

I recognize one as Nolan Ryan in an Astros uniform, another as Earl Campbell wearing the burnt orange of the University of Texas Longhorns, and a third as Roger Staubach, star emblazoned on a silver helmet, dropping back to pass. Each is encased in matching thick, high-gloss black frames.

The wide-plank, light pine floors are bare, except for a black leather sectional in the middle of the room and a pair of media room recliners. They face a large flat screen television that serves as the focal point above an encased gas fireplace with a large, Romanesque limestone surround.

Three regional Emmy awards sit atop the mantel just beneath the television. There's also a Columbia DuPont baton and a bust of Edward R. Murrow. This is the focal point of the room. It's intentional. George clearly wants everyone who sits in the room to see his trophies, to see his worth as a journalist. He might as well have some flashing neon arrows aimed at them.

Mack drops himself into one of the recliners and Bella finds a corner of the sofa. George has walked to the far end of the great room, past a glass dining table, and into his kitchen.

"Does anyone need a drink?" he asks from behind the bar separating the kitchen from the rest of the floor. "I've got plenty of options."

"Johnny Walker Black," calls Mack, "if you've got that option."

"Sure thing," George says and reaches into the frosted glass cabinet next to a large stainless steel range hood. "Mr. and Mrs. Quick, anything for you?"

"Water," Bella replies. Her eyes are closed and she's pinching the bridge of her nose.

"Same." I slide onto the sofa next to Bella. "Headache?" I whisper.

"No, just stress. This is a lot to take in, Jackson." She glances at Mack, whose eyes are closed but whose ears are likely wide open.

I inch closer to her, aware of the eavesdropper next to us. "I get it. You don't trust Mack, and you don't trust George. Frankly, neither do I. What choice do we have?"

"None," she admits. "That's the stressful part. We've engaged ourselves in a fight we cannot win. We've, by complete necessity, aligned ourselves with the least of three evils. This won't end well, Jackson."

"Don't you trust me?" I ask. "Don't you trust my instincts?"

"Yes and no," she says to her lap and not to my face. "That is, I *do* trust you. I know that everything you do, every plan you concoct, every remote hiding place you find, is for our common good. And you've kept us alive for months now. But so much of what we've survived, or escaped, or defeated was by pure luck. You're not James Bond, Jackson. You're not even Mack, when it comes to tactical experience."

Mack grunts from the recliner, acknowledging his interest in our conversation. George returns with his liquor and our waters.

"I'll finish later," she says, shifting away from me in her seat to grab a glass.

"Please, we're all together in this confederacy of dunces. No need to finish later."

"Okay," her eyes narrow as though she's confused. "I've suspended my disbelief up until now, Jackson. I wanted to see you as the hero. I wanted to think of you as infallible, as un-killable. I bought into the idea that you were always one step ahead of everyone else."

"And?"

"And since you dove into the water to rescue that woman," she spits back, counting on her fingers my missteps, "brought us back into the lion's den here in Houston, reunited us with two people who've betrayed us for the sake of the man who killed your parents and has you under his thumb…."

"Wow," Mack chimes in, smacking his lips after a sip of his drink. "Tough room."

"So what do you want me to do?" I yell, pushing myself from the sofa to stand over her. "What would you have me do?"

"I don't know, Jackson." Tears well in her eyes, pooling on her lower lids. "I don't know."

"Let me show you the third floor," George offers to Mack. "There's a great terrace off of the master bedroom. You can see the downtown skyline in the distance."

"This scene is better than any view of downtown," Mack laughs and raises his glass toward me.

"So you haven't changed, then," Bella fires at Mack, blasting the smirk from his suddenly wounded face. "That's what I figured."

Mack nudges himself from the recliner and follows George to the stairwell, disappearing up the flight to the third floor. Bella watches them go and then wipes her eyes with the back of her index fingers.

"I never suggested I was part of Seal Team Six," I say. "I didn't drag you into this. *You* hired *me*. You and Sir Spencer, who you also hired, got me mixed up in this crap."

"That's not fair," she pouts. "I didn't know—"

"I was on my own, Bella. I was surviving, escaping, defeating whatever on my own. You brought me into your fold as nothing more than a desperate survivalist with good aim and a wish for a life free of violence. And you're right when you say I'm lucky. But I'd rather be lucky and alive than James Bond and dead."

Bella turns away, burying herself in the corner of the sofa. She's like a cat trying to make itself as small as possible.

A wave of guilt rushes over me. "How long have you been feeling this way?" I ask, my voice softer.

"Since Hawaii," she says, her back to me. "I mean, it started then."

"When Blogis found us?"

"Yes," she sniffles. "And then when that woman tried to kill me on the beach, the feeling grew."

"What feeling?"

"The feeling that you—we—are in over our heads. I tried to bury it. I tried to ignore that growing, nagging feeling in my gut that we've been making one bad move after another."

"I don't think that—"

"Let me finish, Jackson," she bristles and rolls her eyes.

"Okay."

"I'm carrying around a sense of dread," she says flatly. "It's not going to end well. It's just not. Despite your best efforts, and your uncanny ability to shoot a flea off of a dog, you can't win. And the final straw is this mess with your parents. Your head is spinning in so many different directions at once you can't possibly keep your balance. Are we going after Blogis? Are we going after Spencer? Are we trying to find out who killed your parents? Are we going to kill Spencer? Or Blogis? Or both?"

"I have a plan."

"I *know*," she laughs, out of frustration probably, "and I love that about you. You never give up. It's not enough."

"How so?"

"It'll never end, Jackson. That's the crux of it. That's the dread and the fear and the anxiety all wrapped into one. It's the clarity I've found in understanding it will never, ever end."

"Yes it will," I tell her, pulling her chin up so her eyes meet mine. "It *will* end. That is the plan. Just stay with me on this, Bella." I put my hand on top of her hers.

"I don't have a choice."

"Truth be told," I laugh, "not really."

She nods, swallowing hard. "I'll try."

She leans in to hug me and buries her head in my shoulder. I put my hands on her shoulders and slide them down her back, holding her. It's quiet; maybe the last moment of peace we'll have until this is over, if my plan works. It's likely the last, even if it *doesn't* work.

And then it ends.

***

Bella pulls away from our embrace. "Did you hear that?"

I put a finger to my lips as a door slowly creaks and clicks shut.

"It's downstairs," she whispers.

I catch her hand and pull her from the sofa, quietly leading her to the window overlooking the street.

Parked behind George's SUV is a black Suburban with ridiculously dark tint on its windows. Still, the driver is visible behind the wheel. His aviator sunglasses and military haircut are a dead giveaway: F. Pickle.

I pull Bella's nine millimeter handgun from my waistband and grip it in my right hand. Padding quietly across the room, leading Bella, I'm reminded that George didn't close the garage door. The stairwell is out.

I change direction and lead Bella to the kitchen. Above the sink, there's a wide double window that opens with the flip of a couple of latches. Quietly, I slide one of the panes open and climb into the sink to look outside. It's about a fifteen-foot jump down, but we'd be visible to the Suburban. I flip over and look up. About four feet above the window is the edge of the third floor bedroom terrace. I stuff the gun back into my waistband at the small of my back.

I motion quickly to Bella and pull her into the sink. "We're going up," I whisper into her left ear. "Follow me." Her eyes go wide, but she nods.

There's about a four inch sill outside of the window, which is barely enough for me to use for leverage as I pull myself outside. I reach for the concrete bottom of the terrace, hoping to grab the foot of the iron railing, but it's just out of reach.

"They're coming!" Bella whisper-shouts. "Hurry!" She's crouched in the sink, holding on to one of my legs.

To my left as I face the window, on the same side as the terrace, is a gutter downspout that leads to the roof two stories above us. It's attached to the stucco with a thick metal tie and a pair of bolts. I test the tie with my left foot and push myself up just enough to grab the iron footing above with my left hand. With my right, I wave Bella through the window and she scurries out onto the thin sill. I'm hanging by my left arm, barely braced by the metal tie as Bella steps onto my right leg, which I've braced against the stucco with my foot. She pushes herself upward, nearly causing me to lose my grip, and with her right side pressed against the stucco, gets just enough height to grab the railing with both hands.

Straining against the weight, I look straight ahead, wincing against sweat dripping into my eyes. Through the upper windowpane in front of me, against the glare of the glass and the sting in my eyes, the dark outline of two figures appear, growing larger as they run toward the glass. One of them yells something and the other raises his arm, maybe aiming a gun.

"Hurry!" I yell to Bella. "They're here!"

Scrambling now, she uses me to leverage herself up the four or five feet needed to throw herself over the railing and onto the terrace. Her last push was just enough. It was also too much.

Pop! Pop!

A pair of shots from one gun, or maybe two, crash through the window just as my foot slips from the gutter tie and I swing outward, hanging from the iron footer by my left hand. My fingers lose their grip in super slow motion and as Mack and George peer over the railing, reaching for me, I fall.

The sensation is at once surreal and too real. For what seems like an eternity, the terrace grows smaller above me. A head pokes from the opening at the sink, looking down at me and then up at—

Thud!

Fifteen feet later I'm on my back in a flowerbed between George's house and the one next to it. Stunned, the wind knocked from my lungs, I'm disoriented.

Pop! Ziiiip!

A bullet explodes the rose bush a foot from my head. Rolling over, I reach for the gun to return fire. It's not there.

Pop! Ziiip!

Another explosion into the mulch next to my hip. If this guy were any good, I'd be dead twice.

I roll over again, trying to find cover where there isn't any.

Pop! Pop!

No zip? I look up to the window. The shooter's gone. But one level up is Bella with her nine millimeter aimed at the window.

She grabbed it from me!

"I got him!" she calls down to me. "Are you okay?"

I wave at her and try to get to my feet. "There are two of them!" I call back.

She disappears behind the railing as I stand up to brush myself off.

A deep voice from behind freezes me. "Jackson Quick?"

I'm screwed.

"Quick, look at me."

I consider my lack of options. "Why, so you can shoot me in the face?"

"Your luck is running out, Quick," he snarls, his feet brushing the grass as he moves toward me. "If you won't turn around, put your hands on your head. Clasp them together."

I keep my hands at my side.

"I've got him," the driver says. "We're outside the house. What are my instructions?"

He's obviously communicating with the kill team, or what's left of it, inside the house.

"Got it," he says. "I'm—"

Pop! Ziip!

A bullet zings past me, just overhead. I glance up to see Bella standing on the terrace, a small trail of smoke trailing from the 9MM.

The driver grunts, gasps, and drops to ground. I turn around in time to see him slump forward on his knees. Spinning, I lunge to the ground and grab his weapon, a Glock 19 with a standard 15-round magazine.

I look back up to the terrace and Bella is gone again. I race around the front of the house and back through the garage. I'm halfway up the stairwell to the main level when the shouting gets louder.

Pop! Pop! Pop! Pop!

There's more shouting as I round the last step onto the main floor, sprint past it up the next flight of stairs, nearly losing my balance, and close in on the third level.

Pop! Pop! Pop! Pop! Pop!

The gunshots, coming from at least two different weapons, are louder. Maybe on the third floor.

Bella screams something I can't understand as I find myself between the third and fourth floors and only a few steps behind one of the black suits. He's bleeding, wincing with pain from the shot to his shoulder. I can see the exit wound through his dark jacket to the left of the seam for his right arm. He's turned sideways in the stairwell, and he hasn't yet spotted me. His injury has forced a loss of focus, given him tunnel vision. Behind him, I see the angled, ragged holes in the drywall. The window on the wall at the turn is broken. I level the Glock, take aim, and put just enough pressure on the five and half pound trigger to fire.

Pop!

He's not in pain anymore. Pushed into the wall at the stairwell turn, his body goes limp. Certain there's a second black-suited Pickle further up the stairs, I inch my way up to the dead man's body. Breathing in and out through my nose, I'm trying to maintain the quiet. My eyes focused upward, I don't see anyone. However, when I reach the landing at the stairwell turn, the momentary silence is shattered.

Pop! Ziip! Pop! Ziip!

Two shots fly past my head to the left, one of them nicking the top of my left ear.

Rolling onto my side, ignoring the stinging burn on my ear, I nudge my body halfway under the dead Pickle.

Pop! Thump! Pop! Thump!

Two more bullets lodge themselves into the dead Pickle, this time protecting me from his very much alive partner.

Pop! Pop!

Another pair of shots echoes in the space, farther away.

Pop!

The third shot, from the same distance, is followed by a wail, a guttural moan, and a body sliding down the stairs like a flattened cartoon character until it slams into the wall next to me.

"They're down!" I yell, pushing one body off of me and then stepping over the other one. "It's clear!"

I bound up the final flight of stairs into a hallway. There's a pony wall separating the hallway from a door at the far end. The door has half a dozen smooth bore holes in it, most of them centered near the handle, and another dozen ragged punctures at random spots across its face.

"It's clear!" I yell again, holding the Glock low, in front of me, with both hands. "It's me, Jackson. It's clear."

***

From behind the door I can hear Bella crying. "Oh my God! Oh My God!"

I call to her, shouldering the door to shove it inward. It craters against my weight and I stumble into an office. I'm first caught by the large maps on the walls, the clutter of files and papers on the corner desk, and then, at almost the same moment, my attention turns to Bella.

On the floor, his head in her lap, is George. Bella is rubbing his forehead rhythmically, gently rocking back and forth.

She looks up at me, tears streaming down her cheeks, snot bubbling from her nose.

Mack is sitting with his back against the wall, his favored Ukrainian Fort-12 handgun in his lap. His gaze is fixed on George.

George Townsend, News 4 Houston, is dead.

His eyes are open, his chest is bloodied, his legs are splayed on the floor at odd angles. There is no life left in him. And for some reason, my bottom lip quivers, my chest burns, and the knot in my throat grows painfully thick.

George, the self-centered narcissistic teevee dude, whose "all about me" approach to journalism had won him accolades and awards, had also earned him a fatal bullet to the chest.

Dropping to my knees in front of him, I join Bella in mourning. Putting the Glock on the floor, I grab the fabric of his pants at his knee. The tears are streaming down my cheeks, mixing with the sweat dripping from my forehead.

I've never cried in front of Bella, not like this. It is a draining cry, the kind that sucks energy and will with every whimper. I can't explain it, really. Why am I so emotional about the loss of a man who sold me out more than once? Why is Bella crying over a virtual stranger for whom, mere minutes earlier, she could not hide her disdain?

Maybe this is not about George. Maybe our collective breakdown is about what we know is coming, about what we imagine our own fates will be. We're facing our own mortality through his horribly sudden, bloody death.

Maybe this is about the realization that regardless of Blogis's plans, or those of Sir Spencer, the governor's relentless obsession to see me dead is ultimately unbeatable.

Bella is right when she says I've been lucky, that I'm no Jason Bourne or James Bond, or Mitch Rapp, or any number of super mercenaries capable of outwitting their foes time and time again.

Mack leans forward to put his hand on my shoulder. "Jackson, we don't have time to mourn him right now." He places a hand on Bella's arm. "We can do this later. We need to go."

I loosen my grip on George's knee, push myself to my feet, and wipe my face with the back of my arm, sniffling like a child. "We need to get what we can from this room and get out of here."

Bella closes George's eyes, puts her hands on each side of his head, and gently lays it on the floor.

Breathing deeply, I reach down to pull Mack to his feet. "Look at the walls." I motion around the room. "What do you think?" I offer a hand to Bella, who declines and stands on her own, not able to take her eyes off of George.

"He was doing some extracurricular research," Mack says. "Something outside the scope of his television work."

In the distance, a siren wails.

"We've got maybe two minutes," I tell Mack. "Let's grab what we can and go."

Mack starts pulling maps from the walls. Bella, still transfixed by the dead reporter, stands in the corner with her arms folded. She looks stunned. I haven't seen her like this since our trip to Odessa, Ukraine. The violence there almost sent her over the edge. And here we are, in her hometown, where she's now killed two men and had another die in her arms.

Shaking free of my instinct to hold her, I rummage through the drawers in the corner desk, finding three thumb drives, a 2TB hard drive, and an armful of file folders labeled "Neutrinos."

I stuff the drives into my pockets, tuck the folders into my back waistband with the Glock, pull my shirt over them, and unplug a large MacBook Pro from its high-speed cable connection. The sirens are getting louder, and now there are at least two or three of them.

"We've got to go." I reach for Bella's hand, my eyes still stinging from tears. "Bella, c'mon."

She snaps out of her trance and takes my hand, pulling herself to her feet. Without looking at me she leads us out of the room as though she knows where she's going.

"Bella," Mack says, his arms full of folded maps, "Where are you going?"

"Downstairs," she calls without turning around and starts down the stairwell, past the Pickle bodies, and toward the third floor.

Mack looks at me and shrugs before joining her, so I follow both of them down the stairs and past the carnage on the landing. Two flights later and we're in the garage. The sirens are loud, maybe around the corner on Kirby, and there is an elderly couple standing in the driveway. The woman is on her cellphone, presumably with police.

I grab Bella's hand and, with the laptop tucked under my other arm, lead her quickly past the dumbstruck couple and to the Pickle Suburban at the curb. Doing his best to keep up, Mack trails close behind us.

"Hey, y'all," the woman calls. "You can't just leave. The police are on their way. You need to stay here and wait."

Ignoring her, I split with Bella at the rear of the SUV. She gets in the passenger's side, I climb in behind the driver's seat, tossing the laptop into the back seat, and Mack hops inside next to it. Shifting the SUV into drive, my foot slams onto the accelerator as a pair of flashing blue lights appears in the rear view.

"We're screwed," Bella says, turned to look behind us. "Another cop is following us!"

A second set of lights flashes in the rear view and closes in on us as I narrowly avoid a Honda Civic parked curbside.

I spin the wheel hard and brake, losing the back end of the Suburban as I turn right on Avalon Place, heading west toward another major street called Shepherd Drive. Bella slides into me before finding her seatbelt.

"It won't be long and they'll have a chopper up," says Mack.

"The news?" Bella asks.

"The cops," Mack says, holding himself in place with a handle above the window as I make a sharp right onto Shepherd, turning south toward the freeway.

"Then the news," I add, pushing on the accelerator to give myself a little bit of distance from the Houston Police Department cruiser slaloming its way between parked cars to keep pace with us.

"Don't get on the freeway," Mack says.

"Why?" I ask, flying past a red light at Westheimer, narrowly avoiding a taco truck and a Volvo station wagon.

"You'll be too easy to spot," he says. "Trust me."

I glance at him and then the blue lights in the rear view. So far, it's just the one cop giving chase.

"Look out!" Bella screams.

I cross West Alabama and slide to the left of an oncoming police car, nearly hitting an SUV head-on in the intersection.

"Turn back around," Mack instructs. "Head back the other direction!"

At the next cross street I wait until the last second and whip the wheel to the right, screaming around the corner. The police car nearly misses the turn, but stays with me.

"Where's the second police car?" Bella asks.

"We don't have much time," Mack reminds me. "We lose these cops now, or we're screwed."

I pass another intersection and look to my right. There's the answer to Bella's question. The second cop was running parallel to me and is now heading south to join the chase. The streets narrow, with cars parked on both sides, and I make another turn, heading back towards West Alabama.

"Watch it," Bella calls out. "The light is turning!"

I gun it through the yellow light, hitting the intersection after it turns red. We clear the cross street and hear a loud crash behind us. Bella tells us that the first cop car is out.

"He clipped another car and spun out," Bella says. "The second one's not far behind."

"Westheimer's up here," Mack tells me. "Turn left."

I follow his instructions, accelerating out of my turn on Westheimer, almost losing control of the car before realizing there is no way we're escaping this time.

"What time is it?" I ask.

"16:55 local," answers Mack in military time.

"Rush hour," I lament, my foot on the brake, stuck in traffic, and blue lights flashing five cars back.

***

Bella opens the passenger door just wide enough for her to slip out. It takes me a second to realize what she's doing. I grab the laptop from the back seat and Wordlessly, Mack and I follow her, sliding out of the SUV, crouching low as we weave our way past the left lane of traffic and onto the sidewalk.

We're walking quickly, but as nonchalantly as possible away from the police car with the hope he doesn't spot us. It doesn't work.

"Stop!" We hear over the loudspeaker on his car. "The three of you, this is the Houston Police Department. Do not walk any further."

We bolt around the corner. Mack, carrying the maps, is hustling with as much speed as he can muster. We reach the other side of what looks like a church, chugging through a parking lot. In the distance, the familiar whip of helicopter blades is growing louder.

"We have got to get out of sight," Mack huffs. He's right. When that helicopter spots the three of us, we're done.

We round a corner of the building, running next to a baseball field behind the church.

"We should split up," I suggest. "They'll be looking for the three of us. Let's go our separate ways and meet up in Conroe at the airport."

"It's 5 o'clock," Mack says, still running. "Let's meet no later than ten o'clock and get out of here." Mack disappears between a couple of small buildings next to the field.

Bella is maybe three strides ahead of me. She hasn't turned around, so I pick up my pace to pull even with her as we pass a street sign that reads "Fairview". She turns right and then left, and I follow her down another narrow street called Peckham.

"Bella, did you hear Mack?"

Still running, she replies, "Yes, you want to split up. Meet back at the airport."

"Can you do that?"

"Yes." She keeps her eyes ahead, not looking at me. "Whatever gets us out of here," she says between heavy breaths. "If you want to be on your own, I'm fine with that."

"Good," I tell her, acting as though I'm too stupid to realize she's baiting me. "I'll see you by 10PM."

She stops cold. "What if you don't?"

"What if I don't what?" I stop too, listening for the helicopter, looking for the cops.

"What if you don't see me by 10?" She looks all at once hurt, frightened, and angry, an amazing combination of expressions.

"Let's stick together then. If we go down, we go down together. We don't have time to debate this."

She squeezes my hand and pulls away. "No, you're right. Let's split up. I'll see you at ten."

She darts off to the left, between a couple of houses. The helicopter is getting close, so I take off in the other direction and into the parking lot of the Petco Animal Supplies store.

I take a deep breath and slow my walk past the automatic sliding doors of the store and relish the overly air-conditioned smell of wet dog and cat litter. I weave my way unnoticed down an aisle to the aquarium section, pretending to look at the fine selection of Neon Tetras and Crowntail Bettas.

I've got five hours to get fifty miles north to Conroe. Cops will be looking for me, George's death will be on television soon, if it isn't already, and thanks to our visit to his station, we'll be the last ones seen with him. Bella and I, even under false names, will be identifiable as the former CEO of a major Houston company and the turncoat political aide who sent a governor to prison. Anyone who looks at the station's security video will see that.

Mack will be okay. He's smart enough to get his way to the plane without getting caught. Bella will be okay too. She knows this city. She has friends who'll help. She's ridiculously resourceful when she has to be. She's saved my life twice today, despite her loss of faith in me.

As for me…I've only gotten this far because of luck. Bella said it.

I need help. I need someone who doesn't trust the government, someone who'll believe I didn't kill George, and someone who can get me a weapon without asking any questions. Staring at the Grade A Koi fluttering around the air bubbles in the tank, the answer comes to me.

I know exactly who to call.

CHAPTER 6

My shrink called it a "repression mechanism". She told me, during our many sessions together, I'd chosen to forget key elements of my childhood to escape the pain of them.

I told her there were, what I called, "black holes" in my memories: long periods of time for which I couldn't account. People would ask me questions about things I couldn't remember. It's not that there was some hazy recollection. There was nothing. A black hole.

Then there were the things I thought I remembered, but didn't actually happen to me. They were what the shrink called "substitute memories." I'd created them as a coping skill, false memories to mask the ones I didn't like.

I've read a lot about this stuff and there's research that backs it up. Incredibly, there are two opposing parts of the brain that account for the suppression and the substitution of memories. Apparently it's pretty common among people who suffer from post-traumatic stress.

I guess my childhood, or what was left of it after my parents died, was post-trauma. It makes sense. I've got to be honest, though. I didn't really buy into it until I started remembering snippets of my parents' involvement with Sir Spencer and Liho Blogis.

I'd forgotten their visits to our house, the arguments my parents had over my father's job, my dad's contention that, in some way, my mother was responsible for his line of work. The memories came back in snippets, short unconnected visions that made little sense to me in and of themselves. But the more of them I experienced, the farther down the rabbit hole I chose to fall, the more they made sense.

At this point, I can't be sure what really happened and what didn't. I've got so many of these substitute memories floating around with the real ones, I can't tell the difference sometimes. It's like watching a television show of your life, not sure which parts were made better by Hollywood.

The crazy thing is that my adult life, the part I can't escape, seems more like some Hollywood action flick than anything I endured as a kid. I'm messed up.

I've dragged the only woman who's ever *really* loved me, other than my mother, into hell. True, she took the first few steps willingly, but I yanked her through the remaining eight circles.

Limbo, check. Lust, check. Gluttony, Avarice, and Wrath, triple check. Heresy, I guess. Violence, definitively. Fraud, assuredly. Treachery, obviously. Lust may have been the only one she consciously chose. The only thing missing is Morgan Freeman finding a head in a box while Brad Pitt blows out Kevin Spacey's brains.

She's lost faith in me. I can't blame her, given how deeply we've descended. I know, however, I can fix it. I can free her and give her a better life, a life more closely resembling the one she had before I entered it.

My plan is to ensnare the two men who I repeatedly removed from memory. I'll play to their unbridled greed. I'll plot them against each other. Whether I survive or not is irrelevant. If I die in the process, all of the memories I suppressed or substituted will die with me. It'll be like they never really happened in the first place, as my mind would want.

***

"*Here's what we know now,*" a youngish, bottle blonde reports earnestly, gripping her microphone a little too tightly. "*There are three people dead inside this Upper Kirby home. There is a fourth person outside of the house. He is also deceased."*

The four people bellied up to the bar at Kenneally's Irish Pub, across the street from Petco, are glued to the flat panel television hanging above the top shelf liquor. The volume is up loud.

I joined them ten minutes ago, waiting for my ride. I'm in a booth, nursing a Guinness, trying to remain as incognito as possible. The barkeep was kind enough to let me use his phone.

"Police sources tell me that all four people are men, all of them were killed in what appears to be some sort of shootout, which happened within the last hour." The camera moves from the reporter to a live picture of George's house. The television crew is apparently across the street, outside of the yellow crime tape that stretches the length of George's property. *"We also know that homicide detectives are en route to the scene here, as are a crime scene unit, and the Harris County medical examiner."*

The live picture zooms in to an upstairs window in George's house, through which I can see the dark outline of police inside. There are fire trucks, ambulances, and police cars cluttering the street and driveway. The camera zooms out again, reintroducing the reporter into the frame.

"Again," she says with as serious a face as she can muster, *"this happened in just the last hour. And we do understand that at least three people fled the scene. HPD gave chase, but lost the suspects near Westheimer and Kirby. One officer was involved in a collision during that pursuit."* Video of the crash I last saw in my rear view mirror fills the screen.

"Nobody was seriously injured in that crash, we are told. And while investigators haven't given us a description of the suspects, the woman who called 9-1-1, first alerting police to the shooting here, can tell us a little bit more about them. She joins us live."

Oh crap.

"Her name is Maxine Landiss." The reporter turns to the woman who was on the phone as we ran from George's house. *"She tells me she saw the trio run from the house and get into a black SUV."*

"That's right," the woman confirms, glancing back and forth between the reporter and the camera, *"I saw two men and a woman come from the garage. One of the men was missing a leg. The woman looked familiar to me, but I can't place her. She was pretty. The other man was young. He was carrying a laptop computer."*

"You say," the reporter presses urgently, *"that one of the men was missing a leg? Tell me more about that."*

"Well, he had a prosthetic leg. And even though he was an African American, he had lighter skin in spots."

"Anything else you can tell us?"

"I don't think so."

"Okay." The reporter nods at the woman and turns back to the camera. *"That's the latest from here. We, of course, will stay on top of any new developments and get them back to you as quickly as possible. Reporting live in Upper Kirby, Kandy Bellman, News 4 Houston."*

The screen switches from the reporter to the anchors in the studio. The woman anchor looks down at a ragged piece of paper before addressing the camera.

"I've just been handed some information that is particularly distressing for those of us here at News 4 Houston," she says. *"The address of the deadly shooting is a home owned by our own George Townsend. We do not have confirmation that George was home at the time of the shootings, that he is one of the victims, or is in anyway involved. But in full disclosure, we wanted to let you, our viewers, know every bit of information about this fluid, developing story."*

"I know that dude," says one of the men at the bar to nobody in particular. "He's the reporter who did all of those reports on the governor. He won, like, an Oscar or something."

"An Oscar is for movies, idiot," says the older guy next to him.

"Whatever," says the movie fan. "He won some award. I saw them running commercials on it. He's a big deal."

"Now turning to our local weather forecast." The woman forces a smile and the screen switches to a wider shot of the anchor desk. It's what's called a "three shot" of the two news anchors and the meteorologist. *"We understand there might be a chance for rain tonight?"*

My beer is already getting warm. I take a sip and swallow. Alcohol is probably not the best choice right now. Staring at the glass, relishing the sour aftertaste of the beer, I lose myself for just a beat. Sitting in the bar, alone, I almost feel normal. The four guys at the bar are normal. A couple of them are in dress pants and dress shirts. Their ties are loosened at their unbuttoned collars and the gel in their hair has lost its grip. They're finished for the day at their customer service jobs or sales positions. They're drowning what they perceive as the mundane, repetitive nature of their lives before heading home to an empty apartment or a house full of kids.

They've got no idea how lucky they are.

The other two look like blue-collar types. They're wearing jeans and heavy boots. One of them is wearing a dingy t-shirt with a large marlin sprawled across the back. The other is in a short-sleeved collared shirt. I'm guessing it has some company's logo on the breast pocket.

This is their place to unwind after a physical day in the heat and humidity, to talk shop before stepping outside to smoke a couple of cigarettes. Their girlfriends or wives don't expect them home for a couple of hours.

What I'd give to have their lives…

"Hey." A thin man standing at my table raps arthritis-thickened knuckles on the laminated wood in front of me. "You awake?"

I snap out of my trance and focus on the man. He's in his early sixties, with deep creases along his brow and stretching from the edges of his nose to his jawline. He's tanned, with thinning hair slicked back against his narrow head. His eyes are powerful and pained.

He's wearing a tan cotton jacket, despite the heat, and it's zipped up to his neck.

He squints and asks again, "You all there, Jackson? I got here as quickly as I could. Thankfully, I was on this side of town running errands."

I nod and offer him the seat across from me. He sits down and wraps his fingers around my beer, asking me for a drink without saying anything.

I nod again and he swigs from the glass until it's empty of everything but foam. Licking the leftovers from the gray stubble above his lips he knocks on the table again.

"Shall we go?" He stands, not really waiting for my answer.

"Sure thing," I say and follow Roswell Ripley to his truck.

***

Roswell Ripley owes me. That's the only reason he'd help me. Our relationship, or at least what exists of one, is complicated.

While I was working for the governor, his opponent, Bella's father, was shot during a campaign rally in Houston. He survived it and, as we all later learned, ordered the hit on himself to gain sympathy and political momentum.

Ripley was framed for it. He was a well-known activist who supported Texas seceding from the union. My boss, sensing the political winds, often talked about secession on the campaign trail as a way of appealing to a large block of fringe voters like Ripley.

Bella's father thought connecting a perceived nut like Ripley to an "assassination" attempt would be political gold. Apparently he was a fan of the Tim Robbins movie, *Bob Roberts*.

Ripley's son, of the same name, was a scientist at Rice University. His research was critical to a new technology in the oil and gas sector. It was worth untold billions, if not trillions, of dollars. It was also the centerpiece of the conspiracy into which I had unknowingly involved myself by agreeing to deliver information-laden iPods around the globe on behalf of my boss.

Dr. Ripley had gotten cold feet about his work and went into hiding. George and I found him and tried to help him shortly before he was killed. We ultimately took down the people responsible for his death and cleared the senior Ripley of any wrongdoing.

He promised George and me on the day he was released from jail, if we ever needed anything he would be there to help.

Here he is delivering on that promise, driving me north in his beater of an F-150, no questions asked.

Almost.

"So did you kill George?" Ripley has one hand on the wheel, the other gripped around the gearshift. He's rubbing his palm back and forth on the top of it.

"You have to ask me that?"

"That's not an answer, Jackson." He glances in the rearview mirror. He's either checking the traffic behind us or the Smith & Wesson M&P15 semi-automatic sport rifle he has on a rack attached to the rear window.

"No, I didn't kill him. The governor's people did."

"He's still got people, does he?" Ripley sneers. "Ain't he locked up good and tight?"

"Mr. Ripley, you're a smart man. You know how these things work. You know better than most how conspiracies work, how far-reaching the tentacles of a powerful person can be."

"I guess." He pulls a sweating Styrofoam cup from the twin cup holders between us, takes a long sip, sucking in his cheeks, before replacing the cup and dropping his hand back onto the gear shift knob. "So, tell me what we're up to, Jackson?"

"What do you mean?"

"Mr. Quick," he chides, "you're a smart man. You know what I mean. Far-reaching tentacles and such." He raises his right hand from the shifter and wiggles his fingers.

"Good point." I exhale and begin to tell him about the last few months of my life.

I detail the effort to piece together the process, the people killed, the people still alive. He listens without saying anything. By the time I've finished, we're on the North Freeway past Beltway 8 and halfway to Conroe.

"So," he finally says, "you're a walking, talking death magnet. Is that about right?"

I nod without saying anything and turn to look out the window at the endless stream of strip shopping centers, fast food joints, car dealerships, and gas stations lining the feeder road on the north side of the freeway.

"Look, Jackson," he says, "you're a victim of circumstance, right? But these circumstances are of your own making. You can whine to me all you want about how much of a victim you are, how lucky you are to be alive. It don't matter much to me."

He takes another swig from the Styrofoam cup, slurping what has to be melted ice and backwash by this point.

"I was a victim, right?" he asks rhetorically. "That rich girlfriend of yours... her dad seized on my political leanings, my affection for a twenty-thousand dollar Knights SR-XM110 Rifle that was perfect for a sniper. He framed me. He *victimized* me. My son was a victim too. He died because of his intelligence, because he was the first one in the world to figure out how change gas mileage with nanobots or something."

There's an almost imperceptible change in his facial expression when he talks about his son. The deep crevice in his forehead shallows a bit. His eyes widen and become glassy. He's wistful.

"He put himself in that position, just as I put myself in a position, just as you have, Jackson. And that girlfriend, Bella, she done the same thing. She put herself in this pickle."

"What's your point?"

"Stop getting so philosophical about the whole thing," he says. "I talk to God all of the time." He pulls a silver cross from under his shirt, his thumb beneath the thin chain holding it around his neck. "You know what the good Lord tells me? He tells me to take responsibility for my life. To believe in Him in all I do, but to know that what I do is of my own free will. I choose which paths to take. I choose how to walk them. Are you God-fearing, Jackson?"

I shrug. "I believe in a higher power. I believe I'll have to answer for the things I do."

"All right then," Ripley says. "You need to understand the awesome power that comes with being a believer. You need to stop lamenting what's happened. Ask for forgiveness. Move on. You are responsible for what happens next."

"*You're* being pretty philosophical for telling *me* not to be so philosophical."

"Having faith and being philosophical are two different things, Jackson," he says, wagging his finger at me. "You can have faith without wallowing in the ethereal worlds of 'What if?' and 'What have I done?'"

"Why are you telling me this?" I shift in my seat, turning toward him. "Are you suggesting I let go of my regret and angst and whatever else it is I'm feeling so I can *live my best life*?"

"I'm being serious," he says, apparently sensing my sarcasm.

"So am I."

"I'll be honest here, Jackson," His eyes darting between me and the road ahead. "I don't know you hardly at all. Frankly, I don't care to know you given the crap-filled hole you always seem to find yourself in, but this really isn't about you or your *best life*."

"Then what's it about?"

"It's about killing every last one of those dickweeds responsible for my son's death," he spits, the crease in his forehead deepening. "I need you to have a clear head. I need you to let go of all that metaphysical crap bouncing around in your thin skull and focus on what you have planned."

I don't tell him that his call for revenge goes against everything he just told me. Instead, I focus on the intent in his eyes. Even with the short glances back and forth between mine and the road, the desire, the anger, the pain is evident. He's prepping me for battle. I'm Rocky and he's Mickey. I'm Maximus and he's Proximo. He's telling me to do as he says, not as he does.

"Sir Spencer has got to go," he says. "And that Blogis fella, too. If he's connected in any way to all of this, I want him dead. These Pickle people you talk about, something's got to happen to them too."

"They're just pawns," I tell him. "They're doing what the governor pays them to do."

"Then I guess we gotta kill the governor. You got a plan for that?"

"I'm working on it."

"Then," he says, his voice lowered and tone softened, "there's the matter of your girlfriend."

"What about her?" Maybe I should tell him that both Mickey and Proximo die in their respective films.

"She's clean in all of this?"

"How do you mean?"

"She had nothing to do with my son?" He tightens his grip on the steering wheel, not looking at me as he asks.

"Not that I know of," I tell him. "I really don't think—"

"I got it. She's clean. At least as far as you're concerned. And let's be truthful about this. If you take care of Sir Spencer, Blogis, and the governor, I got no quarrel with your girl."

"Understood." I let out a deep breath and sink into my seat. The whole point of this, my *raison d'*être, as it were, is to free her from this.

"Now," he says, speeding up ahead of a car to his right and sliding over to take the next exit, "we need to get you armed."

***

Ripley's storage unit is unremarkable. With a construction orange, manual pull-up, metal door, it blends in with the sixty or so other units that line the short concrete runway on either side of the property.

He grunts as he bends over to yank up on the handle of what is essentially a heavy garage door. "I bought this place right after Junior died," he says, pushing on the bottom of the spring-loaded door so that it slides all the way past the door opening.

"The storage unit?"

"No," he says, stepping into the sixteen by sixteen space and flipping a light switch to his right. "I bought the whole place. All fifty-six units." He sweeps his arm toward the units on the other side. "Needed something to do after the dust settled, and I didn't want to keep my doomsday supplies at the house anymore."

He slides a bar across the door to lock it from the inside and walks to the back of what resembles a small military surplus store. The floor to ceiling cinderblock walls are spotted with memorabilia that speaks to who Roswell Ripley is, or better yet, who he *was*.

On the wall at the rear of the unit is a large green flag. It hangs vertically and is emblazoned with the emblem of the United States Army. At the center is an eagle with a U.S. flag shielding its chest. Its wings are spread wide, olive branches in one talon and a quiver of arrows in the other.

To its left is a second, larger flag. It also hangs vertically, but is black and more sinister in appearance. At its center is a large human skull wrapped in a cobra. The snake's jaws are open, its fangs out. Underneath the snake and skull is a pair of bullets arranged in an X. At the bottom, stretching horizontally between the bullets is the Latin phrase Julius

Caesar sent in a letter to the Roman Senate after defeating Pharnaces II of Pontus: *Veni, Vidi, Vici.* "I came, I saw, I conquered." The sentiment is amplified by another motto in larger letters, "One Shot - One Kill."

Beneath the flags, and running along the length of the walls, are shoulder-height metal shelving racks. They are filled with rifles, shotguns, handguns, sights, scopes, and components I don't even recognize.

In the center of the unit is a wide, wooden planked table. On it sits a couple of disassembled Remington rifles and some boxes of ammunition. There's a black Kevlar vest hanging off one corner of the table. I put George's MacBook on the table along with the 2TB hard drive I took from his apartment. The trio of thumb drives are still in my pocket.

"I'd say you're ready for doomsday," I laugh nervously. I'm certainly comfortable around firearms, but this is intimidating.

"Never too prepared," he says, running his hand along the table as he walks to the back of the unit. "Close that behind you, would you?"

I reach up behind me to pull the door closed. It clangs with a deafening echo against the walls.

Ripley spins on his heel and folds his arms across his chest. "So, what do you think you need to get 'er done?"

"I don't know." It's like I'm looking at a dessert menu with too many choices. "What do you recommend? You're more of the survivalist than I am."

"Ha! I haven't killed near the number of people you have, that's for sure."

I slink toward him. "All I've got is a nine millimeter." I pull it from the small of my back and palm it onto the wooden table. "There's a six-shooter on the plane, and our cohort Mack has a Ukrainian-made handgun of some kind. I used to have a lot more at my disposal, but I've kept downsizing."

"Time to upsize then," he says. "Let's start in the back. Here in the left corner."

I follow him to the back of the space, beneath a Texas flag with a rattlesnake coiled in the center of it. The words, "Don't Tread On Me" are proudly stitched in yellow against the red bar across the bottom of the flag.

"These here are my Barretts," he says, leaning against a waist high shelf, gesturing at a row of nasty looking rifles. "My favorite is the 821A semiautomatic. It's got a Leupold scope on it and has a ten round detachable magazine. Comes with a nice case."

I run my hand across the stock. "Looks heavy."

"About thirty pounds," he says.

"Anything lighter?"

"I got a 98B. It fires thirty-threes, has a nice pistol grip, and only weighs thirteen pounds. But it doesn't have a sight or a scope."

"I don't need one."

"Sold!" He claps his hands and pulls the fully assembled rifle to the center table, laying it next to the Remingtons.

"Maybe." There are so many choices; I'm not ready to commit.

"Now if you want something new and super light to carry, I've got this beauty over here. I haven't even taken her for a spin yet." He pulls out a military style rifle that looks like a cross between a lightweight M16 and an AK-47. "This is an Arsenal SLR-106."

"It looks like it carries more rounds than the Barrett," I remark, observing the long curve of the magazine.

"Nope." He shakes his head. "It's deceiving. This only holds five rounds, but they're nice and big. The buttstock folds, you have the pistol grip, and it weighs just over seven pounds." He snorts with glee. "Crazy, right?"

I nod and he puts the Arsenal on the table. He claps his hands again, rubs them together. He shakes his finger at me and moves to another shelf, closer to the entrance. "You want light with a large capacity. Let's look at the Rock River."

"What's that?" I move toward him as he pulls a mid-length rifle from its space on the shelf.

"This is a Rock River LAR-15. It's about the same weight as the Arsenal, shoots the same caliber too, but it has a thirty round magazine." He runs his hand along the forward curve of the magazine like a *Price Is Right* model. "There's the traditional pistol grip and a two stage trigger. Really nice semiautomatic."

"It looks cheap."

"Well, you can't have everything. This one runs about a thousand dollars. The others are between five and ten grand."

"I don't mean cost," I clarify. "I mean quality. I don't want it jamming."

"No worries," he assures me. "This is quality. You'll be good."

"You have two of them?"

"I have five."

"Why?"

"I buy in bulk and it saves money."

I move to another shelf, where it appears he's stocked shotguns. Turning a corner, there are handguns. I stop and try to assess the options.

"I've got Glock, Sig Sauer, Smith 7 Wesson, Olympic, Walther, Kel-Tec, and Colt. Oh, and I have Taurus too. Maybe just bought me a couple of 809's." He rummages through a couple of shelves and then pulls a small box from the back. "Yep, here's an 809. Holds eighteen rounds. Pretty much your standard nine millimeter."

"What about the Kel-Tec?"

"Another high capacity magazine. I have the PMR-30. It carries thirty rounds. It's a little heavier than some, but it disassembles with a single pin. Really nice."

"And the Walther?" I like the irony of using James Bond's preferred weapon.

"It's the slim police version. Fires seven rounds of a forty caliber Smith & Wesson or eight of a standard 9mm. It's half again as heavy as the Kel-Tec, but it's a heavy punch."

"I need the capacity over the power," I explain. "I'll take the Kel-Tec."

"Done," he says and locates the small box containing the PMR-30. "Now, you'll need a small sidearm, something you can hide."

"What do you suggest? An old single shot Derringer?" I smirk.

"I have one of those, but you said capacity was the key." He scoots around me to another shelf on the opposite side of the room. He's like a mad professor, knowing exactly where to find just the right beaker amongst a laboratory full of them. "So I would go with the Kimber Micro Carry. It holds six rounds but has a barrel less than three inches long. It's got a thumb safety on the side."

Ripley pulls out a case from the back of the shelf, pops open the tabs, and reveals a shiny aluminum thirty-eight caliber handgun. "I've even got the ankle holster if you plan on wearing pants."

The whole scene is surreal to me. I'm in a storage unit off the side of a freeway, ordering up high-powered weapons like items on a dollar menu. A wave of dread washes over me.

Are we being watched?

I mean, Ripley *is* a known dissenter. He was accused of shooting a gubernatorial candidate. His son was assassinated.

How can they not *be watching him?*

The fear grows darker.

There are surveillance cameras nestled into each of the unit's four corners, where the walls meet the corrugated steel roof. I remember spotting one at the entrance to the property, another as we rolled into the aisle of units, and a third perched on a short light pole to the right of Ripley's storage space.

"Aren't you worried about all of this?" I ask. "Doesn't *Waco* mean anything to you?"

He laughs, pulling a large olive canvas bag from underneath the center table. He spreads it open at the zipper, and starts placing boxes of ammunition into its corners.

I glance at one of the security cameras, certain someone with a badge is watching a monitor on the other end. My throat's getting dry and I try to swallow past it.

"Of course it does. And nothing's changed since 1993. Koresh is still God to the Davidians and the ATF still overreaches in its authority. But that ain't gonna stop me from exercising my second amendment right to keep and bear arms. You know as well as anyone, with the blood you've seen, that a well-regulated militia is what keeps us from turning into Moscow or Beijing or Havana."

"So they don't know about this stash?"

Maybe my flush of worry was overblown. Or maybe the door behind me is about to rumble open, revealing a cadre of paramilitary troopers.

"Hell, they probably *do* know. But what are they gonna do about it?"

"Take them," I state. "Arrest you."

"Think about the optics of that," he says, rummaging through the bag to check its inventory. He makes room for the MacBook and the hard drive and places them inside the bag, alongside the Kel-Tec and a large first aid kit. "I was falsely arrested and paraded through the media as some wacko, neoconservative gun nut. Then I'm released and the district attorney publicly apologizes to me for the 'rush to judgment.' You think they're gonna come after me again without probable cause?"

"They could."

"They could," he nods. "But this is still Texas. People like their guns and their right to own them. They like to use them to hunt and protect their property. All of these weapons are legal. I got paperwork for all of it."

"If they're watching you," I counter, "and you're hanging out with me…" I let the thought waft in the stale air for a moment.

"They're not watching. All of these cameras I'm watching you ogle are encrypted. The pictures go to a private server. Nobody but some professional Chinese hacker is getting into the system." He lugs the bag over his shoulder and walks around the table toward me. "Jackson, what's going on in that head of yours?"

"Coming here was a bad idea," I say, stepping back toward the wall. "I don't think you can be sure that nobody's watching."

"Nobody's watching," he tries to reassure me. "You're understandably spooked. But let's be honest, if *I* ain't paranoid, you shouldn't be either." He pulls an iPhone from his pocket and slides his finger across the screen before punching up an app.

He hands me his phone. "Here, this is the video feed from the cameras mounted on the outside of the unit. What do you see?"

On the screen is a live view of the storage units opposite the one in which we're doing business. To the left of the view is the cab of Ripley's well-worn F-150. There's no movement.

"Push the little icon on the bottom left. It'll switch the view to the camera at the front gate."

I touch the orange triangle at the bottom left and the screen fills with a menu.

BREAKNECK SECURITY
REMOTE OPTIONS
CAM1 CAM2 CAM3
CAM4 CAM5 CAM6

"Which one?"

"Camera one."

I press the icon.

Nothing.

"It's not working." I hand him the phone.

"Let me see that." He pushes the same spot on the phone a couple of times, each touch more aggressive than the previous. "I'll try camera two. It's also at the—" His eyes grow wide at the same instant the blood drains from his face.

"What?" I move a step toward him as he holds up the phone, revealing a screen filled with flashing blue and red lights right before the screen goes black.

They *were* watching.

"We've got to get you out of here." Ripley slips the phone into his pocket and shoves the duffle bag into my chest. "Take this."

I laugh incredulously. "Where am I going to go? There's no way out of here."

"Yeah there is," he says. "But I need your help."

Quickly, Ripley moves to the back of the storage unit. He grabs the vertical frame of one of the shelving units and pulls. One half of the shelf slides away from the wall, leaving just enough space between it and the adjoining shelf for a person to fit through.

I hadn't noticed it before, but there are tiny plastic discs on the bottom corners of the shelf, making it easier to slide, and the hinge midway along the shelf was nearly invisible.

Ripley pulls a key ring from his pocket and slides through the opening. He mumbles something to himself and reappears less than thirty seconds later.

He puts his hands on my shoulders, gripping with his fingers. "There's a door behind there. I just unlocked it. Go through it, turn to the left, and you'll be fine."

"What's to the left?"

"A way out."

"You coming too?"

"No."

"Why not? You don't have to sacrifice yourself for me."

"I'm not doing it for you, you narcissistic prick," he spits, his fingertips and thumbs digging into my shoulders. "I'm doing this for my son. You are the only way I see justice. Plus, somebody needs to stay behind to lock the door and slide the shelf into place. I'll buy you time to escape."

He slips me his phone, tells me the PIN code, and pushes me into the opening between the shelves. I duck through the door, feel a slight shove from Ripley, and tumble into the tight, dank passageway. The door creaks behind me and clicks shut just as the cops start banging on the metal garage door at the front of the unit.

I'm in total darkness.

***

Lying on my side in a quasi-fetal position, I push the home button on the iPhone. The dim glow from the screen illuminates the passageway enough for me to see a couple of feet in front of me.

The space is maybe five foot cubed. The walls are cinderblock, as is the ceiling, but the floor is concrete. It's probably the unfinished slab beneath the building. It's cooler in the tunnel than in the storage unit, though the air burns my nostrils with the sting of mildew.

Maneuvering my body one hundred and eight degrees, I press my ear against the door. Ripley's muffled voice yells something about the Fourth Amendment, but it's mostly unintelligible.

I thumb the home button on the phone and enter Ripley's PIN code to turn on the flashlight function. It illuminates the corridor better than the dim backlight of the screen.

Dragging the duffel alongside me, I push through the cramped tunnel maybe fifty yards or so before it turns to the left. I can't quite stand and find it better inching along on my knees so there's less stress on my back. Even though my knees don't care for it, it's the most efficient way to move.

I turn the corner to the left, and the space becomes more confined. Above my head are a series of white PVC pipes running parallel to one another beneath the ceiling. I aim the small flashlight on the back of the iPhone at the ceiling, and a pair of tiny, reflective yellow eyes peer back at me before disappearing and scurrying off. The pipes disappear upward into the ceiling at elbow joints at various points. The joints are slathered in the dried blue and purple expo plumbers use on plastic pipes to affix them to one another. Still, some of them glisten with leaks. The dank odor of the catacomb is strongest here.

The light, aimed directly ahead of me, illuminates the darkness. This hallway is longer than the one before it, but within a couple of minutes I reach another turn. I crawl to the right this time and am met immediately by a dead end and what best resembles an attic access panel. There's no handle or lock or obvious mechanism for opening what has to be the exit.

I run my fingers along the raised edge of the panel and find a pair of small grooves at each end, tugging to loosen the panel.

This is the way out.

Before I pull the panel inward, opening the tunnel to the outside world, I sit down and lean against one of the concrete walls. Punching Ripley's code again, I unlock the phone and turn off the flashlight. Double clicking the home button reveals the list of open applications on the device, and I scroll to the surveillance program Ripley showed me earlier. I find it and thumb it open. The screen fills with orange and black lettering against a white background.

BREAKNECK SECURITY
REMOTE OPTIONS
CAM 1 CAM 2 CAM 3
CAM 4 CAM 5 CAM 6

I punch cameras one and two before remembering that both are disabled. Camera three is the view Ripley first showed me. It's aimed at the storage units across from the Ripley's armory. His truck is still to the left of the screen, but now there are at least half a dozen armor-clad troopers positioned outside the door.

Several of them are kneeling, semi-automatic rifles aimed at Ripley's unit. A couple of them are standing behind the truck, using the hood to brace their weapons. I push the small triangle at the bottom of the screen and switch to camera four.

It's mounted on the opposite corner of the unit and provides a similar option as camera three. From this angle, it's easier to see the sniper team resting on top of the building opposite Ripley.

He's not getting away.

Camera five is inside his storage unit. Mounted high in the front of the unit and to the left, it provides a fisheye perspective of Ripley in his lair.

He's pacing back and forth, and despite the lack of audio, I can tell he's shouting at the men outside. His arms are gesticulating wildly as he talks, as if he's a flightless bird frustrated with his lot.

Ripley's unarmed, unless you count the endless supply of weaponry surrounding him. He's not stupid. He knows when those officers force their way into the unit, his only chance of survival is being empty handed with his arms raised above his head.

Camera six provides a better perspective of what's coming. It's affixed to the back left corner of the unit and offers a view of the garage door. Ripley's pacing back and forth, clearly anxious about what he knows is coming.

I turn off the phone. I can't watch it. Placing the phone on the ground next to me, I reach into the recesses along the top of the panel and pull it toward me. After resisting for a moment, it slips easily from the wall and provides an escape from the tunnel.

I don't know what to expect on the other side of the opening, but it's certainly not what I find. Ripley is a freaking genius.

***

I feel guilty for doubting Ripley's intentions. Maybe I merely underestimated the all-consuming desire of revenge. He called it justice. He wants the men responsible for his son's execution to share the same fate.

I don't judge him. It is what it is. As far back as Hammurabi's Mesopotamia, men were exacting what they called justice. Four thousand years later, we haven't changed much.

Power. Greed. Revenge. They're fundamental to who we are. I've accepted it. I appreciate it. I also appreciate Ripley's foresight.

Emerging from the tunnel that wound its way secretly through the walls of the storage facility, I find myself inside another unit. A motion sensing light hums to life an overhead fluorescent light. Taking a deep breath, free of mold, I rise to my feet and pull the bag into the room.

It's roughly the same size as the armory, but this unit is empty except for two things: a large refrigerator and a silver Toyota Camry. This is my escape pod.

The refrigerator is stocked with bottled water and Gatorade. I grab a twenty ounce bottle of the fruit punch flavor, unscrew the cap, and guzzle it before picking up a couple of waters for the road.

The door to the Camry is unlocked, so I toss the waters onto the passenger seat and reach next to the driver's seat to flip the trunk lever. It clicks and the trunk thumps open. Aside from a road hazard kit, the trunk is empty, so I heave the weapons bag into the space and unzip it to pull out the Kel-Tec. In the middle of swigging the Gatorade, I realized I left the 9mm on the table in the armory.

Popping out the magazine on the Kel-Tec, I quickly fill its thirty round magazine and palm it back into place. It's a nasty looking gun, lightweight and lethal. I hold it in my right hand, testing its feel, wrapping my fingers around the front strap. The nylon grip is comfortable against my palm.

With the duffel reorganized and zipped, I reach up and pull the trunk closed, careful to make as little noise as possible. The keys are in the ignition and on the sun visor is a remote control for an automatic garage door opener with two buttons.

Only now do I notice the mechanized arm attached to the bay door of the unit and I'm about to push the button when I stop short. Opening the door, with its humming and whirring, will make too much noise. I get out of the car, stand on the edge of the doorframe, and reach up to pull the emergency release cord on the opener's gearbox.

Thunk!

The door separates from the automatic opener, allowing me to slowly, quietly, roll the door upwards manually. I only raise it a foot before lying flat on my stomach to peek out from under the opening.

It's dark outside now. The only light is the dim yellow glow of the overhead lamp a few units down to the left. In front of the unit, and to the right, it's black. My eyes adjust to the darkness and survey the landscape.

I'm at what must be the back of the property. There's a narrow asphalt driveway running between the storage units and an eight-foot wooden fence. At the edge of asphalt, about fifteen feet directly in front of me, is a wrought iron gate. Beyond the gate, as best I can tell, is a dirt path that leads into a thicket of pine trees.

The stormtroopers haven't found this part of the property yet, so I quietly roll the garage door the rest of the way along its tracks and slide back into the driver's seat.

Before starting the engine, I flip the headlights on to get a better look at the gate. It's mechanized, with a control arm on its far right side. The gate opens outward and into the trees.

Figuring it has to work, I push both buttons on the remote control on the Camry's visor, and the gate slowly hums to life and swings outward. It's fully open by the time the Toyota's rear wheels spin past the gravel beyond the fence line. I punch the buttons again to close it behind me and navigate the dirt path away from the storage unit. The clock on the Camry's dash tells me I've got ninety minutes to make it to the airport. I check Ripley's phone to confirm the time before I toss the potential tracking device out of the window and into the brush.

***

Within a quarter of a mile, the dirt road gives way to a dead end street at the back of a neighborhood. The homes are modest but well kept, the yards lined with recently planted oak trees all equidistant from the curb. It's the developer's attempt to make the neighborhood more appealing, but even in the darkness of early evening it seems forced.

With a decent sense of direction I maneuver my way out of the neighborhood to a feeder road for the highway. I look to the left before turning and notice a grouping of flashing red and blue lights before realizing Ripley's self-storage business is right next to me.

The flashing illuminates a pair of white vehicles parked awkwardly against the edge of the feeder road. One of them is a small SUV, and on its hood is a logo for one of the local news radio stations, NewsMachine 88.5. The other is a van with a small satellite dish atop its roof. It belongs to News 4 Houston, George's station.

How did they get here so fast?

I'm tempted to sit at the intersection and gawk, but that would just call attention to me. And I'm running out of time to get to the airport in Conroe. I tune the radio to 88.5 FM, and turn right onto the feeder road.

"*...for about a half hour,*" the radio reporter says breathlessly through the tinny resonance of his cell phone. "*A source tells me the people inside the storage unit are wanted for questioning in the deadly shootout in southwest Houston earlier today. We have confirmed, among the dead, is thirty four year old KCLA television reporter, George Townsend.*"

I press the accelerator to merge onto I-45 and head north. There's very little traffic, aside from some rumbling eighteen-wheelers, so I should make it in time.

"*Investigators here at the scene are not talking to us yet, but we do see what appears to be SWAT officers positioned across the expanse of this property. And a quick records search tells us that the owner of this self-storage business is Roswell Ripley, who you may remember,*" the reporter slows his cadence to stress the importance of his next point, "*was accused of shooting a gubernatorial candidate. Though he was later released and cleared of any wrongdoing, he is known for his fringe political views and a penchant for weapons.*"

That was not at *all* biased.

"*Our source would not confirm Ripley is a suspect, only that he and at least one other individual are persons of interest. Of course, we'll be here at the scene, bringing you updates as they happen. For the News Machine in north Harris County, I'm Bill McNeal. Back to you, Catherine.*"

"*Thanks for the update,*" the anchor says. "*Recapping our top story, the Department of Public Safety and the Harris County Sheriff's Office are in a standoff with a person or persons of interest in the mass shooting early this evening in Southwest Houston at the home of a local television reporter. We will keep you updated on this breaking story as it warrants. You're listening to the News Machine. I'm Catherine Duke. Now for an update on this evening's forecast let's get an update from meteorologist Max Lewis...*"

I tune out the weather report. The speedometer tells me the Camry is cruising at seventy miles per hour.

It's a good moment to take inventory.

Hopefully Bella and Mack will beat me to the airport. I'm out of cash, spending my only five dollars on the beer at the bar, but Bella had money and I imagine Mack did too. They should be able to make their way north without a problem, especially now that there's so much attention focused on Ripley. If we can get onto the plane, take off, and hit cruising altitude, we'll be okay.

"*Thanks Max,*" says the radio anchor. "*You're listening to the News Machine. I'm Catherine Duke,*" she repeats. They do that on radio. A lot. "*We have some developments in our top story this hour. Bill McNeal is*" *at the scene of a tense SWAT standoff along the North Freeway which may be connected to the deaths of four men earlier tonight. Bill you have new information for us?"*

"Yes, Catherine," he says through his phone. *"We just saw a bright flash, followed a couple of seconds later by a loud boom. We're being kept back by caution tape and can't see the activity firsthand. But we can surmise troopers and deputies may have gotten impatient with the people holed up inside a storage unit."*

"Were shots fired?" Catherine Duke asks. *"Or do you think deputies were using what's called a flash-bang?"*

"It was a flash-bang," answers Bill McNeal. *"Which is technically a stun grenade. It produces a very bright flash of light and a loud bang, hence the name. It's intended to stun a criminal suspect long enough to give the advancing officers an upper hand. It temporarily blinds the person, for maybe five seconds or so, deafens them temporarily, and causes him to lose his bal—"* The reporter stops talking, and there's a loud commotion in the background. It sounds like he's talking to someone there next to him.

"Bill are you there? Are you okay?" Catherin asks.

"U-uh," he stutters, *"Uh. Yes, I'm here, Catherine. We're distracted here by an orange glow coming from beyond our line of sight. It seems the building the SWAT team has surrounded is on fire."*

"On fire?"

"Yes!" the reporter's voice cracks. *"On fire. There's now a large column of thick black smoke, evident even at night because of the large spike of flames coming from the building. It could be the flash-"*

Boom! There's a loud explosive sound in the reporter's transmission, followed by another. *Boom!*

"Catherine!" the reporter says, sounding as though he is running. *"We're being pushed back. We're being moved away, south along the feeder road. It seems there are explosions, a pair of them, pushing the flames and smoke higher into the sky."*

The ammunition! The flash-bang must have ignited the tons of ammunition stored inside the unit.

I've reached the exit off the freeway and merge onto the feeder road. There's a gas station to the right. I pull into a parking spot and turn off the ignition. The radio is still on and the reporter is describing the horrific scene unfolding in front of him.

There's no way Ripley survived. He couldn't have.

Another life ended because of me. I'm like the grim reaper. The dread and misery I've been trying to keep at bay leaks back into my mind.

"*Catherine,*" the reporter says, out of breath, but still working to provide information as best he can, "*we have a spokesperson here from DPS who is about to give us some updated information. I'll let you listen in.*" There's a shuffling noise as he presumably adjusts his phone.

"*Hello,* I'm Lieutenant Penny Rogers with the Texas Department of Public Safety."

"*Could you spell that?*" someone in the background asks the lieutenant. She spells her name.

"*We're going to have to ask all of the media to move to the other side of the freeway at this point,*" she announces amidst grumbling from the reporters and photographers. "*It's just too dangerous now. We have multiple fire units on the way. They need access here. You need to head north, turn around, and gather on the southbound side of the freeway. We'll have someone over there to assist you and provide updates.*" More grumbling. There are sirens in the background now.

"*Listen,*" she says in a firmer voice, worthy of her rank, "*this is not a debate. You need to move now. The only information I can give you right now, and this is only so you'll move along quickly without hassling me anymore, is the following.*" She clears her throat. "*We have two injured DPS troopers. Both of them seem to have minor burns and lacerations. We have three Harris County deputies with similar injuries. None are life threatening. As for the fire, it appears there may have been some sort of flammable product inside the building our team was targeting. We can't tell you more than that.*"

Somebody hurls another question at Lt. Rogers.

"No more questions," she says. *"Now, for your safety and ours, please move as instructed."* There's a crackle on the phone and Bill McNeal, the reporter, returns.

"So you heard that, Catherine," McNeal adds. *"Two DPS troopers and three deputies injured but okay. No word on the person or people inside the storage unit. I'm going to move now, as instructed, and will get back to you with more information once I've set up in the media staging area across the interstate."*

"Okay, Bill," says Catherine, exhaling as she speaks. *"Thank you for the incredible update. Live radio, folks. That was Bill McNeal reporting from the scene of what is now an inferno burning at a storage facility on the North Freeway in Harris County. I believe Bill has already sent some photos into the station and we've got them posted on our website. Incredible pictures of the fire, which, we believe, was ignited by a flash-bang thrown at a building during a tense standoff. And all of this somehow connected to a shooting earlier today that left at least four people dead. I'm Catherine Duke and you're listening to the News Machine 88.5 FM."*

The harder I work to dig myself out of this quicksand of a hole, the deeper I slip. Every move I make to excise the violence from my life creates an unwitting butterfly effect of harm, injury, and death. I should be numb to it by now. But I'm not. Not when people who should be sitting at home watching *American Idol* or *Game of Thrones* are, instead, burning alive inside of a storage unit. Not when five law enforcement officers, doing their jobs to keep people safe, are nursing shrapnel wounds and second degree burns.

I remind myself, however, this nasty, blood-spilling, back-stabbing world has always existed, I just didn't know about it. It wasn't until I took an iPod on a plane to London that I became enlightened.

With a deep breath, I throw the Camry into reverse.

I've got a plane to catch.

PART TWO
NIGHT VISION

"Nature is relentless and unchangeable, and it is indifferent as to whether its hidden reasons and actions are understandable to man or not."
—GALILEO GALILEI

CHAPTER 7

Straight Line FBO has its own terminal at Conroe's Lone Star Executive Airport. It's what's called a fixed base operator, providing A to Z support for private aircraft, pilots, and travelers.

The fifty thousand square foot hangar was big enough to house the white-and-gold Bombardier Global 5000 jet we flew here from Santa Rosa. The aircraft, rented under a pseudonym, of course, is top notch. It's big for a corporate jet and can cross the Atlantic with its awesome range. It's a shame we're flying it under these circumstances. It makes it difficult to appreciate the luxury of it. Let's put it this way: the pilot's cockpit is lined in double-stitched leather and chrome.

We told the attendant at the FBO we wouldn't be more than a day or so, and that we'd need the plane fueled and ready to fly with little notice. The pilot and copilot were on standby when we left this morning. It feels like a month ago.

Exiting off the freeway, I head east and then north on a loop around the city of Conroe, until there's a sign directing me to the airport and Straight Line. The radio distracts me for a moment and I almost miss the turn. Bill McNeal is back on the air with an update.

"*...got word from DPS that they believe there are two fatalities inside the storage unit, which is still on fire. Sources are telling me the people inside that unit were Roswell Ripley, the owner of the facility and well known for the assassination attempt of former gubernatorial candidate Don Carlos Buell, and a man named Jackson Quick. You may remember him for his* *involvement in the prosecution of the former governor. He was a political aide for the governor who turned against him and gave prosecutors valuable information as they sought a conviction for a host of crimes."*

They think I'm dead?

"Where this gets more complicated," McNeal adds to the drama of it with a pregnant pause. *"Quick was the source for much of George Townsend's award-winning coverage that put the governor in the legal crosshairs. Townsend was also the first television reporter to interview Roswell Ripley when he was wrongly arrested for the Buell shooting. Now Townsend, as we mentioned earlier, is dead after a shootout in his home earlier today. Piecing the parts together, with the help of our sources, it seems Ripley and Quick were the 'persons of interest' authorities sought to question about Townsend's death. Catherine, that's all I have for now. Back to you in the studio."*

"Great work out there, Bill," Catherine crows. *"Really fantastic information on this developing story. I'm Catherine Duke and you're listening to the News Machine on 88.5 FM Houston. For more on the mass shooting that left reporter George Townsend and three others dead, let's go to reporter Matthew Brock. He's joining us live from southwest Houston. Matthew, what are authorities there telling you?"*

"Catherine, this upscale neighborhood isn't used to this kind of crime. Police have marked bullet casings in the yard between two homes, there are trajectory sticks poking from the windows of a three-story townhouse, and yellow crime tape is everywhere. The body of one victim is covered in a sheet, still on the ground.

"Inside the home, police say there are three more bodies, all of them adult men. One of them is local television reporter George Townsend. Investigators here tell us that they believe at least three different weapons were used, and some of the victims were shot with more than one weapon. Witnesses tell me they saw three people leaving the house after they heard gunshots. There were two men and a woman. They have no suspects in custody, we're told. But we don't know if either of the men seen leaving this scene are connected to the

*standoff and deadly fire some twenty miles north of here. Catherine, we'll
stay here for the latest information and get it to you when we can. From
southwest Houston, I'm—"*

I turn the radio off, processing what this new information means.
It means I'm dead. At least until the arson team fails to find my body.

That's probably a good thing. Until they discover I wasn't in the fire,
I've got a free pass. Nobody looks for a dead guy. I press the brakes and
slow the car to make a left turn.

Once off the loop, the absence of streetlights makes the drive dark
until I reach the modern Straight Line terminal looms, glowing from its
lobby lighting. It's impressive through the twenty-foot tall single pane of
glass surrounding the front entry and facing the parking lot. The sight
of it makes my heart beat faster. A cold sweat blooms on my forehead.

Will Bella be there? Mack?

I steer the Toyota into an empty parking space next to a black
Silverado and crank the car into park. On truck's side is the Straight Line
FBO logo; two red dots connected by a straight brush stroke of black.
This place is vacant. I hope I'm not the only one here. That wouldn't be
good. I'm bothered less by the lack of activity on the other side of the
windows, however, than I am by the information that radio reporter got
from anonymous sources.

Would DPS or Harris County really have pieced all of that together
so quickly, especially with HPD handling the scene at George's house?
It just seems so—

Then it hits me.

It seems so… Sir Spencer.

✳✳✳

My mother was a gardener. She always planted seeds, believing that
growing vegetables or fruit from anything else was agricultural heresy.
We had a small, elevated garden in the backyard and she worked the

plot year round. I can't even tell you the number of times my dad and I found her elbow deep in compost.

"Your mom has got to be the most beautiful woman in the world," my dad would say. "She is unbelievably sexy."

"Gross, Dad," I'd complain. "I don't need to hear that."

She *was* beautiful. Even in soil stained overalls and bright yellow rubber boots, she carried an elegance unmatched by any of the other moms I knew.

The garden was as much a hobby as it was an escape for her, and it was a daily part of her routine. She treated it like a job. A labor of love.

My mom was meticulous with that garden. She'd split the plot into four equal sections and she'd alternate plantings to keep the soil fresh.

"It rejuvenates the nutrients," she told me one day as I helped her clip a snake of black irrigation tubing around her plantings when I was about ten years old. "Plus it helps keep pests away."

"How?" I asked her.

"Different crops need different things from the soil," she explained, wiping the sweat from her forehead with the back of a gloved hand. "Some plants, like tomatoes or corn, suck out the nitrogen. So if I plant tomatoes and corn in the same places, year after year, that part of the garden will lose its nitrogen faster than the other parts. If I rotate where I plant the tomatoes and the corn, it balances out the soil."

"What about the bugs?"

"The bugs are less of a nutrient problem and more of an appetite issue. You want to rotate plants so that you confuse the bugs and they don't set up shop in one spot expecting the same meal season after season."

She liked planting bulb onions, pole snap beans, summer squash, and tomatoes at the end of the summer and into the fall. In the spring, she'd plant cucumber, chard, radishes, and kale.

"The key, Jackson, is balance. That's the key to life, really; balance in all things."

In the winter, it could get tough sometimes to keep the plot healthy, but she worked at it. There could be ice or snow on the ground, and she was outside with a shovel or a hoe in her hand.

My dad might admire her from the back porch, but he didn't venture into the dirt. Maybe he didn't like it or, better yet, he didn't want to interfere on her turf. He'd surely enjoy the salads and side dishes she put on the dinner table, though.

"Have you thought about raising cattle?" he'd joke. "I mean, if you can grow vegetables like this, what's to stop you from ranching a mean steak?"

"You're the hunter and gatherer in this family," she'd said. "You bring home the steak."

My dad, as I've discovered, was the hunter. If I believe Mack, my mom had a lot to do with that. She was the one who introduced him to the life that killed them and sent me on this Greek tragedy of a life path.

One warm day in the garden, I remember, I was harvesting cucumbers. I'd take a set of clippers and cut them from their sticky, prickly stalks, carefully brush off the dirt, and place them in a canvas bag my mom gave me. There were maybe five or six of them in the bag when my mom cried out in pain.

I turned around to see a tangled piece of chicken wire sticking out of her forearm. She'd lost her balance pulling a weed and, in stopping her fall, caught her arm on the wire intended to keep out snakes and rodents. There was an extra thick layer of barbs along the top of the fence, some of which had burrowed their way beneath her skin.

"Mom!" I shrieked, sounding more like a teenage girl than a young boy. "Are you okay?"

"I'm fine," she grunted. "It looks worse than it is." She was on her knees, bracing herself on the top edge of the limestone, trying not to tug on the chicken wire. Most of it was still in the ground, except the part connected to her arm.

"Do you need help?" I asked, moving to her side.

"Yes," she said, smiling through the pain. "I need you to pull it out."

That was not the help I was expecting to give. But my dad wasn't home and she couldn't balance herself and pull free from the barbs buried in her arm. So, without really thinking, I took the clippers and started cutting the wire about six inches from my mom's flesh.

"I'm cutting you free of the fence first," I explained, snipping through the flexible galvanized steel mesh. "Then you can sit up straight and it won't hurt as much when I have to yank on the parts of the fence stuck in your arm."

"Good idea, Jackson. Very good idea."

I clipped through one hexagonal gap after another until she was free of the fence, then ran inside the house. A minute later, I emerged with a bottle of hydrogen peroxide and a pair of needle nose pliers.

"Sit here," I told her with what I now know was a remarkable sense of calm for a kid my age. I gently pulled her arm into my lap by her wrist. There is a three-inch section of fence protruding upward with at least four barbs to pull out.

I pour a healthy dose of the peroxide on the punctures and it bubbled ferociously around the edges of the barbs.

"Okay, Mom, this might hurt." Wincing as I did it, I surgically plucked each of the four prongs with those pliers. It took several minutes, which felt like hours, and tears were streaming down my mother's face by the time I'd removed the last of them and doused the wounds with another slug of H_2O_2.

She didn't think they were deep enough to warrant a trip to the emergency room, but she slathered the cuts with a healthy dose of Neosporin. I was carefully unwrapping a large square Band-Aid when I noticed something on her forearm I'd not seen before.

Right at the point where her forearm met the lower part of her bicep, there was a small, raised, circular scar. It looked like a bullet wound.

I pressed the edges of the bandages onto her skin, careful to avoid the wounds themselves. "Mom, what's the scar on your arm?"

"What scar?" she said, feigning ignorance.

"The one on your arm." I pointed to it. "It looks like it hurt."

"Oh, *that* scar," she said dramatically. My mother wasn't much of an actress. She rubbed her thumb on it. "I'm not sure."

I'd never known my mom to lie to me. She was, as far as I could tell, a straight shooter.

"I mean, who remembers all of the bumps and bruises they collect growing up?" she said.

I looked at the scar again. It wasn't a scrape or a cut. It was scar from a serious injury. I'd bet my money it was a bullet wound. I was as taken off guard by her denial as I was that I'd never really noticed it before, though I wasn't going to press.

"I guess not," I shrugged. No point in arguing with her. My parents clearly had secrets they wanted to keep. I had to assume they had good reasons for it.

***

A whoosh of cold air and the soulful sounds of Chuck Mangione on his flugelhorn greet me at the entrance to Straight Line FBO's terminal. The expansive space is essentially empty, the polished travertine floor reflecting the bright spotlights hanging high above. The half-dozen modern, low back, white leather chairs in the waiting area are empty. The magazines are fanned perfectly on the spotless glass tables next to each chair. My heart sinks, thinking Bella and Mack haven't made it.

At the far end of the terminal past the waiting area, a young businessman is manipulating a single serve Keurig coffeemaker. He's spinning the lazy Susan next to the machine, presumably looking for the right flavor.

There's also a pilot sitting at a computer terminal inside an office adjacent to the coffee bar. His back is to me and he's working a mouse with his left hand. A half empty twenty-ounce bottle of Mountain Dew Code Red is on the desk next to a crumpled cellophane wrapper.

I swing to the left after pushing my way through the double doors and head to the main service counter. It's alit with the led logo of Straight Line FBO across the front. Across the wall behind the counter are five digital clocks: one each for Los Angeles, New York, London, Tokyo, and Conroe, Texas. The local time is 9:54 PM.

There's a young woman in a dark blue blazer, her pressed white collar laying evenly on the lapel of the jacket. Her hair is pulled tightly into a bun, her tanned cheeks dusted pink with blush. It gives her the appearance of a business suit ballerina. She wasn't the attendant at the desk when we landed earlier in the day, though I swear Mangione's *Feels So Good* was playing then too. Maybe it's on a loop of inoffensive, instrumental, medium rock.

"May I help you?" She glances at the heavy duffel I'm lugging. She's not nearly as warm as the trio of FBO attendants who treated us like celebrities upon our arrival. They greeted us on the tarmac, at the end of a red carpet, with chilled bottles of Fiji water and fruit. Their smiles were genuine, their hospitality appreciated despite the circumstances. This one in front of me is on the night shift for a reason, I imagine.

"Yes. I'm looking for a young woman. Beautiful, dark complexion, about this tall." I hold my hand at about Bella's height.

The woman narrows her glare and holds up the back of her left hand, revealing a nice-sized diamond on the back of her ring ringer. "Sir, I'm flattered. But I'm enga—"

"Not you," I shoot back, darkening the pink on her cheeks to an embarrassed red. "I'm looking for another woman, a passenger. She and a coworker of ours should be here." I realize I should have described Mack from the start. "He's an amputee, short haircut."

She purses her lips to an F sharp from Chuck's flugelhorn and tugs on her jacket. "Oh, um…" she looks past me toward the tarmac and the hangars. "I apologize, Sir. I believe the two of them just boarded that aircraft." She points to the familiar, oversized Global 5000 on the other side of the floor to ceiling glass framing the outdoors.

Without turning back to thank the betrothed ballerina, I slug the duffel onto my back and bolt for the plane. A pair of automatic doors slide open as I approach and the smell of jet fuel swims into my nostrils. The engines are running, the beacon is on. Mangione is replaced with the high-pitched whistle of an idling jet.

I eagerly jog to the front of the plane, excited and relieved that both Bella and Mack are aboard, and start to climb the retractable steps. I smile at the flight attendant and start to move past her. She stops me.

"Sir," she holds out her hand like a Supreme. "This is a private flight."

"I'm aware," I say, stuck a couple of steps from the cabin. "I'm one the passengers."

"I don't think so," she says. "We have a manifest here with only two passengers and they're on board."

It's not even ten o'clock. Only two passengers? Were they going to leave me here?

"I was on this flight on the way here," I remind her. "You served me a Diet Dr. Pepper."

"Sir," she says, "I cannot—"

Mack appears from behind the flight attendant, his face brightening when he sees me. "Jackson? You're alive?"

"Yes, the reports of my death have been greatly exaggerated."

"Let this man aboard." Mack motions to the flight attendant to get out of the way. She sheepishly moves to the left and I duck into the cabin.

"You thought I was dead?" I ask, dropping the bag on the leather sofa.

"We did. We heard it on the news. They said you were killed in a fire."

"Where's Bella?"

"Bella's in the back of the plane, in the bedroom." He motions to a part of the plane hidden by a door at the rear of the plane. "She's… emotional…"

I nod and start to walk to the back of thirty-foot cabin when a voice stops me.

"Sir, would you like me to store your bag?" asks the co-pilot. He reaches for my bag and I wave him off.

"I'm good. Just leave it there, thanks." It's probably not a good idea to have him handling the portable weapons cache.

"Will do." He salutes. "By the way, we're fueled up and ready to go, but we can't take off until we know where it is you want us to fly."

"Give me five minutes," I tell him. "Just sit tight." Then I think better of it. "On second thought, chart a course for Washington, D.C."

He nods and returns to the cockpit.

I turn the handle to the bedroom door at the back of the plane and take a deep breath.

***

The "bedroom" is small. It's maybe eight feet squared with just enough room for a queen-sized bed and two nightstands. The light is dimmed and it takes my eyes a moment to adjust to the figure curled up in the middle of the bed, the cream colored duvet pulled over her. She's crying softly.

I've never before interrupted someone mourning my death.

"Bella? It's me." I sit on the edge of the bed, my knees hitting the wall of the tight space.

The whimpering stops and she throws back the comforter. Her eyes widen with confusion before blinking rapidly, processing what they're seeing. She throws her arms around me, almost knocking me off of the bed. The whimpering turns into heaving sobs as she pulls tighter against me.

Overwhelmed, an unfamiliar lump grows in my throat. My eyes well and my hands move from her shoulders to the small of her back. My eyes start to burn so I squeeze them shut to press the tears from them.

"We thought you were dead," Bella sniffles, her voice nearly unrecognizable. "We thought you died in a fire. They said you were dead."

"I know," I whisper, "but I'm okay. I'm here."

She pulls away from me, her hands still on my arms. "What happened?"

I laugh nervously. "Long story. I was there at the storage facility with Roswell Ripley. He picked me up at —"

"Roswell Ripley?" she interrupts, the confusion consuming her face. "The guy who they said shot my dad?"

"Same one," I say.

"Why him?"

"I figured I could trust him," I explain, thumbing a tear from her cheek.

"Could you?" she sniffs.

"I think so," I nod. "He picked me up not too far from where we separated and took me to the storage facility. He owns—uh—owned it. He had this armory of weapons in one of the units. He gave me a bag full of them. And when the troopers showed up, he helped me escape. I was gone before the fire started."

"I thought for sure you were..." she can't bring herself to finish and throws herself into me again. I give her a minute before pulling away to look her in the eyes.

"I'm okay," I reassure her. "I'm here. I'm not going anywhere."

"Right, like I believe that." Her face hardens. "You left me, Jackson. I mean, right in the middle of a crisis, you just left."

"That's not—"

"I know you're on this 'You're better off without me' kick, or whatever, but it's just not true. I can try to distance myself from you, try to emotionally shut myself down, but it doesn't do any good."

"I don't—"

"Just shut up for a second," she snaps. "I'm saying something important here."

I close my mouth.

"You can't keep believing that this is going to end with you running away from me. I'm not going to let that happen. I'm no safer without you, I'm not better off without you, and let's be honest here, Jackson, I saved *you* too. You need me as much as I need you." She licks the tears from her top lip. "It's like a light bulb went off or something when I thought you were dead."

"Is that all it took?" I joke.

"Seriously, whatever you think your plans are, they include me."

"Understood."

"Don't placate me, Jackson. I get why we split up. I get that you think you're bad for me. That's not your decision to make."

"The two have nothing to do with one another, Bella. I understand what you're saying about not wanting to distance yourself, that you want to be with me despite my fears that I'll get you killed."

"So…"

"So me splitting up with you in Houston was to protect all three of us. There was no way we'd make it out of there if we'd stuck together. We had to go our separate ways to give ourselves a chance."

She nods.

"How did you get here?" I finally get around to asking.

"Uber."

"What?"

She looks at me like I have green horns growing out of my head. "Really? Mr. Espionage doesn't know about Uber? The taxi service?"

Well that escalated quickly. She went from heartfelt sentimentality to sarcastic derision in a split second.

"No, what is it?"

"It's a person-to-person taxi service. It's super cheap. I had the burner phone you gave me. I downloaded the app, clicked it, and ordered a ride."

"From whom?"

"From Uber."

"No, who picked you up?"

"Some woman in a Prius," she says. "The location services on the phone gave her a location through the GPS. The app finds the closest driver. I picked the cheapest option and paid her cash."

"Did you have to give them a credit card or anything?"

"No, just my cell phone number through a text. I left the burner in the car, Jackson. There's no way to trace me or follow me or anything."

"How'd you know about it?"

"Nanergetix invested in it," she explains. "Goldman Sachs, Google, and some others were on board too."

"Is it really safe? I mean getting into cars with strangers?"

"Less safe than having to escape from a burning storage unit?"

"Point taken," I concede. "What about Mack?"

"I haven't asked him. I was a little preoccupied with your death."

I smile at her and run my fingers across her forehead. She's so beautiful. Even with reddened eyes, puffy from crying, she's mesmerizing. She moves closer to me to offer a kiss when there's a knock at the door.

"Sir, I'm sorry to interrupt," says the copilot. "We've got an issue. The pilot needs to see you before we take off."

***

"I'm your captain, Chris Secousse," the pilot says when we step into the cockpit. He turns in his seat and reaches over his right shoulder to offer his left hand. "I've got a few questions for you, if you're the one in charge."

Captain Secousse is young but confident. It's obvious in the way he grips my hand, looks me in the eyes. He's clean-shaven with a high and tight haircut underneath his captain's hat. He's chomping on a piece of gum in a way that reminds me of Matthew McConaughey accepting an Oscar. That, and he has a West Texas drawl.

"I don't think I'm in charge," I say after the handshake. "But I'll make the decisions."

"Ha!" Secousse laughs, a big smile revealing the neon green gum nestled between his molars. "I'm the one who makes the decisions compadre." Definitely McConaughey. "This is my ship. However, you can feel free to make suggestions."

"Understood. What did you want…Captain?"

"Well, we're fueled up and ready to go, but I don't know where you want me to head. That's kind of an issue."

"Washington, D.C. I told your copilot." I nod in the direction of the second in command, who's standing behind me outside the cockpit entrance.

"There are no fewer than twenty-two airports around D.C. I could pick one, but that doesn't mean it's where you want to go. And depending on which one you choose, there could be an FRZ."

"What's that?"

"A flight restriction zone. I have to have special clearance, with an access code, and I have to file the flight plan by physically talking with the good people at the Lynchburg Flight Service Station. It's a real pain."

"Let's try Washington Executive," I suggest. I remember Sir Spencer mentioning it as a convenient landing spot with a lot of discretion among its workers.

"Washington Executive is a tricky one. That runway isn't really built for a plane this size."

"Really?"

"Well, if we were in, say, a Citation Sovereign or some other nice mid-sized jet, we'd be good. This Bombardier is a beast by comparison."

"So you can't do it?" asks the copilot from behind me. "I've seen these planes land there before."

"I didn't say I *couldn't*," the pilot bristles, clenching the gum between his teeth. "I said it was tricky. And what do you know 'newbie?' You've had next to nothing in the way of flying."

"I have six hundred and seventy-three hours," the copilot says.

"Well then, *Manfred Von Richthofen*," says Captain Secousse, "climb in and let's get going." Secousse winks at me and smiles. "We can make it happen, boss."

The copilot, red-faced after challenging his superior in front of me, squeezes by and maneuvers his way into his seat. I brace myself against the cockpit door.

"Lone Star Clearance," Captain Secousse says into the radio, "this is Global N seven hundred X-Ray Charlie. I'm at Straight Line Aviation with information Romeo and requesting our IFR clearance to Washington Executive."

There's a crackle over the radio and the tower responds. *"This is Clearance Delivery, Global seven hundred X-Ray Charlie. You are cleared to Washington Executive via the Alexandria Six Departure, as filed. Maintain four thousand and expect Flight Level four ten, ten minutes after departure. Departure control one one nine point seven, three two four six."*

Captain Secousse reads back the clearance into the radio, repeating exactly what the tower just told him. He turns to the copilot and slaps his leg. "I didn't mean to get snappy with you, boss. I apologize for that."

"No offense," the copilot says. "I was out of line for questioning you in the cockpit."

"You *were* out of line," Secousse laughs.

"Global seven hundred X-Ray Charlie, read back correct contact ground when you are ready to taxi," the tower requests over the radio.

Secousse runs his finger down the notepad on his wheel and then flips a couple of switches. There's a loud rumble and whir as the second engine ignites.

"You can stand there for a few minutes," Secousse says to me. "But once I get set to take off, you gotta go sit down and buckle up."

I turn around and see Bella and Mack sitting in adjacent captain's chairs along the right side of the cabin. They're talking to each other. Bella sees me looking at her and smiles weakly.

"Lone Star Ground," the copilot keys his mic, "Global seven hundred X-ray Charlie is ready to taxi."

"Global seven hundred X-Ray Charlie," Control responds, *"taxi to Runway Three Two via taxiway Golf."*

"Global seven hundred X-Ray Charlie," the copilot confirms, "taxi to Runway Three Two via taxiway Golf."

The plane lurches forward and I grab the doorframe to avoid losing my balance. It's a short taxi, maybe a couple hundred feet from Straight Line to the end of the runway. The plane eases to a stop, its nose facing the flat stretch of concrete

"Global seven hundred X-Ray Charlie," says the copilot. "Ready for takeoff."

The tower responds, *"Global seven hundred X-Ray Charlie, after departure, turn right heading Zero Three Zero. Cleared for takeoff Runway Three Two."*

The copilot repeats the instructions and Captain Secousse pulls the wad of chewing gum from his mouth, sticking it on the wheel's clipboard. "Here's where you take a seat, boss," he instructs without turning to look at me. You can leave the door open when you leave. Make sure you buckle up."

I go find a seat next to Bella. No sooner has the buckle snapped at my waist when the gravity of the accelerating jet presses me into my seat. Captain Secousse's hand is on the throttle, like he's about to shift into overdrive in a racecar. A few seconds later, we're airborne and on our way to Washington.

CHAPTER 8

Bella's eyes are dry, but still swollen and red. She's exhausted. Mack appears unfazed by it all. He's squeezing lotion from a small tube and rubbing it on his elbows and hands. Neither of them are talking.

"So I guess it's my turn," I say. "Since both of you are jumping to discuss what's next for our merry band of travelers."

"Bella was just telling me about your escape," Mack says. "Pretty incredible. I guess the Ripley guy is dead though, right?"

"I'm pretty sure," I say. "I got this sense from him he was ready to go."

"Really?" Bella asks. "Why would you think that?"

"I don't know." I shrug, loosening the belt a little as the plane levels off at altitude. "He knew what he was doing by helping me, arming me with his weapons. He knew the risk and took it anyway."

"I knew the risks by sticking with you," she says. "I don't have a death wish."

"I'm not saying that. I'm not suggesting he wanted to die, only that he'd accepted it. He wanted revenge for his son's death, and if that came at the cost of his own life, he was willing to pay it. He could have escaped with me if he'd wanted. He stayed behind to make sure I had enough time to get out and keep my promise."

"What promise it that?" Mack says, jumping on my admission like a Marine on a hot meal.

"I told him I'd kill the people responsible for his son's death."

"Really?" Bella looks surprised. Mack doesn't. "How does that fit in to what we've already got going on here? I mean, our plate is full."

"It fits in," Mack says in my defense. "We already plan on handling Sir Spencer. From what he told me, the only other people involved in that mess were your father and the governor. Your father, God rest his soul, has already passed on. So that leaves the governor. That's the only piece which might not fit, and we could make it fit."

"I don't know," Bella says. "Maybe we can just forego the 'eye for an eye' part of this and focus on what we already have on our plate."

"Are you hungry?" Mack asks, putting his hand on Bella's arm.

"Why do you ask?"

"You keep talking about plates."

"Actually," she laughs, "I am. We haven't eaten in, I don't know, forever."

Mack unbuckles his belt and pushes himself to his prosthetic foot. "I'm gonna get us some grub." He walks to the front of the cabin toward a small galley and the flight attendant.

"So we're headed to Washington?" Bella asks.

"Yes. We're going to find Sir Spencer. He set me up in Houston, giving information to the media."

"How would he do that? Better yet, *why* would he do that?" Bella questions. "He knows you're trying to get him the entirety of the process. He knows you want to take care of Blogis."

"How?" I look at her like she's nuts. "He makes a phone call or two to the television stations. He tips them off that I'm involved in George's death. The reporters then call their sources at Harris County or DPS and confirm whatever Sir Spencer told them."

"Okay," she concedes. "That still leaves 'why.'"

"Because he can. He didn't like the fact that for a moment I had the upper hand, that I was calling the shots. So he gently reminds me of his power, his reach. I don't think he actually thought they'd catch me.

I don't know if he was even aware I'd reached out to Ripley. I just think he was giving me a big middle-fingered salute."

"So what are you going to do when we get to D.C.?" she asks. "Do you know where he is?"

"I know he's staying at the Hay Adams Hotel. If he's not there, we'll ask around. We'll find him."

"And once we find him?"

"We get whatever information he has about Blogis." I swivel the captain's chair toward Bella and, out of habit more than anything else, lower my voice. "He wants that process. He knows Blogis wants it too. It's too valuable. And with the instability in the Ukraine, Gaza, and Syria, the bidders are chomping at the bit. You know they are."

"But the plan is to get Blogis on our side," she reminds me. "How is wasting our time in D.C. hunting for Sir Spencer going to help us?"

"Sir Spencer is our ticket to finding Blogis. That's the whole reason we risked going to Houston in the first place, remember?"

Bella sighs and sinks a little into the comfort of the cream colored leather of the captain's chair. She runs both of her hands through her hair and squeezes her eyes shut, then blinks them open.

"We know Blogis is still hunting for the process. It's too valuable for him to have given up on it. We know Sir Spencer wants it."

"You're repeating what I already understand, Jackson," she says. "But why do we have to go *see* Sir Spencer?"

"We need to surprise him. I need to let him know we're in control. He has to believe he needs us. And as long as we stay a half step ahead, we'll have that in our corner."

"He's right, you know," Mack says, returning from the galley carrying a bowl of bar mix and a cheese plate. He slides the plate onto the table between his chair and Bella's and plops into his seat. "Sir Spencer is a gamer. He's all about the tradecraft, so to speak. He needs to know we're players. We surprise him on his turf? That's a point for us. He'll give us what we need and we'll be on our way."

"All of this is beyond me." Bella shakes her head and pops a piece of cheddar into her mouth. "You just tell me what to do."

"We need to look at the stuff from the reporter's apartment," Mack suggests. "It'll help us understand what Sir Spencer already knows about Blogis and the process. Then we go in armed."

"Good idea." I reach into my pockets and pull out the thumb drives. "I've got the laptop and the hard drive in that bag over there." I unbuckle and go to unzip the duffel.

"I've got those file folders and the maps," Mack adds. "There in a backpack next to your duffel."

I open the backpack and find the files, along with a stack of folded maps. All of it finds a place on a long burled wood table that runs four feet along the side of the cabin opposite our chairs.

Mack moves over to the table and leans on it. "As we start to look at all of this, let's remind ourselves of the score."

"What score?" I ask.

"The pieces of the process," Mack says, spreading out one of the maps. It's too big for the width of the table and hangs from it like a tablecloth. "If I remember correctly, Blogis had one piece. He managed to find the piece hidden in Toulon, France, correct?"

"That's what Sir Spencer told us." I start scanning the map. It looks more like a blueprint than a map. "He said there were four pieces. Blogis had one. We had the other three."

"Until you destroyed the hard drive," Mack reminds me, his eyes still on the table.

"I'm sure the Germans and the Israelis were devastated," I say snarkily, referencing the buyers Sir Spencer suggested were interested in obtaining the complete process.

"I'm sure."

"So these are blueprints?" I ask. "It's not a map?"

"No, " it's not a map. It's a detailed rendering of Brookhaven National Laboratory. Building 197."

"What's in Building 197?"

"I'm not sure," says Mack. "But this is detailed down to the number of inches in a hallway, the thickness of the walls, the materials used in construction."

"I know what the building is," Bella says, walking over to us. She's sipping from a glass of water. "Building 197 at Brookhaven is the Nonproliferation and National Security Department building," she says, placing the empty glass next to the blueprint. "They do neutrino research."

"In this building?" I ask.

"Not officially, no. They have other places on the campus where they conduct their public neutrino work. They partner with Fermi National Accelerator Lab in Illinois. They're part of what's called the Daya Bay Neutrino Project. They partnered with Japan in the Super-Kamoiokande experiment. Some of the work they're doing actually connects to Homestake."

"In South Dakota?" I ask, shocked I haven't heard this before, given our history at the bottom of the Homestake Mine, a mile beneath the Earth.

"The very same," she says.

"I'm confused," says Mack. "How do you know all of this?"

"Really, guys?" she's says incredulously. "I was CEO of Nanergetix when we were developing the process, when we were secretly funding the research. Of course I know about all of this."

"So what's going on in Building 197?" I ask.

"That's where the unofficial neutrino work is happening," she says. "It's no coincidence that they call it 'non-proliferation'. The federal government was working on the process too. We weren't the only ones. Building 197 is where we believed they were conducting that research."

"Why didn't I know about this?" asked Mack. "I was your go-to guy, wasn't I? I mean, you trusted me to kill Dr. Wolf at Homestake. Why wouldn't you have told me about the government's work?"

"Nobody knew everything, Mack," she says. "It's called plausible deniability. We were spying on the government. If things went south, not everybody could be in on it, especially the one who killed Dr. Wolf."

"Things sure went south, didn't they?" I understate, and Bella shoots me a look suggesting it was an ill-advised question.

"So why did George have this in his apartment?" Mack asks.

"My goodness," Bella says. "The two of you... for being so smart, you're both idiots."

"Don't lump me in with him," I say. "George has it because he thinks there are existing pieces of the process in that building."

"That's my guess," says Bella. "We knew they were working on something. Wolf believes they were a good six months behind him. But we also had evidence he was secretly collaborating with someone at Brookhaven."

"Wouldn't this have been helpful to know before we traipsed all over Europe?" I complain. "We could've started at Brookhaven."

"Not really," says Mack. "Look at this map." He unrolls another large document that more closely resembles a map than the one already on the table. "Look at all of this security. There's really only one way in for the public. Here, off of West Princeton. There's a security building before you get anywhere."

"They have a Laboratory Protection Division," Bella adds. "It's a government installation under the Department of Energy. You need badges, passes, vehicle authorization, and placards. It's not as easy as walking up, knocking on a door, and asking for top secret information on technology that doesn't officially exist."

"Oh," I roll my eyes and laugh. "And finding a single piece of the process in the hidden back room of a liquor store inside an irradiated exclusion zone in the country in the midst of a civil war is easy."

"I didn't miss your sarcasm when I thought you were dead," says Bella with a smirk. "I'm just saying that given how we were flying by the seat of our pants, breaking into a heavily guarded government installation wasn't on the list of things to do."

"Got it," I say without sarcasm.

"What's this?" Mack points to a handwritten note on the corner of the document. "It says, 'Corkscrew'. And there's an email address and a series of numbers."

"That's an IP address," says Bella. "Those numbers are a server location for a computer."

"Could mean anything," I shrug. "Could be a passcode or a username for something. Keep it in the backs of your minds."

"So once we go through the rest of this stuff," Mack waves his hand at the laptop and stacks of file folders, "and determine that there are pieces of the process hidden at Brookhaven, what do we do?"

Mack and Bella both look to me, the man with the plan.

"We break into a heavily guarded government installation," I answer, "and we take what doesn't officially exist."

***

The amount of information George was hoarding in his apartment was worthy of an investigative reporter. He'd done his homework. Amongst the files, both paper and electronic, we found security protocols for Brookhaven, emergency procedures, and staffing levels at every one of the campus's seventy-five buildings above ground.

We knew about the underground facilities, more than a dozen of them, that weren't on the Star Maps tour guide for Brookhaven. We had hi-resolution images of badging for all of the laboratory's divisions and placards for all of its parking lots.

Based on George's extensive research, a lot of which we imagine was aided by Sir Spencer and his deep government ties, we had a good idea about where in Building 197 we could find the government's version of the process. And from what we could decipher from handwritten notes,

Sir Spencer and George believed that one of the labs actually contained an early draft of Dr. Wolf's work.

There were also bank records on one of the flash drives, detailing payments from one Swiss account to another; likely payments from Sir Spencer to George. That would explain the reporter's lavish lifestyle.

Most importantly, we come to the conclusion that "Corkscrew" is some sort of computer expert. There are multiple references to Corkscrew and the information he was able to relay to George and Sir Spencer. It appears as though this research was months, if not years, in the making.

"So," Mack concludes as he begins to fold up the maps and blueprints, "we have enough here to formulate a plan. Don't you think?"

Bella nods. "I can't believe how much of this information George had just sitting in his house. I mean, all of this classified material out in the open."

"Sir Spencer has a long reach," Mack says. "He has access to a lot people and places. You know he was at Thatcher's side during the Falklands War? And he was one of Reagan's advisors ahead of the Granada invasion."

"He *was* knighted," I say as if his influence was obvious. "It wouldn't shock me if he tried to singlehandedly overthrow a government someday."

"Who says he hasn't already?" Mack jokes. Sort of.

"And he claims to have less of a handle on things than Blogis," I add. "He said Blogis is more connected, more powerful than he is."

"Do you believe that?" Mack asked.

"I don't know what to believe," I admit. "All of this is so far over my pay grade, it's ridiculous. It's like there's this whole class of people secretly running the world."

"You mean secret societies?" Mack questions. "I believe in that stuff. Illuminati. New World Order. It's real."

"No," I say, waving him off of his conspiratorial cliff. "I don't mean that. I just mean the real power lies in the money, the industry. The kind of thing that Eisenhower warned against. You know, the Military Industrial Complex and such."

"It's all the same," Mack says.

"Still," Bella says, "it never ceases to amaze me what people are willing to do for money or power."

"Really?" Mack laughs. "That sentiment coming from a Buell?"

"Good point," she acknowledges.

"The one question I have," I say, "is why Sir Spencer hasn't already gone in and gotten what he thinks is there."

"Good point," Bella agrees. "If he had access to all of this information, why couldn't get access to the process itself?"

"We don't know that he hasn't," Mack says. "My guess is that he hasn't found anyone willing to take the risk. If a nun can get three years in prison, imagine what some mercenary with a Swiss bank account will get."

"A nun?" Bella asks.

"Yeah," Mack laughs. "An eighty year old nun broke into a uranium processing facility in Tennessee. She and a couple of other guys in their fifties were protesting. The guys got five years and she got thirty-five months. It was big news when it happened. There were lots of questions about security at nuclear facilities."

"How'd they get in?" Bella asks.

"They cut through fences," Mack says. "They spent a while in a secure area. That meant the Department of Energy had to enhance its security measures at all of its facilities."

"Then maybe that's *why* Sir Spencer hasn't tried it yet, assuming he hasn't," I suggest. "It's too risky. He can't afford a failed break-in to come back to him."

"So we're going to do it." Bella's now the one beaming with sarcasm.

"If Ethan Hunt can break into the CIA and steal the NOC list we can handle Brookhaven," I say..

"Ethan Hunt," she repeats, "Wait... I got it... *Patriot Games!*"

"No," Mack says, "that was Jack Ryan."

"Jack Ryan broke into the CIA?"

"No, Jack Ryan is the hero in *Patriot Games.*"

"Ethan Hunt is Tom Cruise's character in *Mission Impossible.* Hunt gets framed for killing his MI team and to earn his reputation back, he steals the NOC list fr—"

"I got it," Bella waves me off with a giggle. "You have more useless crap stored in that brain of yours." It's good to see her laugh. She's run the gamut in the last month, week, and hour. Any moment of levity is good.

It's cut short when the flight attendant interrupts. "Mr. Quick, the captain would like to see you."

***

Captain Secousse is playing Angry Birds on his iPad when I peek into the cockpit. The gum is still stuck to the notepad on the wheel.

"You wanted to see me, Captain?"

"Yeah!" He snaps to attention and turns in his seat to look at me. "We're getting close. I just talked to a briefer at LFSS."

"LFSS?"

"Lynchburg Flight Service Station," he clarifies. "I reconfirmed our flight into the FRZ. The rules are super strict, boss."

"And?"

"Well," he thumbs his hat back on his head a bit, "as I explained before, we're a big plane for that runway."

"Okay..."

"It's not really something we should be doing," he says. "We need about twenty-six hundred feet of runway to land this jet. There's right at three thousand feet at Washington Executive."

"Okay..."

"So," he adjusts his cap again, "landing a fifty-million dollar jet in less than optimal conditions, especially with a bag full of weapons on board, that's tricky. Thankfully we have cooler than normal temperatures and some low level clouds. But that's not the hard part."

"I'm really against this," the copilot speaks up. "I don't think we should be flying to this airport. We could easily land in Baltimore. That would alleviate all of the problems."

"I didn't ask your opinion," says Secousse. "You're fresh of out of a classroom, right?"

"Checked out with highest marks possible."

"So you know, then, that we can land where the customer is asking us to land." The captain lowers his chin, looking down his nose at the book smart copilot.

"Yes. But with the possibility of rain we—"

"I can handle it," Captain Secousse snaps.

"And then the takeoff," the copilot goes on. "That's the bigger problem.

"What do you mean?" I ask both of them.

"The hard part is after you've gotten off of the plane," Secousse explains. "This bird typically needs five thousand feet to take off. I mean, I can get her in the air quicker than that, but on that runway, we don't meet what we like to call the *Balance Field Requirement*. If I have an engine failure or some other issue as we're accelerating toward liftoff, it would be a super long day. Or a short day!" He laughs. "I'm just saying that once *your* trip is over, I've still got work to do. We probably have to liftoff again without refueling, to lighten the load so to speak. And I have to hope we've got some headwind."

"Again," the copilot shakes his head, "this isn't a good idea. I'm not sure the FAA, or our owners for that matter, will be thrilled with this."

"Without risk," smiles the pilot, "there is no reward." He glances back at me. "Am I right? Or am I right?"

"How much is it going to cost me?"

"Boss, I don't want any cash." He looks at his copilot. "I just want you to know how accommodating a pilot I must be to land there, and how talented I must be to take off again."

"Right," I smirk. "How much do you want?"

"What would you tip a good waiter, boss?" He chuckles.

"Seeing as how you make the decisions, Captain, you tell me."

"Ohhh!" he says, punching his copilot's shoulder. "We got a live one here, Greenie." The copilot, turning his attention to the instruments in front of him is clearly uncomfortable with the discussion. "Let's say a twenty percent gratuity on the thirty grand you spent on this here leg of the trip would be fair," he says, turning back to Angry Birds. "But I'm up for suggestions."

"Let's suggest this," I tell him, tired of his games. "I'll figure what's fair when we get on the ground safely. Sound good?"

"Okay by me," Captain Secousse says without looking at me. "We've only got maybe fifteen minutes until we land. Might want to take your seat, boss."

I suddenly hate Matthew McConaughey.

"What is it?" Bella asks, obviously sensing my irritation as I walk back from the cockpit.

"Captain Jerk up there is blackmailing us." I drop into my seat and pull the buckle across my lap. "He wants a tip commensurate with his ability to land and take off at an airport he says isn't really suitable for this aircraft."

"And you're surprised?" Mack asks.

"More irritated than surprised. Everybody's out for a buck."

"How do you think I got to the airport?" Mack says.

"What do you mean?"

"From George's apartment, when we split up. It's not like I exactly blend in with the crowd," he says, gesturing to his prosthetic and then the pigment-less spots of skin on his face and hands.

"What did you do?"

"I ducked into a car wash," he says, "and I looked for the most expensive, cheap car I could find in the line."

"What does that mean?"

"Like a Chrysler or a Honda that's tricked out. I figure someone who takes a twenty or twenty-five thousand dollar car and puts a five thousand dollar paint job and a three thousand dollar set of wheels on it has got to need some quick cash. I see this ridiculous two tone metallic green Civic," he says. "It's got a set of swangas on it worthy of a chariot race."

"Wait," Bella interrupts. "What are *swangas*?"

"The rims that stick out beyond the wheels themselves."

Bella nods. The plane pitches up quickly before nosing downward.

"So there's this Honda getting washed, going through the spinning brushes, and there's this young kid watching it. He's walking along slowly as the car moves through the rinse cycle."

The flight attendant steps over. "Is there anything else I can get for you? We're about to land." We decline her offer and she quickly returns to her jump seat next to the cabin door.

"I ask the kid if the Honda is his car," Mack continues. "He says yes. He's proud of it and tells me he bought it himself. He did the paint job, worked two jobs to pay for the rims. He's beaming like he's talking about his child going to an Ivy League school. So I ask him if he wants to earn a little extra cash. I just need a ride. I show him my identification and some cash.

"The kid was a little suspicious at first," he says. "But when I explained I needed a ride to the airport, that I didn't have a car, and I couldn't wait for a taxi, he was cool with it."

"He never asked how you ended up at the car wash without any transportation?" I ask.

The cabin rattles against the weather outside. Maybe it's worse than Captain Secousse anticipated from the radar.

"Nope," he says. "The cash answered all of his unasked questions. Two hundred bucks. That's all it took. Name was Chris Donald. Good kid. Easy as pie."

The co-pilot's voice blares over the cabin speakers. "We're approaching Washington Executive Airport. The landing will be an aggressive one, so please stay in your seats with your belts fastened. We should be on the ground in about five minutes."

"What's first on the agenda?" Mack asks. Another rumble.

"We rent a car," Bella says. "We can't be taking public transportation or cabs. Jackson is a wanted man and who knows if they've identified us by now, Mack? I mean, I *was* stupid enough to use my name when we signed in at the television station."

"I'm dead," I remind her. "Remember? Nobody's looking for me yet."

The plane shudders as we dip into the clouds. Water beads on the windows.

"Good point," Bella acknowledges, gripping the armrests of her chair. "Still, probably better to have our own car, right?"

"Agreed," Mack concurs.

"We're gonna need fake identification," I say.

We dip and rise quickly in what is clearly a rainstorm. The lights flicker in the cabin.

"I still have one set of documents," Bella says. "I have one for you too, Jackson. They're in the pack over there, with what's left of my cash and our last burner phone. Outside zipper."

"We'll need new ones," I tell them as the plane tilts aggressively to the left and then levels again. "I'll take care of that after we deal with Sir Spencer."

"I'll get the burner phones," Mack says absently. "I know a place."

All of us are focused on the impending landing in a plane that's too big... on a runway that's too short... in weather that's not good.

"So this is where it gets fun," I joke.

Nobody laughs as we feel the weight of the jet sink to the tarmac at Washington Executive. Something is wrong.

***

I don't know if it was intentional, but one of the pilots keyed his microphone a minute before we hit the tarmac. I wish he hadn't.

"We've got one shot at this Greenie!" shouts Secousse. "I need your focus."

"We're going too fast!" the copilot answers. "The tailwinds are too much. The tarmac will be wet. We're not going to make it!"

"I need your focus!" Secousse says, angry now. "I don't need your doubt. Help me put this bird on the ground! We've got twenty-seven hundred feet to land this and park it. That runway is three thousand."

"Exactly my point!" says the copilot. "Exactly why I was against this airport. This is totally wrong."

"With the anti-lock brakes, the thrusters, and my experience, we're good," snaps the pilot. "I've never lost a plane. We're good. We're good. Just read out the data."

Bella grabs my hand, squeezing it. Her face is pale, her upper teeth dug into her lower lip. Mack's eyes are closed. He's mumbling. Or praying. I'm convinced now that discretion is not the better part of valor. We'd have been better off at an airport with a bunch of TMZ paparazzi awaiting our landing than this alternative.

"We're heavy and too fast," repeats the copilot. "You need to decrease speed. Approach a stall and drop to the front of the runway."

"I'm attempting that now!" shouts Secousse.

"Stop attempting!" snaps the copilot, the stress exploding through the cabin speakers. "You need to reverse thrust as soon as we hit the ground."

"I've got it," Secousse says with a renewed sense of calm. "I've got it!"

Bella's fingernails are digging into my palm. Mack is still meditating.

"Go around!" urges the copilot. "Nose up! Go around! Power up! We're coming in too fast. We will not make it. There's too much tailwind."

"I'm not going to pull up!" yells Secousse. "I've never missed a landing and I'm not about to mi—" The radio crackles and shuts off. The heated conversation is replaced by the sound of the engine whining and the rattling of everything inside the cabin. It's as though I'm at the end of a wooden rollercoaster. Then the pilot rekeys the mic.

"Our landing is going to be a little rougher than normal," Secousse says in his best smooth jazz deejay voice, unaware we've just heard the conversation between him and his copilot. "I'd suggest you stay strapped into your seats until we come to a complete stop."

Just as it seems we're about to touch down, there's a large gust of wind, pushing the plane to the right. My stomach drops. Bella looks green.

Mack, his eyes pressed shut, is singing the Marine's hymn, "Our flag's unfurled to every breeze, From dust to setting sun..." He's tapping his prosthetic knee with his hand. "We have fought in every clime and place, Where we could take a gun."

Without warning, we slap the ground hard. Instantly the engines scream as the pilot reverses thrust and applies the brake. The safety belt digs into my gut. All three of us are thrown forward. It's like we're test dummies in a vehicle crash test. Our bags go flying into aisles, tumbling toward the cockpit. The flight attendant is bent over at her waist, her hands wrapped around the back of her head.

I can hear her huffing from between her knees, "Oh lord, oh lord, oh lord!"

But as much as we feel the inertia of the pilot's effort to stop the plane, it's obvious we're not slowing enough. Instead, the plane is fishtailing as its rear tires try to grip the tarmac. The anti-lock brakes are struggling to engage.

The frame of the cabin is shuddering, vibrating with such intensity I'm sure it'll crack open. It's then that the front of the plane pitches forward and to the left, pulling my midsection harder against the safety belt. There's another rumble before we abruptly stop.

The engines wind down and the lights flicker again before shutting off.

It's dark and silent, like a cocoon.

***

"You okay?" I whisper to Bella. She nods and tries to sit back in her seat, but the forward lean of the aircraft makes that difficult. She grips the sides of her chair to slide back and hold herself in her seat more comfortably.

Mack has stopped singing. His eyes are open and he's trying to peer out the window next to his seat. It's fogged and, despite cupping his hand around his face and pressing it to the acrylic window, he can't see anything.

"We need to get out of here," I say.

"Agreed," Mack says.

"We made it," says Captain Secousse, throwing open the cockpit door. It's dark, but I can vaguely see him emerge from the cockpit as my eyes adjust. "We're nose deep in muck," he chuckles, "and about seventy-five feet off the end of the runway, but we made it."

"We need out of here," I call to him. "We can't afford to wait around for anyone in a uniform."

"We can get you out on the over-wing exits." He calls back to the copilot, "Get out here, Greenie, and give me a hand with these bags. Our guests need to scoot pronto."

"I don't think the FAA or NTSB is going to be good with that," interjects the copilot. "They're going to ask a lot of questions. The passengers need to stick around."

"Understood," says Secousse, handing me the duffel without looking back at his by-the-book subordinate. "But once we tell them to exit the aircraft, which is procedure, we can't control them. What they do is what they do."

"But you're telling them to leave," the copilot whines. "That's *not* procedure."

Even in the dark, the frustration is obvious on Secousse's face. "I've had about enough of your holier-than-thou act, Greenie." He turns and pokes the copilot in the chest. "This is my plane, my call. I'll handle the feds. You help them with their gear. That's your job right now."

The copilot silently moves to grab Bella's pack from the floor in front of the flight attendant. She's still bent over at her waist, her hands wrapped around the back of her head.

"The exit door is to your right," Secousse points to his left toward the wing. "There's a quick release latch on the top and a hand grip underneath the window."

I meet Mack by the window over the right wing. He slides his left hand into the handle at the bottom and then grabs the latch with his right.

"That door is heavy," says Secousse. "It's almost fifty pounds and it's awkward."

Mack motions me to his side for help. He pulls on the latch and tilts the top of the door toward himself before lifting up. The door clicks against the hooks holding it into place, coming free. I grab the side of the door and help Mack lower it into the cabin. We're immediately pelted with rain.

"Bella, I'll go first. Slide me the bags before you slide down. I'll be at the bottom to catch you. Mack, you good?"

"Oo-Rah," he grunts. "I'll need your help at the bottom. These legs'll make it interesting when I drop from the side."

"Hey," calls Captain Secousse. "My tip?"

"Really?" I ask. "We nearly crashed."

"We didn't though," he says. "You're okay, boss."

"Bella," I nod to her. She rolls her eyes and unzips her bag, pulling out a roll of one hundred dollar bills and tosses it to the captain.

"This buys your silence," she says. "You can't describe us, you don't have names, your log is vague, and your memory fuzzy."

"Without a doubt," Captain Secousse says.

I have my doubts about how quiet Secousse can keep his copilot, but that's beyond what we can control. Hopefully, we're long gone by the time anybody figures out anything.

The opening is about three feet by maybe a foot and a half. I grab each side and pull myself onto the wing one leg at a time, slipping a bit on the wet wing. Sitting with my legs extended in front of me, I push myself forward and slide down the wing to the ground below.

Wiping rain from my face, I look back to the emergency exit. Bella pokes her head out and slides her backpack first, followed by Mack's, and then my portable arsenal. I grab each of them and drop them on the ground, putting them underneath the plane to minimize how wet they get.

Bella slides down easily, grabbing my hands at the last second before hitting the ground on her feet. Mack struggles to climb out of the exit, but has no trouble with the descent once he situates himself on the wing.

We grab our bags and start walking away from the mess. In the distance, sirens wail and at the far end of the runway to the left, red and white lights strobe against the falling rain.

"We need to move quickly."

Neither Mack nor Bella say anything, but they're already ahead of me, moving away from the plane.

✳✳✳

The trudge through the damp, boggy grass is brief, maybe only a hundred yards or so, until we reach a two lane road running parallel to the runway. A thin line of trees border the road on either side and, despite the darkness, we navigate our way into a thicket of pines on the other side. There's a short dirt driveway and a trio of older model cars parked on the grass in front of a small mobile home.

We trek around the house, farther from the road into a clearing surrounding by an expanse of woods. The sound of emergency sirens in the distance lessens the farther we walk. The accompanying flashing lights also dim, making it more difficult to see.

"Do we keep going this way?" Bella asks, shrugging her pack higher onto her shoulders, grunting a little.

"Let's get into those woods," says Mack, "and I'll check my GPS. We can reassess there." He has his bag over one shoulder. He's the slowest of us right now, struggling a little bit with the wet, soft earth.

"You okay?" I ask him. "Do you need help with your bag?"

"No," he snaps. "I carry my own weight." He raises his chin and looks forward toward the trees.

The rain is coming down harder now, cold drops pelting my eyes and cheeks. I look at Bella, walking a few steps ahead of me, and think of Chernobyl. It was raining like this when we recovered a piece of the process in that forsaken place. The only thing we're missing here is the teeth-rattling thunder and bullets flying past us. Just another reminder of how far we've come and how far we haven't.

The rain isn't as bad underneath the canopy of the trees. The three of us huddle together to look at Mack's burner phone and its built-in GPS mapping application.

"Looking at this," Mack says, rubbing his finger dry on his pants before attempting to swipe the phone's screen. "That road we just crossed is called Piscataway. We're standing a few hundred yards due south of the end of the runway. East of us, through these woods, there's a neighborhood. It's on the other side of Tippett Road. If we walk maybe a mile, there's a park there. Due west is farmland, trees, and some truck business or warehouse. Hard to tell."

"What other options do we have?" Bella asks, dropping her pack to the pine needled ground under our feet.

"If we head north," Mack swipes his finger downward to reveal more of the surrounding area, "parallel to Piscataway, there's a church. That might be a good spot to call for a cab."

"What's that up there?" I point to what looks like a big building in the upper right portion of the screen.

"That's a Wal-Mart," Mack says. "Even better than the church. We can buy some dry clothes, kinda reorganize."

"Wal-Mart," I laugh. "We could be on Mars and there'd be a Wal-Mart within walking distance."

"How far a walk *is* that?" Bella asks, rubbing her left shoulder with her right hand. "It looks far."

"Let me check," Mac manipulates the options in the GPS. "Almost three and a half miles. Maybe a little more than an hour walk. Could be closer to four miles if we want to stay off the main road."

"So about an hour and a half then. Okay," she sighs. "I can do it."

"How about you, Mack?" I turn to the proud Marine.

"I'm good," he says. "Oo-Rah!"

"Where does that come from?" I ask him, wiping my hand through my hair to temporally stop the waterfall pouring from my head. The duffel, rain soaked now is remarkably heavy.

"What?" Mack asks.

"Oo-Rah?"

"Oh," he laughs. "It's a Marine thing."

"I know that. What's its origin?"

"There's some debate about that," he explains. "But pretty much anyone with a brain agrees it came from recon Marines stationed in Korea in the 1950s."

"Why there?"

"They were in the 1st Amphibious Recon. They were always on submarines. And as you know, when a sub dives, a dive alarm has a distinct sound." He stops for a second to adjust his pack and then keeps moving. The trees are thinning out as we approach a neighborhood to the east.

"It's like aa-RU-guh, aa-RU-guh, right?" I ask, mimicking the sound I've heard only in movies.

"What are you doing?" Bella stops and turns. "I thought we were trying to be discreet."

"Sorry, you're right. I'll keep it down."

"Yes," Mack whispers above the sound of raindrops falling from the leaves above us. "But Marines, who do everything as economically as possible, shortened it to 'Oo-Rah' and would call it out to signify their enthusiasm or readiness."

We hit the clearing adjacent to the neighborhood and a road heading north toward the Wal-Mart. The rain lessens to a sprinkle as we trek along the shoulder of Thrift Road. It's an annoying mist more than anything. We'll be on this road for a couple of miles until we hit highway 223. We'll turn right, go maybe a quarter of a mile before we hit the Wal-Mart parking lot. Looking at my watch, I estimate we've got about an hour to go. It's three-thirty in the morning.

***

My neck and shoulders are screaming as we approach the large parking lot near the intersection of highway 223 and Branch Avenue. It's a long expanse of asphalt that extends to our left. We pass a Chipotle

Mexican Grill to our right and make the turn into the lot. The low-pressure sodium bulbs of the overhead lights cast a ridiculously bright light onto the empty rows of parking spaces running the length of the lot. At least the rain has stopped.

"The Wal-Mart is at the far end," Mack huffs, keeping pace with me. "It would be, right?"

All three of us are drenched. We're exhausted. Bella has dropped back behind us by a few paces. She's been quiet most of the trek. Occasionally, she'll stop and adjust her backpack. I've offered a half dozen times to carry it and she politely declines each time.

Imagine, one of the wealthiest women in the world chugging along back roads in Southern Maryland so she can buy some dry clothing at Wal-Mart. I should be embarrassed about the depths to which I've dragged her, but the thought of her shopping the racks in the women's section, adjacent to frozen foods, makes me smile.

The smile evaporates when I look at the sign on the glass doors of the Wal-Mart, barricaded by shopping carts.

The store is closed.

"Are you *kidding* me?" Bella asks rhetorically, pulling the pack from her shoulders and dropping it to the cement in front of the door. "Since when is Wal-Mart not open twenty-four hours?"

"Since it doesn't open until six," says Mack. He peers into the store. "There are people in there," he adds. "They're stocking shelves and sweeping floors."

"We've got less than an hour," I say calmly. "It's a couple minutes after five."

"I'm not waiting," Mack bangs on the door. "We've got places to be."

"So much for being incognito," Bella says.

"There's another entrance over there," I point farther down the lot. "Maybe those doors are unlocked for the employees."

"Nobody heard me anyhow," Mack laments. We might as well try it."

At the second set of doors, we're met by a security guard armed with a walkie-talkie. He's taller than Mack, younger than me, and interested in Bella.

"Can I help you ma'am?" he asks, his mop of blond hair leaking from the bottom of his ball cap. "I'm security here." He's wearing a black and gray short-sleeved uniform that matches the ball cap. His badge is actually a yellow patch. It reads SEMPER VIGILO SECURITY. His sleeves are adorned with two chevrons. So he's a corporal.

"Yes." Bella smiles and holds out her hand. "Thank you so much, Officer ...?"

"Corporal Sanders," he beams, firmly grasping Bella's extended hand. He shakes it earnestly. "I'm the night shift supervisor for this property."

"Great," Bella giggles. "You're exactly the man to help me."

He lets go of her hand and places both of his on his hips. "How can I help?"

"I know the store doesn't open until six o'clock," she says, "but I am soaking wet. I am uncomfortable and afraid I'm going to get sick."

He eyes her up and down, likely not anxious to have her out of the clingy, wet clothes. "Uh, huh," he mutters.

"I would appreciate it so much if we could go into the store early," she pleads. "That way, we could get some dry clothes, do the rest of our shopping, and be ready to check out right after the store opens."

"I don't know..." He glances at Mack and me.

"Please, Corporal Sanders?" She puts her hand on his forearm. "My friend here is a war hero. He needs to change the socks that help his leg stay in the prosthetic. Otherwise he could get a horrible rash."

"I'd need to check with the manager," he says. "I can't guarantee anything. I mean, I'm just security. I don't run the store."

"I trust you," Bella says. "You can convince them to help us."

Corporal Sanders holds up a finger for us to wait and marches into the store.

"You were working some magic with Colonel Sanders there," Mack says under his breath. "Playing the wet t-shirt card? I would have thought that beneath you, Bella."

"Haven't you learned anything about me, Mack? When it comes to surviving, I'm like everyone else. I do what I have to do. This is survival."

Mack nods, coming to understand what I knew about her months ago. She's as tough as nails when she has to be. She's resourceful. Delicate and fragile at times, an instinctive killer at others. She's me, but hotter.

"We can help you," Corporal Sanders comes bounding out of the store, double-timing it straight to Bella.

"Great!" Bella lights up. "We appreciate it so much."

"The only catch is," he says, "you can't check out until after the store is open. And the manager has to check you out."

"Thank you so much." Bella touches his arm again. "I knew you were the perfect person to ask. We really appreciate it."

"No problem," he says, and motions into the store. "And sir," he looks at Mack as we pass him, "thank you for your service to our country." He stands ramrod straight and salutes.

Mack stops and salutes the corporal. "My honor, Corporal."

"Feel guilty about the *Colonel Sanders* crack now?" I whisper to him as I grab a shopping cart.

"A little," he says, pulling his own cart. "Just a little."

"I'm going to call for a car," says Bella. "Mack, give me your phone."

"What kind of car?" Mack reluctantly hands over his phone as we pass the grocery section.

"A rental," she says. "I'm calling one of those places that'll pick us up." Bella makes the call, answers a few questions, and tosses the phone into a trashcan next to the pet food section.

"Let's save some time by hitting different parts of the store," I suggest. We divvy up an agreed upon list of "must haves" and go our separate ways.

Forty-five minutes later we're loaded for bear. All of us have changed into clean, dry clothing, and we've loaded our carts with a variety of goods.

Mack spent a lot of his time in the hardware and electronics sections. Bella went to the pharmacy. I bought a couple of new backpacks and, at Mack's instructions, a handful of disposable cameras and a half-dozen packages of Tic-Tacs.

Each of us is armed with a new burner cell phone.

There's a green sedan parked in front of the store when we emerge. An amiable woman in an Enterprise Rent-A-Car shirt is standing at the passenger door.

"Greta Hammershmidt?" the woman says to Bella.

"Yes," Bella says. "That's me." She walks to the woman and pulls an Illinois driver's license from her new black canvas cross body purse.

"Wonderful," she says. "I'm Sally. I'm here to take you to the office so we can fill out the paperwork. May I help you with your bags?"

"We've got it," I say. "Thank you though."

Sally pops the trunk to the car and Mack and I load it up with our gear. We empty the Wal-Mart bags into the new backpacks before closing the trunk and climbing into the backseat of the Ford.

"You have a lot of bags," Sally comments on our five backpacks and large duffel. "Are you campers?"

"Yep," Mack says. "We're actually doing some research in the northern part of Virginia. Takes a lot of gear."

"Oh," says Sally. "How fascinating. What kind of research?"

Bella glares at Mack from the front seat before answering inquisitive Sally. "It's complicated. Essentially, we're examining the survivability of certain types of mold found in wooded environments."

"Mold?" Sally asks. "Wow!"

"Yeah," Bella says. "It's pretty boring if you're not into that sort of thing. My research team and I have spent much of our lives up to our elbows in it. By the way," she changes the subject, "I'm so surprised you were open so early."

"We're open twenty-four hours basically. We don't deliver until after six o'clock, though, so your timing was perfect."

"Thanks for being on time," Bella says.

"We should be to the office in just a minute." Sally accelerates and turns on the radio. "Is jazz okay?"

"Perfect," says Bella. "Absolutely perfect."

CHAPTER 9

The Hay Adams Hotel is haunted. Really.

Clover Adams, the wife of one the hotel's original owners, died in the hotel in 1885. She ingested photo-processing chemicals. Some say she killed herself; others think she was murdered. Regardless, her ghost haunts the fourth floor. Maids say she's called them out by name, guests report doors opening and spontaneous music from their clock radios.

Despite Clover, the hotel is expensive and popular. My guess is it's because it's situated on Lafayette Park opposite the south lawn of the White House. Location. Location. Location.

We pull into the semicircle drive on 16th Street and I hop out of our rented green Ford Taurus, leaving Bella and Mack to fend off the kind but overly eager valets. There are tourists milling around the sidewalk, pointing at the White House, taking photographs before crossing the street to the park. The sun is rising to my left, casting an ethereal glow on the eastern side of the stone exterior. I remember reading somewhere that it takes five hundred and seventy gallons of paint to cover the White House. The air feels as thick as paint, come to think of it, now that the rain has cleared out and the morning light brings with it heat. It's been a while since I've visited Washington, and I'd forgotten how humid it can get.

At the far side of the park, on Pennsylvania Avenue, there's a group of poster board-carrying demonstrators. I can't read the signs, and their chanting is unintelligible, but they seem passionate.

Past the limestone facade of the hotel, inside the hotel lobby, the building's age is evident. It's clearly been restored, but there's a definite nineteenth century vibe to the place. To the left of the entrance is the front desk.

I approach the young clerk with a smile. "Excuse me. I'm looking for a guest of yours. I'm a friend, and he asked me to meet him here."

"Yes sir," says the clerk, fastidiously dressed, jet black hair coiffed impeccably. He's tall and thin, his nose pointing upward at the end. His eyes are narrow and deep set underneath his brow. He's polite but wary. "And the name of this guest would be?"

"Sir Spencer Thomas," I say, noticing an immediate recognition on the clerk's face.

"I can confirm he is a guest at the hotel," he says, typing on the keyboard on the desk in front of him. "I cannot give you any additional information, but I'd be happy to take a message. Perhaps you'd like to leave a note?"

"Can you connect me to his room? Do you have a house phone I might use?"

"He's not in his room," says the clerk, pressing his lips into a duckbill. "So a phone call would prove fruitless, I'm afraid."

"It's nine o'clock in the morning. Did he leave for a meeting or something?"

"I wouldn't have that information, sir. Would you like to leave a message for him?" He places a piece of stationery and a pen on the counter ledge in front of me. "I'll be pleased to insure he receives it upon his return."

I look toward the port-a-cache and the valets looking to help guests coming and going. "No, thank you." I slide the paper and pen back toward the clerk. "I'll just come back later."

"Whatever you wish." The clerk removes the pen and paper and waves the next guest to the counter. "How may I help you?" he asks a classy looking middle-aged woman dressed like Barbara Bush.

I push through the double-doored entrance and step outside. There's a gray-suited valet standing to the right. His shoulders are back, a brass nametag on his left coat pocket, a whistle tucked into his vest.

"Mr. Davis?" I ask, reading the nametag.

"Yes?" he says, somewhat surprised I called him by name. "May I help you?"

"I'm looking for someone. A guest of the hotel. He left this morning, and I need to find where he went."

"I'm not sure I can help," he says. "We have so many people."

"Older gentleman," I describe. "Tall and heavy set. Has a proper British accent."

"Sir Spencer Thomas?" he asks, the smile spreading wider across his cheeks.

"That would be him," I nod. "I have a meeting with him. I lost the address. So I thought I'd come here, hoping to catch him."

"He's already left, I'm afraid." Davis waves a taxi past him, under the overhang and back onto 16th Street. "I put him in a car myself maybe half an hour ago."

"Do you know where he was headed?"

"A bar," he says, the smile sliding into a knowing grin. "The Cato Street Pub."

"At eight thirty in the morning?"

"I don't ask questions, sir," he laughs. "I just put the man into the car."

"Great." I hand the man a twenty dollar bill and start toward the Ford Taurus. "Do you know is the address?"

"Yep. It's a big hangout for political types. Twenty-one Hundred block of Pennsylvania Avenue, Northwest. Two-story red brick building. Easy to spot."

"Thanks so much!" I trot off to the Ford and climb into the front seat next to Bella. "He's at a bar not far from here."

"Really?" Bella asks. "At nine o'clock in the morning?"

"That's what I said," I laugh. "He should still be there. He left a half hour ago. It's called the Cato Street Pub."

"I know that place," chimes Mack. "Spencer took me there. It's a dive, but it's popular. I saw Ted Cruz there. He was having a friendly conversation with Harry Reid. Weird."

Mack guides Bella to the bar.

The red brick two-story building is squeezed between a drug store and a Vietnamese restaurant. It has the look of an 18th century London home. The two windows on the second floor are twelve panels with white paint on the trim and sheer white draperies drawn on the inside.

Bella finds an empty spot at the curb across the street and pulls in. "Are we all going in?" she asks. "Or you think you're okay by yourself?"

"Let's all go," Mack says.

"Let's," I say, hopping out of the car and leading our trio across the yellow brick road to visit the wizard. If I only had a brain.

The large, solid wood doors at the entrance are painted brothel red. Affixed to the brick, to the left of the doors, is an engraved brass plaque bearing the bar's name and its hours of operation. Surprising, it is open at nine o'clock in the morning.

***

I pull open the door on the right, expecting to walk into a Stanley Kubrick film, and let Bella and Mack walk ahead of me. It takes a moment to adjust to the dark interior, which is wall-to-wall hickory. There's a long, lacquered wooden bar to the right. About a dozen matching tables dot the dining portion of the space. Opposite the bar, on the far left wall, are four red velvet booths.   On the walls are black and white photographs of some of the politicos who've spent time imbibing, or deal-making, or both, atop the brass and leather stools. There's one great shot of former House Majority Leader Tom DeLay chatting with Speaker of The House Felicia Jackson. Another photograph features Tip

O'Neill. There's Strom Thurmond and Robert McNamara with a much younger former Attorney General Bill Davidson.

Behind the bar is a slight, thin man with even thinner hair. What's left of it is a smoke stained white. He's sucking on a cigarette, a pack of camels in his shirt pocket. His cheeks and nose are redder than the rest of his face. He looks unhappy.

"What is Zimbabwe?" he snaps at the television hanging above the bar behind him where there's an episode of *Jeopardy!* on the screen. "Idiot! Everybody knows it's Zimbabwe."

There's a younger man, maybe in his twenties, sitting at the bar nursing a beer. He's hunched over, his suit jacket riding up his shoulders and back. He hasn't shaved and his eyes are bloodshot. He looks as though central casting sat him at the bar and told him to stay put. Next to him is a young woman in a black hoodie. She's on a laptop.

Sir Spencer isn't here.

The man behind the bar notices us in the commercial break before *Double Jeopardy.* "Can I help you? You need a drink?" He eyes Bella and Mack, who've taken a seat in one of the booths.

I sidle up to the bar. "I'm good right now, but I am looking for someone."

"Yeah?" The Camel hanging on his bottom lip wiggles while he talks. "Who you want?" He walks toward me, flipping a bar towel over his shoulder.

"I'm Liho Blogis," I tell him, offering my hand.

"Blogis?" He warily grabs my hand and shakes it. "What kinda name is that?"

"Ukrainian."

"Hmmph." He lets go of my hand and takes a drag. Smoke swirls into his nostrils. "I'm Jimmy Ings. This is my place. I know everybody who comes and goes."

"I'm looking for a British man," I start, but I don't have to finish. Ings' eyes grow wide between his crow's feet. He glances across the bar at Bella and Mack again.

"They lookin' for him too?" He nods in their direction.

"Yep. You need a name? I haven't told you—"

"Nah," he sucks on the cancer stick. "I know who you're lookin' for. I'll get him."

Jimmy Ings walks to the other end of the bar and picks up a phone. He punches some numbers, mumbles something I can't hear, and cradles the phone in his neck. "He's on his way down."

"I'll take that drink then," I smile. "Single malt, whatever brand you have. My friends will have the same. I'll be over at the booth with them." I slap a twenty on the bar.

Ings turns to the liquor shelf. "Scotch, eh? You must be a friend of the man," he snickers.

I slide into the booth next to Bella, leaving Mack with the open seat. "He's on his way down."

"You ordered scotch?" Bella looks surprised but thirsty.

"Another message to our friend. You don't have to drink it."

Bella smiles. "Oh, I'll drink it."

"As will I," Mack adds. "A Marine never turns down a drink, especially when he's about to a face the man who nearly killed him."

"Funny," I respond, "I'm facing the man who nearly killed *me*."

Mack's smile fades and Ings struts across the bar toward us. He slides a tray onto the table, sloshing the scotch in the glasses. "No ice," he says. "You didn't tell me you wanted it on the rocks."

"That's good," Mack says, gripping his glass the instant Ings puts it on the table. He toasts the barkeep and takes a swig. "Oooooeeeee!" He smacks his lips.

"Aberfeldy," says Ings, unloading the other glasses in front of Bella and me. "Twelve year. Single malt, like you asked."

"The twenty-one year variety is far more satisfying," chimes a familiar, distasteful voice from behind Ings. His eyes dance across us as though he'd expected us. "It's a bit more pricey, and Jimmy here doesn't carry it, but it's quite worth the expense." He slaps Ings on his back hard enough to break him. "I'll take a Glenfiddich twenty-one. It's on your top shelf, to the left.

Ings trudges back to the bar.

"May I?" Sir Spencer asks, motioning to the empty seat next to Mack.

Mack slides over without saying anything.

"You look good, Mack," he says, exhaling when he relieves the weight from his aging knees. "As do you, Bella. But Mr. Blogis, good man, you have changed so. I liked you better before the plastic surgery." He laughs at himself.

"You knew it was me."

"Of course," he scoffs. "Jackson, as I've told you before, I know you better than you know yourself. Though I must admit I'm taken aback at how early in the morning it is for you to have ordered a drink." He leans back against the booth, giving his girth more room to breathe. He's wearing a dark three-piece suit, tailored to his size. His golden tie pops against his pale blue shirt.

"Where's Blogis?" I ask, not interested in niceties.

"That's complicated, Jackson. Where is he now, where was he this morning, where will he be tonight? Specifics untangle the complexity of it."

"Help us then," Bella interjects. "Give us specifics." Bella swirls the caramel colored liquid around in the glass but doesn't drink.

"He's here on the East Coast," Sir Spencer offers. "Looking for the same pot of gold we seek."

"Where is the pot of gold?" Mack asks, drawing the last of his drink to his lips.

"This is information I should just give you? I'm still not certain I should be placing my proverbial eggs in your basket."

Jimmy Ings delivers the Glenfiddich. Sir Spencer thanks him and the barkeep returns to his post.

"Jimmy is a good man," Sir Spencer says, raising his glass in Ings' direction. "He's trustworthy. He keeps secrets. He's of the same... ideological mindset."

"Is that so?" I remark.

"He's not betrayed me," Sir Spencer says, pulling a sip between his lips. "He's not abandoned me or threatened me. He's a team player, Jackson."

"What are you getting at?"

"Aside from my distaste for ending a sentence in a preposition," he says condescendingly, "I can't be at all certain you are the right man anymore."

Mack runs his finger on the rim of his empty glass. Bella leans forward on the table but says nothing. The man at the bar is laying his head on the lacquered finish. It's too early in the morning for this, too late in the game not to play along.

"Listen, I'm sick of the platitudes. Let's be straight up here, Sir Spencer. You need me. If you could get the process without me, you would have done it."

"That's assuming I know where it is."

"You know where it is," I say.

He doesn't bite. Instead he aggressively swigs from the glass.

I dangle another hook. "C-H-1-0-0-2-3-0-0-0-A-1-0-7-2-3-4-3-6-4."

The glass still to his mouth, his eyes grow wide. For a moment there's a hint of panic before his calm takes control. He slowly lowers the glass to the table.

A knowing smile slowly spreads across Mack's face. He gets it.

"I know," I say, just above a whisper. "Dramatic." Stanley Kubrick would have loved it.

"Dear George," says Sir Spencer. "He couldn't keep things between us. Just as well. He'd have been good as dead to me anyhow."

"How could you say that?" Bella snaps loudly enough that it draws Ings' attention at the bar. "That's heartless. The poor man's been dead less than a day."

"Heartless?" laughs Sir Spencer. "Please. There's no room for hearts in this game. That's your problem, you know," he aims his glass at Bella and then me. "Your heart's involved. It's going to get both of you killed."

"Back to the subject," I say, "we need what you have on Blogis. Before we risk everything to get the process for you, I need that collateral."

"So you have my Swiss bank account number," he says. "You think that's enough to force me to jump in the boat with you and paddle merrily in the same direction?"

I remain silent and keep my eyes squarely focused on his until he blinks.

"What is your preoccupation with Blogis?" he asks, releasing a sigh of resignation. He knows he needs my help, and he doesn't like it.

"He killed my parents." I still haven't looked at Mack's thumb drive. I haven't had the time or, frankly, the constitution to find out what information it holds about my parents' deaths. If what Mack told me is true, that Sir Spencer had them killed, he'll bite on this hook, line, and sinker.

Sir Spencer draws a final sip from his glass and sucks an ice cube into his mouth. He's on the rocks as much as his drink at the moment, trying to measure me. Is he nibbling?

"I never knew how to tell you that, Jackson," he says, his voice softening. "I was afraid it might cloud your judgment, make it difficult for you to see the task at hand. I understand, though," he says. "I really do. Vengeance is a very powerful motivator. It's second only to survival as a practical application to success."

"So what do you know?"

"I know he was looking for you. He followed you west before you disappeared for a bit. I understand, however, the governor's mates located you without too much trouble."

"He keeps finding us," Bella says.

"Such is the way of the sword," says Sir Spencer. "Discipline to one's task."

"Go on," I say, trying to keep him on the hook.

"Yes," he says, refocusing. "Blogis. He's here in Washington."

What?

"He's here?" all three of us say at the same time.

"For now," he says, rubbing the slight scruff on his chins, "he's visiting some venture capitalists. I use that term loosely, of course. They're more like civilized mercenaries, really. But I digress."

"Is he trying to assemble a team?"

"Perhaps. He had a team in Japan."

"Japan?" I ask. "Why there?"

"T2K," answers Bella.

"Exactly." Sir Spencer raises his empty glass to her.

"It's a huge antineutrino beam project in Japan," Bella explains. "They're not interested in the nuclear aspects of neutrinos like Nanergetix was. The team there is looking to explain the origins of the universe. They're looking at matter and antimatter. It's a whole different approach to the neutrino problem."

"They created a neutrino beam that stretched two hundred ninety-five meters across Japan," adds Sir Spencer. "And then they had the accident."

"Accident?" asks Mack.

"In 2013 the poor chaps suffered a radiation leak. A beam was too strong and it leaked radiation into the labs. That exposed some workers to the radiation. Then, a researcher restarted the beam and caused a bigger problem. The radiation got out, contaminated the environment around the facility. They shut down the project for more than a year."

"But they reopened," Bella says. "It was incredibly fast. Most thought it would take a lot longer to get back up and running, especially in the wake of Fukushima and the radiation concerns surrounding that facility."

"It was incredibly fast because of our mutual friend," Sir Spencer tells us. "Blogis believed the closest thing to the process existing on the planet was T2K. So he found 'investors' who paid large sums of yen to get that facility up and running. In exchange for his generosity, he was granted access to the research."

"And?"

"And nothing," shrugs Sir Spencer. "They weren't producing the results he needed. His venture capitalists, who I understand were promised a tidy return on the investment, were not happy."

"Does he know about Brookhaven?" Mack asks.

"Ahhh," Sir Spencer nods. "Brookhaven. Clearly George *did* tell you everything. I thought this was merely a financial shakedown, what with my bank account number committed to your memory. You really *do* want the process."

"That's why we're here," I say. "I told you. I owe you the process. In exchange, we get back some semblance of a life and whatever you know about Blogis. Then we go our separate ways. Forever."

Sir Spencer looks at me as though this is the first time he's considered the proposition. He must have thought I was bluffing, or lying, or playing him in some way.

"What makes you think the process, as it were, is still in Brookhaven?" he asks. "What makes you believe it's not gone already?"

"Nothing," I admit. "I don't know it's still there. But we know Blogis doesn't have it, right?"

"I'd have heard from my business partners if he had it in his possession."

"And you'd have already told me if you have it, right?'

Sir Spencer tilts his head to crack his neck and raises his hand to get Jimmy Ings' attention. Ings has his back turned, his eyes on *Final Jeopardy.*

"Ridiculous," mutters Sir Spencer. "Him and that silly game show of his." He raises his voice to get the barkeep's attention, "James! Another, please."

Ings waves at his friend without turning around, then he holds up a finger asking Sir Spencer to wait a moment. He's engaged in whatever query Alex Trebek has posited. The girl in the hoodie turns around. She's got big, round eyes, almost like an anime character, and a big diamond poked into the side of her right nostril. Her skin is as pale as velum and a shock of fluorescent green hair is spilling out from under her hood. She turns back around to her laptop.

"You are correct in your assumption, Jackson," he says. "I do not have what it is I seek."

"A soul?" Bella retorts.

"Perhaps that too, Bella," he says before leaning in and lowering his voice. "But I wouldn't be so quick throw stones, Miss Buell. Your means are a result of your daddy's willingness to blur the lines of morality. No man of success, of wealth, reaches such heights of power and influence without a rationalized compass."

Bella bristles, grabbing my leg under the table. She grips hard to maintain her composure. "I had no idea you were so thin skinned, Sir Spencer. If I'd known the depth of your insecurity, perhaps I would have never partnered with you in the first place."

He throws his head back and laughs heartily. "It's not insecurity, dear girl. I've no illusions about my weaknesses. I'm merely not one to let hypocrisy go unrecognized."

Bella's grip tightens, her fingernails digging into my thigh. I bite the inside of my cheek. Both of us are now concealing our pain: mine physical, and hers emotional.

Ings arrives with a fresh glass of scotch and then floats back to the bar. It's the commercial break before the answer to the final clue.

"Back to the point at hand, Jackson," he shifts his heft toward me, away from Bella. "I do not have the entirety of the process. I do, however, believe there is an exact copy of it within the well-guarded walls of Brookhaven."

"Why haven't you gone after it already?" Mack asks. "And why doesn't Blogis know about it?"

"Second question first," Sir Spencer answers after a sip of his drink. "He may know about it. He considered, as do I, that Brookhaven is too heavily guarded to attempt the theft. For him, Japan was an easier target."

"First question?" Mack prompts.

"The same reason Mr. Blogis hasn't tried. That's not to suggest I haven't offered a king's ransom in exchange for the effort."

"Nobody's willing to do it?" I ask.

"Not to this point. George was the intermediary. He completed much of the research on my behalf. I'd provide him with some of the classified information, of course, but he did a yeoman's job in completing the picture. It was he who convinced me the rest of the process is there."

"What about Corkscrew?"

"What?" Sir Spencer's ego melts into a puddle on the floor. I've surprised him for the second time in minutes.

"Corkscrew."

"What about it?" He slips his index finger inside the collar of his shirt and tugs.

"He's a hacker. He's working for you. He's discovered a lot of the intelligence you have about Brookhaven."

"Is that a question?"

"What else is there?" I push. "What other information does he have?"

"Why don't you ask Corkscrew yourself? You have the email, I assume."

"She won't respond to me. She won't know who I am."

"I'll tell her to expect a message," he says. "She can choose how to proceed from there. She may decide to ignore you. Or she may choose, at my gentle nudging, to assist you as she's assisted me."

"By hacking into government systems?" Mack surmises.

"You make it sound so blasé." Sir Spencer pulls a handkerchief from his pocket and pats the beads of sweat forming on his brow. "Hacking into a secure government facility isn't as it appears in film or on television. It's not just a point and click endeavor. It can take weeks or months, maybe years, to effectively infiltrate said system."

"Is that how you know Dr. Wolf left the process there?" Bella asks. "This Corkscrew person found evidence in Brookhaven's servers?"

"Oh no," he laughs. "It wasn't that complicated. Rather it was the Freedom of Information Act. Visitor logs. It's a government facility. Whoever visits is catalogued. That catalogue becomes a public record. Our dear friend, Dr. Wolf…" he points the glass at Bella. "*Your* Dr. Wolf, visited Brookhaven six times in a three month period."

"We never tracked him there." Bella glances at Mack who, at the time, was in charge of the surveillance on the late scientist. "Europe, Asia, Canada," she lists with her fingers, "but not Brookhaven."

"*Au contraire,*" Sir Spencer contradicts. "Your Mack here did know about Brookhaven. It was among the options we considered during our last adventure together. I recall mentioning it to you when we discussed Blogis' successful foray in Toulon."

"I didn't say we were unaware of the connection to Brookhaven. I'm just saying we don't remember that we were certain he'd been there." Bella looks down at the table, maybe trying to recall the conversation.

"Well," he counters, "we *did* discuss it. One can't blame you for letting it slip from memory. You've had so much on your mind lately."

"We know, then," I say, "Wolf gave them the process?"

"We don't know," Sir Spencer says. "We can suppose he did. The logs are for the main entrance to the facility and not specific buildings."

"It's too coincidental," Bella says. "It has to be there."

"What is?" I ask.

"I told you about Building 197, right? I mentioned what they do there? The research? That they partnered with Japan in the Super-Kamoiokande experiment? How all of it came back to Homestake?"

"Yeah?"

"That Super-K project is part of T2K," she says, "the project Blogis was helping get back on its feet."

"Very good, Bella," Sir Spencer says. "Now that you've pieced together the puzzle, it seems you have a job to do."

"Do we?" I ask.

"Oh yes," Sir Spencer smiles. "I'll give you Blogis. You give me whatever you find in Building 197."

CHAPTER 10

My dad was a jack-of-all-trades and master of all tradecraft. Looking back, there really wasn't anything he couldn't do. He was a master marksman, he could catch, filet, and grill fish with one hand while changing the spark plugs in his car with the other. He was also a skilled boater.

We didn't own a boat, though we'd frequently rent one. Sometimes it'd be a simple johnboat for a day of fishing or a small ski boat for fun. Other times, he'd rent a nine-foot Lightning sailboat. He liked that class of boats because it was a challenging sail for one or two people and there was room for four in the cockpit. That meant ample room for the two of us, and my mom too, on the rare occasion she'd venture out on the water.

There was a large lake, maybe an hour from our house. In the summer, when my dad wasn't traveling, we'd go there a couple of times a month.

Aside from our time at the gun range, it's what my mom called "male bonding time." My dad always laughed at that. He'd tell her he knew *women* who liked guns and boats. She'd giggle back and tell him she needed to meet those women. Dad would pull her close and say she already knew the most important one.

When witness to it, I would suggest that what they were doing was "couple bonding time," and I didn't need to see it. That only pressed their flirtation into hyperdrive.

They were, from a kid's perspective, flawlessly happy. Aside from the occasional argument, which was pretty rare, they were always doting on each other.

But my mom, sensing the importance of the time my dad spent with me alone, would give us space. Even when invited, she would most often decline.

So she wasn't with us the day I saw my first dead body.

We were on a Lightning. The wind was calm and so there was no need for the spinnaker. There was barely use for the mainsail and jib. My dad was keeping them close-hauled. The sails were in tight and he was working as close to the direction of the wind as he could without pointing up directly into it. It was a tough job and he was a little frustrated. We were one of three boats on the water that day.

He'd already tried reaching, which meant we were running perpendicular to the wind and he had the sails out as far as he could to capture the breezy gusts. It hadn't worked well, so he'd employed the alternative strategy.

"Why don't we try running with the wind?" I asked. "You know, going with it instead of against it? That'll give us speed." I'd been reading a book about sailing and thought I'd impress him with my newly gained knowledge.

"Been studying I see," he smiled, the tension on his face easing a bit. "I'm impressed. That's too dangerous with you on board though. We could accidentally jibe and you could get knocked into the water."

"I'm wearing a life vest." I always did. I hated it. It was uncomfortable and uncool.

"Doesn't matter," he said, one hand working the main sail and the other on the tiller.

I moped, my shoulders drooping for effect, and looked off the port side of the boat, watching the small bubbling wake along the edge of the Lightning. My dad laughed at me. "You're hilarious," he said. "Trying to make me feel—" He stopped cold, which caught my attention.

"Make you feel what?"

"Hang on." He looked past me, toward something in the distance, the tension returning to his face. "There's something out there." He took his hand from the line running the mainsail and pointed off the port bow.

About two hundred yards away, halfway between our dinghy and the shore was a white and red object, bouncing with the roll of the lake's surface. It looked a little like a buoy or marker of some kind. Our speed slowed as my dad navigated the boat toward the object.

"What is that, Dad?"

"I'm not sure yet, Jackson." He leaned forward and squinted to get a better look. As we neared the object, it became increasingly clear it was something not meant to be floating in the middle of a lake. My dad put his hand on my back. "Jackson, I don't want you to see this. Shift to the starboard side of the cockpit and look out that direction."

He was too late. I'd already figured out what it was.

A man's body: ghostly white, almost gray in appearance. He was bloated, bobbing face down, his red T-shirt clinging to his swollen back. It looked like someone had filled his body with too much air. He was a balloon about to pop.

"I know it's a body," I told him, my eyes willing themselves to stay fixed on the aqua-corpse. "I know it's a person." I turned to look at him, and the intensity in his face was replaced with sadness. I didn't know then why he was sad. It was much later, in my counseling sessions, I'd understood he was lamenting a loss of innocence in his son. I was witnessing something no child should see. Childhood was about life, not death. That came soon enough. For me, that body was a warm-up for the death to come in my life.

"Why does his body look like that?" I asked as we approached within twenty yards. "All puffy?"

"It's from gas. When someone drowns, they sink to the bottom pretty quickly. When the body decays, that causes gasses to build. Once there is enough gas, the body is lighter than the water and rises to the surface."

My dad pointed directly into the wind and the boat slowed to a stop, drifting with the slight movement of the lake water. The body remained close enough for me to study it, but far enough away it wouldn't bump into the boat.

"I'm going to call this in, Jackson," he says. "We may have to wait here until police arrive."

"Okay."

Eventually, a sheriff's boat pulled alongside us. My dad had anchored us, so we stayed out while they started their investigation. I'll never forget the sight of two deputies pulling the man's distended body from the water. It was, and is, the most disgusting image ever seared into my memory.

Years later, in school, I wrote a fictionalized account of our discovery. I spent days researching what happened to a drowning victim, and made sure to include it in my essay.

I imagined the man struggling for air, panicking as he realized those were his final moments. Then the blackness enveloped his eyes, the burning in his lungs stopped as they filled with water. That fresh, cool water pumping from his lungs into his bloodstream, diluting it rapidly so that it couldn't carry oxygen. He was dead. His body, heavier than the water would sink as the pressure condensed the remaining gas in his lungs and abdomen.

Once he hit the bottom, he stayed there for days or weeks, the fish or other freshwater creatures tasting his flesh, pecking at his eyes. Then the bacteria grew inside him as the decay intensified. Slowly those gases filled the cavities of his body until he became so light he slowly rose to the surface, emerging like a beach ball held under water too long.

The teacher, a young woman only a couple of years in the profession, gave me an A minus. Her only comments at the top of the first page, written in red ink in that perfect cursive handwriting only teachers seem to have, were, *VERY DARK!!*

If she only knew the half of it.

The weird thing about seeing that body was that every time my dad took me out on the lake after that, I'd look for another one. I couldn't help myself. I'd scan the horizon for anything bobbing up and down, anything bloated beyond recognition.

It was almost as if I expected to see another "floater," as my dad called it. Any second a body might bubble to the surface. It was bothersome and all-consuming at the same time.

My dad sensed it too. He'd try to give me more responsibility on the boat to keep me occupied. I'd handle the tiller and the mainsail for stretches at a time. He'd let me run the spinnaker if the weather called for it.

I started bringing binoculars. Every little white chop on the water was a potential discovery, another call to the sheriff, another glimpse at a life ended.

"What are you doing?" my dad asked, likely aware of my preoccupation.

I dropped the binoculars around my neck but kept my eyes on the water. "Nothing. Just looking for stuff."

"Bodies?"

I didn't know how to respond. I mean, it wasn't normal to be so interested in death, was it? I didn't want my dad to think less of me.

"Jackson?"

"Yeah?"

"Are you looking for bodies?"

I turned in the cockpit to face my dad. He cleated the mainsail line and wrapped his huge mitt of a hand around my knee.

"I can't help it," I exhaled. "I can't stop thinking about it."

"I know," he said, squeezing my knee enough to simulate a hug. "I'm the same way."

"Really?"

"You've no idea," he said. "I half expect to see death around every corner. I anticipate it. I understand."

I didn't bother asking him why he *expected* to see death around every corner. At that age, I was so self-consumed and narcissistic I didn't stop to consider why my dad, a traveling technology consultant, would worry about death. I should have asked.

He probably wouldn't have given me a straight answer. It's not like he would have told me he was an assassin-for-hire, working with the nasty power brokers of the underworld and black markets.

***

Planning to steal from a secure government facility is not as easy as movies would have you believe. The CIA isn't going to let in a handful of firefighters with axes, as it did in *Mission Impossible.* Auric Goldfinger isn't about to break into the U.S. Bullion Depository and render all of the gold radioactive and useless, as was his plan in the James Bond flick *Goldfinger.*

But truth is stranger than fiction. Otherwise, a former military veteran never would have been able to race across the White House lawn, through the north entrance, past the staircase to the presidential residence, and into the East Room before being tackled. An armed felon with a history of assault never would have ridden on an elevator with President Obama and his security detail at, of all places, the Centers for Disease Control.

So our plot seems reasonable as we coordinate the particulars in our third floor hotel room on F Street NW. It's a sparse, two-star hotel in what's called the Foggy Bottom area of the city. We're not far from the Potomac or George Washington University.

"Why did we choose this hotel?" asks Mack, slapping at a roach. "Are we low on money?"

"I have my reasons," I explain. "I've gotta make a call."

Bella has the lone chair pulled up to the bed, where she's spread out the maps and blueprints. She's taking notes.

Mack is sitting on the small apartment sized refrigerator, mumbling to himself, rifling through the Wal-Mart backpacks.

My call connects. "How quickly can you have them to me?" I ask.

"I have them sent overnight," says Wolodymyr, a Ukrainian friend of mine who is my closest connection to the black market. I haven't talked to him since he helped Bella and me traipse across Europe undetected by border agents. "I get you sets of everything you need. Send to encrypted email please."

"Okay. It'll come through a Gmail account. Look for it in within the hour."

"You got it, Jackson Quick," Wolodymyr confirms. "Always happy to help my American friend. Everything I can do."

"There is something else…"

"What is it?" he asks. "Good Cuban cigar? Nice Vodka? Ukrainian bride? I can do it."

"I know," I laugh, "What can you tell me about Corkscrew?"

"Corkscrew?" His voice drops with the seriousness of the question. "Are you on secure line?"

"I'm on a burner. It's not secure."

"Let me just say," he clears his throat, "that is a very bad person."

"Why? You know Corkscrew?"

"I know *of* Corkscrew," he says softly, as if someone's listening to us. "Corkscrew is what we hackers call a Black Hat."

"What is that?"

"There are different breeds of hackers," he says. "I'm like most. I'm Gray Hat. I do some good, some bad. It is in eye of beholder, yes?"

"Okay."

"There are White Hats. They are goody two shoes. Hackers who only exploit systems and servers for good."

"So Black Hats are the bad guys. Like the Old West. The bad guys wear black hats."

"Yes," he says. "Corkscrew does the bad things. Most hackers use tools from open source. They get Metasploit or Subterfuge online, download it, and follow the directions. It's like Easy Bake Oven for hacking."

"Corkscrew doesn't do that?"

"No," he says, his voice still hushed. "Corkscrew created new LINUX distro and hacks with code from that. Super powerful. Super secure. Super smart."

"What's a LINUX distro?"

"LINUX is an operating system like Windows or Apple Yosemite," he explains. "It provides bridge between hardware and software. But it is special."

"How so?"

"LINUX was created in early 1990s by man named Linus," he says. "He didn't like people paying for operating systems. He created new one, called LINUX, and put its code on the internet for free. Anyone could see how it worked and make changes to fit what they needed. These are called 'distributions'. It is distro for short."

"So Corkscrew created a unique version of LINUX just for hacking?" I'm getting it now.

"All LINUX is good for hacking, some better than others. Corkscrew's is the best. Better than BackTrack, and that is saying much." He snorts a short laugh before catching himself. "Why you ask about Corkscrew?"

"We may be working together."

"You kid me," he says. "This is big joke, Jackson Quick?"

"No."

"Be careful."

"What do you mean? We're talking about a hacker, not a killer."

"Hackers are worse," he says. "A killer ends your life, a hacker ruins it."

"Tell me more."

"If you contact Corkscrew," he says, "do it from a computer and a connection that has nothing to do with you. Use an internet cafe or a library. Use an email account you don't care about with a password you don't use anywhere else."

"Why?"

"Corkscrew doesn't know you," he says, "won't trust you, and will try to dig into your system. You don't want that."

"Have you ever dealt with Corkscrew?"

"No. As good as I am at what I do, I'm not as good. Hackers like Corkscrew laugh at what I do."

"Thanks for the insight. I'll send you the mailing info for the stuff I need you send."

I give him some of the details and provide the rest in my email. He thanks me for my trust, quotes me a ridiculous price he knows I'll pay, and hangs up.

"Was that your Ukrainian bromance?" Bella looks up from a blueprint, her finger marking a spot on the drawing. "Wolodymyr?"

"Yep. He's going to be a big help."

"What do you think?" Mack asks me, holding up an odd-looking device. It's a clear Tic-Tac case with a couple of batteries inside.

"What is it?"

"It's a homemade taser." He smiles. "We don't want to kill these people at Brookhaven, right? But we might need to defend ourselves."

"How'd you do that?" Bella asks, intrigued. "Let me see that."

Mack tosses it to her. "There is a piece of metal inside the lid of the candy case. I ripped the circuit board out of a disposable camera. It's connected to the batteries and can deliver right at six hundred volts. It's not enough to kill or knock unconscious. But it's enough of a shock to give you time to get the upper hand or get away."

Bella presses a small red button protruding from a cut in the plastic. There's a click and a low hum. "Is that it?"

"Touch the screws," Mack tells her. There is a pair of screws extending from the top of the case.

Bella touches them, while keeping the button depressed, and jumps. "Ouch!" She drops the stun gun onto the bed. "That *does* hurt." She shakes the sting from her hand. "It's more surprising than painful, but still..."

"That one's yours," Mack says. "I made three of them. Here's yours, Jackson." He tosses me an identical looking weapon. "There are easy to hide. Just keep them in your pockets. The batteries are new, so they should deliver a nice, steady current."

"Do they have to charge?" I ask, moving to the window and turning the device over in my hand, admiring its simplicity.

"Nope. There's no capacitor. It doesn't need a charge. Of course, that lessens the jolt, but we're not trying to hurt anyone with these. Like I said, a nice non-lethal complement to the weapons you're toting in that bag."

From the window of our crappy hotel room I can see into at least a dozen other rooms across a courtyard from us. I call it a courtyard, though it's more of a concrete weed factory with a bench and a large standup ashtray.

There's a couple sitting in deck chairs outside of their ground floor room. The sliding glass door is open. He's reading a magazine. She's on her iPad. I'm guessing, from the way the rooms are laid out in the place, they're in room 104.

Above them and one room to the left is a child with thick, curly hair, pressing his face against the glass. The curtains are drawn, and he's hiding from whoever is in the room with him. The kid is probably three of four. Room 206.

Directly above the curly haired tot, on the third floor, there's a man sitting on the edge of his bed. The curtains are halfway open. The television is on, as is a lamp on the desk next to the T.V. He's talking on the phone, his free hand moving wildly when he's not running it through his hair. Room 306.

"I found him," I say, my eyes on the desperate man at the edge of his bed.

"Who?" Bella asks.

"Blogis."

"Where?" Mack joins me at the window, Bella follows.

"Room 306." I nod in the direction of the third floor room. Blogis is standing now, pacing back and forth. He's rubbing his temples as he talks.

Bella puts her hand around the back of my neck and squeezes, rubbing her thumb back and forth. "Now what are you going to do?"

"Good question," I answer. "I guess I better figure that out."

***

There's only one exit to the hotel, so as long as Blogis remains in his room, we're in good shape. If he leaves, we can follow him.

Mack is downstairs in the rental car, awaiting the word. Bella is keeping watch at the window. I'm on George's laptop, connected to the internet through an ethernet cable. This hotel is a piece of junk, but it has a super-fast connection.

With the camera on the laptop, I take photos of the Brookhaven identification cards we found in the reporter's apartment. Then I save them to the desktop and go to my Gmail account.

I long ago learned the benefits of encrypted email. This was certainly a prime opportunity to employ its secrecy. I hit COMPOSE and open a new email window. At the bottom right of the screen is a downward pointing arrow. I click it and open MORE OPTIONS to switch back to an older COMPOSE function. Once the message to Wolodymyr is finished and the photos are attached, I look under the SUBJECT line and check a box to encrypt.

The system then asks for me to fill out a question and answer form. I make sure it's something Wolodymyr will be able to figure out. I click on SEND + ENCRYPT and send the email.

Easy as pie.

"He's on the move," Bella says as the SENT confirmation pops up at the top of the screen. "We need to go."

I flip the laptop closed and slide it into a backpack. Inside the pack are my favorite six-shooter, the Kel-Tec PMR-30 handgun, and some ammo. I pull out the loaded revolver and slip in the small of my back. I follow Bella out of the room and into the hallway. She sends a text to Mack, letting him know we're on our way.

"So what exactly is the plan?" she asks me as we round the corner to the stairwell. She swings the door open and we race down the flights of steps toward the first floor, the echo of our steps loud in the metal and concrete of the enclosed well.

"Mack follows him. We follow Mack."

"You called the cab?"

"It's across the street at a gas station waiting right now. Mack will tell us what direction he's heading, and we'll follow. That's as far as I've gotten. I've been so focused on finding him, I never really pieced together what I'd do when we did."

"Oh, Jackson," she sighs, tugging open the heavy exit door on the ground floor. "You're too much."

The stairwell opens into the end of a first floor hallway. We walk quickly across the carpeted floor, trying not to announce our arrival as we near the lobby and the bank of elevators.

Bella slows and we turn the corner into the lobby at the same time, just as Blogis passes through the automatic doors leading to the street. There's an SUV awaiting him just past the doors, and he slides into the back passenger's seat. The SUV speeds off.

Bella stops in the middle of the lobby and texts a message to Mack, who we see turning right onto the street as we pass through the automatic doors ourselves. The weight of the humidity almost knocks me back into the hotel.

"It got hot out here," Bella says, checking her buzzing phone. "Mack sees him. He's about two cars back, heading east on I Street Northwest."

Our taxi is sitting across the street, the driver reading a newspaper, his left arm hanging out of an open window. Bella and I sprint across 25th Street, just beating a Volvo riding its horn as it speeds behind us. The cabbie looks up at the commotion and sees us coming. He drops his paper and waves at us.

"Head to I Street and go east, please," orders Bella once we're in the back of the cab.

"Where are we going?" the cabbie questions, looking at us through the rearview mirror.

"We don't know, exactly," Bella tells him between heavy breaths. "Just head east on I for now."

The cabbie grips the wheel, accelerating into traffic. Neither Mack nor the black Cadillac SUV carrying Blogis are visible. Bella's sitting behind the cabbie, my backpack between us. She leans into me.

"Any idea where he's going?" she whispers into my ear.

"The driver or Blogis?"

"Blogis."

"I'm not sure, but Sir Spencer did say he was in trouble with some of his investors. He looked distressed in the hotel room. My guess is he's on his way to meet with those investors."

Bella's phone vibrates and she checks the text from Mack. "They're on New Hampshire, passing GW Hospital. Driver, please make a left on New Hampshire."

The cabbie nods.

Washington D.C. is a city laid out in grids. In this part of the city, between K Street and Constitution Avenue, the east and west streets are identified by letters. The streets running north and south are numbered.

Then there are intersecting diagonal streets that meet at traffic circles. They're named after states.

The cabbie turns left onto New Hampshire, toward Washington Circle Park, and drives northeast. We pass the hospital and the George Washington University Medical Center and enter the traffic circle.

Bella's phone vibrates again. "Exit onto K Street," she tells the driver. "Head east and then turn right onto 21st."

The cabbie exits the circle onto K Street before he immediately steers south onto 21st. He glances in the rearview mirror, maybe looking for more instructions from his navigator.

Bella's phone buzzes as if on cue, telling us to turn right onto H Street. The cabbie nods at Bella's request and turns back west.

"We are going in a big circle," he says, driving his car into the heart of the GWU campus. Almost immediately the phone vibrates again.

"We need to get out," Bella says. "Can you drop us off at the corner of 23rd and H?"

The driver passes 22nd and slows at 23rd. He pulls up behind Mack in the rented Ford Taurus. "You need me to wait?" he asks, punching a button on the front of the meter.

"No thanks," Bella says, opening her door and passing forward a pair of twenty dollar bills "We're good."

I slide out behind Bella, flip the pack onto my back, and meet her at Mack's driver's side window. He's already talking to her when I join them.

"… out of the car here and walked north on 23rd," Mack is saying. "I'm pretty sure he went into the Metro Station up there."

"Was he alone?" I ask.

From street level the station is just a pair of escalators rising and dropping to the sidewalk. The only distinguishing feature is banks of newspaper machines flanking either side of the entrance.

"He got out of the SUV right here and immediately went into the station," says Mack. "I'm pretty sure he got onto the escalator to the right and went down to the station."

"Let's go," Bella says. "We're not stopping now."

"I don't know," says Mack. "I don't trust it."

"What's not to trust?" asks Bella. "If he's meeting with some dangerous investors, it's probably a precaution to make sure he's not followed to their location."

"You watch too many spy movies," I say.

"I don't watch *any* spy movies," she counters before realizing I'm joking. She smirks. "We don't have time for this. I'm going." She slaps her hands on the doorframe of Mack's open window and starts jogging north toward the station. I shrug and follow her.

"Tell me where to meet you," Mack calls after us and I wave to acknowledge him.

It's a block to the escalators and I've caught up with Bella by the time we descend underground. It's crowded and we politely push our way past commuters to reach the bottom. The space opens up into a wide lobby area, lined with automated fare card machines.

"What do we do?" Bella looks at me. "Where do we go?"

"Just buy two fare cards to anywhere. We'll figure it out once we get past the gates."

Bella navigates the machine and purchases two cards, hands me one, and leads me past the tollgate. There's a narrow hallway to the left and another set of stairs leading down to the tracks. We quickly make our way down, hoping to spot Blogis.

The crowds are flowing like rush hour traffic on and off the trains as they squeal in and out of the station. It's hard to tell one dark suited businessman from another, with their cell phones in one hand, computer bags in another.

Bella's straining to look for him, standing on her tiptoes. "There are so many people."

I take her hand and wedge us into the crowd, fighting against the throngs exiting the train on the left side of the platform. Groups of people push past us, a couple of them glaring at us for swimming upstream. Within a minute or so, the crowd evaporates up the stairs behind us. To our right, there's another swell beginning to pool as the next train approaches.

We work our way into the crowd, and the rumble of the train intensifies. A bright light glows from the tunnel. More people stream down the steps, rushing to make it in time. The train screeches past us, slowing as it nears the tunnel on the opposite end of the tracks. It stops and the doors whoosh open on the opposite side, allowing passengers to exit.

A moment later the doors in facing us slide open and Bella gets pushed toward the track from the wave of people surging onto the train. She fights her way against the push and tightens her grip. Then, as the wave subsides, and we relax our hold, hands grip my sides just beneath the bottom of my backpack.

Before I react, I am shoved forcefully onto the train. I lose hold of Bella's hand and trip into the cabin of the train car. Grabbing a floor to ceiling pole to brace myself, I turn around in time to see the doors shutting closed behind me. Bella's standing on the platform, mouth agape, unable to speak. Her eyes aren't on me, though. She's staring in disbelief at the man between the door and me.

Liho Blogis smiles at me, winks, and grabs the pole just above my hand. As the train jolts forward and accelerates, he turns to the window and blows a kiss to Bella.

"She's a pretty girl, Jackson," he says. "You're clearly out of your league in every sense of the word."

CHAPTER 11

Memories are funny things. They're either there or they're not. A memory to me is what tells me I'm alive. My memories are the sum of me. They dictate, to varying degrees, who I am and how I got here.

If I'm missing one, if there's a part of my past I've blocked out, it's as if part of *me* is missing. Given the number of memories my shrink suggested I've handled with a "suppression mechanism," it's not inconceivable that the Jackson Quick walking around today isn't the Jackson Quick I was supposed to be.

Every day since this violent odyssey began, since I delivered that first iPod an eternity ago, snapshots have flashed back into my consciousness, filling a missing puzzle piece.

Maybe they don't flash. It's more they pop to the surface, like that dead body in the lake. My memories sank to the bottom of my mind, drifting among the black muck of things I don't want to remember. And then, suddenly filled with air, they found their way back. Now I expect to find memories around every corner: a loud sound, a familiar odor, a building or street sign, a spot on a map—all of them are triggers.

I don't know what it was that made the memory of my mother and Liho Blogis find its way to the surface, but it did. She called him Frank. He looked sad and she looked angry.

My dad and I were back from an outing. I can't remember if it was the lake or the gun range or just a quick trip to the hardware store. My dad parked the car in the driveway and told me to go ahead, that he had something to do in the garage.

I remember running inside the house, bolting through the front to back family room to the wall of windows facing the backyard. I reached for the handle to back door and stopped cold.

A man had his hands on my mother's shoulders. She was cross-armed, her hands in gardening gloves. They were standing next to the tomatoes. He was talking, she was listening. I could tell, even without the ability to read lips, he was pleading with her.

She wasn't buying what he was selling, despite his efforts. More than wondering what he might be saying to her, I was more interested, more bothered by the way he touched her. It was obvious he'd had his hands on her before.

My mom shook her head, trying not to look at him as she did. He made himself smaller, attempting to face her at eye level. The more I looked at this stranger, the more I recognized him.

He was the man who'd pulled up in front of our house months earlier. He drove a black BMW and, when I last saw him, wore reflective aviators. His voice sounded like he gargled with gravel. We'd talked about him at dinner. He'd offered dad a job he didn't want.

There was something comforting and, at the same time, terrifying in that recognition. When he'd last visited us, showing up unannounced, upsetting my dad, my mother had acted as though she had no idea who he was. Not until dinner that night had she admitted she knew him, pretending his age and a different haircut had fooled her.

What was she hiding from me?

I turned the handle and walked out back. The sound of the door creaking open spun both of them on their heels. My mother looked worried about what I might have seen or heard.

"Hi, Mom," I said, trying to pretend like nothing was wrong, though my eyes probably gave away my confusion.

"Hi, Jackson." She extended her arms to me, pulling me to her side as I approached. "I didn't know you were home. Jackson this is Frank. He's a—"

"College friend of Dad's, I know. And he works with him, too. He was here before, right?"

Frank's eyes centered on mine, his head tilted. He was studying me. He extended his hand. "You were playing in the front yard," he said. "I remember."

"I remember too," said my dad. He was standing at the back of the house, his frame filling the open doorway. "Frank, I thought I told you unequivocally you were never to come to my house again. I *was* clear, right?"

Frank moved his head back and forth, pouting like Robert DeNiro about to deliver judgment as Al Capone in *The Untouchables*. "Perhaps." He stuffed his hands into his pockets.

My dad's nostrils flared, his jaw tightened. "I was *clear.*"

Frank held up his hands in surrender. "Gotcha." He reached into his pocket and pulled out a pair of reflective aviators, sliding them on and pushing them up the bridge of his Roman nose. "I was just asking your bride here to reconsider. That's all. No harm done. Yet."

"There's a gate around the side of the house." My dad indicated with his head. "Leave."

Frank strolled past my mom, gently squeezing her shoulder as he moved.

"Beautiful garden," he said. "But your squash needs tending." He stopped, his back to my mom and looked over at my dad. "You've got vine borers. You can kill them with praying mantises."

My dad bristled but said nothing as Frank disappeared around the corner. The metallic clank of the gate signaled Frank was gone.

I didn't see him again until we met along a riverbank in Germany twenty years later.

***

"You can't kill me on a public train," I state.

"Ha!" Liho Blogis laughs, the deep creases around his mouth darkening with expression. "Of course I could. Your naiveté amazes me, Jackson. Despite your skill, your passion," he shakes a fist for emphasis, "you still lack the awareness, the street sense of your father. Hell, for that matter even your mother was more savvy."

My hand tightening on the pole, I pull myself closer to him. "Don't talk about my mother."

"Touched a nerve, did I?"

The train rumbles around a curve and the lights flicker. The car is full. People around us are reading papers or magazines. A couple have their eyes closed. Almost nobody is on a phone since the service is spotty underground.

"If I wanted to kill you myself," Blogis informs me, "I would have done it on the banks of the Nekar River. Instead, you tried to kill *me*."

"What do you want then?"

"I should be the one asking that question, Jackson," he replies, shifting his weight to stay balanced around another curve. "You were following me."

"How did you know?"

"Aside from the idiot in the Ford Taurus who followed me too closely..." he pulls an iPod from his pocket, "there's this." He thumbs a code across the face of the iPod and opens a video. He hits PLAY.

The screen fills with a graphic that reads, "The Nation's Most Watched Cable News". It dissolves to a woman reading a news story. I can't hear what she's saying, but her name, Vickie Lupo, is on the screen. I recognize her and her earnest delivery of the day's events. She leans into the camera and then looks down dramatically as video replaces her face on the display.

The video is of the outside of George's house swarming with police and roped with yellow crime tape. There's what looks like an interview with a police officer and then another with the couple that saw Mack, Bella, and me leaving George's garage.

Then the scene switches to the bar where I stopped to wait for Ripley. It's color surveillance video of the interior of the place. I'm there, sitting at the table when Ripley walks up to me. There's a quick flash and the surveillance video shows the two of us getting into his truck and driving off.

I look up from the screen at Blogis. He points me to the screen again. I still can't hear the report, but it's not necessary. There are three photographs on the screen: Bella, Ripley, and me. They look like old driver's license photos. Mine's at least four years old.

That's followed by bright orange video of the conflagration that enveloped Ripley's storage facility. There's an interview with the same DPS Trooper Rogers from the car radio. She's pointing across the interstate and talking about the mess behind her, I assume.

Vickie Lupo is back on the screen, waving her hands while she talks. She has a bright red marker in one hand she occasionally taps on the desk for emphasis.

"This is the best part," Lupo says. *"You'll love this."*

Vickie Lupo points off screen and more video appears. This time it's the scene of a plane crash.

Before I can react, Blogis says, "Yep. That's your plane." He chuckles.

There's shaky video of the Global 5000 in the muck off the end of the runway. It cuts to a scene of firefighters and paramedics jumping out of their emergency vehicles. It looks almost like cell phone video taken from the opposite end of the runway.

"Somebody who worked for the airport shot this," Blogis tells me. "But here's the kicker."

The screen fills with the face of the plane's copilot. He's talking to a reporter, pointing to the plane behind him before a graphic replaces him. There are three images. Bella's photo and mine appear again. Next to ours is a silhouette with a question mark in the middle of it. That likely represents Mack.

The train slows quickly as we approach a stop. I grip the pole with my free hand and brace my legs for the momentum shift.

"Don't think about getting off the train," Blogis snarls and shifts his position to block me from moving toward the door.

"Why would I do that?" I ask. "This is the good part, right?"

Vickie Lupo reappears. Next to her, along the right side of the screen is a summary of what she's just reported:

-*Two Suspects In Death Of Houston TV Reporter Identified*

-*One Suspect Also Connected To Deadly Fire*

-*Two Suspects & Accomplice Involved In Airplane Crash Landing Near D.C.*

"So you knew I was in D.C." I've watched enough and hand him the iPod, trying to play it cool. "That doesn't mean I was looking for you. That doesn't explain how you found me."

The train stops and the doors slide open. Only a few new passengers join us. With the car nearly empty, I notice this is one of the older Metro trains. The floor is carpeted in a burnt orange color. The seats, which are in pairs on either side of the narrow center aisle, are molded plastic with vinyl cushions that alternate blue and red with every row.

"You were staring at me from your hotel room, Jackson. I wasn't sure at first it was you. Then I saw the report on the television. I called for a car service and paid attention. Your guy, the silhouette with the question mark where his face should be, isn't as good as he thinks he is."

"He's better than you think."

The doors slide shut.

"You really do need to get better at covering your tracks," he suggests. "It took me no time to find you in Hawaii."

"How?"

The train lurches forward and we jerk with the acceleration.

"Banking. I know people. If you're not using a Swiss account or something in Liechtenstein, you're advertising where you keep your money. Every time you pulled money in regular increments from the islands or Europe, I could see it. I have people who look for things like that. Put that data together with surveillance images from the Bank of Hawaii every time you went to make a withdrawal and voila! Nice pop culture reference, by the way."

"What do you mean?"

"You used the name Richard Denning," he reminds me. "Bella was Peggy Ryan. Both of those are names of actors in *Hawaii 5-0*. But it was another giveaway."

"Nobody else found us."

"Not true at all, Jackson," he scolds, wagging a finger at me. "Your good friend, the governor, found you. Then he had his people follow you to northern California."

"How did—?"

"I know things," he says, slipping the iPod into his pocket. "I know iPods, for example, are the bane of your existence. They're what got you into this rabbit hole of an existence in the first place, am I right?"

My silence acknowledges the truth of it. I lose my balance as the train rumbles around a curve. Blogis grabs my elbow to steady me. I pull away and grip my hand more tightly around the pole.

"The problem is," he says, "if I know you're here, so does everyone else. You're not going to able to walk around without somebody or some camera identifying you. You'll be lucky if it's the Feds who find you first."

"We'll be fine," I assure him. "We've got a plan. It involves you. That's why I'm here."

"What do you want, Jackson?" He stares into my eyes with an uncomfortable intensity.

"I can get you the process."

Blogis cocks his head like a curious dog, his eyes still boring holes into mine, before he laughs. It's a genuine laugh and loud enough to draw the attention of the few people in the train car. Then he coughs and clears his throat.

"Seriously." It's a question as much as it's a request that I level with him.

"Seriously."

"How in the world—" He looks around at the others in the car and lowers his voice. "How in the world do you think you and your ragtag band of underachievers are going to accomplish what nobody else has been able to do?"

"Brookhaven."

"What about it?"

"That's where it is."

"That's not the information I have," he says, the words not oozing with condescension as they were moments ago.

"Is that information from the same sources that made you waste your time in Japan? Is that information coming from the same places that have you indebted to some people more dangerous than you?"

His pupils flash larger like the aperture of a camera. "Where are you getting *your* information?"

"I can get it."

"Even if that's the case, that facility is airtight. There's no way."

"Make me a deal." The doors slide open and nearly everyone gets out of our car.

"What? Assuming you do the impossible, what's the deal?"

I tighten my grip around the pole and put my other hand on his shoulder, pulling him close enough for me to whisper into his ear. "Kill the governor." A couple in jogging suits and headphones gets on the train, choosing blue seats at the opposite end of the train.

He pulls away and studies me for a moment, measuring the seriousness of my offer. He rubs his chin and then runs his hand through his hair, as he'd done on the phone in the hotel room. It's his tell.

I've got him.

"Deal," he says. "You get the process for me and I return the favor. He's had it coming for a while now anyway."

"Good."

"Jackson, you need to know something before we move forward." He licks his lips and runs his hand through his hair. "That photo of your dad and me…"

"From college," I clarify.

"Yes."

"What about it?"

"Your father and I were friends. We were very good friends."

"I don't remember it that way. I remember my dad being hostile toward you."

"That's a long story," he starts, but the train jerks around a corner and he loses his grip on the pole. I move to help him and catch a reflection in the window at the back of our car.

The couple in the sweatsuits has moved to red seats a couple of rows closer to us. The woman appears preoccupied with her phone, but the man is watching us. I'm sure of it.

"Why don't we sit down," I suggest to Blogis. "This pack is killing me."

Blogis nods and moves to a red seat in front of the exit doors. I sit next to him, swinging my backpack on to the floor in front of me. Before he can resume his heartwarming tale of friendship and betrayal, I unzip the pack, pull out the Kel-Tec, and place it on my lap.

"If you were *ever* my dad's friend," I tell him, "then I have to trust you with this."

Blogis looks at the weapon and then at me. I tilt my head back, motioning as subtly as possible to the joggers at the far end of the car.

"I'll give this back to you," he promises, "after I borrow a few bullets." He checks the magazine and measures the weight of the gun in his hand, flipping it over to look at it.

"You can have the bullets," I tell him, sucking in a deep breath to prepare for what I know is coming. "There are thirty of them."

He takes my gift as I reach around to the small of my back and pull out the Governor. It's fully loaded with traditional bullets. I'm out of shotshell.

"Kel-Tec?" he whispers. "Odd choice."

"It was on sale. One hundred percent off."

He chuckles as the lights flicker, go completely dark, and the joggers make their move.

***

Thump! Thump! Thump! Thump!

I don't know who fired first, but in a confined space like a moving Metro train, gunfire is deafening. When the lights went out I slid from my seat, across the aisle, and took cover behind the seats on the opposite side. Glass shatters and showers over me.

Amidst the cacophony of fireworks, one of the joggers approaches quickly, firing off at least four quick rounds before the lights strobe back to life.

The flash from his gun gives away his position, but I'm not able to return fire immediately. I'm pinned behind the seats, but certain the first of the two joggers doesn't notice I've moved. The gunfire stops for a brief moment.

I pop up on my knees and, without stopping to consider the physics of a moving train, quickly pull the trigger twice as the car jerks to the right, affecting my aim.

Pow! Pow!

I hit the jogger in the left shoulder once, knocking him back and forcing a guttural moan. He drops his weapon, before I fire a third shot, Blogis unloads a triplet of twenty-two caliber bullets from the Kel-Tec. They hit the jogger in a tight pattern below his left eye. He crumples to the orange carpet with a thud, banging his bloodied head into the chrome pole in the middle of the aisle.

As he falls, I spot the other jogger. She's hunkered down, like me, behind a pair of seats. I've got four shots left. Blogis has twenty-seven. We're in good shape.

I look over at Blogis, who nods he's ready, and I slide into the aisle in a catcher's stance. The jogger is still hiding behind the seats.

"Give up!" shouts Blogis. "You're not getting out of here unless you do." He braces his arms against the back of the seat in front of him.

The jogger raises her empty hand and then tosses her weapon into the aisle with the other before slowly pressing herself up, using the seat for leverage.   "Who are you?" Blogis demands, working to maintain his balance, even though I'm pretty sure we both know the answer. I brace myself against the side of the seats to my left. The Governor is leveled at the jogger.

She's a pretty blonde with an athletic build. Even in the hoodie, it's apparent she's in outstanding shape. Her hair is pulled tight in a short ponytail, revealing wisps of her natural hair color over a Botox filled forehead absent any wrinkles. Even contract killers fight the effects of aging.

Her fingers are long and skinny, almost manly in appearance as she holds them above her head. The headphones are draped around her neck. She looks like a club deejay.

She doesn't answer Blogis' question. Instead, she starts to tremble and looks to her partner on the floor of the car, his blood staining the burnt orange a macabre brown. She starts to cry.

"You killed him," she whimpers, drawing Blogis' attention to the body for a split second. In that narrow space of time, she slides a knife from the sleeve of her hoodie and whips it at Blogis in a fluid, chopping motion.

"Knife!" I yell at the moment it leaves her hand and empty my remaining rounds into her chest.

Pow! Pow! Pow! Pow!

She staggers against the force of the barrage and sinks into the red seats behind her. She likely doesn't see her blade clang into the pole next to Blogis' head and bounce harmlessly to the floor.

The jogger's lungs rattle out her last breath of air as the train slows to a stop. Her last Botox treatment was a complete waste of money.

The doors hiss open and I move to grab my backpack from the floor. I start to get off the train but Blogis stops me.

"Wait," he grabs my arm. He kneels down over the male jogger's body and pulls something from the man's pockets.

A small group of people, maybe seven or eight, trudge into the car as we squeeze out onto the hexagonal, red brick platform. From behind us, a woman screams.

"Call 9-1-1!" shouts someone else. "Somebody's been shot."

"Keep walking," says Blogis, pushing his way against the crowd eager to join the commotion at the train car. He tucks the Kel-Tec in the front of his pants and pulls out his shirt, covering the bulge at his waist. "They're so distracted by the bodies, they won't be able to describe us."

"Yeah, but those cameras will," I remark without looking at the surveillance cameras perched strategically throughout the terminal. I've already slipped the six-shooter back into the pack, which I've slung over one shoulder.

"We'll be gone by then," he says, quickening his pace up a set of stairs. "Plus, you're already a wanted man. What's another murder added to your growing list of charges?"

We reach the top of the stairs and push our way out onto the street. A sign at the doors reads *METRO CENTER*.

"We're close to the White House," I say.

"So? Want to stop for a tour?"

"I'm just saying there's a lot of law enforcement around here. We need to get away from this part of the district. There are a gazillion different agencies patrolling this area."

"They're everywhere," he says. "It doesn't matter. Just follow me."

We hit 11th street and Blogis stops at a bank of red bicycles. He reaches into his pocket and pulls out a wallet.

"Is that the jogger's?" I ask.

"Yep." Blogis pulls out a credit card and flips it over. "Thank you, Mr. Franklin." He takes a couple of steps to a red kiosk and inserts the card. He punches a few buttons, consults Mr. Franklin's driver's license, and then chuckles.

"Figures," he says and holds up a corporate identification card for F. Pickle Security Consultants. "Probably paid you a visit courtesy of your former boss."

"Probably."

"I'll give the hair sack this much: he's persistent." He rubs his hands together. "All right then. Grab a bike."

"What?"

"Grab a bike and start peddling," he says. "We need to get out of here. Two wheels are faster than feet."

"What about you?"

"I'm grabbing one too," he says. "I'll meet you back at the hotel. We can talk later." He pulls out a wad of bills from the wallet and hands them to me, then tosses the wallet into a nearby trashcan. "It amazes me how many people still carry cash."

He pulls a red bike from the rack and hops aboard, standing as he pedals north on 11th Street. I pull another bike from the rack but instead of heading north, I go east on F Street, the pack bouncing only back as I pedal.

It seems Bella, Mack, and I have a new partner.

Three blocks from the bike stand, there's an internet cafe that doubles as a coffeehouse. Maybe it's the other way around. Either way, it's a good place to duck inside for a minute.

The barista lets me tuck the bike just inside the entry, next to a small cafe table facing the street. There's a computer terminal littered with small post-it sized notes with rules and payment options. I've got a couple bucks left from our Wal-Mart excursion and the cash Blogis handed me, which will more than cover the cost of ten minutes online.

The barista happily takes the money and gives me a credit card, telling me to swipe it through the card reader attached to the terminal. He says the computer will automatically return to the login screen when my time is up. I won't get a warning.

I swipe the card and log on to Gmail to create a new account from which to email Corkscrew. I don't want a hacker having access to anything that matters. And if he's as good as everyone seems to think, it's better safe than sorry.

In a new window I start typing my message:

```
I am Sir Spencer's contact. He suggested
I email you for more details about the
Long Island project. We're moving to the
next phase. We need to talk. Here's my
cell. Text me.
```

I encrypt the message and send it to the email address I've memorized from the document we recovered from George's townhouse.

I've got four minutes left on the computer, so I decide to read a little about myself. I Google my name and a list of news articles pops up on the screen. There are articles from *The New York Times*, *People Magazine*, *USAToday*, *The Houston Chronicle*. I click the most recent, which is only a couple of minutes old. It's from the news/gossip website

PlausibleDeniability.info and it's written by their lead investigative reporter, Dillinger Holt. As soon as I click on the link and read the headline, I wish I hadn't.

BREAKING NEWS BREAKING NEWS BREAKING NEWS

DC METRO DEATHS LINKED TO ON-THE-RUN KILLER?
By Dillinger Holt, Lead Investigative Correspondent

Washington DC - Multiple sources are telling PD.info there is a breaking development in the search for wanted killer, Jackson Quick. DC Metro Police confirm they are on the scene of a double homicide inside a metro train.

They will not confirm causes of death or the origin/destination of the train. But we do know there is surveillance video of two people exiting a train car in which two bodies were found. One of the men may be Jackson Quick, the suspect in a multiple homicide in Houston, Texas.

Quick, authorities warn, is linked to other violent crimes and could be traveling with Bella Buell, the daughter of deceased energy magnate Don Carlos Buell. It is unclear if the second person on the videotape is a woman or a man.

Both are believed to be in the Washington metropolitan area. The pilot of a plane that crash landed at Washington Executive Airport in Clinton, Maryland reports his passengers included Quick, Buell, and one other unidentified individual.

That aircraft left southeast Texas within hours of a mass shooting at the home of Houston television reporter George Townsend. The award-winning journalist was among those killed in what Texas authorities describe to PB.info as a "bloodbath".

We are working to get new information and will update this article as warranted.

How is this even possible? I mean, I can still hear the gunshots ringing in my ears and this guy, Holt, has "sources" telling him I'm responsible. I look at the photographs accompanying the brief article. There's me, with my goofy grin in a driver's license picture. Bella's mug is next to mine. She's smiling too, her hair down over her shoulders. She can't take a bad picture.

I click through the gallery to find shots of George's house, a publicity photograph of him, and a link to his station biography page. There's also a blurry shot of Ripley's burning storage unit, the light from the flames overexposing the shot.

I try clicking a link to "related article" when my time runs out and the screen returns to a generic login screen which instructs me to slide a card through the reader. I really don't need to see anymore. Thankfully the barista hasn't recognized me. Otherwise, I'm sure I'd be in cuffs by now.

Without turning to face the barista again, I push back from the computer and move to grab my bike. It's time to put some distance between the metro station and me. I don't know where to go, but I've got to get rid of the bike and find my way back to the hotel.

***

After riding for fifteen minutes, I reach Union Station. I hop off the bike at North Capitol and F Streets and lean the bike against another bike share rack, intentionally not "returning" it so as not to leave an electronic record. It floors me sometimes how much privacy we *don't* have anymore because of technology. The same advances that are supposed to make our lives easier also complicate things like anonymity.

Looking over my shoulder and turning around to get a three hundred and sixty degree idea of my surroundings, I half expect to see jack-booted agents descending on me from every direction. Instead it's the stereotypical Beltway crowd of smartphone-typing, Starbucks-swigging young professionals communicating, negotiating, and backstabbing through Bluetooth earpieces surgically attached to their heads. I move my hand to the small of my back, checking my six-shooter. It's empty and this isn't the place to reload it, but it's comforting knowing I have it there.

There's a bench just off the plaza leading to Union Station. It's empty, so I find a seat and drop my backpack next to me on the bench. Sitting is a bad idea.

Almost immediately, my legs feel thick. Not having run in months, except for my life, my muscles feel hot. The lactic acid thumping through them from the pedal pushing is increasingly painful. The additional blood flowing to push oxygen through my thighs and calves creates the sensation of thousands of pinpricks across the surface of my skin.

The adrenaline that's pushed me for the last hour evaporates and I wonder how comfortable the bench might be if I lay down. A security camera fifty yards away staring me straight in the face changes my mind. Inhaling deeply through my nose, the air provides a momentary boost. I close my eyes and take another breath, telling myself exhaustion is a state of mind.

I reach over to the backpack and pull my burner phone from an outside pocket.

I punch the contact list and text the only listing under the letter B.

u ok? i o good.

I stare at the screen, praying for a quick response. It's not until I look away that the phone vibrates.

yes. where r u????

I thumb in the response. *not far. meet u at crap hotel.*

how do i know it's u? Good question.

ask me something.

favorite food truck in hawaii? she types. Clever.

leonard's malasadas. I love those doughnuts. So worth the drive from the North Shore to Waipahu. I breathe in through my nose, almost able to smell the sugar and fried dough. My shrink says smells are the best memory triggers. I don't know whether it's true or not, but I'll admit the smell of soil makes me think of my mom. It's the metallic, acrid sting of a discharged weapon that reminds me of Dad. Appropriate I guess.

i was afraid you were gone. 2nd time in a day. :-(

What is it with texting and emojis? I've never quite gotten it. It took me a while to accept the bastardization of English that is text lingo. Emojis are an entirely different level of brevity that's beyond me.

sorry. nothing i could do. pushed onto train too quickly. I hit send.

what happened on train?

2 much 2 txt. Understatement.

try. :-)

i'm ok but pickle people showed up.

My phone buzzes again. This time it's a call.

"Hello?"

"Jackson?" It's Bella. "How did they find you?"

"I don't know." I press the phone close to my face so I can speak softly. "How do they always find me? You haven't had any trouble, right?"

"No."

"So you're okay?"

"Yes," her voice quavers. "Mack brought me back to the hotel. What happened? Is Blogis with you? Are you hurt? Where are you?"

"I'm not hurt, but the Pickle people aren't doing so well. In fact, I might have drawn more attention by how we handled it."

"What do you mean?"

"In case you haven't noticed," I sigh, "we're all over the news. You and I *are* a regular Bonnie and Clyde. George was right."

"I hadn't noticed."

"Also, we killed both of the Pickle people. On the train."

"We?"

"Blogis and me."

"Is he with you? You never answered me. Where is he? Did he let you go?"

"Blogis isn't with me right now, but we're going to meet up with him at the hotel."

"What?"

"He's on board," I explain. "I'll fill you in when I see you."

"How is he *on board*? He was trying to *kill* us."

"I'm not sure he was…"

"He kidnapped me in Germany!" Bella reminds me. "We had to shoot our way out of the Russian Embassy! Does that ring a bell?"

"I opened fire first, remember?"

"He tried to kill you near the river," she says.

"I shot him. It wasn't the other way around."

"So now he's a saint?" she grumbles, the pitch of her voice changing with her rising frustration.

"Do you trust me?" I ask.

"Yes."

"Then trust me. I'll see you soon."

***

I haven't walked three blocks, my head on a swivel, when a familiar Ford pulls alongside me. Mack rolls down his window and slows to a stop. "Get in."

I duck into the front passenger's seat and thank him for coming to get me. He nods and merges back into traffic. The car smells stale, like cigarettes.

"Do you smoke?"

"Occasionally," he admits. "When I'm stressed."

"I've never smelled it on you before." I find the button for my window and crack it.

"I was out of them." He checks the rearview mirror and changes lanes. "There's a machine in the hotel lobby. I grabbed a pack."

"A cigarette machine? I didn't even know those still exist."

"Yeah, I know. Nasty habit, right? Gonna kill me someday." He clears his throat and accelerates past a taxi.

"I don't know," I shrug, glancing at the reflection in the passenger side-view mirror. Paranoia has me looking for death around every corner. "We could bite it at any second, Mack. A cancer stick is the least of your worries."

"Wow! Thanks for the pep talk."

I shrug. "Just keeping it real."

Mack bites his lip, his upper teeth digging into the pinkish blotch of skin that surrounds his mouth. His knuckles, wrapped around the steering wheel, bear the same resemblance. It's on his elbows, his eyelids, and the tops of his ears.

"Can I ask you a question, Mack?"

"As long as you keep it real." He brakes for a red light and rubs his chin again before craning his neck to either direction to ease the stress.

"How did you get the vitiligo?"

"I don't know." He examines his knuckles, using one hand to rub the back of the other while we wait for the light to turn green. "Just lucky I guess."

"How old were you?"

"Thirty-five when I first noticed it. It was on my knuckles first. They were itching constantly. At first the doctors gave me hydrocortisone cream. It didn't help. Then I spotted it on my eyelids. I guess I would have gotten it on my knees if they weren't already scarred up from Iraq."

"It's a virus, right?"

"That's what they tell me," he says. "They don't really know how anyone gets it."

"Does it bother you?"

"In what way?" The light turns green and he presses the gas pedal.

"That you have it. Does it bother you?"

"It used to, I guess. People would ask me if I had been burned. They thought it was related to my injuries in Iraq. I still get looks and questions, but it doesn't bother me much now. I mean, after nearly dying twice and losing my wife, loss of skin pigment is kinda irrelevant."

"What happened in Iraq?"

"Man," he says, making a right turn, "you're Mr. Inquisitive today. What's up?"

"Just wondering. I mean, I'd like to know more about the man who nearly killed *me*."

"*The* man?" he laughs. "I'm like one of a *hundred* people who've tried to kill you. And I bet I'm the only one who's apologized."

"You're the only one who survived," I say, deadpan. It's not actually true. But it sounds good.

"It was an RPG, a rocket propelled grenade. I never saw it coming. Lucky I even lived."

"Tell me about it," I say in my best shrink voice. I might as well have said, *And how does that make you feel, Mack?*

He shoots a curious look at me. His eyes are glassy, he's blinking rapidly. Maybe I shouldn't press.

"We were on patrol. It was six days after President Bush gave Saddam and his sons a warning to get out of their country." He pulls into the hotel parking lot and finds a parking space. "We'd been there for a few days. The shock and awe of the start of the war was killing them. There were pinpoint attacks, targeted bombings from the air. We were relentless."

"I remember shock and awe," I tell him.

He leaves the engine running and unbuckles his seatbelt. "We advanced quickly on the ground, plowing along the Euphrates for more than one hundred and fifty miles.

"The brass was using the air to our advantage," he says, his eyes distant now. He's there, I gather, in the desert. "Saturday night and Sunday morning it was a blitzkrieg. We were hitting them with drones. The Navy and the Air Force were flying hundreds of sorties."

"It seemed like we were going to end the war as soon as it started," I say, trying to engage him. He's long gone, though, lost in the memory of March 23, 2003.

"I was in Nasiriya. That's a city in the southeastern part of the country. It was bad."

"What happened?"

"I was one of the explosives experts in our unit. I had a lot of training in IEDs, nuclear, other weapons of mass destruction. That day we were charged with securing a pair of bridges. One of the bridges was over the Euphrates. The other crossed Saddam Canal. They framed the city from the north and south.

"We knew we'd face resistance there," he continued. "There was regular Iraqi army, Republican Guard, and Fedayeen all working together. It was a hornet's nest. But we're Marines. We poked the nest."

"They fought back," I say as much as ask.

"They fought," he nods without looking at me. "A lot of people remember some of the Iraqis surrendering in those early days of the war, so they assume all of the ground troops surrendered. They think the pushback came later, once Al-Qaeda started infiltrating and ISIS grew in strength. That's not what happened.

He sighs. "They just kept coming. We got hit with a lot of small arms fire. One of our AAV's got hit by an RPG first."

"What's an AAV?"

"Amphibious Assault Vehicle."

"Oh."

"We were taking so much fire, the medics couldn't get to us. They couldn't land a helo. Nothing. We were on our own for a while. We were taking mortar fire. Our position was north of the canal. Communication among the companies was bad. We were in the middle of what became known as Ambush Alley."

Mack stops talking and rubs his chin and then his nose. I sit quietly, waiting for him to continue. He blinks a couple of times and inhales deeply through his nose.

"Even though there was a lot of vegetation along the banks of the river, there wasn't much cover once we got a couple hundred yards past the water. So when the mortar fire got accurate, starting tagging us pretty bad, we were looking for anything that would help. On one side of the road, there were little drainage ditches and canals. We dove into them and the shells exploded around us. It was wet and marshy, and it smelled like a port-o-john in that ditch. I can't walk by a construction site without thinking about lying in that ditch, waiting to get blown up."

"Is that where you got hit?"

"No," he shakes his head. "Others got hit. We loaded them on AAVs and started heading back, trying to get them to an LZ where they could get help. Somebody ordered us to head back south. We got hit again by RPG fire. And then air support came."

"So they helped you get out?"

"No. They fired on us."

"What do you mean?"

"A-10s," he says flatly. "Warthogs. Somebody thought we were the enemy. We were heading south. There was so much confusion, so little communication, air support saw our convoy and thought we were

Iraqis. They strafed us. In the confusion of it all, we took more RPG fire. My AAV got hit."

"That's how you lost your leg?"

"Basically," he says, unconsciously grabbing his knee and rubbing it. "I mean, I got lucky. Eighteen Marines died that day."

"How many were injured?"

"I don't know. The numbers aren't accurate. There are so many different versions of that day."

"How'd they get you out of there?"

"I don't remember. I was unconscious. Sometimes it feels like I never got out."

I don't know what to say to that. I never served my country in war. I've never been on foreign soil, fighting for democracy. My battles have been self-serving, self-preserving.

He laughs.

"What?"

"They say that history is written by the victors," he opines.

"Winston Churchill said that."

"Whoever said it, they were only partially right."

"How so?"

"The victors write like a million versions of what happened. Then somebody who probably wasn't even there takes the juiciest bits and pieces and it becomes the gospel."

"You think?"

"Look at what's going on with you, Jackson. You're not winning right now, and all of the media types are writing your history for you. Shoot," he laughs, "with the way the internet works now, I'm not sure there's even one history anymore."

"You're not making sense to me."

"It's just as well." He pulls on the door handle to get out. "I'm just some crazy, one-legged black man with a question mark on his face."

"You know about that?"

"Yep. That's my history unless we do something about it." He swings his leg around and gets out of the car. He pokes his head back in and stares at me. "We gonna do something about it?"

***

I can't quantify or accurately describe the level of awkwardness in our dank hotel room when Liho Blogis walks through the door.

It's five o'clock in the evening. There's the orange light of early dusk beaming through the courtyard window as the sun sinks below the hotel roof opposite our room. The colony of dust dancing in the air makes me want to hold my breath.

Blogis strides past the three of us and sits on the edge of the bed without introducing himself to Bella or Mack.

"You've been watching this?" he points at the warped flat screen television in front of him tuned to cable news coverage of our escapades. "They just made the connection to our skirmish on the Metro."

He finds the remote and turns up the volume. The three of us are still standing near the door, dumbfounded.

"These surveillance cameras are everywhere," he says, looking over at us. "Am I right? And the quality… wow! I can see you need to shave, Jackson. The picture is so crystal clear."

Vickie Lupo is on the screen, pointing her pencil at the camera, her overly mascaraed lashes batting in Morse code.

"Now this band of marauders is out of control," she spits. *"I mean, this Jackson Quick fellow, who we've learned from federal law enforcement sources is really named Jackson* Ellsworth, *is dangerous to all of us."*

My photograph is in a graphically enhanced square over her shoulder. At the bottom, it reads, *"Serial Killer?"*

"We know he's the same man who had no compunction about opening fire on live television during the last Texas gubernatorial debate. There are reports he was suspected of assault in South Dakota. Interpol had concerns

he might have been connected to violence in the U.K., Ukraine, and Germany."

Blogis turns to look at me and offers a thumbs-up. I can feel Bella and Mack staring at me from behind.

"How is it that someone who is best described as a serial killer walks around like nothing's happened? For an answer to that question, we turn to our law enforcement analyst and former second in command at the Federal Bureau of Investigation, Bernard Francis. He now runs the private sector security and information firm Wignock Homeland Intelligence Group."

The screen changes to reveal the guest on the right side of the screen. Lupo's image slides to the left.

"Thank you for having me, Vickie," says Francis. He's a distinguished man with a smile far too kind for the kind of work he likely did in his former life. *"Always good to speak with you."*

"We don't have time for this." I reach across Blogis for the remote but he grabs it before I get to it.

"Yes we do," he says. "It's not as though you can go out for a jog right now."

"Quick is a unique case, Vickie," he says. *"Here's a seemingly normal kid who's working for the Governor of Texas. Then he ends up trying to stop the assassination of his boss's political opponent. He kills that assassin, a man named Crockett. And then he disappears for more than a year."*

"Well," Lupo interrupts, *"let's be clear, Bernard. Most people suspect that it was Jackson Quick who provided the damning video evidence that ultimately led to the governor's conviction and lengthy incarceration. So he didn't fall off the face of the Earth."*

"No." Francis smiles widely. *"You're correct, Vickie. He didn't. But he did lay low for quite some time. Then his image was recorded on a city bus in San Antonio. Three people were killed. Jackson Quick was the only one to walk off the bus alive."*

"So much for the normal kid," Lupo interjects.

"*True,*" says Francis. "*But let me postulate something here that might upset some people.*"

"*Please,*" says Lupo, eyes widening at the prospect of ratings gold. "*Go ahead, Bernard.*"

"*What was it that forced this normal kid to become a killer?*" He leans into the camera, measuring his theory carefully before uttering it into the microphone on his lapel. "*I suggest, contrary to what most law enforcement believes, he is the victim here.*"

"*How so?*" Lupo almost explodes, slapping her hands flat on her desk. "*He's a killer. We've got a reporter, among others, killed in Houston. Two people, a couple in jogging clothes, are murdered on the subway in our nation's capital. The good Lord knows how many bodies he left in his wake across Europe.*"

"*Let me just suggest,*" he raises his hands as an animal trainer would to a crazed lion about to pounce, "*he is defending himself.*"

"*That's absurd, Bernard.*" Lupo rolls her eyes. "*I'm sorry here. I respect you. I really do. But—*"

"*Ask yourself this, Vickie,*" Bernard is still smiling, "*why would he try to heroically save a man's life on live television, kill random people on a bus eighteen months later, and then, after causing havoc across three countries, come back here to kill a friend of his?*"

"*You're suggesting George Townsend was his friend?*"

"*We know they were acquainted,*" says Francis. "*As you said, most suspect it was Quick's video that put the governor away and gave Townsend a tremendous story. Townsend has publicly praised Quick's bravery in the past.*"

"*Go on,*" says Lupo, somewhat tamed.

"*And you've forgotten the connection to Bella Buell.*" Francis is gaining steam. "*Her father was killed on live television, she takes over his company, now she's a cold blooded killer? A Bonnie to Quick's Clyde?*"

"There it is," Bella snipes from behind me. "I was waiting for that."

"I would say so," says Lupo. *"Or maybe he's got her under his control. Maybe she's not with him of her own free will."*

"That's enough!" Bella charges Blogis. "Give me the remote."

"Hold on now." Blogis holds up his hands, the remote in one of them, then slides off the bed. "This is not only entertaining theatre," he says, backing into the mini-refrigerator, "it's also important we learn what they know. Consider this counter-intelligence."

Bella searches for the power button on the television, running her hands along the bezel like she's giving it a TSA pat down. She can't find it.

"Now that we've heard the fringe theorist on this," Lupo sneers from her bully pulpit, *"let's get a sane perspective from the always level-headed Dillinger Holt. He's a reporter with the popular beltway website Plausible Deniability Dot Com."*

"All right," Blogis points the remote at the television. "I can't handle that blowhard. We've done enough recon." He turns it off.

"Finally," huffs Bella. "I can only handle so much." She walks back to the other side of the room, near Mack. He hasn't moved since Blogis sauntered into our space. He hasn't said much at all, really, since our conversation in the car.

"We've been watching," I say, moving a step closer to Blogis. "We know there's more heat on us than before."

"You!" he points at me. "The heat's on *you*. They don't know who *I* am."

"There's heat on you," I remind him. "Your investors. They're applying every bit as much heat as any federal agent could. I'm going to guess your friends don't care about Miranda rights or due process. Am I right?"

Blogis sits on the edge of the bed. He shifts his weight and leans back on his elbows, crumpling one of the large Brookhaven diagrams with his weight.

"So Jackson tells me you're on board," Bella says. "Whatever that means." She shoots me a look before her eyes dart back to our guest.

"It means I like the terms of our agreement," he says. He pushes down on his forearms, bounces forward on the bed, and stands up.

"And what is that?" Bella's question is for both Blogis and me.

"I want the process," he says. "My investors want the process. Your boy here tells me you can get it."

"He said that, did he?" Bella doesn't look at me this time. Her arms are folded in front of her. She's clearly irritated that we're now allied with three men who neither of us trust. She knows it is a necessary evil.

"Are we not on the same page here?" One of his eyebrows arcs higher than the other. He looks at Bella, shifts his gaze to me for a moment, and returns to Bella.

"We're good," I say. "I've told him, with a little help from his network of computer experts, we can get into Brookhaven. We believe we know where a duplicate of the process exists. We'll provide it for a price."

"What's the price?" Mack's first words in a while.

"Oh!!" Blogis seems intrigued I haven't discussed that with my partners. "Are we suffering from a lack of communication here?"

"No," Bella steps in. "Like Jackson said, we're good."

"So then you know my payment to you, other than leaving you alone in perpetuity, is offing the man who keeps sending sour Pickles your way."

Mack bites his lower lip and nods. "How will you do that? He's in prison."

"Please," Blogis waves him off. "It's because it's a prison, I tell you I can do it without equivocation."

"You can't get into Brookhaven." Mack takes a couple of steps. "So tell me how you'll kill the governor."

"You tell me how you're getting into Brookhaven," Blogis snaps, "I'll tell you how I will take care of Jackson's predator."

"Do we need to get our rulers?" Bella asks. Neither man knows how to respond, so she ends the Mexican standoff. "The truth is none of us trust each other. We've all taken shots at one another. But if we want to achieve our goals, we've got to work together. So get over yourselves and understand if there's any double-crossing or back-stabbing, I'll put a bullet in you."

"I'm turned on now," Blogis laughs. "Mr. Ellsworth, you've got yourself quite the woman."

"Don't I know it," I say, offering my smile to Bella. She smiles back. We're good.

***

Despite what some might tell you, there's only one proven photo of Billy The Kid. It's a tintype of William Bonney, taken around 1879 outside of a saloon in New Mexico. He's wearing a crumpled hat, a long-sleeved sweater, some worn boots, and baggy pants. The infamous outlaw is holding a Winchester rifle in one hand and a Colt .45 on his hip. His crooked smile is unforced and genuine.

It is a famous photograph, published in newspapers even before Billy The Kid was shot and killed less than two years later. Still, most wanted posters had just a sketch of him or, more commonly, a description of his five-foot-three inch, one hundred and twenty-five pound frame.

I'm not living in the late nineteenth century. This isn't the Old West. My face is everywhere. It's on television, on websites, and it's trending on social media. There's even a hashtag—#QuicklyFindQuick—that cable news outlets have branded on the bottom left of their breaking news coverage. Neither Frank and Jesse James nor Bonnie and Clyde had that.

I'm public enemy number one, it would seem. And except for some former FBI suit, everyone thinks I'm a dangerous serial killer. That makes my job a little bit more difficult.

It would be tough enough to break into Brookhaven draped in a cloak of anonymity. Now, it seems all the more impossible. Before we even get to the lab, we have to get three hundred miles north.

"I'll take care of it," Blogis says. "We'll get you two different cars. You'll be a target in no time in that rental car."

Within an hour there are a pair of black Chevy Suburbans parked at the side exit of the hotel. Bella and I take one of them, while Mack and Blogis take the other.

"I'm only with you for a few city blocks," he says, holding onto the outside of the SUV, his foot planted on the running board like George Washington crossing the Delaware.

"I'll have someone from my team meet you in New York," he says. "I'll text you the meet details. That'll be your hacker. I won't see you again until you deliver what you've promised."

"And the payment?" I ask, my door still open.

"It'll happen," he promises and drops into the SUV, slamming the door shut behind him. Mack pulls out ahead of us and motors down the street into the darkness. Once his taillights blur and disappear, I accelerate in the opposite direction.

It's a five hour drive from Washington to Upton, New York. Driving at night should make it easier, and allow for us to get fewer looks on the road.

Most of the trip will be up I-95. We'll drive through Baltimore, past Wilmington, Delaware, and the outskirts of Philadelphia. We'll hang a right at Teaneck, New York and head east on Long Island.

"You have your new burner?" Bella asks me, checking the signal on hers. "And you gave the number to Blogis?"

"Yes." I make a right and slow behind a motorcycle puttering along at the posted speed limit. "He's got it."

"I still don't know about this," Bella says, turning down the fan on the air conditioning. "We're playing a ridiculously dangerous game, Jackson."

"How so?"

"Really?" she punches my right thigh. "Don't play stupid. You're trying to run two parallel deals here. It could blow up in your face."

"I know that." I do. There's a point at which my luck has to run out, right? Maybe it already has. "I don't know what else to do. This is my best shot, Bella."

"How does this play out?" She folds her arms across her chest. "Walk me through it."

"First we have to get to New York. Then we steal the process."

"That's a big leap from step one to step two. I need to know what's going on in that head of yours. Since we left California, I haven't felt a connection. I'm trying. But—"

"A connection? What is this? *The Bachelorette?* I don't get what that has to do with anything."

"Lord, you are dense sometimes. We're a team. But you keep trying to treat this like it's you against the world. It's like I'm a tagalong or something."

"That's ridiculous." I shake my head and merge onto the interstate. "I never—"

"You don't have to say anything; it's obvious. You make all of these decisions without asking. You run off by yourself at critical times. At least twice, you'd be dead if it weren't for me."

"Look, I know you saved my life. More than once. I know that."

"You have to open up," she says, apparently stealing a page from my shrink. "If we're going to make this work, you need to trust me as much as you want me to trust you."

"Are we talking about *us* here? Or are we talking about this scheme I've concocted?"

"There is no *us*, Jackson," she chides, "if we don't make it through this scheme. So no, I'm not talking about *us*, right now. That's a conversation for much later."

I stay in the right lane and set the Suburban's cruise control at one mile below the speed limit.

"So fill me in. I need to know how this is going to go down once we've miraculously recovered the process." She adjusts the seatbelt and leans back in her seat, propping her feet on the dash. She's in for the long haul.

I tell her my plan to play both sides of the proverbial fence, explaining why we can get both men to a single location after we have the process.

Neither of us is convinced that we've fooled either Sir Spencer or Blogis. For all we know, they're working together and we're the odd-men out. We can't worry about that, we decide. We have to act as though we have the upper hand.

"Best case," she says, "we survive this, the world forgets about us, and we live happily ever after on some island. Sir Spencer and Blogis get their just desserts. Mack finds happiness somewhere with someone."

"Worst case?" I know the answer and so does she.

"Let's be positive, Jackson. I'm trying to look at the bright side." She turns on the radio.

"...*was Billy Joel,*" says the deejay, "*performing 'The Ballad of Billy The Kid', live at the Hollywood Bowl on May 17th, 2014. It was the Piano Man's first ever performance at that iconic venue. He did three dates there in a ten day span. All three were sellouts. Next up, the Steve Miller Band with their classic tune 'Take The Money And Run.'*"

"I always liked Billy Joel," Bella says. "My dad was a big fan." Her eyes are closed while she hums along to Steve Miller.

We've long since merged onto I-95, and I've taken the SUV off of cruise control to keep myself engaged. It's close to midnight by the time she falls asleep, her head bobbing with the movement of the road. I press a preset on the radio, changing it to news.

"...*hotel clerk says he thought the guests looked familiar, but it wasn't until he logged onto his computer he was certain about who they were,*" a radio reporter apes in a ridiculously nasal delivery.

My grip on the steering wheels tightens and I accelerate into the left lane, passing a slow-moving Volkswagen. The driver's texting on her phone, the bluish glow illuminating her face in the dark of her car.

"*I looked at my homepage and there they were,*" says the clerk, who I picture standing behind the small check-in desk at the crappy Foggy Bottom hotel. "*The man and the woman. I know it was them. And they were with another man too. He had one leg, and his lips looked funny.*"

I slide the SUV back into the right lane, maintaining my speed.

"*The man and the woman are Jackson Quick and Bella Buell,*" says the reporter, "*a couple wanted by local, state, and federal authorities for a variety of violent crimes. The second man is as yet unidentified, but law enforcement in Texas say that description matches that of an alleged accomplice seen at the home of a murdered television reporter in Houston. Here is Houston Police spokesperson Stephen Davis.*"

I close in on a Subaru wagon in the right lane and push into the passing lane, pressing the pedal to speed past. Checking my rearview, I slide back into the right lane and put distance between our SUV and the Subaru.

"*We believe,*" says Davis, "*there were multiple weapons discharged inside the residence. We have three bodies inside and one outside. Each of the decedents was shot multiple times. All of them are adult males in their thirties or forties. There are three persons of interest who left the residence shortly after gunshots were reported by neighbors.*"

Bella leans her head against the space between the headrest and the door. Her feet are curled behind her on the passenger's seat. I check my rearview and see a set of lights growing in size as the vehicle moves closer to us. I'm guessing the Subaru driver wants to pick up the pace.

"*Again,*" the reporter says through his nose, "*authorities are looking for the suspects. They are believed to be in the D.C. metro area. You can look at their photographs and read more about them at our website.*" I turn off the radio and cruise in silence. I've heard enough.

The lights behind me are blinding in my rearview. The Subaru is tailgating me now. I push the pedal to put some space between us when I realize it's not the Subaru on my bumper.

The lights in my rearview start flashing, alternating blue and white. It's not the Subaru. It's a cop. I check my speedometer. I'm going eighty-five-miles per hour and there's a decision to make.

Do I slow down and pull over? Or do I gun it and try to run?

Without thinking, I push the pedal and accelerate, dimming the flashing lights in my mirror.

PART THREE
CLARITY

"It is mine to avenge; I will repay. In due time their foot will slip; their day of disaster is near and their doom rushes upon them."
—DEUTERONOMY 32:35

CHAPTER 12

They call the Astrodome "The Eighth Wonder of the World". At least they used to call it that. When it opened in 1965, it was the world's first multi-use domed stadium and it was impressive.

It was the concept of the dome that convinced Major League Baseball to award a team to Houston. First named the Colt .45's, the team was renamed the Astros when they started playing inside the new dome. It was instantly a hit.

This was the place where Muhammed Ali knocked out Cleveland Williams, and where Billie Jean King defeated Bobby Riggs in tennis's "Battle of the Sexes." It saw Earl Campbell, tattered jersey and all, run through, over, and around opposing defenders for seven seasons. Modern college basketball television coverage started inside the Astrodome. The 1968 game between UCLA and the University of Houston was the first ever regular season college basketball game televised nationally in prime time. The Dome even hosted the 1992 Republican National Convention, likely since Houston was the hometown of then President George H.W. Bush.

"It was a big deal to play there because the Astrodome was a big deal." Billie Jean King said that.

Now, it's a shadow of its former self. Since sixteen thousand Hurricane Katrina evacuees slept on its floor, the Dome has fallen into disrepair. It just sits there, deteriorating alongside the larger, sleeker stadium built right next to it.

It's sad. Nobody knows what to do with it. Some want it torn down for a parking lot, while others can't bear to see it go. It's like a dog nobody wants to put down, even if it's what's best for the animal.

I choose to remember it in its glory days, having once attended a game there. I don't remember the year, but the Astros won the game. It was an incredible, overwhelming experience.

The dome was so big, especially to a young kid. We were sitting along the first base line, maybe three or four rows above the top of the Astros' dugout. Across from us, in left field, was a huge Marlboro billboard. In centerfield, beneath the lowest part of the dome arch, was a huge American flag.

The Astroturf field was an unnatural shade of green. At first I thought it was real grass.

"It's what they call Astroturf or artificial turf," my dad told me. "They put it in here because there's not enough sunlight coming through the roof for real grass to grow."

The sound the ball hitting the bat was suffocated by the crowd's reverberating cheers. The noise and the size of the place made the game feel more like a carnival or a circus. The Astros trailed most of the game, but the fans were raucous anyhow.

There was a man next to me in that famous rainbow Astros jersey that matched the pattern of the seats in the upper deck. It was probably a size too small for him, but he didn't seem to care. He was too entrenched in the game and the bag of peanuts he was shelling onto the floor.

"C'mon ump," he called out to the umpire behind home plate. "That was a steee-rike! Get your head in the game!"

He seemed to live and die with each pitch. An Astros hit or great defensive play would drive him to his feet, peanut shards flying into the air from his lap, his belly sticking out from the bottom of the untucked jersey.

"Whoop!" he yelled. "That's it 'Stros! Let's go!"

My father watched me watching the man. He laughed out loud when the man's loud and sudden outburst would make me jump with surprise.

It was late in the game. The Astros were at the plate in the seventh or eighth inning. They had a man on first. They were trailing by a run after having come back from a deep hole. One of the players hit a deep ball to right field. Everyone in the Dome stood as if on cue. The roar inside the Dome rose to a deafening crescendo when the ball stayed inside the foul pole and sailed into the first row of seats. The Astros took the lead.

Peanut Man bounced up and down, his arms in the air. "That's it Astros!" he yelled through the constant rasp in his voice. He turned to me and reached over my head, high-fiving my dad before punching at the air like Ali.

"That's what I'm talking about!" he said to nobody and everybody, his arms extended to the domed roof. "Nobody keeps Houston down. Never say die! Never give up! That's H-town baby!"

The Astros won the game. When we walked out to our car, my stomach was full of hot dogs and soda and I was toting a Houston Astros felt pennant. My dad had his arm around my shoulder.

"What did you take away from that game?" he asked. It was the first and last time we'd go to a Major League game.

"Make sure my shirt always fits?" I joked.

"No." He laughed and tousled my hair. "A larger life lesson."

"That was a pretty big lesson," I replied before seriously considering his question. It was a long walk to the car, through the maze of a packed parking lot.

"Seriously," my dad said. "What one really good lesson could you learn from watching the Astros today? The big guy next to you so much as said it."

I thought back to the Astros' go-ahead home run and Peanut Man's gesture toward the roof. "Never give up?" I answered as much as asked.

"Exactly." My dad patted by back. "Never give up. No matter the odds against you, without consideration for what's already transpired, look ahead. Be positive. Never quit."

***

"What do you mean you're running from the cops?" Bella has the glazed over look on her face of someone who's just woken up in a strange place.

"There's a cop behind us," I repeat. "I'm running from him."

"Why?"

"We're dead meat if we pull over. Everybody and their brother is looking for us."

"I am aware of that, *Jackson*, but aren't you making it worse? You can't outrun a police car. They've got supercharged engines."

"I am so far," I say, referencing the distance I've managed to put between us and the flashing lights.

"Then maybe it's not a cop," she says, spinning around to look out the rear window. "Maybe it's someone impersonating a cop."

"Right. Who would—" I don't even have to finish the question before I know the answer.

"He would," she confirms.

"I don't have a tracker inside my leg anymore," I say, reminding her of the nifty device Sir Spencer surgically implanted in my knee. He tracked me for months without me being the wiser. It wasn't until a doctor found it in an X-ray that I knew anything about it. "He can't find us."

She plops back into her seat, facing forward. "Well those damned Pickle people keep finding you. Maybe you have an implant in your brain."

"Very funny. What do you want me to do? We've almost lost whoever it is."

"We could keep speeding along and catch the attention of a real cop," she said. "Or we could stop and confront Sir Spencer. Clearly he has something to say."

I'm cruising at just over ninety miles per hour, zooming past cars and trucks in the slow lane. She has a point. I ease off of the gas pedal and even out at a respectable seventy-five miles per hour. The lights in the rear view grow brighter as the pseudo-cop approaches with a no-supercharged engine.

"What if it's not Sir Spencer?" I ask, glancing over at Bella, who's already pulled a nine millimeter out of the glove box.

"Then we deal with it," she shrugs. I love her.

I'm sliding the Suburban into the right lane when my phone buzzes. The screen lights up with a text message.

"What's it say?" I ask Bella, who picks it up to read the screen.

"Pull over."

I slow the car another five miles per hour.

"No," she holds up the phone. "Whoever's texting you is telling you to pull over."

The cop car is gaining on us, its lights still spinning. There's no siren. From the glare, I can't see who's driving or how many people might be in the car. Not good.

"Who's it from? What's the area code?"

"It's blocked," she says. "There's no number. Wait." The phone buzzes again.

"What's it say?" My attention is more on the phone than the road and I swerve to stay off the shoulder, bouncing off rumble strips to regain control of the SUV.

Bella looks at me the moment the Suburban slows, jerking to a lower gear. Pressing the accelerator doesn't help. It's spongy and not responding.

"Are you stopping?" Bella asks.

"No." I press on the gas pedal like it's connected to a bass drum. "It's stopping on its own. It won't accelerate."

The speedometer drops to zero and I pull the wheel to the right, stopping the SUV on the side of the road. Without bothering to put the Suburban in park, I reach into the backseat and pull out the loaded LAR-15 rifle.

"A bit much?" Bella asks, referring to the nine millimeter in her hand.

"Better to be over prepared." I place the rifle across my lap, the business end aimed at the driver's side door. "I don't think this is Sir Spencer." I glance at the rear view again, seeing the bright lights of the car behind us, the blue and white flashing brighter than the blinding high beams blasting into our SUV. I can't see anything behind me, so I try adjusting the mirror to lessen he glare. Then it hits me.

"OnStar."

"What about it?" Bella asks.

"That's how we got stopped. There's a remote stop. OnStar is a GPS. They know our coordinates, they pop a signal that shuts us off."

She's agitated, trying to look at the car behind us. "I get that. But I thought only law enforcement could do that? I mean, the car would have to be reported stolen, right?"

So maybe it is a cop.

"We're screwed if that's the case, Jackson. And we're better off unarmed. She reaches to put the semi-automatic in the glove box.

"I'm not sure about that. There was no siren, there's no backup. This doesn't seem right." My phone buzzes again.

"Press the OnStar button," Bella says. "It's telling you to press the button."

I push it. A large eighteen-wheeler rumbles past, rocking the SUV.

"Good evening, Mister Quick," says a pleasant woman's voice. "How may I help you?"

Still nobody has emerged from the car behind us. The lights rotate silently, illuminating the cabin of the Suburban in alternating beams of blue and white. Neither Bella nor I respond to whoever it is on the other end of OnStar.

"Miss Buell," says the voice, which could pass for Siri, "I presume that's you in the front passenger seat of the vehicle."

Bella whips around, pushing herself to her knees, and aims the nine millimeter directly at the car behind us. "Who are you?" she demands.

"There's no need for that, Miss Buell," she says. "I'm unarmed."

"Who are you?" Bella says, the gun shaking with emphasis. "What do you want?"

"Well," says Siri, "let's flip that around for a moment and ask ourselves what it is *you* want."

"I want you to turn off the lights," Bella says.

The lights shut off. We're sitting in the dark now.

"You're welcome," says Siri. "Now what?"

"Who are you?" I ask. "You're clearly not law enforcement."

"No." There's a hint of a smile in the response, a playful sarcasm Siri often employs, "Clearly I am *not* law enforcement."

Bella grabs my leg. I glance down at her hand without moving my head. She has one finger extended, tapping my thigh.

There's only one person in the car.

"Who are you, then?" I repeat, slipping my finger onto the trigger of the LAR-15 without turning to look into the car behind us. Glancing at the rearview, I make out a vague shape in the driver's seat. Whoever it is is dressed in dark clothing, maybe a hoodie, or wearing a skullcap.

"You should know, Jackson," says Siri. "You gave me your cell phone number."

I did?

"I'm Corkscrew."

***

In the empty parking lot of a Golden Corral just west of the Maryland/Delaware border along Interstate 95, Bella and I meet the genius hacker, Corkscrew.

She's about five-foot-nothing, with a slight build. The diamond in her nose sparkles more than her cartoonish large round eyes. A green tuft of hair pokes out from underneath her black hoodie. Her black Doc Martens are loose and unlaced.

"You were in that bar in D.C.," I say, gripping her hand as I shake it. "Sitting with a laptop."

She smirks, her lips drawing closed like a cat. "That was me," she admits and turns her attention to Bella. "Miss Buell?"

"Call me Bella," Bella shakes her hand and then folds her arms across her chest. She's already looked the hacker up and down. "How did you find us?"

Corkscrew puts her hands on her hips and takes a step back. "I'm a hacker."

"How did you find us?" Bella asks again. "This time, with a little less sarcasm."

"Your boy here gave me his cell phone number. That's an easy place to start. There are about a zillion websites that'll track cell phones if you know the number and the carrier."

"How'd you find out the carrier?" I ask. "I didn't give you that."

"I assumed you were using a burner. There are only a couple of companies doing that on the cheap. I kept checking until it hit. I saw you were moving, so I followed you."

"Then you hacked OnStar?" Bella looks at me while asking the question, then turns to Corkscrew. "While you were cruising along the interstate in a fake cop car."

Corkscrew scrunches her nose. I can't tell if it's in disgust or condescension. "First, It's not a fake cop car. It's a car with flashing lights. Big difference." It's condescension. "And second, yes. I checked the plates, found the owner, got the VIN, and went from there. OnStar is like any other system. There are back doors everywhere."

"Back doors?" I ask. I've heard of them, but don't really know what they are.

"When programmers create a system they create alternate entry points during testing. That way, when they're coding, or checking for bugs, they have a faster way in and out. A lot of times they leave the back doors open after the system, or program, is completed."

Bella looks at me again. "So now what?"

"Well," Corkscrew puts her hands on her hips again, this time giving Bella the onceover, "if you two are finished with remedial hacking, we can get to what's next."

"We need help getting into Brookhaven," I tell her flat out. "We know you've accessed their systems already. We need control of the security system so that we can get into a particular building there. It's a very secure building."

Corkscrew purses her lips, maybe considering what I'm asking. "I've been working at this for months, you know." She tugs on her hoodie, pulling it down farther across her forehead. "Hacking isn't like the movies. You can't just push a few buttons and 'Bang!' you're hacking the CIA. It doesn't work like that."

"So you can't help us?" Bella challenges her.

"I didn't say that." Corkscrew tugs on the strings at the sides of the hoodie. She looks like a fifteen-year-old emo kid trying hard to not fit in with "regular" kids. "I said I'd been working at this for months. Planning an attack takes time. First you have to figure out what you want. Then you have to determine how you'll get the information you want. You're reverse engineering a system, essentially. What software will you need? What are the system's vulnerabilities, if any?"

"Enough with the remedial hacking," I interrupt. "We're standing here in a restaurant parking lot in the middle of the night, a good distance from where we need to be."

"Whatever. Yes. I can do it. But I need help."

"What kind of help?"

"The way their system is designed is top notch. There are different layers to it. I can access certain parts of it remotely. That's how I got a lot of the data you apparently possess. But there are certain layers that need a physical connection to the system. The attack has to be internal."

"Meaning what?" Bella asks.

"I was able to get what I got by finding out the names and email addresses for a few key people at the facility. I researched them, figured out passwords and security questions to access certain data files using their information. I was in and out, and nobody knew I'd ever been there. The security layer is deeper. I can't hack it from the outside. I need to have a physical terminal inside their servers to alter the protocols."

"We think we know what building we need to access. So you'll be able to control the security to that building, if we can get you physical control of the security."

"Yep," Corkscrew nods, hands back on her hips. "I will."

"Doesn't that mean we'll have to break into Brookhaven *twice*?" Bella asks.

"Yep," says the hacker. "It does."

***

492C Cedar Lane in Teaneck, New Jersey is one of a trio of businesses in a building that looks like it's a half-century overdue for a facelift. Sharing space is an "international" beauty supply store, a "fine" art gallery that also does custom framing, and a UPS Store.

Atop the building runs unfinished, vertical planks of wood which boast the placards for the businesses. Each has a recessed, narrow glass door flanked by picture windows displaying their wares. We're parked in the short-term space against the curb in front of the building.

"This is the place?" Bella appears as unimpressed as I am. "You couldn't have done better?"

"Given the time constraints, probably not," I reply. "As long as we get what we need, does it matter?"

"No," she says, fiddling with the steering wheel. She's been driving since we left the Golden Corral parking lot and our new friend, Corkscrew. "As long as it's there, we're good."

"It opens in five minutes." The digital clock on the dash reads 8:25 am. We've already seen DHL and FedEx make deliveries. "Have you heard from Mack?"

"Not in a few hours." Bella rubs the back of her neck. "He should be in place by now. He dropped off Blogis in Baltimore and last I heard from him he was making good time."

"When was he supposed to check in with you?"

"Not for another half hour," she says, eyeing the clock before looking over at me. Her eyes are glassy and bloodshot. Dark circles are spreading underneath her eyes from either side of her nose. She smiles weakly, as if it's taking every bit of effort she can muster. She glances past me through the front passenger window. "Hey, the guy's opening up the shop."

He is his late twenties to early thirties. He's got a shaggy mop of jet-black hair that makes his pale skin even more sallow. There are gauges in both floppy earlobes. He looks a little like Corkscrew, unlocking the door with a key attached to a chrome-colored chain hooked into his belt loop.

A bell clangs to announce my arrival at exactly 8:30. Edward Scissorhands is the only one in the store. He's behind the counter, leaning on his elbows and scrolling through his phone. He looks up at me as I approach and his earlobes wiggle from the weight of the gauges. His nametag reads *Will E.* It's written in Sharpie.

"Can I help you?" he asks in a tone suggesting he'd rather not.

I smile. "Yes, Will E. I have a package awaiting pick up."

He frowns before the light bulb goes off and he looks down at the nametag. "And you would be?"

"Here to pick up the package."

"What's your name?" He puts his phone on the counter and slinks over to a computer at the cash register.

"Abraham Zapruder," I tell him, using the name of the man who captured President Kennedy's assassination on film. "With a Z."

"Did it come FedEx?"

"That or DHL."

"I'm not seeing it in FedEx's system," he says and looks up at me. "It's not here."

"Did you check DHL?"

"No," he shakes his head, rattling his earlobes. "Should I?"

"Please."

He pecks at the keys for another thirty seconds and then runs his finger down the side of the monitor. "Here it is," he says. "Prepaid delivery. Let me go get it."

"Thanks."

Will trudges to the other end of the counter and through an entryway into a back room. A minute later he emerges with a yellow envelope and slaps it on the counter.

"You're good to go," he says. "No signature needed."

I grab the envelope and coolly saunter back through the door to the Suburban. Bella's thumping the steering wheel impatiently.

"You get it?" she asks. "Everything there?" She pulls away from the curb.

I tear open the strip at the top of the envelope and reach inside to pull out a stack of documents bound together with a rubber band. There's a note scribbled on a coffee stained piece of yellow paper at the top of the stack. The writing is barely legible, and calling it chicken scratch would be offensive to the birds.

These should be good for you. You have couple choices. I think they pass. No problems. If you need more tell me. I work quick for you. Please you be careful with Corkscrew. You cannot trust —Wolodymyr

"What's it say?" Bella asks, trying to catch a glimpse of the scrawl while navigating her way back to the highway. I shuffle through the various forgeries our friend has supplied. A third of them have my photograph on them, a third have Bella's, and the remainder are for Mack. Everything seems to be here, and they're likely flawless reproductions to the untrained eye.

"It looks like it." I hold up one of the false identification badges with her image on it. "They look good too."

"What's the name on that one?" She squints to read the small print above the photograph. "Olivia?"

I turn the card to read it. "Olivia Jacobs."

"Do I look like an Olivia?" She pouts her lips, probably deciding she doesn't look like an Olivia.

"Does it matter?" I ask. "It's the name of someone who works in the facility at another location. It'll get us in if Corkscrew does her job."

"What's your name?"

"Alex. Do I look like an Alex?"

"Not really. *You* look more like an Olivia."

"Funny."

"C'mon," she punches my leg, "you've gotta laugh now. Things are about to get real."

I wrap the rubber band around the bundle and stuff it back in the envelope, "Where did *that* phrase come from?"

"Just trying to lighten the mood. Do I head north on I-95?'

"Yes. Everything is north and east to get to Long Island. It becomes 495. You'll take that all the way to the rendezvous point."

"The *rendezvous* point?" She giggles mockingly.

"Yes. You know what that means in French, right? You speak French."

"It means appointment," she says, rolling her eyes.

"No it doesn't."

"Yes it does," she argues. "Did you take French?"

"Nope."

"Then what's it mean, Jackson?"

"Place where it gets real."

We both laugh. A good laugh. The kind we haven't shared in a while. It's not even over something that funny but it doesn't matter. We're blowing off the stress building under the surface, allowing ourselves to feel something positive, because she's right.

It *is* about to get real.

CHAPTER 13

Taco Bell may be the cheapest fast food meal on the face of the planet. It's also a good place to organize ahead of phase one. It's only a couple of miles from the main entrance to Brookhaven.

Bella and I are on one side of a plastic-molded booth, our backs to the counter. Corkscrew is on the other. We've already devoured our bean burritos and chicken soft tacos when the hacker lays it out for us. She hands us the envelope containing some of the IDs Wolodymyr prepared for us. She says she tweaked them. Then she reaches into a messenger bag and pulls out a sleek black laptop.

"I need this netbook hooked into their system," She slides the laptop across the booth. I'll be waiting. I'll know when it's live. If you have a problem drop me an email. I'll find you." She pulls on the strings of her hoodie, slides out of the booth, and disappears through the exit without saying anything else.

"That was weird," says Bella, slurping the last of a Diet Pepsi through her straw.

"You want more?" I ask her, grabbing my empty cup to refill it with caffeine, sugar, and chemicals.

She hands me her cup, minus the lid and straw, "Sure, thanks." Her eyes are on a television mounted near the back of the restaurant. It's on cable news and despite our mugs flashing on the screen a half-dozen times, the teenagers behind the counter haven't recognized us.

Still, I walk to the drink counter with my head down. No need to make it easy for the kids folding tortillas and microwaving cheese. I'm walking back to Bella with two full cups when the news breaks on the screen.

The volume is off, but between the large graphics on the screen and the closed captioning scrolling across the lower half, I know what's happened. So does Bella. She spins around, her face as ashen as Corkscrew's natural complexion.

I slide into the booth, hand her the drink, and try to keep up with the captioning. My heart's pounding.

"What have we done?" Bella whispers. "What have we unleashed?"

I don't respond except for a reflexive head shake. I can't take my eyes off the words in the news ticker scrolling across the screen.

FORMER GOVERNOR OF TEXAS FOUND DEAD IN PRISON CELL. NO FOUL PLAY SUSPECTED. INVESTIGATION UNDERWAY SAYS TEXAS DEPARTMENT OF CRIMINAL JUSTICE. GOVERNOR SERVING 55 YEAR SENTENCE FOR CONSPIRACY, FRAUD AND OTHER CHARGES. FORMER AIDE, WANTED MURDER SUSPECT JACKSON QUICK CONNECTED TO GOVERNOR'S CONVICTION.

The closed captioning reads like a conspiracy theorist's dream, *"Incredible coincidence or is something more sinister at play here?"*

The news anchor's lips are moving to too fast to read as he highlights the series of events unfolding in the last twenty-four hours. *"First, George Townsend, the reporter whose work on the governor's transgressions helped put the crook behind bars, is murdered in a bizarre shootout in his home. Then, Jackson Quick is connected to the killing. Quick is a former aide to the governor, and most suspect he's the one who provided key evidence in secret Grand Jury proceedings prior to the groundbreaking indictments against the Lone Star State's former favorite son."*

Bella reaches for my hand and pulls it into her lap, rubbing her thumb across mine. She leans into me but says nothing.

"Then, we learn he may have an accomplice in Bella Buell. She's the former CEO of Nanergetix, a Fortune 20 company, and the daughter of the late Don Carlos Buell. He was assassinated while running for governor. But it doesn't stop there."

The screen fills with the orange and yellow images of the fire at Ripley's place. *"Roswell Ripley, who was charged and later exonerated in a separate assassination attempt on Buell, is seen with Quick and later dies in a fire at his self-storage facility in Houston, Texas."*

"Let's bring back Dillinger Holt," reads the captioning. *"He's been leading the way on the unbelievable developments of the connect-the-dots crime spree. He writes for the popular website Plausible Deniability, also known as PDInfo."*

Dillinger's face appears on the screen. He's sitting in a newsroom. People are frantically working the phones and working at their desks behind him. He adjusts an earpiece and starts talking.

"Here's what we're learning about the former governor's death," reads the captioning. *"The governor was found in his cell, face down on the floor. The last person to see him alive was another prisoner assigned to the motor pool. The governor's job while in prison was maintaining buses in the prison system's fleet. That prisoner, we're told by a well-placed source, says the governor was drinking coffee and reading the bible during a break. He told a supervisor he didn't feel good, vomited at least once, and was told to go to the infirmary. He never showed. Then, an hour later, he was found dead in his cell."*

"Do they suspect a heart attack?" the anchor asks, appearing on a split screen.

"No speculation right now," says Holt, shaking his head. *"They're saying they do not suspect foul play. But that's a difficult conclusion to accept given the other events of this week."*

My phone, on the table in front of me, buzzes. The number's blocked.

"Blogis?" Bella whispers.

I nod, squeeze her hand, and answer the phone. "How did you do it?" I ask.

"Anti-freeze," says Blogis matter-of-factly.

"What?"

"The addict drank ten cups of coffee a day," he explains. "Anti-freeze is sweet. Well, really it's the ethylene glycol in the anti-freeze that's sweet. It's toxic, colorless, and odorless. It's also readily available in auto shops."

"You poisoned him?"

"I didn't poison him any more than you did," snaps Blogis. "A well-placed friend took care of the barista duties. They'll think he had a heart attack. They'll never test for anti-freeze poisoning in a prison morgue."

"I don't know," I say, shaking my head, "the timing is bad. There are already conspiracy theories running rampant."

"Let them run," he says dismissively. "It's the least of your worries."

"So what now?"

"How about a thank you?" he sneers. "I held up my end of the deal. Your Pickle problems are over. The governor is gone. Now live up to your part."

"Thank you," I say in the most convincing tone I can affect.

"Now go get it done," he commands. "Let me know when we're even and you're prepared to deliver." The line clicks and falls silent.

"So?" Bella asks, her elbows on the table, hands grabbing at the sides of her head.

"He had him poisoned with anti-freeze. Put it in his coffee."

"That's like the doctor in Houston," she says. "The cancer doctor who tried to poison her lover with anti-freeze by putting it in his coffee."

"Did she kill him?"

She exhales. "No, but she's in prison for it. She probably thought she had the perfect murder. But she was too smart for her own good. The scheme failed."

The best laid plans...

***

After my parents' deaths, and I worked my way through the legal system, I went home only once. My cousin picked me up from foster care and drove me to the house I'd shared with Mom and Dad. In just a few short weeks, it had lost its warmth and charm. It wasn't *home* anymore.

"Go ahead and grab whatever you want," my cousin told me. "The stuff you don't want will get auctioned off. Then we'll put the money in your bank account. The movers have already taken some of the things of value to the auction house."

She said it like I was browsing a garage sale. She'd never been here before. She didn't understand the significance of the ivory tchotchkes my mother kept on a hutch near the fireplace or the cubist painting that hung above the bed in my parents' bedroom.

It wasn't her fault. My cousin was a good person tossed into a maelstrom. Keeping her head above water was plenty to ask. But she was an accountant by trade and everything had an assigned value. There was nothing more to it and nothing less.

I picked up one of the ivory pieces on the hutch. It was a rocking chair, delicately carved with incredible detail. My mother had inherited the collection from her grandmother. There was a tiny tea set, a miniature chess table, and a horse rearing on its hind hooves. There was no rhyme or reason to the odd variety of pieces, but she cherished them all.

"You can have these," I told my cousin, holding up the rocking chair. "They meant a lot to my mom, so I don't want to sell them. I'm afraid I'd break them."

She blinked, taking the rocking chair from my hand. "Thank you, Jackson. That is very thoughtful of you."

Looking around the room, I noticed the glass dining table was gone, as was the rug that covered the floor under it. The wood flooring was a lighter shade of oak where the rug had been. The living room was devoid of furniture. My mother liked antiques. They were valuable, I guess.

I walked past the fireplace and to the entry into my parents' bedroom. At the opposite end of the room was their unmade bed. For whatever reason, the movers hadn't touched the bed or the tables on either side. The pillows were askew, the cream-colored sheets rippled atop the brown blanket. I walked to the foot of the bed and looked above the oak headboard at the painting my dad loved.

It was a large replica of a famous painting. At least that's what my dad told me. He called it a "print." He was proud of it.

It was an abstract with blues and grays and browns. The browns were supposed to represent a card table, my dad had explained. And the other items dotted across the painting were items on the table.

There was a bunch of grapes, a teacup, and a bunch of lines that made no sense to me. Some random letters graced the middle of the print, adjacent to a pair of playing cards. One was a spade, the other a heart.

"It's simple," my dad once told me, admiring the work one morning, "but it's not boring. I could see myself there."

"It looks like a mess," I'd said to him. "I don't get it."

"I don't really get it either," he'd admitted. "I just like it."

The artist was Georges Braque. The piece was Still Life With Playing Cards.

My dad liked cubism. He said the world was so crazy, but most people couldn't see it. He said they saw everything as ordered and linear, but that cubists saw life as it really was; jumbled and chaotic. All the pieces were there, he told me. He said they were just struggling to fit into the right spot, if in fact there was a right spot for them at all.

That only confused me further. But as an adult, whose life is jumbled and out of sorts, I get it now.

I thought about offering the print to my cousin, but didn't. I walked back to the doorway to their room and shut the door. Apprehensively, I walked back to the bed and stood on my father's side. Dad was always on the side of the bed closest to the door. My mother felt safer that way, she'd explained.

At first, I couldn't bring myself to touch the sheets. It was like a force field was preventing me from moving my hands too close. Drawing in a deep breath, the force field gave way and I pressed my palms flat onto the bed and gripped the sheets, squeezing the handfuls of threaded cotton as tightly as I could. Then, without thinking, I threw myself face first onto the unmade bed, burying myself in the linens. I could smell them; the soap they used in the shower, the aftershave my dad applied to his neck and chin, the baby powder lotion my mom used on her arms and legs. They were alive!

And for the first time since their deaths, I felt that thick, dry lump in my throat. It burned, and my eyes welled. Muted by the sheets, I wailed. I remember feeling my tears in the dampness of the fabric. Each time I inhaled, on the verge of hyperventilating, I could sense their presence in the scents they left behind.

I was in a time capsule, visiting the past in which my parents were alive. My chest heaving up and down, slobber drooling from my mouth, I expected them to walk in and comfort me. I prayed that, in their bed, I was dreaming and being here would wake me up.

Of course, it didn't. I cried myself dry and my cousin knocked on their door. It was a soft, reluctant rap, as if she'd been thinking about whether or not to open the door and walk inside their room.

"Jackson?" she called. "Are you okay?"

Of course I'm not okay! I wanted to scream at her. *How could I be okay? My parents are dead and I'm to blame!*

I sat up on the edge of the bed and wiped my face with the back of my arm. "Yes," I told her. "I'm fine. I'll be out in a minute."

She was standing at the door, with the rocking chair in one hand, her handbag in the other. I forced a weak smile, but tried to not make eye contact with her and walked past.

My mother's garden was unrecognizable. Every bit as much as my parents bed was a warm hug, the garden was a knife to the gut. It was littered with dead, pest-eaten leaves. The vegetables were shriveled or blackened from inattention and a lack of water. The wooden paint-stirrers she used to label each section were faded or missing.

It's only been a few weeks, I thought to myself. At the edge of the plot, I knelt down onto the dry, sinking mulch that lined its exterior. A large spider moved up a thread onto the web it had woven between two staked vines.

I considered crawling under the web and onto the soil, planting myself amongst the wasted crops. I felt like the plants, abandoned and dying, unable to seek what I needed to survive without the help of my mother.

Closing my eyes, I remembered the afternoons spent in the garden with my mom. I thought about her smile and her laughter. I could hear her giggling at my fear of earthworms, and how I'd insist on wearing gloves to handle them.

High above the garden, the leaves of a neighboring oak rustled from a breeze. I opened my eyes, still swollen from tears, and looked up at the branches swaying back and forth, waving at me. Another gust carried with it a handful of leaves, which floated and swirled above me before dropping into the yard behind ours.

"Jackson?" I turned to see my cousin standing in the open doorway. "What are you doing out here?"

"Nothing," I brushed past her into the house without looking back at the garden again. I wanted to try and remember it the way my mother had kept it; bright and vibrant, healthy and thriving.

Bounding up the stairs, I found my way to my room. It was warm, uncomfortably so, and dusty. I looked around at the posters on the walls and the assortment of Little League trophies perched on a bookshelf. There were a couple of Choose Your Own Adventure books and a catalog's worth of comic books about super heroes on the shelf. It was a nice mix of DC and Marvel. I didn't discriminate between the Avengers or the Justice League. Both fought for good.

Under my bed was a blue lock box. It had a keyhole and a combination lock on its face and a handle on its top. I popped it open and carried it to my dad's office.

The office was actually a spare bedroom he'd converted into a study. On his desk was an electronic chessboard. He'd play against the computer for days, making maybe three or four moves in a week if he was playing a difficult level. I grabbed a pawn from the board. It was cool to the touch, the black marble reflecting the light peeking in from the room's lone window. On the edge of the desk was a brown leather photo album. It was a Father's Day gift from my mother and she'd filled it with family photographs.

Flipping through it I saw the three of us in Key West, posing by the famous marker for the southernmost point in the United States. There was a photograph of my dad's college rifle team. There were a couple of pictures from a trip my dad took to Ukraine and a few from my parents' honeymoon. I folded the album shut and placed it in the box.

I moved to the closet and swung open the accordion doors. His gun safe was gone. There was a single red shotgun shell on the floor. I picked it up and put it in the box.

"We need to go," my cousin called up the stairs. "I have to get back to work, Jackson."

When I got to the bottom of the steps, she reached into her pocket and pulled out some jewelry. "These were your mom's. She was wearing them when…"

"Thanks." No need to hear more. I reached into her hand and pulled my mom's wedding ring and a pair of diamond earrings. They found a place in the blue lock box and we made our way from the house to her car.

My life to that point had been reduced to the contents of a container I could carry with me. It hasn't changed all that much.

***

Mack's waiting for us at the 7-11 across the street from the Taco Bell. He's sitting in his SUV, slurping on a Big Gulp when we climb inside.

"You ready?" I ask him. "Our hacker says everything is ready to go."

"You have what I need?" Mack checks his side view mirror. "Everything has to be good to go for this to work."

I hand him the netbook and the documents Wolodymyr prepared. "They'll pass."

"Let's do this, then," Mack plops the drink into the cupholder. "I'll have my phone dialed in so that you can hear what's happening. Cool?"

Bella checks her phone. "Cool. I'm tracking your movements, so we'll be able to see where you are."

"If you get caught, you need to run," I say.

"As best I can," he says, gesturing to his legs.

"Understood," Bella and I hop out of Mack's SUV and he spins out of the parking lot and heads south toward Brookhaven's main entrance.

Bella and I return to our SUV and wait for the fireworks. She pulls up the tracking app on her burner and shows me the screen.

There's a flashing blue dot moving along a map. It looks like Google Maps with different colors. Within a couple of minutes, the app indicates Mack is in the Visitor Center where he'll check in. I connect my phone to the Bluetooth in the Suburban so we can listen to Mack, who's wearing a wireless earpiece for his phone.

"Hello," a woman says. The audio is somewhat muffled. "Welcome to Brookhaven. May I help you?"

"Yes," says Mack. "I have an appointment. I'm here to run a diagnostics test on the mail server." Corkscrew came up with that terminology. She said it was vague but plausible. Access to the mail server might be an easier target than anything more secure. It would also provide access points through passwords and other secretive information carelessly sent through intraoffice email.

"Do you have your boarding pass and driver's license?" the woman asks. The boarding pass is a barcoded document allowing access to Brookhaven. All visitors have to create an online account and go through a verification process before being allowed access.

Wolodymyr took care of the boarding pass and false identification. Corkscrew handled the appointment. The hacker made certain that Mack was "employed" by one of Brookhaven's legitimate contractors.

"Mr. Johnson," she says. "David Johnson? You're with one of our contractors, Ravenscroft Data Partners?"

"Yes," Mack says. "Here's my company identification and my boarding pass."

"And your health insurance?"

Mack produces a false health insurance card.

"I see you have a bag," the woman notices. "Can you confirm you are not carrying with you any of the prohibited items you see listed on the paperwork I just placed in front of you?"

"Yes. No weapons or nuclear devices." Mack chuckles.

"It's not a laughing matter, Mr. Johnson," the woman chides.

It's quiet for a moment before the woman speaks again. She's likely on a phone or intercom. "I have a Mr. David Johnson here to see Hector

Nieto in IT. Could he please come to GUV to escort Mr. Johnson to the mail server facility?"

Minutes go by before there's a new voice. "Mr. Johnson? I'm Hector Nieto," says the man. His voice is friendly with the faintest hint of a Hispanic accent. "I'll be your escort."

Mack greets Nieto and the two of them carry on an innocuous conversation on their way to the server facility. Bella checks the GPS tracker application on her phone. They're right off the main street running east and west through Brookhaven's main campus.

"This is building 515," says Nieto. "It's the Information Technology building. It's lunchtime, so most everybody is out. It'll be just you and me in the server room." The sound of doors opening and closing resonate through the SUV's speakers.

"Now," Nieto huffs as he walks, "I'm confused."

"How's that?" Mack says, playing it cool.

"Why do we even need this diagnostics check? We just upgraded this server a month ago," Nieto says.

"I couldn't tell you," Mack says. "All I know is that my company tells me where to go and what to do. I go and I do. I don't ask questions."

"I get that," Nieto replies against the sound of a repetitive beeps, like he's entering a code. "It just seems odd. I don't know why we'd contract out this sort of thing. I checked the paperwork and it looks legit. I know Ravenscroft has done work with us in the past."

"Look, Hector," says Mack. "I'm not trying to take anyone's job if that's what you're worried about. Last time I checked, government work was about as secure as it comes."

"I guess," Nieto grunts and there's the sound of a metallic hum and click. "Here we go. This is the server room. Nobody is ever in here. Mail is over there on the left. I'll wait right here."

After a few seconds of what sounds like Mack getting himself in position, he whispers, "We're good. I'm just looking for the right port. Then I'll hide it and I'm done."

There's a shuffling sound and Mack starts humming, singing, "The Battle Hymn of the Republic." "*Mine eyes have seen the glory of the coming of the Lord...*"

"Hey," Nieto says from a distance, "are you a Marine?"

"Yes I am," Mack says in a voice loud enough that it distorts the speaker. Then softly again, "I can't find the port."

"You serve overseas?" Nieto's voice is getting louder, as if he's walking toward Mack. If he sees exactly what Mack's doing, we're toast.

"Yes," Mack says, "Afghanistan and Iraq. Why do you ask?" Mack whispers again, "I'm close. Hang on." He's breathing more heavily as he presumably works to finish what he's doing.

"Hey!" There's an urgency in Nieto's voice. "What are you doing?"

Uh oh.

Bella looks at me. She's biting her lip, running a hand through her hair.

"What's that?" Nieto asks, his tone sharpening.

"What's what?" Mack says, playing clueless. There's a zipper closing as he answers his own question. "It's my netbook."

"Why is it plugged into the system like that?" Nieto asks. "That doesn't look right to me."

Mack is screwed.

"What do we do?" Bella mouths to me. She's rubbing her palms on her thighs.

I don't have an answer for her. I shrug.

"I'm gonna need an answer, Mr. Johnson," Nieto says. "That connection seems unnecessary."

"Do something!" Bella pleads.

I hang up the call with Mack and immediately dial back. It rings. Rings again.

On the third rings Mack answers, "Dave Johnson. Can I help you?"

"Tell him he doesn't have the clearance to know specifically what you're doing. But, to be a nice guy, you can tell him this is new diagnostic software just approved by the GAO for use at all government installations."

"I'm in the middle of something," he says to me. "Hang on." His tone changes.

"Look," Mack says to Nieto, "you need to back off. You should not confuse your rank with my authority, if you catch my drift, Hector."

"I asked a simple question," Nieto snaps. "You haven't answered it."

"I have to consider whether or not you have the clearance to be in the loop on this," Mack says. "You probably don't."

"I have Confidential Clearance," Nieto says. It's the lowest of the three security clearance levels. I know this from my time with the governor and his meeting with the State Department on immigration issues. Mack likely knows this from his military experience.

"Yeah," Mack's says, "that's what I thought. Frankly, it's why this is above your pay grade. But because you're here and I'll assume you're a fellow jarhead, I'll give you the basics."

"I d-d-didn't—" Nieto stutters, backing down.

"Of course you didn't think or consider or defer or whatever it was you *weren't* doing," Mack chides. "Now hang on."

"Can I call you back?" He says to me. "I've got a knucklehead here who's challenging the new Security Protocol." He pauses for effect. "You heard that? No. I won't tell him anything above his clearance. No."

"You've got it from here," I say and hear him pretend to hang up.

"Now here's the deal," Mack says to Nieto, "DOD is testing a new security protocol. They've got these netbooks loaded with invisible software that surfs for keywords in emails. It uploads the keywords and email addresses and sends them straight to our Counter Terrorism folks."

"Seriously?" Nieto sounds impressed. "They've been able to do that for a while." Or not. "This is bogus—you're not who you say—"

"Stop right there," Mack snaps. "I've killed men for less attitude than you're giving me right now. You have a problem? Take my phone and call whoever it is you think is gonna tell you the truth. Go ahead."

Silence.

"That's what I thought," Mack says. "Bottom line. I'm not telling you squat. You don't have clearance. You're the flunky who they sent to babysit me. Now go back to your corner and wait for me to finish what I'm doing. I'm leaving this terminal hooked up to your system for twenty-four hours. Look at the order. I'll be back tomorrow to take it back."

"I looked at the order already and—"

"And nothing!" Mack is amped. "I'm labeling this with a piece of tape and a marker. It reads *Do Not Touch—Security Protocol Testing!!*" The marker squeaks out the letters as he writes them. "Now go back while I finish the setup. Otherwise, I'll report you to your superior for insubordination and the Office of Personnel Security and Suitability will make sure your five year review happens early and often."

"Fine," Nieto ignores his first instinct and succumbs to Mack's force of will.

"It's good to go," Mack whispers to me. "Corkscrew can go to work." He disconnects the call.

"That was close," Bella exhales and sinks in the driver's seat. "Thankfully it's done."

"Oh," I laugh. "It's just getting started."

CHAPTER 14

"Do we have to face west?" Bella lowers the sun visor to block the nuclear orange glow blasting into her eyes. "This is killing me."

"Corkscrew told us to meet here ahead of tonight's adventure," I remind her. "Sunset is in twenty minutes."

"So why are we here already?" Her blood sugar must be low. "We could be grabbing something to eat." Bingo.

"Better to be early than late." I toss her an energy bar from Wal-Mart. "I've been saving this for you."

She rips open the foil and bites off half of the bar. "You're such a gentleman." She squirrels a huge chunk in her cheeks and takes another bite.

"Whoa!" I raise my hands. "Nobody's fighting you for it. The bar's gonna be there."

She laughs, spitting out a little bit of the bar, which makes me laugh. She's adorable even when cranky and malnourished.

"I love you."

"I love you too," she says, though it sounds more like, "I grub boo too."

We're still laughing at each other when a black Suburban pulls up next to us in the parking lot behind a vacant warehouse. The driver rolls down his window. I roll down mine.

"She coming?" Mack asks me, handing me George's laptop.

"As far as I know," I say, tossing the computer onto the back seat. "She indicated you did what you needed to do."

"Any chance she'll double cross us?"

Bella leans across me to say to Mack, "There's always a chance. Right, Mack?" Her tone is sarcasm mixed with energy bar.

"Point taken, Bella," he says with a salute. "I'm out of here, if you're good with it. I'll get things set for phase two."

"Okay," I nod. "Good work today." I thank him for his help and he speeds off to catch a commercial flight with his airtight false identification.

"You think we can pull this off, Jackson?"

"I don't know. But we're a third of the way there."

Bella washes down the bar with bottled water as another vehicle pulls into the lot. It's a plain white bread truck with Pennsylvania plates. Rays of sunlight are fighting against the horizon, hanging on as long as they can. The van pulls directly in front of us, parking perpendicular to our SUV. The rear door slides open with a bang and the hacker emerges. She hops onto the gravel lot, dust kicking up dramatically as she trudges to Bella on the driver's side.

"You ready for this?" She asks, sniffing and crinkling her nose like a rabbit. "It's gonna happen fast. You'll have to be on your game." She pulls her hoodie off of her head, revealing an avant garde haircut that says, *"I'm so different, I'm just like everyone else who wants to be perceived as different."*

It's shaved along the right side, her ear decorated with a half dozen piercings. The left side is longer, curling forward toward her chin. A severe part, missing the green die staining the rest of her hair, gives her face an angular look not as obvious with the hoodie up and drawn tight. Still, her eyes are round, the whites bright and the pupils large.

"We're ready," Bella assures the hacker. "We know what to expect."

"Here are some earpieces." She opens her hand, revealing two flesh colored beans. "I'll have to talk you through security as I work the system. They're one way. You can't talk to me."

"These work through phones or what?" I ask.

"They're radio," she nods at the piece in Bella's hand. "VHF digital. Good penetrating capabilities. Less line of sight needed," she says. "I don't want to rely on a cell signal for this. Plus, there's supposed to be rough weather tonight. A front's moving through. Two-way is better."

"How will you know where we are?" Bella asks. "I mean, how will you know what security to punch at the right time?"

"I'll be tracking you with these," Corkscrew produces two rectangular white boxes. They fit in the palm of her hand. "Got them on Amazon. Cheap but effective. Slip them in your pockets and these little dudes will pinpoint where you are."

"What are they exactly?" Bella takes both of them, flipping them over in her hand. "GPS trackers?"

Corkscrew nods. "Real time. Accurate to within five feet. Batteries last a couple of weeks. I can set up alerts if you're heading outside of the desired path. It's satellite and map view of your location. It also leaves breadcrumbs for your return trip out of the facility."

"What does that mean?" Bella hands me my device. It's lightweight and feels cheap.

"Breadcrumbs are electronic markers," Corkscrew explains. "They're like real breadcrumbs you'd leave to prevent yourself from getting lost in the woods. It'll help me more than you. I'll have you pulled up on one of my displays."

"Why not use the OnStar in the Suburban, since you hacked into it before? Doesn't it have GPS?"

"Yessss," Corkscrew says, sounding like a frustrated fifteen-year-old whose mother just asked her to make her bed. "But it's not the same. It doesn't track the same way and it's not as accurate."

"Why can't we communicate with you?" Bella asks

"I don't want you talking. Enough questions, okay?" Corkscrew pleads. "I know what I'm doing."

"I get that, but—"

"Remember when the Chinese hacked the U.S. Postal Service or the time when they got into the servers for the National Weather Service? They shut down their satellite access for days, remember?"

"Vaguely," Bella responds.

"It wasn't the Chinese," Corkscrew folds her arms across her chest, arching her back to stick out her chest. She looks like a rapper on a cheaply produced music video.

Bella rolls her eyes. "Good for you."

"I've done a lot of homework," Corkscrew explains. "Your friend Spencer and I have been working this up for a while. We just needed…" she searches for the right word with her hands until she finds it, "partners to help us execute it."

"You say 'us' like you're a team," Bella infers.

"Not a team so much," Corkscrew smirks, her face splitting into the closest thing to a smile she can muster. "I'm a gun for hire." She forms her hand into the shape of a gun and puts her index finger to her lips, blowing onto it. "No different than the two of you. I'm just more expensive."

"Make sure he pays you up front," I warn.

Corkscrew throws her hoodie back over her head. "You won't see me again," she says. "Either way this goes down, I disappear."

"Okay," Bella says, not impressed with the drama as she starts to roll up the window.

"One more thing," Corkscrew says, slipping her hand onto the window. "Your buddy the governor is dead."

"We heard," I acknowledge.

"Sir Spencer's kinda wondering how that happened." She looks at me, the semblance of a smile gone. She raps on the windowsill and spins on her booted heel, walking back to the van.

"What is that supposed to mean?" Bella watches the hacker climb into the van and tug the door closed.

"It's a warning."

"You think he knows we're working with Blogis too?" Bella whispers, as if the hacker could hear us.

"Maybe, maybe not. It could be a bluff."

"If it's not?"

"Does it matter?" We're in so deep that we can't stop now. We can't call it off.

"Probably not." She shifts into drive. "We're screwed no matter how this ends." It's the first time I've heard her parrot my negativity. She turns and blows me a kiss. "I still love you."

"I love your enthusiasm," I say pulling my seatbelt across my lap as she accelerates into light traffic. Can't ever be too careful.

***

The trees lining Upton Road near Brookhaven National Laboratory are rustling from the slight breeze sweeping across Long Island from the Atlantic. A low-pressure system swirling offshore has the temperature dropping by the minute. I can feel it in my knee. The ache grows with every incremental drop in barometric pressure.

The moon peeks out from behind some clouds, backlit by the satellite's reflected sunlight, before disappearing again. The clouds are moving quickly from the southeast. In the distance, there's the faint flash of lightning.

"Of course," says Bella. "The weather would turn on us."

"It was worse at Chernobyl," I say, reminding Bella of our adventure in that radioactive wasteland, securing a part of the neutrino process before getting chased, lost, and barely escaping with our lives. "Plus there were a lot of bullets flying at us."

"Good point." Her shoulders are raised, held tight against her body to protect her from the chill that's settled into the SUV. The engine is off and we're awaiting the go-ahead from Corkscrew.

We're parked off of Upton Road, near the facility's North Gate. It closes at 5:30 and is accessible with a pass card. Corkscrew is parked in the apartment area, south of the main facility, next to the laundry building. She figured she could park her van there, amongst the other cars and trucks in the lot, without anyone noticing. I suggested we park there too, but the hacker had her plan set in stone. She said security was easier to work if we came in from the North.

Brookhaven is laid out like a college campus with probably close to one hundred buildings. Aside from the two dozen in the apartment area, BNL is a series of laboratories and research centers.

It's as if Arthur Hailey named the buildings. There's the *Tandem Van de Graff Cyclotron*, the *Linac Isotope Producer*, the *National Synchrotron Light Source I and II*, and the *Star Detector Wide Angle Hall*.

Star Detector is as close as I can get to understanding what goes on inside any of them. And I'm just guessing that's where they detect stars.

Brookhaven gets most of its funding from the U.S. Department of Energy, so there's a lot of high level work happening here and has been for decades. I read online it was opened after World War II on the site of a former Army post specializing in post-war rehabilitation. It makes sense. From the pictures I've seen of it, it looks like a military installation with a utilitarian feel.

"It's eight o'clock," Bella says. "She should contact us in five minutes."

"She's testing the earpiece." I tap my left ear. "She's playing Taylor Swift."

"Seriously?" Bella pinches the earpiece between her thumb and index finger, inserting it into her right ear. "Oh lord," she sighs. "This is akin to the stuff I've heard the CIA does to soften up detainees."

I check my revolver, ensuring all six chambers are loaded.

"Why are you bringing that?" Bella asks. "We're not supposed to hurt anyone."

"Better safe than sorry," I explain and hand her the Kimber Micro-Carry. "Take this."

"I don't—"

"Just take it, Bella."

"What about the tasers Mack gave us?" she holds up the crude device made from a disposable camera. "Why don't we just take these?"

"We can take those," I agree. "But they're for close-up, stun-someone-for-just-a-second-to-gain-the-upper-hand, kind of stuff. They won't really protect you if it comes down to it."

"Fine." She relents and takes the handgun. "It's loaded?"

"Yep."

The Taylor Swift music goes silent mid twang. "If you can hear me, text me the number three six nine," says the hacker. "If Bella can hear me, text the number two four six."

I punch both sets of numbers into my phone and hit send.

"Good," says Corkscrew. "I see both of you on the GPS map, so the tracker's working." Her fingers are clacking away at a keyboard. "I need you to put the Suburban in drive and move south on Upton Road. Do not exceed thirty miles per hour."

Bella pulls onto Upton Road and turns right, heading south toward the main campus. To our right, traffic whirs by in both directions on a parkway running parallel to Upton. In less than a minute we approach a gated entrance. The guard booth is dark. There's an automatic card reader alit in red on the driver's side.

"Give me a second," says Corkscrew, typing feverishly. "There."

The red light turns green and the gate arm swings up. Bella drives past the gate. "So far, so good," she mumbles.

"You're going to make a left just past the Linear Accelerator," says the hacker. "That's Michelson Street."

Bella turns left onto Michelson, driving past a long narrow building which is glowing orange from the lights illuminating its facade. "I guess that's the Linear Accelerator," she points at the facility.

"Follow this road until it forks," Corkscrew instructs. "Go left and drive past building 938. It'll be on your left. It looks like a shed. Then make a left. It should be coming up… now."

Bella swings the steering wheel to the left. The headlights sweep onto the short road in front of us, freezing a mole in the middle of the pavement. Bella slams on the brakes, jerking me forward into a locked seatbelt.

"Whoa!" I snap, bracing myself against the dash with my forearm.

"Sorry," she says, "I just didn't want to hit that mole."

"Too late." The rodent is in a defensive posture, fighting off two birds intent on eating him. One of the birds hops toward the mole and pecks at his back, and then the other takes its turn. "He's already dying."

"You're stopped," says Corkscrew. "I didn't tell you to stop. Keep going. You're there. The road curves to the right and then sharply to the left. There's a short concrete path to the right between two clumps of trees. Park there between the two buildings closest to that path."

Bella follows Corkscrews directions, navigating between the trees and onto the worn path. There's a long, narrow space between two parallel wings of Building 197 extending toward the path. Bella drives past the space about a car length and then reverses, slipping the SUV in between them tailgate first.

"Just in case we need to leave in a hurry," she explains, "it's probably better to back in. Right?"

"Good idea!" I pull a set of ID badges from the glove box, handing Bella hers and slipping mine around my neck with the attached lanyard. "Here you go, Olivia."

"Very funny, Alex." She shuts off the engine and we sit in the dark for close to a minute, awaiting instructions from Corkscrew.

"Okay," the hacker says, breaking the silence. "We should be good to go. There should be a rear entrance to the building. Get out of the SUV and walk back toward the road. At the end of the wing to your left, facing some trees, there's an access panel and coded door."

We hop out of the Suburban and quietly shut our doors. I shove the six shooter into my waist band, covering it with my untucked shirt.

"It's gotten colder," Bella comments as we turn the corner to the end of the building. "And it smells like it's about to rain."

"You should see the panel now," Corkscrew interrupts. "It's to the right of the door."

It looks like a miniature ATM with a key panel at the bottom, a slot for a card to the side, and a camera at the top. In the middle is a 6x6 inch screen. Above the wall mounted machine is a black placard inscribed with plain white lettering: *Nonproliferation & National Security Department*

"There's a three step process here," Corkscrew explains. "I've input your data here. Both of you will have to run through the protocol, or an alarm will sound when you pass the threshold of the door."

Bella looks over at me, the dim light casting a dark shadow across her face. "I'm not so sure about this."

"We'll be fine," I assure her, putting my hand on her shoulder. "Just do exactly what she tells us to do."

"Bella," Corkscrew says, "ladies first. Step to the panel and slide your BNL access card through the card reader. It should activate the LCD screen above the keypad. I'll give you ten seconds."

Bella swipes her card through the reader and the screen illuminates.
Brookhaven National Laboratory, DOE

NNSD Building 197, Main Campus
Welcome Dr. Olivia Triblet!
Please enter facility access code

"It should be asking you to enter a code," Corkscrew chirps. "Enter your birthdate. Punch in the two-digit month, two-digit day, four-digit year. Then follow the instructions on the screen. When you're finished, the door should unlock. Go inside by yourself. Let Jackson repeat the process and enter on his own. I'll give you both a couple of minutes."

Bella enters the eight-digit code and the screen changes.

Brookhaven National Laboratory, DOE
NNSD Building 197, Main Campus
Facility Access Code Accepted for Dr. Olivia Triblet
Please stand in front of blinking green light for scan

She shifts to the right and bends her knees to position her face in front of the blinking light. The screen changes again.

Brookhaven National Laboratory, DOE
NNSD Building 197, Main Campus
Scanning...
Please stand motionless, Dr. Olivia Triblet

Bella holds her position until the green light stops flashing. It turns blue at the same instant a loud metallic hum signals the unlocking of the door. Bella pulls on the handle and steps into the darkness beyond the threshold.

"I'll wait right here," she whispers. The door automatically shuts, the humming stops, and the screen in front of me returns to its home screen.

Lightning flashes in the sky above us followed a few seconds later by a loud thunderclap. The storm is here.

✳✳✳

Following the same steps as Bella, I swipe my card, enter the eight-digit birthday code, and stand for the facial recognition scan. The green light blinks rapidly.

Brookhaven National Laboratory, DOE
NNSD Building 197, Main Campus
Approval & Recognition
Please enter building Dr. Alex Dennis
Single entry only.

The metallic hum unlocks, I tug on the heavy steel door and enter, where Bella's standing just inside. We're in a long hallway that has a series of doors on either side. At the end of the hallway, maybe thirty feet ahead of us, it appears as though the hallway splits to the left and right. There's an eyeball camera dropped from the ceiling at that intersection. I can't tell which way its lens is directed.

"I flipped the light switch when the door shut," she says pointing to the plastic switch plate on the wall. "Otherwise it was pitch black in here."

"Where do we start?" I ask. Both of us are speaking just above a whisper.

"I'm not sure. We'll have to wait for—"

"Okay cherubs," says the hacker, "you're inside. Next step is finding the right lab. Hang on."

"Shouldn't she have already figured this out?" Bella says, moving toward the first door to the right.

"You'd think," I agree, inspecting the door to the left. It's key coded. Above the keypad is a nameplate.

"We've got some good options," Corkscrew says. "Start moving down the hallway until it splits. You're looking for what's called the Radiation Detector and Non-Proliferation R&D Group. It's one of the three divisions in this building, and it was a scientist in that group who Dr. Wolf kept visiting."

"Who was the scientist?" Bella whispers, treading lightly on the linoleum floor.

"The scientist was Aleksey Diozegi. I don't have a lab number for him specifically, but—ah! There we go. I can see you now."

I look up to the camera above us. At this distance I can see the lens and the LED infrared detector encircling it.

The hacker tells us to go to the left. She thinks that's the most likely spot for Aleksey Diozegi's office.

"From the emails I checked this morning, he's working with neuron detectors for arms control verification. Sound familiar? It's like a cover for what's really going on."

It does sound virtually the same as Wolf's "process", by which a concentrated beam of solar neutrinos could identify and melt a nuclear arsenal stashed anywhere in the world without detection. Switch *neurons* with *neutrinos* and *arms control verification* with *destroy* and it's the same thing.

That's why it was so critical the process not fall into the wrong hands, why I couldn't let Sir Spencer or Blogis have it. They'd sell it on the black market and it would end up with a country, or worse, a disparate group like ISIS or Al-Qaeda with permanently bad intentions against the United States. Whoever controlled the process could systematically destroy the nuclear weapons cache of any nation it saw fit to attack.

And given the U.S. had to invest more than seven billion dollars to fix its fledgling nuclear program after the Secretary of Defense said they'd "taken their eyes off the ball," there might be nobody minding the store to recognize the breach until it was too late.

I was right to destroy what I thought was the only copy of the process when I did it. I felt good about it, even as I lay dying from a gunshot wound on the stone floor of a medieval German castle. Now I'm on the verge of opening Pandora's box for the second time.

"There are three lab possibilities," Corkscrew says amidst the loud hammering on her keyboard. "One of them is up here on the left. It's room A32. I'm working on the key code now."

Bella stops at the door closest to her on the left. There's a Lucite file holder on the wall next to the door. It's empty, but there's a label on the folder.

Outgoing Data: Do Not Remove Without Permission
Thank You, RDNP R&D

"This could be it." Bella's eyes widen, as does her smile.

"Try the door," I say. "Couldn't hurt."

Bella tries to turn the handle, which doesn't budge.

"Hang on," Corkscrew chirps. "Don't go trying doors without me. I'm there. I'm trying to reset all of the door codes in the building to a single set of numbers. That'll speed things up."

I glance farther down the hall and see another surveillance camera. It's similar to the one we passed at the T-intersection.

"You notice the smell of this place?" Bella asks, her nose crinkled. "It smells like something familiar. I can't place it."

"Moth balls. You know, formaldehyde?"

"Maybe." She sniffs again. "No, it's more familiar than that."

I inhale through my nose, trying to find the answer on the tip of her tongue. "Latex?"

"Yes!" she pops me on the arm, making a sound louder than the whispering we're using to communicate. "Latex. Like latex gloves or balloons."

"Okay," says Corkscrew, "stop talking. Time to get busy. Punch in the number one, nine, three, and two. You'll need it to exit the room too. All of the labs require the code to enter or exit."

Bella presses the combination on the keypad and it blinks and beeps, then the door lock clicks. She turns the lever and again and, this time, it opens. "So far so good," she says.

***

An overhead fluorescent light clinks to life automatically when we enter, casting a harsh light on what looks more like a police precinct than a laboratory. There are four metal desks in the middle of the room. Each desk has a matching banker's lamp, a black multi-line phone, and a computer terminal. The desks are maybe four feet wide and two feet deep. They have three keyed drawers on the left side of wheeled and worn wooden chairs. There are no Dilbert calendars or family photographs. It's sterile.

I'm guessing the government hasn't updated the decor in here for decades. The room is windowless and has a single through-the-wall air conditioner, so ancient that Willis Carrier, the man who invented modern air conditioning, may have installed it himself.

On the far wall is a floor to ceiling white board, decorated with an indecipherable collage of formulas, equations, and hypotheses scribbled in a rainbow of dry-erase markers. On the other side of the room, is a laminate counter running the width of the room from front to back. There is a sink and a calcified glass carafe on a vintage commercial coffee maker sitting at one end of the otherwise empty, waist-high expanse.

The door automatically closes and locks behind us.

"Where do we start?" Bella asks. "We've got all of these locked desks and the cabinets. Where do you want to begin?"

"I'll take the cabinets," I offer. "If the desks are locked, I'll help you figure it out."

Bella moves to the first desk while I try the cabinets closest to the door.

The first upper cabinet is stuffed with Styrofoam cups, as is the second. The rest have sugar, powered creamer, and coffee mugs in varying states of cleanliness.

"Nothing in the first desk," Bella says loudly enough for me to hear, but not so loud as to draw attention should anyone walk by the office. "It was unlocked and all three drawers are empty."

"There's nothing in these cabinets either," I'm rifling through the under-counter cabinets now and there's nothing except for the plumbing delivering water to the coffee maker and the stainless sink.

"The second desk has nothing," she says. "But this third one is locked. Can you help me?"

I cross the room to the desk closest to the white board. There's a desk organizer with a couple of pens, a rubber band, and a few paperclips. I grab one of the clips and start bending it, pulling both bends straight and then use the edge of the desk to press a tiny ninety-degree turn at one end.

"Are you going to pick the lock with a paperclip?" Bella says incredulously. "Seriously?"

"Yep." I bend down in front of the lock on the top of the three drawers. "This is a basic tension wrench. It should work on a rudimentary lock like this one."

"How did you learn how to do that?" Bella squats next to me, watching me manipulate the clip inside the keyhole. "Because this is a major turn-on, Dr. Alex Whoever-You-Are..."

"YouTube," I admit. "It's unreal the stuff you can learn by watching videos."

"And I thought all of that time you spent on the computer was useless."

"You should know me better than that, Olivia." I close my eyes to feed the clip through the mechanism.

"It's about the amount of pressure I apply to the lock," I explain. "Too much pressure and it'll twist the paperclip. To light, and it's not enough to pick the lock."

I'm guessing the lock opens to the left so I try that first, followed by a slight twist to the right. There's less tension to the left, so I'm right. Sliding a second straightened clip back toward the top of the hole I start raking the clip back and forth trying to set some of the pins.

"Have you ever practiced this?" Bella asks, clearly not impressed with my skills.

"A couple of times and it didn't work either time."

"Oh."

One pins gives and then another. Three of them. Four. Five. "All of the pins are set."

There's a loud bang of thunder, rattling the air conditioner, followed immediately by the drumbeat of heavy rain on the roof.

"Anyone ever tell you that you stick your tongue out like Michael Strahan when you're concentrating?" she whispers.

"Michael Jordan."

"What?"

"It's Michael Jordan who stuck his tongue out," I correct her. "He played basketball. Strahan played football. Plus, they look nothing like one another. And Jordan is probably ten years older."

"Well, who was the one in the Looney Tunes movie that played on cable over and over again?"

"Michael Jordan."

"What about the Gatorade guy? The 'I wanna be like Mike' guy?"

"Jordan."

"Shoes?"

"Are you clueless?" I stop picking the lock and glare at her, because of both her complete lack of cultural awareness and the distraction. "I'll take pop culture for a thousand, Alex."

"Alex?"

"Nevermind," The lock clicks and drawer slides open. "Got it!"

"I was kidding!" Bella says.

"About what?" I stand up to look through the contents of the drawer. There's a pack of Juicy Fruit gum, some napkins, a plastic fork, and a couple of hot sauce packets from Taco Bell.

"The shoes," she says. "And the Gatorade."

"What about Alex?" The second drawer is full of file folders. They're labeled with dates. I pull a stack and drop them onto the desk.

"Trebek," she winks and starts shuffling through the files. "These are meeting notes. Project deadlines, assignments, and stuff like that. I'm not seeing—"

"Are you getting anywhere?" the hacker interrupts us. "Might want to speed it up. I can't see you in the room, and I don't mean to slip you some gangster pills, but I do see someone standing outside the door."

CHAPTER 15

The most useless, but entertaining class I took in college was Theatre Appreciation. It was a survey class in a huge auditorium. There were maybe two or three hundred kids in that class. It was at seven o'clock in the morning, but the professor was so enthusiastic, I found myself sitting in his class every Monday, Wednesday, and Friday, Starbucks in hand and anxious to learn something I'd never, ever use in my professional life. Other students must have felt the same way, because the class was always packed.

I remember one thing in particular from the class, other than the James Lipton-esque quality of the professor's lectures, and that's the term *Deus Ex Machina*. It is the most clever and least creative of literary devices.

Deus Ex Machina, literally translated as "god from a machine," was how Greek or Roman playwrights would extricate the hero from an impossible situation at the end of the drama. In those plays, a god would appear on stage, by means of a crane or stairway, and miraculously save the day.

Here now, locked inside a windowless room, with virtually nowhere to go and someone standing at our only exit, Bella and I could use a *Deus* or a *Machina* or both. But this isn't a Greek play. Sophocles isn't writing my story.

"Hello?" a raspy voice calls from outside the door and Bella and I freeze. Bella's holding one of the files. I'm still squatting next to an open drawer.

"Hello?" he calls again. "Is someone in here? I'm Jenkins, from the Laboratory Protection Division. I'm doing my rounds, and I see the light coming from underneath the door."

Without thinking, I answer him, "Yes! We're in here, just catching up on some project notes."

Bella glowers, apparently disagreeing with my decision to play along. Without taking her hex of a stare off of me, she joins in, "We won't be long, Jenkins."

"Uh…could you open the door, please?" Jenkins asks. "Protocol requires I offer you the opportunity to let me in before I code in an entry. I don't want to stumble onto anything above my classification."

I move to the door and Bella takes a seat at the desk, pretending to pore over the files on the desk.

The six-shooter is tucked neatly in my waistband and hidden by my shirt before I enter the code, tug on the door and open it to the large, drooping security guard named Jenkins.

"Like I said," he steps into the room without waiting for an invitation, "my name is Jenkins. I'm one the guards here at night."

"Keep your cool," Corkscrew urges. "Just remember your cover. Make something up. He'll buy it."

I offer my hand, "I'm Dr. Alex Dennis and this is my colleague Dr. Olivia Triblet."

Jenkins takes my hand and shakes it with pudgy, calloused fingers. He nods and looks at the identification badge hanging around my neck. "May I take a look?" He lets go of my hand and glances at Bella.

"Sure." I extend the lanyard so Jenkins can look it over through his swollen, reddened eyes. His wide nose is decorated with the signs of alcohol abuse. He sniffs as he holds Wolodymyr's handiwork, flipping it over for good measure.

"We're finished for the night," I say. "Heading to a nearby bar for a drink after we leave. Any suggestions?" I swallow against the pulse intensifying in my neck. I take a deep breath to maintain my calm.

"Momo's Sports Bar is good," he says. "It's next to the Outback on Holbrook. If you're hungry the Steak Tidbits are popular." He lets go of my lanyard and waddles toward Bella in a way that suggests his feet hurt. "You not from here?"

"No," Bella answers. "We're visiting researchers."

"Yeah?" he asks, handling Bella's identification when she offers it to him. "Where you from?"

"The University of Florida. We work in their nuclear engineering program. We're just here for a few weeks."

"Florida, huh?" Jenkins puts his hands on his hip and I notice he's armed. He turns back to face me. "I don't recall seeing either of you here before."

"We've only been here two days," Bella says. "We're just getting settled in and thought it'd be a good idea to be here when there's not a lot going on."

"Makes sense." Jenkins yanks on the wide patent leather belt holding up his pants. He turns to me, his back to Bella. "I'm just gonna need to call this one in to the Platoon Captain. You know, since badging is closed."

"Platoon?" I ask, trying to stall him as he reaches for the radio mic on his lapel.

"We have three platoons in our police group. Each one has a captain in charge." He starts to press the mic and turns back toward Bella.

"What's your rank?" I ask, trying to think of something.

"I'm a—ARGGH!" Jenkins tenses, convulses and drops to the floor like a felled tree, banging his head on the desk next to Bella. He's unconscious but not bleeding.

"What happened?" I take two quick steps toward Jenkins and see Bella holding Mack's homemade taser.

"I just shoved this as hard as I could into his groin and pressed the button," she shrugs.

"Well it worked." I kneel down next to Jenkins; he's breathing. I grab his radio and his nine millimeter. "We don't have much time now."

Bella joins me at the door, just as a deafening explosion of thunder rattles the building. The lights flicker and then go dark.

The power is out. The door won't open. We're locked inside.

***

"The feed's dead," says Corkscrew. "I'm guessing from the blackness in the apartments across from me that the power went out. That last lightning bolt was a direct hit. I can't see you and I have no access to anything."

I'm huddled next to Bella, having made my way to her side with the flashlight on my cell phone. She has her flashlight app trained on the unconscious Jenkins. He's started moaning. He'll wake up any second now.

"Are you hearing her? We're flying blind," Bella says, tapping her earpiece. "And the battery on my cell is dead."

"We can figure this out. Jenkins might be helpful. He probably knows exactly where Aleksey Diozegi works. He can lead us to the right place."

"Maybe," Bella says with uncertainty

"There's a backup generator," says Corkscrew. "It takes five minutes without power for it to kick on."

"Five minutes," Bella whispers, holding up the fingers on her left hand. "We've got five minutes."

"I'll be right back," I say and walk quickly to the cabinets next to the coffee maker. Above the sink are stacks of napkins. They're bound with large plastic ties, which I grab and take over to Jenkins. He's lying on his side, so I roll him onto his stomach and, using three of the ties, manufacture some crude binds around his wrists. He mumbles something unintelligible as I shove him back onto his side, drool slobbering down the side of his face. Then I take the handcuffs from the sleeve on his belt and close one cuff around each ankle.

I run the flashlight from the blueish-yellow bruise on his forehead along his body, checking for any other weapons he may be carrying. Nothing. But he did piss himself.

Poor guy.

"Will those hold?" Bella asks, her flashlight dimming to nothing.

"Probably."

I stand over Jenkins and look back toward the door. My eyes have adjusted to the darkness. It's quiet except for the thumping of raindrops on the roof and the grumble of thunder distancing itself from Brookhaven.

"You've got maybe a minute," Corkscrew interrupts the silence. "Then the generator will kick on. It'll be a couple of minutes before the security system resets itself. Then I have to regain access. I won't be able to see you until after that."

No sooner has she finished speaking when there's the sound of a diesel generator roaring to life and the fluorescents flicker, washing the room in light that seems brighter than before. The numeric control panel at the door is still off.

"What happened?" groans Jenkins. "Wait! What…my hands…I… Who the…" He struggles against the ties on his wrists, flopping on the floor like a beetle on its back.

I kneel down, close to his face, speaking softly and evenly, "Jenkins, keep calm. We're not going to hurt you."

"I kinda did already," Bella interjects. "Sorry about that."

Jenkins snarls, finally able to wrestle himself into a sitting position. His face is crimson, camouflaging the bruise.

"We're going to need your help," I tell him. "Understood?"

"I'm not helping you," he spits. "Who are you? You realize the amount of trouble you're in right now? Do you have any *clue*?" He winces, squeezing his eyes together as if he's making a wish on a lamp. "My head…"

"Yeah, when my friend tased you, you fell and hit your head. You have a nasty bruise and maybe a concussion. You were out cold for a couple of minutes."

The pulse of his headache must have calmed him. He's looking at me with less malice. The snarl relaxes into a frown. "Who are you?"

"We're here looking for some information a coworker of ours may have shared with a scientist at Brookhaven," Bella says.

"What scientist?" His chest is heaving with each breath. He's wriggling against the ties, but I must have done a pretty good job. They're holding.

"Aleksey Diozegi," I say. "You know him?"

Jenkins nods, squeezing his eyes shut again.

"Do you know which of the R&D offices is his?" Bella asks, peeking around his back to check on the ties. "We need to know where he keeps his paper files."

"His office is in another wing, a few hundred feet from here." His chin drops to his chest. "I need something for my head. I can't open my eyes without pain."

"You show us where to go, don't give us any trouble, and you'll be getting the help you need pretty quick. I promise."

He doesn't acknowledge me. He's puffing like a Lamaze instructor. "Understood?"

"Understood," he clenches his teeth and a look of recognition washes across his face. "You know this is gonna end badly for you."

"Yeah." I help him to his feet just as the coded panel at the door resets and powers up. "It probably will."

***

Aleksey Diozegi's office is a study in chaos. It's like a paper factory exploded inside its four walls.

"Good luck," Jenkins grumbles. I've sat him in a chair in the corner of the room after clearing it of a stack of academic journals. "You're going to run out of time."

"I've got nothing for you," says our helpful hacker. "I'll keep an eye on the cameras, though and give you a heads up if you get more company."

"That's helpful," Bella mumbles, standing in front of a bookshelf, arms crossed in front her.

"I know who you are," says Jenkins. "I thought I recognized both of you. Now I'm positive."

Neither Bella nor I say anything. She's stopped admiring the bookshelf and is digging through vertical file folders looking for anything remotely familiar. I'm at the desk, picking through the debris.

"You're the two killers on the run. I saw you on the news. You killed that reporter in Texas and then crashed a plane in Maryland."

It's tempting to correct him, but I don't.

"Then you killed two people on a subway in D.C. I know it's you. I recognize you."

Bella's scanning through the files, thumbing past page after page. She's shaking her head, biting her lower lip. That's not a look of confidence.

"There's no way you're getting away with this." Jenkins is struggling against the plastic ties, but they're not loosening. "Your run ends here."

Pulling Diozegi's chair from under his desk, I plop down into the seat, trying to organize my thoughts. Aside from the piles of papers, a couple of framed family photos, and an empty Brookhaven coffee mug, the only other thing on his desk is a large Mac computer. It's decorated with yellow and pink sticky notes. The words and numbers scribbled onto the notes mean nothing.

This is a fool's errand.

"I found something!" Bella shrieks. "A safe."

She's kneeling in front of an open cabinet door at the bottom of the bookshelf. There's a black safe with a combination lock and a key. The key is in the safe.

"It won't turn," she says. "I'll need the combination."

Jenkins is doing his best to see what Bella's doing. But from his position, even with his necked craned, he can't. "You can't be doing this!" he yells at her. His struggling becomes more violent as I reach him in his corner seat. There's an extra tie holding his binds to the chair behind his back. He spits at me, spraying my face. I wipe my face with my hand, then my hand on his shoulder.

"Keep your voice down," I say with the six-shooter pressed into his protruding belly. "Is that clear?" The threat doesn't seem to bother him at first.

"Help!!" he yells at the top of his lungs. "Help!!"

I pull the hammer on the gun and move the business end from his girth to the side of his head.

"If you know who I am then you know I won't hesitate to use this. If I'd kill a friend of mine and a couple of strangers on a train, what makes you think I won't add you to the list?"

Jenkins licks his lips and swallows.

"Are you going to be quiet?" I push the barrel into his temple.

He nods.

"I need some help," Bella calls. "I can't open the safe. We need a combination. Do you see anything?"

"No," I say, then I remember the sticky notes. "Wait, maybe."

Two of the dozen sticky notes have only numbers on them. One of them looks like a phone number; the other could be the combination.

"Try this. Ten to the left. Thirty-five to the right. Then eighteen to the left."

Bella spins the lock and then tries the key. "No."

Our earpieces crackle to life. "You guys are about to get some visitors," Corkscrew says. "There are two security guards. Armed. You have maybe three minutes."

Bella's eyes widen and she runs her hands through her hair. She tries the combination again.

Nothing.

"There are three of them now," Corkscrew says, her voice quavering. "They're moving pretty fast. They're checking every room and forcing entry. You're running out of time."

"Did you skip thirty-five the first time?' I ask Bella, moving to her side.

"What?"

"Spin it all the way around. Haven't you opened a safe before?"

"Not with this kind of lock. Always electronic or keyed."

"Even on your high school locker?" I start working the combination.

"I went to a prep school," she reminds me. "We didn't have locks on our lockers."

I finish the combination and turn the key.

Bingo.

Bella reaches into the safe and pulls out a stack of folders. One of them is labeled with Wolf's name.

"This could be it!" Bella exclaims.

"They're two doors down," Corkscrew says. "I might be able to help you out if they all go into the room." The clicks on her keyboard intensify. "Maybe…buy…you…a…few…"

The line goes silent and then, "There!!"

Bella moves to the door. She looks at the keypad then turns to Jenkins. "What's the override code?"

He looks at her like she's stepped off of Mars and says nothing. I march over to him, aiming the revolver at his face. "Is there a code?"

He stutters, "I-I-It's-It's—"

Corkscrew interrupts and I hold up a finger to silence Jenkins. "They're locked inside the room two doors from you. There's no camera in the room, so I don't know if they've figured it out yet. They're stuck until they figure out to input the override code. I'm trying to change it, but that'll take some time. I may not be able to reprogram it."

"What's the code?" Bella asks.

"Speak," I instruct our hostage. He's staring at something on the desk behind me.

His radio is on the desk with his leather gun belt. The volume is low, but the audio indicator is flashing. Someone's trying to talk with him!

"Jenkins?" calls a voice. "Ten-eighteen. Ten-twenty. Please advise. Over." It repeats twice.

"Have they been trying contact him all along and we had no idea?" Bella asks.

"I didn't think about it," I admit through clenched teeth.

"I told you you're done," Jenkins sneers. "I told you this was the end of the road."

"Jenkins?" the voice calls again, "Where are you? Are you okay? Please advise. Over."

"What's the code?" Bella says. "We need the override code."

"I'm not giving it to you," he says. "You can kill me. I'm not letting you out of here."

"By the way," the hacker updates us, "just so you know. You're locked inside too. You won't be able to get out until they do."

"Start punching numbers," I tell Bella. "We've got nothing to lose."

She taps a combination into the keypad and the light flashes red. She types another. Same result.

"Uh oh," Corkscrew delivers the news. "They're punching in the override. They're on their way. Only one more room before you."

I look around the cluttered office. Bella's punching the keypad with unbridled futility. There's paper everywhere. The safe's unlocked.

Jenkins is smirking. Everything's crashing down around us. I look up and see salvation.

"Sorry about this," I say to Jenkins, ball my fist, and clock him as hard as I can across the cheek, knocking him unconscious.

***

"Did you have to hit him?" Bella whispers. "I feel bad we beat up on the guy so much."

"Keep moving," I tap her on the rear, encouraging her to push ahead without discussion. "We'll talk about this later."

"I don't know how you're doing this," says Corkscrew, "but you're moving right past them. I mean, it's like you're ghosts floating over them. Whatever you're doing, you're good. Keep heading that direction."

I fight back a sneeze from the dust coating the inside of my nose and my eyes water. We're in a large air duct between the ceiling and the roof. It's just wide enough for us to move, on our stomachs toward an exterior vent.

There were two things that made me think of the air duct. First, an asbestos tile in the ceiling was loose. The metal bottom of the duct was visible in that space where the tile was dislodged. That reminded me of one of the diagrams we'd pulled from George's townhouse. It was the HVAC blueprint from the building, detailing the entire ventilation system for the heating and cooling installed throughout the building. There was a single duct that ran the length of the building, emptying onto the backside of the facility, not far from where we parked.

Bella climbed onto the bookshelf and popped open a tile adjacent to the return vent. With my help, she climbed into the duct. I followed her, having just enough room to pull the ceiling tile back into place behind me.

"This is kinda funny," Bella whispers, intent on giving away our location, inching along through the duct. "Didn't they climb through an air vent in *Mission Impossible*?"

"Yes."

"In the CIA headquarters, right?"

"Yes."

"This is life imitating art."

"I guess that makes me Tom Cruise."

"Shhh!" she says. "You're going to make me laugh."

The air conditioning is on, and so, while it's uncomfortable with the air blowing, it dampens the noise we're making along our path to freedom. It's a straight shot to the exit.

Or at least I thought it was.

"We've hit a dead end," Bella says. "I can't go any farther."

"Are you sure?" I ask, trying to look past her. I can't see around her body. The space is too and too dark.

"I'm positive," she says. "It just ends. There's no exit here."

"We're going to have to back up. We passed a split maybe twenty yards back. We'll take the split."

She inches backward, her feet hitting my face. There's a slight rumble, a vibration in the metal and the air conditioning shuts off.

I'm using my elbows to retrace our path feet first, pushing against the metal floor of the duct.

Bella stops. "Shhh! I hear something."

I stop, blinking sweat from my eyes. Without the air conditioning to blow it off my brow, gravity's pulling it straight down my face. Holding myself as still as possible, I'm struck by the lack of room inside the duct, the stagnant air. If I were claustrophobic, this would be bad.

My mind flashes to the recurring dreams I suffered through for so many years...

Trapped in a school locker. Banging on the door. Screaming for help. Pushing against the walls closing in like a compactor. A lack of air.

Banging. Screaming. Pushing. Pain. Panic…

"Did you hear that?" Bella whispers. "Jackson? Did you hear that?"

She shakes me back to the present, my heart thumping blood into my neck, pounding faster against my chest. Closing my eyes, I push away the dream and suck in a dust-laden breath, slowing the pulse of adrenaline.

There's a strong vibration in the duct and it trembles. "Did you feel that?"

"Yes," I whisper.

Another tremor. And voices.

"What do you think it is?" Bella asks. "What's happening?" Another rattle. This one, stronger.

"I don't know." I'm afraid to tell her what might be happening. "We need to move and get to that split." Looking over my shoulder, I start scooting back as quickly as I can. It's dark, but as I slide back, my hand rubs against the wall of the duct.

Push. Slide. Push. Slide.

I'll know when we hit the split. It opens to my left.

Push. Slide. Push. Slide.

Another tremble. This one lasts longer. It's louder.

Push. Slide. Push. Slide.

"Are we close?"

"Yes." I have no idea.

Push. Slide. Push. Slide.

"You're moving back to where you came from," Corkscrew says. Finally. "You're going in the wrong direction. I saw the security dudes go into your room. They never came out. I don't know where they are."

Great.

Push. Slide. Pu—

Yes! The opening to the split.

"Bella! We're here at the split. I'm going to keep sliding past it and let you go first. Once you're in, I'll follow you."

I push past the opening, giving Bella enough room to move past it and then enter the split headfirst. She slides in, her feet disappearing into the split, just as a loud rumble shakes the duct.

Catching my breath, trying not to cough from the dust, I raise myself up on elbows and shift my weight to follow Bella toward what I hope is an exit.

There's another rumble that sounds like metal pots clanging together.

Something grabs my ankles and pulls.

***

"Don't move!" commands the gritty voice behind me, a pair of hands gripping my legs.

I pull my knees toward me, one at a time, and kick back. The fifth kick connects with something hard and the man grunts.

I roll onto my side and try pulling myself around the corner of the duct into the split, but he recovers and manages to grip one foot with both of his hands. He tugs and I lose my grip.

The duct is rattling against the struggle when I connect with another kick. My foot hits him square in the nose.

Still, he claws his way closer to me, using my pants to climb even with me. He's behind me, trying to wrap his arms around me.

I push off the wall of the duct in front of me, near the opening, pinning him between my back and the wall behind me. I relax and push again, knocking the air from his lungs.

He gasps and grabs at my head, gripping a fistful of hair and yanking back. I return the favor with an elbow to his throat and he lets go with a sick gargle.

Another elbow to his chest and I'm able to free myself, feeling for the opening. Finding it, I pull my weight into the split.

My chest is burning, the sweat dripping from my face and neck onto the metal duct. I am halfway into the split, my legs still in the main stretch of the duct when it shifts under my weight.

And falls.

The quick descent, which takes less than second, feels like an eternity. It's like I have time to consider my life, my death, my mistakes, Bella, my parents, Sir Spencer, the governor, Charlie, George, Ripley, Liho Blogis, faceless Pickle people, my cousin…

Time stretches in a deafening silence before it ends just as violently with the sound of metal and bone crunching, glass breaking, the scream of the man in the duct.

I'm surrounded by blackness. I can't tell if my eyes are open or closed. My back hurts, my neck hurts, my knee feels worse than it has since the day it was surgically repaired.

It's good my knee hurts. It means I'm not paralyzed.

The darkness dissolves into a flickering light. I'm on my back, on the floor, staring at the shredded asbestos ceiling ten feet above me. There's a fluorescent light hanging next to the hole, cracked with its twin tube bulbs exposed but functioning somewhat.

A wave of recognition slams into me.

I'm in building 197. Brookhaven National Laboratory.

The motion sensor must have triggered the light.

My fingers work, my toes work. I'm alive. I'm good.

I'll just rest here for a second. I'm so tired. Just a second.

"Jackson?" my earpiece, somehow, is still lodged in its place. "Jackson? If you can hear me, Bella is outside of the building. I'm reading from the tracker you're still inside. You need to exit as quickly as possible. There's backup headed your way."

Maybe not.

"Whatever you're doing in there is getting a lot of attention," the hacker says. "I mean A LOT."

"U.S. Marshals, F.B.I., Suffolk County. They're all headed your way. You have got to get out of there. Meet Bella where your car is parked. She's there."

I'm underneath part of the duct and pieces of asbestos ceiling. Managing to sit up, despite the pain in my lower back, I scoot out from under the debris. Next to me, unconscious but breathing, is the duct attacker. He's wearing a uniform identical to Jenkins'. His face is bloodied and he might be missing a couple of teeth, but I think he'll be okay.

"Jackson," Corkscrew's voice is an octave higher, "you need to go now! There are three guards headed your way. And one of them, a bigger guy, looks really intent on getting to you. He might be the first one who found you."

Jenkins!

I use a chair to help me to my feet. Everything is spinning and out of focus.

The mess of a room looks similar to the other labs and offices. It's got a bookshelf on one side, a bank of cabinets on the other. There's a white board on one wall, an unplugged wall unit air conditioner, the door and its electronic entry panel.

"You've got maybe ten seconds," Corkscrew warns. "Jackson!! I'll work on the key panel again. But you don't have time."

Gaining my balance with the help of a desk, I grab the broken leg of a chair and maneuver my way to the door. I grip the chair leg like a baseball bat and shove the end of it into the key code panel. I crack the panel, but it's still lit. I slam the butt of the leg into the panel a second time, sparking a short. The lights blink and shut off. I hit it again for good measure.

That should keep them out of the room for a minute.

Dragging another chair to the opposite wall, I struggle to the other side of the room. I step up on the chair with one foot and place the other on the bookshelf. Reaching up, I take the chair leg and use a protruding screw to rip into the caulk lining the edge of the air conditioning unit. There's no trim molding around the unit, making the impossible job a little more feasible.

Once I've made my way around the entire unit, I take my fingers and start prying the caulk. It's old and cracked, which makes the job easier. My head is spinning; a sharp pain is pulsing above my right eye. My lower back is tightening by the second.

"They're at the door," Corkscrew says. "They're punching in a key, but it's not working."

Good.

"Their weapons are drawn, Jackson!"

Not good.

I don't have time to finish removing the caulk, so I grab at the face of the unit and pull. It comes off and I swing it to the floor. That does me no good.

I'm not getting out this way.

"Jackson," Corkscrew's voice is softer, like she realizes there's no point in the urgency anymore. "They're working on the panel. You've got a few extra seconds to figure something out."

I bang on the air conditioner, praying that all it needs it a shove or two to come loose and open a hole big enough for me to squeeze through. No such luck.

The air duct attacker is still unconscious. His face is covered in blood from what I figure is either the fall or my elbow to his face.

I can't tell how old he is or what he looks like, except that his hair is my color and about my length. It's short, cropped on the sides, a bit longer than a high and tight military style cut.

Hopping down from the chair, I push aside part of the vent and move to the guard. Standing over him, his chest moving up and down with short, shallow breaths, I have an idea.

***

I've never been one for uniforms, but in this instance I'll make an exception. It's ill fitting, a little loose in my shoulders and tight in the waist, but it'll do.

My face is covered in ceiling dust, palmfuls swept from the floor and generously applied across my cheeks and forehead. There's a little blood too, thumbed from a puddle on the floor next to guard. It's streaked like war paint above one eye and on my ear.

It was a lot easier getting the uniform on than it was pulling it off an unconscious man. Then, getting him dressed again, in my clothes, all while keeping one eye on the door, was ridiculous.

It's taken the guards fourteen minutes to open the door. I've spent the last thirty seconds banging on the door, calling for help.

When the door finally hums and swings open, three guards, including Jenkins tumble into the room. All of them are wide-eyed, trying to take in the chaos in front of them.

"He's alive!" I assure them in a hushed voice, strained from screaming for help. I don't even recognize it as my own. "I got him. But I'm hurt. I'm bleeding. Jenkins, get him first. Secure him. Then help me."

My head is hanging, one of my hands cupped over my eyes. I'm leaning against the wall next to the door. The men are frozen for a moment before Jenkins and one of the other guards picks their way to the man lying face down on the floor.

"That's him!" Jenkins calls back. "That's Jackson Quick! I know what he was wearing. That's him!" The second guard has his weapon trained on the unconscious suspect.

"Go help him," I wave off the guard standing next to me. "That guy's dangerous. I'll go call 9-1-1."

"We've already handled that," he says, putting his hand on my shoulder. "The ambulance will be here any minute."

"Go help them with Quick," I order the guard. "I'm okay."

He nods and, without questioning the instructions, wades his way to Jenkins' side. He kneels down to check the suspect's pulse. "He's got a pulse," he nods and then turns his attention back to the suspect.

I slip out of room, shutting the door behind me. And I run.

My right eye feels like it's connected to a surging electrical socket. My lower back screams with every pound of my feet along the linoleum floor of the long hallway.

I have no idea if I'm headed in the right direction. I can't focus.

"Jackson!" Corkscrew calls to me. "Jackson? You're not moving. You've stopped moving."

She doesn't know the guard is wearing my clothes. I left the transmitter in the pocket.

"Bella," she says. "Bella, Jackson is caught. He's not moving. You need to leave."

No!!

I bite down on the inside of my cheek and refocus. My right eye closed to dull the edge of the pain, ignoring the throb in my lower back, I push forward.

About twenty yards ahead is a glowing red EXIT sign. I'm there.

"Bella," repeats the hacker. "You need to go now. There's a caravan of cops closing in on your location. If you head north now, you'll avoid them."

I'm almost there.

I reach the door and tackle it, slamming it open into the dense midnight air. The humid, cold air pushing me backward. With the last bit of energy I can muster, I run through the doorway and—

I'm on the wrong side of the building!

In front of me is a parking lot. A half-dozen cars are parked amidst the twenty spaces lining the entrance to Building 197. The door swings shut behind me. In the distance there's the flash of red and blue lights against the low, water-filled clouds.

"I see you, Bella," says Corkscrew. "Turn right onto Michelson and the right onto Upton."

She's gone...

I can hear the sirens wailing now. They're getting closer.

Sinking down to the sidewalk, I collapse next to the curb. Rolling onto my back, my right eye still closed, I stare up at the sky. Puffs of vapor obscure the view with every breath.

I clasp my hands across my chest, resigning myself to what's about to happen, when I find something in the left breast pocket of the uniform.

Keys!

Reaching into the pocket, I pull out a set of keys, and dangle them above my left eye to get a better look. Two of them look like building keys, but the third and its accompanying fob belong to a car.

I press the unlock icon on the fob and hear the familiar chirp of doors unlocking. I turn my head to the right, toward the cars in the lot and press the button again. The taillights of a Chevy Cruise flash.

Pushing myself to my feet, I hobble to the Chevy, and climb inside. The car starts and I pull the belt across my lap as I slip it into reverse and pull out of the lot. I find the headlight switch and turn it to the OFF position.

Knowing Upton runs north and south, I turn right out of the lot. Guessing I'm heading in the right direction, I make another right, turning north. It's Upton. I might only be five minutes behind Bella. When I gain some distance from Brookhaven, I'll call her. In my rear view mirror, a cavalry of cops are racing toward the same lot I just left.

My body feels like it's been run through a grinder, the pain acute in too many places to count. But I'm alive.

CHAPTER 16

I've never really finished anything. True, I graduated from high school and college, but other than that, my life has been a series of incompletes.

Whether it's the job-hopping or the inability to maintain relationships of substance, I've found ways to skip out early. My shrink thought I had Attention Deficit Disorder. She even considered the possibility I was bipolar.

She concluded it wasn't either of those diagnoses, but rather, a general fear of completion. I needed to be aware of the pattern and recognize when I was about to run. She made me take notes on every task, however I started and failed to complete.

It was too easy to blame it on my parents' deaths. I couldn't use that as a crutch my entire life. Instead, I should place the blame and responsibility of incompletion squarely on my own shoulders.

She wanted me to research more deeply any project, job, or relationship I was about to undertake. Sketch out goals, outline my expectations, and incrementally move toward resolution.

I was headed there, I thought, when the Governor of Texas hired me. I quickly became a trusted aide, a confidant of sorts. He took me to his ranch, he entrusted me with delicate tasks.

Then I met Charlie. She was everything I thought I wanted in a companion. Whip smart and beautiful, she made me want to be a better person. I opened up to her. I let her in.

Both of them betrayed that trust. Charlie died. The governor went to prison. Now he's dead. You can't get more closure, more resolution, than death.

Now, driving west toward I-95, I find myself on the verge of finishing something I started. It's within reach. I can complete my mission to end Sir Spencer's grasp on me, Liho Blogis' plan to sell nuclear destruction to the highest bidder, and my desire to see Bella free of anxiety and fear.

The clock on the dash reads 12:40 AM. I haven't stopped to call Bella. She doesn't even know I escaped Brookhaven. I'm too afraid to stop. I keep telling myself, "One more exit," and then I drive past it, certain that I'll get surrounded and caught.

I've had the radio off. I don't want to hear the latest about what I've done, who I've killed or maimed, why I'm public enemy number one.

The pain over my right eye is subsiding, or it could be that the ache in my lower back is so concentrated and sharp, it's overpowering my other injuries.

The six-shooter and my burner cell are on the passenger seat. My wallet's in my back pocket. I've got some cash, but no credit card and no identification. I left the fake ID's around the neck of the unconscious security guard. Bella's got the extra burners and additional IDs in the SUV.

She's also got the bag with Ripley's weapons and the thumb drive Mack gave me. I'd forgotten about that thumb drive.

Mack suggested that everything I needed to know about my parents' death was on that drive. He pulled it from the cloud and told me I needed to see it firsthand, learn about the connections between my parents, Sir Spencer, and Liho Blogis.

My shrink could suggest all she wanted that my ability, or inability, to do anything wasn't related to my parents. However, the deeper down this rabbit hole I slip, the harder I work to climb my way out, the more I know that everything in my life was a set up for what I'm about to finish.

One way or the other, I'm ending this. I'm so close to the end, I can see it dancing on the horizon. Just beyond the reach of the Chevy's headlights, it's there. Calling me. Taunting me.

I reach over to the passenger's seat and grab the cell phone to call Bella. She needs to know I'm okay and I need to read what's on that drive.

***

Bella's sitting in the driver's seat of the SUV, parked in a rest area just off the interstate in New Jersey. When I climb into the front seat next to her, she doesn't say anything. Her lower lips quivers, her eyes fill with tears that quickly spill onto her cheeks, and she throws herself across the armrest and into my arms.

Her head buried in my chest, she sobs. I hold her, one hand on the back of her head, the other on her back. With deep, heaving breaths, she cries until the wave subsides. She pulls back from me and kisses my lips. Hers are salty from the tears; the kiss is full and passionate. Her hands move to either side of my face pulling me closer still.

"I can't get close enough to you," she says in a voice on the verge of hyperventilating. "You were right behind me. And then you weren't. And then the crash. And Corkscrew telling me you were stuck. I didn't want to leave. I didn't. I just—"

"I know," I interrupt her, thumbing the tears from underneath her eyes. "I know you didn't. It's okay."

"I thought I had this figured out," she says, wiping her nose with the back of her hand. "I thought I could emotionally detach. You know, I could, distance myself from you just in case."

"I get it."

"But I can't," she admits. "I can't be mad at you. I can't turn a switch and be cold." She sits up and wipes her eyes. "I love you too much."

"I love you too."

"We're finished with this, right? I mean," a laugh emerges from the crying, "we're close to leaving all of this and starting fresh, right?"

"Yes."

"Then let's hurry up and finish."

"You've got the process?"

"I think so." She reaches under the front seat and pulls out one of the file folders from the safe. "Take a look and tell me what you think."

I flip open the folder labeled WOLF to find a stack of papers. On top of the papers is a sticky note.

Aleksey, You are my last hope. Keep this safe, friend.

With deepest admiration, Paul

Under the sticky note, on the first page begins a familiar string of letters, numbers, and symbols. They're indecipherable to me, but I know what they mean.

$$(v\text{-}c)/c = f\hat{A}t \,/(TOFfc - f\hat{A}t) = (2.48 \} 0.28 \text{ (stat.)} \} 0.30 \text{ (sys.)})$$
$$\sim10\text{-}5.i\hbar\, \partial\, \psi(r;t)=H\psi(r;t)\ (1)\ \partial t$$
$$p\hat{}2c2 + m2c4\ (2)\ \partial 22224\ i\hbar\partial t\psi(r;t)= -\hbar\ c\ \nabla +m\ c\ \psi(r;t)\ (3)$$
$$2\partial 2\ 22\ 2\ 24 - \hbar\partial t2\psi(r;t)=-\hbar c\nabla +mc\ \psi(r;t)\ (4)1\ \partial 2\ 2\ m2c2$$
$$c2\partial t2 - \nabla + \hbar 2\ \psi(r;t)=0\ (5)\ 1\partial 2\ 2$$
$$2 = c2\ \partial t2 - \nabla\ (6)\ (\hbar\bar{\ }= c = 1)\ 2 + m2\ \psi(x\mu) = 0$$
$$(7)\partial 2\ .\ \partial 2 - \hbar 2\ \psi(x;\ t) = -\hbar 2c2 + m2c4\ \psi(x;\ t)\ (8)\partial t2\ \partial x2$$
$$2\ \partial 2\ 2 - \hbar\ \partial t2\ \varphi(t) = E\ \varphi(t)\ (10)$$

"This is it!" I look to Bella, who's blinking away her tears, smiling at what we've recovered.

"Yep. You recognize it too?"

"I do."

"So now we need to get to Houston."

"How long do you think it'll take to drive?"

"If we go straight through," she answers, "we can make it in twenty-four hours."

"We can take four hour shifts. You up for it?"

"I'll drive first," she says. "I've already filled up."

"You still have George's laptop?"

"Yes. Mack gave to us, remember? It's in the back seat."

"Have you gotten rid of Corkscrew's tracker?" I ask, having tossed the earpiece miles ago.

"Yes, so unless there's one implanted in my knee, we're good to go."

"Funny." I smirk. "Not funny. But funny."

I take out my phone and take a photo of the front page of the process. I use the filters on the phone to blur most of the image and then text it to Blogis and Sir Spencer individually.

Along with the photograph, I write:

we've got it. we'll deliver this in 48 hrs. tick tock. i'll be in touch.

Bella's merging into interstate traffic as I slip the folder underneath my seat.

Forty-eight hours and miles to go before we sleep.

***

We're in Pennsylvania when I climb into the backseat.

"You need to do this now?" Bella asks, knowing the answer. We've been talking about it for the last thirty minutes.

"Yes. I need to look at it before we get there. Now is as good a time as any." With George's laptop open, I slide in Mack's thumb drive. It opens and reveals a single folder.

ELLSWORTH

My real name. My parents' names.

I thumb the cursor to the folder and, hovering over it for a breath, double click to open it. My heart's pounding, dulling the ache in my head and lower back.

The folder opens and populates a list of files.

ELLSWORTH.JPG
ELLSWORTH2.JPG
ELLSWORTHASSIGN.WAV
ELLSWORTHSURVEIL.DOC

That's it. The truth, as Mack put it, reduced to two photographs, an audio file, and a single document. I click on the first picture.

It's a photograph from our family trip to Devil's Tower, Wyoming. We're standing at the base of a trail that surrounds the formation. I'm standing atop a six-foot tall rock flexing my non-existent biceps, my parents on the cluster of rocks beneath me. My mom is turned to her side, her arms open as though she's presenting me to the world. My father's looking at my mother, laughing at her pose.

I remember the photograph and the kind elderly couple who offered to snap it for us. They were Canadian.

It wasn't long after that photograph that my dad got a call to "go to work". My mom protested, I complained, but we cut our trip short.

"You okay Jackson? You look deep in thought."

"I'm okay." I fake a smile and click on the next photograph.

It's my mom in her garden. She's on a knee, covered in dirt, harvesting cucumbers. My dad's standing to the side, a rake in his hand. They both look tired but content. Happy.

I took the photograph. It was my mom's birthday, the last before they died. She told both of us that she wanted to spend "her" day in her favorite spot with her favorite people.

I stare at each of them smiling for the camera, neither aware of what was coming. Neither of them knowing they'd both celebrated their last birthdays together.

I exit out of the photographs and choose the audio file. Quicktime fills the screen and the audio loads. I immediately recognize the first voice.

"We have an issue with Ellsworth," says Sir Spencer. *"He wants out."*

"Is that Sir Spencer's voice?" Bella asks.

I click pause on the computer. "It's part of the stuff Mack gave me." I click the pause icon to restart the audio.

"So I need you to consider our options," Sir Spencer continues. *"because we cannot allow it to happen."*

"I don't see the problem here," a second voice answers.

"Who is that?" Bella asks, still craning to listen. "Turn the volume up, please. I want to hear it too."

I push the volume button and hold it. "I'm pretty sure it's Blogis."

"The problem, good man," says Sir Spencer, *"is we'll have two rogue agents. They'll be out there in the ether, susceptible to the advances of others."*

"I wouldn't consider them rogue," replies Blogis. *"She hasn't been active for years. He's been loyal. We've no reason to think they'll betray us."*

"That's revealing a naiveté I'm surprised you possess," Sir Spencer laughs. *"There is no loyalty, no allegiance as it were."*

"So what are you saying?"

"I'm merely suggesting we consider the options," Sir Spencer says coyly.

"Which are?"

"We must be the first to the battlefield," Sir Spencer says. *"The victorious do not wait to be attacked."*

"You want them dead."

"Those are your words, good man, not mine. You do what must be done. If you don't, I'll find someone who will."

"Who?" Blogis asks. *"Who else would do what you're asking?"*

"*You know him. He's a man of ambition. A Texan. Good with a rifle, even better with a handshake and a smile.*"

"Who is he talking about?" Bella asks. I shake my head. I don't know.

"*You'd ask him?*" Blogis' voice is warbling, stressed. "*Even amongst the degenerates with whom we work, he has no moral compass. He's about power and money and—*"

"*What else is there, good man? In our world, and you know this, there is power and money. The closer our proximity to the intersection of the two, the more relevant we become.*"

"*I won't have any part of this,*" Blogis says, his voice distant.

"*If you leave,*" Sir Spencer warns, "*I'll be forced to have this same conversation about you.*"

"*Go for it,*" says Blogis, his voice echoing from the distance to whatever is recording the conversation. "*I'm done. And tell your minion to watch his back.*"

Sir Spencer tells Blogis not to interfere, raising his voice. He tells him to stay away from my parents and to let his alternative choice do his job. Then he says the man's name and the blood rushes from my throbbing head. My fingers, hovering over the computer mouse pad, start shaking.

The alternative choice, the man good with a rifle and a handshake, is a name I've heard before. I used to work for him.

He just died in prison.

Blogis had him killed. "*He's had it coming for a while now anyway,*" he said on the Metro when I asked for the favor.

The governor. It was the governor.

***

"Are you sure you're okay to drive?" Bella asks me. We're about an hour outside of Roanoke, Virginia on I-95 South.

"I'm fine." My eyes are focused on the halogen-illuminated highway in front of us. "My head's feeling better."

"You couldn't have known, Jackson."

"My whole life was plotted by the two people who ruined it. Sir Spencer and the governor. What am I supposed to do with that?"

"You're not—"

"It's rhetorical," I snap and then recoil. "I'm sorry. I didn't mean that. I know you're trying to help."

"So what happened?" she asks. "The governor *did* kill your parents?"

There's not much traffic on the road. It's the long, slow part of the night between midnight and dawn. Every once in a while a trucker zooms past us. I'm traveling the speed limit with the cruise control set. It's not worth risking an encounter with a cop.

"Yes. There's no proof. But he was involved. Somebody had tapped the phones in the house and knew when my parents were coming and going."

"Had to be him."

"There were also eyewitness reports of another car involved in the wreck. Two people claimed it caused the crash and fled the scene. The police did a cursory follow up, but decided it was just an accident."

"You think they were paid off?"

"Could be." It's likely, knowing Sir Spencer. "There are also crime scene photographs attached to a couple of the reports. In one of them, in the crowd gathered near the road, I swear he's standing there."

"The governor?"

"Yep."

We pass a mileage sign for Roanoke. We're getting close. It'll be a good place to stop for gasoline and to stretch my legs.

"What did the last document tell you about Blogis?"

"It contained police reports and bank records. That's pretty much it."

"You said that thirty miles ago. Give me details."

"According to what's in the computer," I sigh, "my parents were broke."

"I thought you have a trust fund?"

"I do," I grip the wheel with both hands and shift in my seat to alleviate some of the pressure on my back. "But it's not from them. Blogis funded it."

"What?"

"A little bit of the money was from my parents. The sale of their house and some stocks. But most of it came from Blogis. He set up the trust and most of the money was his. I guess it was guilt money."

"Guilt for what? Not saving their lives?"

"I don't know." An eighteen-wheeler roars past us, shaking the SUV in its wash. "I guess. Or maybe he was trying to minimize Sir Spencer's influence over me in the long run."

"So Blogis wasn't trying to kill us after all," she reasons. "Despite kidnapping me and holding me in a heavily guarded Russian Embassy."

I look over at her. She's sitting with her left side pressed against the seat back so she can face me. I reach over with my right hand and run the back of it along her cheek. "I guess he figured me for a badass."

"Hey!" she cups my hand with hers, holding it against her face. "Remember I rescued myself."

"You did."

"So where does this leave us?"

"I don't know."

***

The left side of the highway is awash in orange and pink as day breaks in Roanoke, Virginia. It's still the darkest part of the night to the right, the sunlight having yet to leak across the sky.

Bella's asleep, her arms folded across her chest and her head leaning on the window. She's snoring. It's a cute-sounding snort every few breaths.

"Hey," I nudge her as I slow to take an exit. "Time to get up."

Her eyes open as I pull into a gas station and stop parallel to a pump. She squints against the overhead canopy lighting and stretches.

I grab her credit card and hop out to fill up the tank. She rolls out of the passenger's side and sleepwalks into the convenience store.

The gas starts glugging into the SUV and a television screen on the pump illuminates with *GAS PUMP NEWS*.

A young, blonde anchorwoman does her best to earnestly present the top headlines in as few words as possible.

"*I'm Chelsea Stallings with your Gas Pump News. We're pumping out the day's top headlines while you fill your tank.*

"*Two suspected killers remain at large. Jackson Quick and Bella Buell were last seen leaving Brookhaven National Laboratory in Long Island, New York. The couple, already considered a modern day Bonnie and Clyde for the gang-style killing of a Texas television reporter, attacked security guards at the secure government-funded facility late last night. Nobody was killed, but investigators fear the couple may have stolen top-secret documents from the Nuclear Nonproliferation Research and Development lab. The couple is considered armed and dangerous and could be anywhere along the east coast of the United States this morning.*"

Great.

If Chelsea and her friends already have this information, then it's everywhere. Apparently everything we do resets the clock on the twenty-hour news cycle featuring the two of us.

The pump clicks off and I finish topping off the tank before locking the SUV and trudging toward the convenience store. My hands are in my pockets, protecting them from the morning chill.

The convenience store looks pretty typical. There are large poster advertisements for snack and drink combos covering the windows.

I notice they're running a special on fountain drinks and Frito-Lay products.

There's a single car parked at the curb which I'm guessing belongs to the cashier.

The same cashier standing behind the register with a shotgun aimed directly at Bella.

***

I'm reminded of the scene in the Coen Brothers classic film, *Raising Arizona*, where Nicholas Cage's character, ex-con H.I. McDunnough, tries to rob the Short Stop convenience store of a package of diapers and the cash in the register. The pimple-faced, paper-hatted teenager behind the counter pulls out a long barrel revolver and takes aim at Cage as he makes a run for it.

This, however, is not funny. Bella has her hands raised above her head, trying to talk the young, pimple-faced teen manning the register out of shooting her with his Remington.

He backs up a step and trains the twin barrels at me when I step into the store and the bell on the door chimes my entrance. He swings back to Bella, his eyes darting between the two of us.

"It's both of you!" he squeals with delight. Or fear. "It's Bonnie *and* Clyde. I knew it. I thought so when I saw you pull up at the pumps."

"Why don't you put down the gun," I suggest, pulling my hands from my pockets and raising them. "There's no need for the gun."

"Ha!" He's jittery, his feet moving like he's Payton Manning trying to avoid a sack. "Right! You two are killers. I'm calling the cops."

"That's fine," I tell him, inching slowly forward. "You call the cops. We get it, right Bella?"

She turns to look at me, her hands trembling above her head, "Right."

"Stop moving!" He points at me with the Remington. "Stay where you are!"

"Okay," I say in a low, non-confrontational tone. "I'm just moving to my girlfriend here."

"Stop!" he says again. "I'll shoot you!"

"You don't want to do that," I glance at the security camera monitor above his head on the wall. The surveillance system is capturing all of this.

His hands are starting to shake and he's unable to maintain a steady aim.

"Look," Bella says, "we're not going anywhere. You can call the cops. That's fine. Just don't shoot."

"Don't tell me what to do!" he snaps, sweat bubbling on his forehead and upper lip. "I'm gonna do what I need to do. You know there's a big reward. Dead or alive. Big reward." He sneers and snorts a weird sort of laugh.

"Here's the thing," I move closer to Bella, my hands above my head, "Bella here is not a willing accomplice."

"So?" The clerk has the gun on my chest, tracking my steps to Bella.

"She's a victim in this," I explain. "I kidnapped her and she's got no choice but to go along with what I tell her to do."

"I don't buy—" he starts, taking his eyes off of me for a split second.

It's long enough for me to dart behind Bella, pull the six-shooter from behind my back and put it to her head. She grabs at my left arm as I wrap it across her chest, pulling her back into me. It's a little rougher than I would have liked, but it adds to the effect.

Bella squeals, pleading with me not to shoot her.

The clerk gulps and licks his lips. "Wait a second!"

"I need you to put down the shotgun," I say, pushing Bella forward. "Put it on the counter and step back."

"I can't do that." He shakes his head. "I'm not gonna do that."

Slowly, deliberately I push Bella closer to the counter. The clerk still has the weapon pointed at us, but his hands are shaking violently.

"Yes you can." I pull back the hammer on the pistol and it makes an ominous clicking sound, letting the clerk know I mean business. The funny thing is, there's absolutely no need to pull the hammer back. It'll happen automatically when I pull the trigger. But it makes for a nice effect.

"I put down my gun and then you'll kill me," he says, his voice quivering.

"You *don't* put it down and I kill *her*." I push the barrel into the side of her head, burying the end of the front sight in her temple.

"Please," she pleads with the clerk. "He'll do it." Bella winces and struggles. She tugs at my arm, feigning an effort to free herself.

The clerk blinks against the beads of sweat dripping into his eyes. He swallows again and licks the dry white spittle from the corner of his mouth. His eyes are darting between Bella and me. He looks like a man whose head is about to explode from confusion.

"C'mon," I take another step toward the counter, careful not to move to quickly, "listen to her. Put the gun down."

The clerk's jaw tightens and his face reddens before he lets out a frustrated grunt and slams the gun onto the counter. He shoves it forward and takes a step back.

I let go of Bella and she grabs the shotgun from the counter. She pulls it to her shoulder and levels it at the clerk. The color evaporates from his face when he realizes what he's done, how we've played him.

"Sit down," Bella orders, and she moves around the counter, the barrels trained on the clerk. "Where's your cell phone?"

He points to the counter and I take the phone, slipping it into my pocket. Behind the counter, next to the condoms and headache medicine, is a wall-mounted phone. I step over and rip it out.

"What do we do with him?" Bella asks. "If we leave him here, he calls the cops."

"Please!" He clasps his hands in prayer, "Don't kill me. Please."

"Have him disconnect the security system and give you the hard drive or the tapes, whichever they're using to record," I tell her. "We can't leave that here."

"And him?" Bella directs the clerk to his feet and he slowly leads her to the DVR where the security video is stored. "What do we do with him?"

"Car keys?" I ask.

"In my pocket," says the clerk, fishing them out and handing them to Bella.

"Keys to the store?"

"On the same ring."

"Any other keys?"

"Just the night manager," says the clerk. "He's not here until six o'clock."

"That gives us some time," Bella says. "Close to twelve hours."

"Okay," I nod. "Here's the deal," I explain. "We're locking you in here. You're not going anywhere until your night manager gets here. And by then, we'll be in Chicago."

Bella directs the clerk to a utility closet in the back of the store. She flips on the light and guides him inside. Apologizing for the inconvenience, she shuts the door and locks him inside.

I find the main electrical box for the store and flip off the main switch. The store goes dark.

Bella follows me outside. We lock the double doors and I jog over to the clerk's car to leave his keys on the front seat.

Bella tosses the shotgun into the trunk and we lock his car. No need to ruin his day any more than we have already. It's just before six-thirty in the morning and we have a full tank of gas.

We should hit Houston by midnight.

CHAPTER 17

I remember my first day working for the governor. It was intimidating and exhilarating at the same time. He invited me into his Capitol office. Just him and me.

"So," he said, chewing on the temple tip of his reading glasses, "tell me a little bit about yourself, Jackson Quick."

The room was comfortable but not overly indulgent. The walls were covered in a pale yellow wallpaper, the wood planked floors hidden with a large blue rug embroidered with the seal of the state of Texas in its center. We were seated at a cherry conference table, the governor seated at one end, and I was next to him, trying to sit up straight in a plush blue chair.

"What would you like to know?" I asked, willing to tell him anything. "Professional or personal?"

"I know the professional resume. Shoot, Jackson, everyone in the office knows about your hopscotch of a professional background. You haven't been much for keeping jobs long."

"No sir," I said. "I just haven't found the right thing."

"It's not a question of loyalty is it?" He tilted his head as if he knew the answer but wanted to gauge my response. "Loyalty is an important commodity, Jackson."

"I agree. And no sir, it wasn't a lack of loyalty. Rather, if I'm not passionate about something, I've found it difficult to give the kind of effort required."

A smile wormed across his face, accentuating the laugh lines around his mouth and eyes. He nodded and offered me a cup of coffee.

"Thank you."

The governor stood and walked over to a credenza opposite the wall of windows overlooking the Capitol grounds. He popped in a single-serve pod and slid a mug under the machine, whistling a non-descript tune while it brewed. A minute later he returned with the coffee.

"Here you go." He placed the blue mug in front of me. "So tell me some of the personal, Jackson. Are you single?"

"Yes," I nodded, admiring the design of the mug. On its front was a geometric shape of some kind. Above it were the words, *Richard B. Smalley Institute for Nanoscale Science and Technology*. At the time, I had no idea what that meant. "I haven't had a girlfriend for a while. I've been too busy working on myself."

"Those sound like therapy words," he said, his eyebrows rising, "No worries," he said. "I've been there."

I didn't know what to say and pulled the coffee mug to my lips.

"Abraham Maslow said, '*Therapy is a search for value.*' Are you searching for value, Jackson?"

I shrugged. "Everyone is always searching for their value. Whether it's real or perceived, we all want to be valued."

"True," he nodded. "That's pretty self-aware for a man who hasn't found his calling. Why were you seeing a therapist?"

"Well," I bought a couple of seconds with another sip of bitter coffee. "It wasn't a search for value, really."

"Hmmm," he sat back in his chair, again measuring me. "You know Abraham Maslow?"

"Not really," I admitted. I'd never heard of him. "Should I?"

"Not necessarily," said the governor. "He was a psychologist who was known for developing what he called The Hierarchy of Needs."

"Which was?"

"Maslow wanted to know what motivated people beyond simple rewards or unconscious desires."

He slipped on his glasses and walked to the coffee maker to brew his own cup of coffee, then turned back toward me, peering over the glasses.

"He said that people are motivated to achieve certain needs and as they meet each need they move to the next, and the next, and the next."

"Simple needs come first?" I ask. "Followed by those which are more complex?"

"Exactly," he said, raising the cup of coffee while walking back to his seat. "The highest of those needs is self-realization. Of course, most people never achieve it. They're too consumed with lower level needs; air, food, sleep, and sex."

"I'd never thought of it like that, but it makes sense."

"Of course it does," he looked over the rim of his glasses. "It's an enlightened few who achieve the higher level of self-awareness, moving past the need for dominance, prestige, and status."

"May I ask you a question, Governor?"

"Of course." He sipped from his cup and crossed one leg over the other.

"What level are you?"

"What level do you think I've achieved, Jackson?" He adjusted his cup on the table and thumbed a drop of coffee from its rim.

"I would have thought you'd achieved the highest level until you asked that question."

His eyes narrowed and he tugged on the lapel of his suit jacket, adjusting himself in the chair. With his lips pressed together he licked the front of his teeth. He said nothing, pushing me to elaborate.

"I mean, if you had achieved the highest level of self-awareness you would not care what I think of you. You'd have moved past the desire for respect."

He scratched his nose, considering my reasoning. He removed his glasses, folded them and put them in his breast pocket.

"Interesting you think that, Jackson," he said, tilting his head like a curious dog. "But you're wrong. Just because I asked what you think doesn't mean I care about what you think. And that, perhaps, is the best first day lesson I could hope to offer."

I pulled the mug to my face, hoping to shield my embarrassment. "I'll remember that."

"Good. Then we'll get along just fine."

"Yes sir."

"Before you go," he said, hinting our meeting was over, "why Quick?"

"Sir?"

"Your real name is Ellsworth. Why did you change it to Quick?"

"A boarding school teacher."

"Yes?"

"I was a challenging kid. I had a teacher at boarding school who told me my middle name should be Quick because I was *quick* to answer without consideration, *quick* to act without thinking, *quick* to anger without contemplation, *quick* to judgment without acceptance."

"When did you change it?"

"When I started my job in television. I wanted to start fresh. New name, new approach, new life."

"That smacks of self-awareness," laughed the governor. "Now get to work. We have a lot going on with the election just around the corner."

I stood from the table, shook his hand, and went to work, excited by the prestige, anxious to please, blinded by power, completely unaware of the Faustian deal I'd just entered and that I'd been destined to shake on it from the moment my mother fell in love with my father.

***

The Astrodome is the perfect place to end this journey. It's an enclosed space with clear lines of sight. Mack suggested it when we discussed how to set up the exchange with Blogis and Sir Spencer. He also employed the help of some friends to make sure everything was prepared to the specifications we'd discussed.

With his security connections, he gained access to the closed arena to do the needed advance work. We'll be able to control the environment and if things go bad, we'll have an escape that won't put innocent people at risk.

I'd have preferred an open air, public place. Bella suggested Discovery Green or Memorial Park. But with the non-stop news coverage and our faces plastered everywhere, there's no way we could get away with it.

We're lucky enough to have made it back to Houston without an alert cop between Virginia and Texas spotting us and putting an end to everything.

Mack and Bella think the plan is good. It's solid. It'll work. I'm having my doubts and with what I've learned about Liho Blogis, I'm not sure our plan is what it should be. He was loyal to my parents. He tried to save them. He helped me without ever trying to take credit for it. And he killed the governor. Half of me wants to alert him, confess what we have in store and enlist his help. Together we could surely rid ourselves of Sir Spencer.

"You can't change the plan," Bella advises. We're in the SUV in the hotel parking lot across from NRG Park, the property that houses the Dome, NRG Stadium, and NRG Arena. "Just because you think he was always on your side, doesn't change the fact that he wants to sell the process to bad guys. It doesn't change all of the other things you read in that file Mack gave you."

"You're right."

He has long affiliated with enemies of the state. After his fall-out with Sir Spencer, Blogis fled to the Soviet Union seeking refuge behind the curtain before it fell.

The hardliners, those not close to Gorbachev, accepted him with open arms.

He was there, and well connected, when the Russian mob filled the economic, social, and power vacuum the Kremlin couldn't control. He, former KGB agents, and military leaders were more than happy to provide support to organized crime.

More than one hundred different cartels dealing in everything from faulty airplane parts to illicit drugs and money laundering took control of the black market in Eastern Europe. That influence spread west and soon enough those cartels became the greatest security threat to the United States and its allies.

Wikileaks revealed the close connection between the mafia and the government in 2013. Blogis was a key go-between, often coordinating the dirty work. He organized a gunrunning operation to help the Kurds destabilize Turkey. His connections provided the weapons used in the hijacking of the Arctic Sea cargo ship in 2009.

In the file, there were photographs of Blogis horseback riding with Vladimir Putin and toasting shots of vodka with Semion Mogilevich. Mogilevich is the man the FBI called the most dangerous mobster in the world. He's Ukrainian-born, ruthless, and closely tied to GazProm, the enormous state-owned Russian energy company. Bella thinks that's where the process will go. She's convinced he'll insist on having the process, regardless of a confession on my part. She thinks he'll forego any allegiance he has to me and save his own skin. His backers, after all, have given him a lot of money and resources to deliver the process. He's as desperate as we are.

I can't overlook that, no matter how much I want to soften. No matter what the file says he's done for me, I can't change course.

Blogis is not a good man.

I pull out my burner phone and text Blogis a message with the meeting information.

in ten hours. n 29 41 5.6868, w 95 24 27.5142

entrance 2. ask for brad

Bella texts Sir Spencer at the same time.

in ten hours. n 29 41 5.5858, w 95 24 27.5142

entrance 9. ask for vince.

The trap is set. We have the bait. Hopefully they bite.

***

Waiting is the hardest part.

Another bead of sweat rolls onto my upper lip. I wipe it with the back of my hand and then run my damp hand through my hair. Bella tugs on the front of her shirt to fan herself.

It's ten o'clock at night. It's dark and humid inside the Dome, which for years has lacked air conditioning. Given our perch high within the decrepit stands, the heat is worse than it would be on the floor.

"Blogis is at entrance two. Over, " Mack whispers into my earpiece.

"And Sir Spencer?"

"There's a vehicle approaching entrance nine," he responds. "We're good to go. Over."

Mack has men stationed at doors on either side of the dome. One of them will escort Blogis to the floor, and another will escort Sir Spencer.

"Are you ready for this?" Bella whispers to me, her hand on my leg. We're crouched beneath a row of seats high above the third base line.

"As ready as I'm going to be. You?"

"I'm ready to move on with our lives," she says.

"Me too."

The plan is to get both men on the floor of the dome. They'll be unarmed and essentially without help.

They'll be confused and probably angry, given that both of them thought this was a simple handover.

Each of them will receive an iPod containing the process. I'll instruct them how to access it, giving both of them the same coded password.

I'll tell them the papers containing the process were destroyed. The only copies which exist are those on the devices in their hands.

What they don't know is that the password is also an activator. The second time it's entered, it engages a tiny explosive placed inside the iPod.

PETN is Pentaerythritol tetranitrate, a primary component of SEMTEX, the explosive used to bring down Pan-Am flight 103 in 1988 and is one of the most lethal package explosives available. It's also used as a treatment for angina, so it's not difficult to acquire.

It was Mack's suggestion we use PETN as our way out. He wanted to implode the Dome. I thought that was a bit excessive.

The iPod was my idea. Poetic in some small way. It was the iPods I delivered around the globe on behalf of the governor that cemented my involvement with Sir Spencer, my leap into the rabbit hole.

Mack, an explosives expert, wrapped the PETN inside the iPods. The explosions would be violent and potentially lethal but unlikely to harm innocent bystanders.

Both men would die or be maimed, and neither could affect our lives or the security of our country ever again.

"Blogis is entering the Dome. Over," Mack says. He's in what used to be an office on the main concourse. Inside the room, he's installed security surveillance at key points. He'll also work the other necessary electronics as the night unfolds.

"Sir Spencer is still in the vehicle," Mack reports. "He's through the gate and outside the door. Over."

"What's the hold up?" Bella asks, pressing a button to key her mic so Mack can hear her.

"I don't know," he responds. "There's no movement. Windows are tinted. Blogis is on the move though. He's to the floor. Over."

"Key the light when he's there," I instruct.

"Even without Sir Spencer? Over."

"Yes."

Far below us, on the floor of the Dome, there's the sound of people approaching from a tunnel. Two of them should be Mack's mercenaries, their heavy boots echoing against the concrete, beams from their flashlights dancing across the rolled pieces of Astroturf partially covering the floor.

"Hello?" calls a familiar voice and, on cue, on pops a blinding white spotlight, focusing on Liho Blogis. He instinctively covers his eyes with his forearm.

"What is this?" he calls out. "Jackson? What are you doing?"

I resist the urge to answer as the two armed, booted thugs push Liho to the center of the floor. He trips on piece of turf, and one of them catches him.

"I don't get this. I was under the impression this was a simple exchange. I lived up to my end of the bargain!" Blogis's eyes are squeezed to slits, his hands trying to block some of the intense light. He spins around, searching for me in the stands. There's something pitiful about him, a bewilderment that makes me sympathetic.

Maybe this is not the right move. Maybe I should let Blogis off the hook.

"I can tell what you're thinking, Jackson," says Bella. "I can see it on your face, even in the dark. Don't trust him. I don't care what he's done for you or what he says. Stay strong."

"Jackson," says Mack, "we've got a problem. It's a big one. Over."

***

"What do you mean he's not here?" Bella asks Mack. "I thought you said he was in his vehicle."

"We never put eyes on him," says Mack. "The only people in the vehicle are the driver and a woman in a black hoodie. Over."

Corkscrew?

"What is she saying?"

"She wants in," he answers. "Says Sir Spencer sent her here to pick up what's his."

"Let her in."

"This changes things," Bella says. "Are you going to give the iPod to her?"

"I don't know. We'll let it play out before I decide."

This isn't good. Already, it seems we've lost control. That's assuming we ever had any semblance of it in the first place. Sir Spencer, as always, is playing us.

He knew this was a set up.

"If Sir Spencer was smart enough not to come," Bella asks, "why did Blogis? He had to know something was up."

"Maybe he trusted me."

Blogis stops searching when he hears Corkscrew and her handlers entering the Dome's floor, emerging from the tunnel. A light blasts onto her from the opposite side. She mimics Blogis in an attempt to shield her blinded eyes.

"Who are you?" she asks Blogis. "What are you doing here?"

"Who am I?" he laughs. "Who are you?"

"I'm repping Sir Spencer."

Instead of responding to the green-haired hacker next to him, Blogis again searches the stadium seats. "Jackson! What are you doing?"

"Play it now," I tell Mack and he initiates an audio file I recorded hours ago. It blares over loudspeakers.

"*This is where it ends,*" says my recorded voice. "*This is where we go our separate ways.*"

Corkscrew is sitting on the floor, cross-legged, leaning back on her hands. Her hoodie is pulled low over her eyes to block the light. She seems bored by the theatrics. Blogis is fidgety and uncomfortable.

"*I am about to provide you both with the only available copies of the process,*" the recording booms. "*The paper retrieved from Brookhaven is destroyed. No other known copies exist. I am not keeping one for myself.*"

"This is not right!" Blogis yells. "You're making a mistake, Jackson!"

Corkscrew laughs.

"In a moment, you'll be handed your copy of the process. I will inform you how to access it. Then you are free to go, to do with the process what you choose."

Blogis starts to move toward the railing that separates the floor from what's left of the stands. Mack's thugs stop him and move him back into the light.

"Mack," I whisper into my mic, "sync my mic with the speaker."

After a second he says, "You're live. Over."

"Corkscrew, where is Sir Spencer?" I ask.

Without moving from her relaxed position on the floor, she answers, "He knew about the set up so he declined your invitation. I'm here instead."

"How did he know?" I ask, my voice reverberating across the expanse of the Dome.

"You may be decent at getting yourself out of a jam, but you're just as good as getting yourself into one. I was tracking your phone. I was listening to your conversations through On Star. Remember? I hacked it."

"And you passed along the information to Sir Spencer?"

"Of course I did," she chuckles. "He's my paycheck, not you. My loyalty lies with the old dude. He knew you were playing both sides and you were trying to pit him against Blogis. I guess this freak over here is Blogis."

He clenches his fists, the anger boiling over. He's pacing now, probably considering his options. He knows he's lost control, whether it's me running the show or Sir Spencer. I'm certain he knows it's not him.

"You're not getting your copy," I tell Corkscrew, "until Sir Spencer shows up. Bottom line."

"Not gonna happen. At least, not on your terms."

"This is deteriorating quickly, Jackson," Bella points out. "What are you—"

"Now!" Blogis orders and the thugs training their weapons on him, aim them into the stands. The Dome explodes with the sound of semiautomatic gunfire. Their first targets are the high-intensity spotlights, which shatter and spark.

In the last bit of light before the spots go dark, Blogis is standing over Corkscrew and she's screaming for her life.

The gunfire stops, its reports echoing against the domed walls and concrete floors, and we're plunged into darkness.

**

This would have been a good time for the night vision goggles that saved my life more than once. With the lights out, I've no idea where Blogis and his newly employed henchmen are.

Their heavy boots give me a vague location, but the acoustics in the Dome make it impossible to pinpoint where exactly they are. Bella's holding my hand as we move higher into the stands toward the highest row. Our hands are slippery, but our grip is inseparable. Crouched low we stop near center field, second row from the top.

"Jackson, this isn't how you saw it playing out is it?" Blogis taunts. "You truly thought you could outsmart both Sir Spencer and me in one ill-conceived swoop? Wow."

His voice sounds as though it's coming from the floor. He hasn't moved from his initial spot, as best I can tell, though I can hear the thugs pushing their way through the stands. There are four of them, if I remember correctly. From their movements, I'm guessing two are about halfway up the first base line and the other two are opposite them along third base.

"Jackson," it's Mack in my ear, "there's another vehicle approaching. Over."

"What happened to your guys, Mack?" I whisper, pushing the mic as close to my mouth as possible. "They turned on us."

"I don't know," Mack admits. "I don't know how they have any connection to Blogis."

"How many did you hire?"

"Six."

"Do you have their locations?" I whisper.

"No, they're all inside now. Someone is getting out of the vehicle at the entra—"

The line buzzes and goes silent.

"Mack?"

Nothing.

"Mack?"

Bella squeezes my hand. She's hearing the same thing I'm hearing.

"Pull your weapon, Bella. You take the left. I'll handle the right."

At least two of the thugs are getting close to us along the first base side, Bella's side.

"What I don't get," Blogis says, "is what made you think you were smart enough to do this? Why would we willingly, and without question, come to the Astrodome unarmed and let you control the situation?

"The thing I pity most in you is also that which I most admire, Jackson. Do you know what that is?"

Bella's holding the nine millimeter we've carried for months. I've got the Kel-Tec PMR 30 in my hand and the six-shooter, loaded with shotshell, in my waistband. I tighten my grip on the Kel-Tec. The thugs on the third base side are getting close. It sounds as if one of them tripped and fell over a seat back.

We're getting squeezed.

"It's your inability to understand how out of your league you are at every turn," Blogis says. "From that first iPod delivery, you were drowning. And yet, here you are with your head above the water. The waves keep coming and coming. You refuse to see them, to understand their power."

Bella and I slide up to the last row of seats and shift toward third base. It'll buy a few extra seconds maybe.

"You keep thinking your one and only marketable skill, firing a weapon straight, is enough to succeed in this game." He laughs. "It's not."

To my right is the outline of a thug. His shoulders and head appear at just the right height and I extend my arm, leveling the Kel-Tec.

"I've got one on my side," Bella whispers.

"Count to three and then go," I reply, my mouth as close to her ear as I can get.

Pop! Pop! Pop! Pop! Pop! Pop!

My first shot finds the thug's head. In the flash from the gunfire, he drops and knocks over a second thug. I track him and two slugs find their way into his body before the echo of the trigger pulls stop reverberating.

I turn to help Bella, but she's already taken out both of her marks. She moves to the two bodies slumped over each other two rows beneath us and just ten yards to our left.

Pop! Pop! She fires one shot into each of them, finishing the job.

I love her.

Following her lead, I move to the heap on my side and fire two more rounds, as a faint yellow light shines through the translucent roof tiles atop the Dome. The clouds have moved past the moon.

Blogis is standing atop of a pile of turf, hands on his hips, staring up at us. Next to him, cross-legged and green-haired is Corkscrew. And walking in from a tunnel opposite us, dressed in a dark suit and hat, is Sir Spencer. His cane clicks against the concrete flooring with each step toward the center of the arena. One of the two remaining henchmen is walking with him.

Blogis steps from his perch and approaches Sir Spencer with open arms. The two of them hug, patting each other on the back like men do, and Blogis leads his mentor back to the hacker.

They're talking, Blogis' hands gesticulating and pointing. Their voices are murmurs at this distance.

"So," Sir Spencer turns toward us, stepping past Blogis and Corkscrew, raising his voice, "this is how you repay me, Jackson? You planned to pit me against Liho, here?"

I grip the Kel-Tec, squeezing it until my knuckles turn white. It's taking everything in me not to aim it at his head and fire. I know at this distance, even with my skill, there's no way I'd hit him.

"It's so disappointing," he says, shaking his head like a stage actor. "To think you would betray both of us. I always thought more of you than that." He takes another deliberate step toward center field.

"And here's what I find so humorous. Liho and I are working together. We always have been. From the beginning. And you never figured it out."

***

Sir Spencer is standing at the edge of the stands. He's leaning on the railing, his fedora tipped back. His necktie is loosened at his thick neck and his three-buttoned suit jacket is open, his heft protruding over his waistline. Even in the dim light, it's apparent he's tired.

"I'm assuming you've read the files, heard the recordings I made available to Mack," he snickers. "I wanted him to find them and give them to you. I wanted you to know who killed your parents. I was hoping you'd have second thoughts about Blogis. I was expecting you'd make a deal with one of us. You exceeded my expectations, I have to say, when you tried to play both sides."

Bella takes my hand, locking her fingers in mine. She's holding the nine millimeter with her left hand.

"Liho was never my enemy, Jackson. He was in love with your mother and refused to kill your parents when I asked. I wasn't pleased, but he was loyal. When he found a home with the Soviets, we opened an entirely new market together. I like to call it *diversification of assets*."

Sir Spencer pulls a red handkerchief from his pockets and dabs his brow. He wipes his upper lip and stuffs the silk into his pants pocket.

"So then," he exhales, "suffice it to say we were searching for the process together. But we needed some way to engage Bella. We needed her insight. We weren't going to get that without a handsome young gunslinger to squire her about the globe."

"Why me?" I yell. My question is asked over again, bouncing off the walls of the Dome. Bella's fingers tighten against mine. I'm sure she didn't like Sir Spencer's misogynist characterization of her.

"Why you?" He laughs and wipes the edges of his mouth with his thumb and forefinger. "You were destined for this, Jackson. We'd hoped to train you. We expected to have the chance to groom you and make you the asset your father always knew you could be. But you went rogue, as it were."

"Rogue?"

"You turned on the governor," he snaps. "You sent him to prison. Despite that, I offered you a role in the organization. You declined. Thankfully, I had a way to keep abreast of your whereabouts." He taps his knee with his cane. "And the governor, not one for bygones, repeatedly flushed you from hiding."

"This is getting old," Blogis calls. "Let's get on with this. Where is the process?"

"In a moment," Sir Spencer says to Blogis. "I'm quite enjoying the conversation."

"Fine," Blogis grumps. "Just hurry up."

"So here we are," Sir Spencer says. "You, not having had the necessary schooling, are falling short of said goal. Whatever that goal was, Jackson, it's obvious now, you aren't achieving it."

"You lose," adds Blogis. "Now where is the process?"

"I have it!" yells Mack from across the Dome as he takes a single shot, hitting the thug on the floor with the LAR-15 rifle Ripley gave to me. The thug, standing next to Blogis, tumbles to the ground, his neck snapping back from the expertly fired bullet driving through it.

Corkscrew screams when the thug's arm drapes across her, his semiautomatic rifle rattling on the concrete floor.

***

Our plan is still alive. Despite the surprises and Sir Spencer's *Goldfinger* speech, it can work. Regardless of my apparent idiocy, we still have a chance to pull it off. We just have to get the iPods into their hands without dying.

"Mack, bring them the process. Give each of them a copy." I wave the gun at Blogis and Corkscrew. "You two: move away from the weapon."

Blogis raises his hands and backs away from the thug's rifle. Corkscrew scoots out from underneath the arms of the dead man and scrambles to her feet. She backs up away from the weapon, the body, and Blogis.

I pull Bella down the steps with me, toward Sir Spencer. He's backed a step away from the railing, leaning on his cane. He pulls out his handkerchief and swipes at his face, not careful this time to maintain the pressed shape of the pocket square.

"You'll get what you came for," I tell him, the Kel-Tec aimed at his chest. "Move over to Blogis."

Sir Spencer turns and walks to the middle of the floor, stepping over the ripped, stained piles of turf littering the concrete. Bella and I are ten yards behind him, both of us with our guns drawn.

Mack limps down the steps. I thought from across the arena, I saw blood spatter on his white shirt. I thought he was shot. Now closer to us, it's evident it's not his blood. Now I know what happened to the fourth thug. His limp is from his prosthetic, which looks damaged near the ankle. He's carrying the rifle at his hip, aiming it toward Sir Spencer and Blogis. He waves it toward Corkscrew, instructing her to join the others.

"We have two copies of the process," I say. "Each one is loaded onto an iPod. You'll find it under Photos."

"How clever," Sir Spencer says wryly. "Bringing it full circle, are we?"

Ignoring him, I say, "Corkscrew, I need you to walk slowly to Mack. He will hand you both iPods. Then you will walk them back to these gentlemen."

With her hands up and her hoodie down, Corkscrew walks to Mack. She keeps glancing over at me, as if I'm going to shoot her while she's not looking. Maintaining his aim with the rifle against his hip, Mack tugs the iPods from his pocket. He tosses them, one at a time, to Corkscrew. She catches them against her sweatshirt and retreats without turning around.

"This is a bit ridiculous, isn't it?" Blogis chides. "The Astrodome, the spotlights, the iPods. Did you get this from a Jerry Bruckheimer screenplay?"

Corkscrew hands the first iPod to Blogis. She starts to hand off the second to Sir Spencer and he stops her.

"No thank you," he waves her off. "Corkscrew, you handle the duties. You are the computer expert, after all."

Bella shoots me a look, which I ignore. "Press the home key and then enter the following numeric code."

"You know," Blogis says to Mack, palming the iPod with one hand, "your guys were pretty cheap. It didn't take much for Sir Spencer here to pay them a few bucks more. You really should look into F. Pickle. Far superior."

"I don't agree with that," I say, and recite the passcode.

Blogis and Corkscrew tap in each number as I say it. Their faces illuminate with the brightness of the screens. They tap their way to the Photos application.

"Does it appear legitimate, Liho?" Sir Spencer leans in to look over Corkscrew's shoulder.

"As far as I can tell, but it will take verification."

"This came straight from Brookhaven," I say. "No alterations."

"Why would you give it to us now?" Sir Spencer takes a cane-assisted step toward me. "After 'all of this' as Liho would put it, I'm unclear why you're just handing over the real process."

"I told you before: I want out. That's all I ever wanted. I played the odds with the two of you and lost. Ultimately, I don't care what you do with it."

"You have no choice about what we do with this," Blogis says, suddenly empowered by the information on the iPod.

"We don't care," Bella says. "We're disappearing after you leave. We're ghosts."

"Good luck with that, dear," Sir Spencer says. "The two of you have never stayed hidden for long. Someone will find you."

"Time for you to go," I wave my Kel-Tec at the exit. "All three of you. Mack, take them with you."

Mack waits for the three of them to pass and then follows them toward the exit tunnel. Bella and I stay behind.

Blogis turns around, walking backward. "This isn't over. I don't like someone trying to play me. I'll find you."

"Come, Liho," says Sir Spencer, "we have buyers with whom to meet. The vodka is getting warm."

They disappear into the darkness of the tunnel. Mack trails behind them, limping but armed.

"Well that was anticlimactic," Bella says. "All of that, and they just walk away."

"They won't make it out of the parking lot. They'll enter the passcode again."

"You think?"

"What would you do? As soon as you get in the car, you'd check it out again."

"Maybe," she concedes. "This didn't go as we planned."

"Nothing ever does," I say. "But we're still here."

***

The explosions happened within seconds of each other. There's no way to know if they were logging onto both iPods at the same time, or if the primary explosion triggered the PETN in the second iPod.

They felt like twin sonic booms from inside the Dome. We'd made our way to their exit, careful to stay back. Mack was on his way back when the blast forced him all the way inside. We helped him up and stepped back outside into the parking lot. Twenty yards from us, a Cadillac Escalade is on fire. The front passenger door is open, and a body is hanging from it.

The front cabin is engulfed in flames; the rest of it filled the thick black smoke pouring from broken windows. There are shards of glass everywhere. There are other indescribable pieces of things smoldering on the asphalt.

With my weapon drawn, I slowly approach the passenger side. When I walk around to the front of the open door, it's obvious the body hanging from the SUV belongs to Liho Blogis. His eyes are open, his mouth agape. Not much else is recognizable. I only know it's him because of the clothing.

There's a driver slumped against his door. I don't recognize him. He's a bigger guy, thick neck, bald head. He's dead too.

The smoke is so thick it's hard for me to see much else. I have to imagine there are people in the back seat, but I can't tell.

"We need to go," Mack says. "Security will be on us soon. My guys at the gate are gone. I'll get the truck."

"Are they all dead?" Bella asks after Mack disappears around the corner.

"I'm pretty sure," I cough, trying to clear the smoke from my throat. "I can't see in the back seat. I know Blogis is dead."

Bella throws her arms around me and buries her head in my chest. There's no sobbing, no laughing, just a suffocating embrace. I place one hand on her head, the other around her back.

Maybe we're finally free. Free.

Mack pulls up in a nondescript Ford F-150. Bella and I climb in and Mack pulls away, barreling through an exit as security descends upon the Escalade. Mack turns left onto Kirby Drive and hits the 610 Loop. He heads toward downtown, and from the rear passenger's seat, looking to the left, I can see the emergency vehicles surrounding the dome.

"What a horrible way to die," Bella says.

"They probably never knew what hit them," I say.

"Where to?" Mack asks.

"We have tickets on Amtrak," I tell him. "They're prepaid with fake names and identification. Sleeping cabin. Once we're on board, nobody has to see us. More private than a bus or a plane."

"Where are you headed?" Mack looks at Bella. "Or is that a secret?"

"We can't tell you, Mack," she says. "It's better if you don't know."

"Plausible deniability," he nods. "I get it."

"There's money in an account for you," I reach out and grab his shoulder. "It's plenty for you to find a hiding place too."

"Beaches," he laughs, "without extradition. That's where I'll be headed. I've got a flight booked already and will be long gone before anyone connects me to any of this."

Mack takes an exit to downtown and slows for a light when my phone rings.

"It's an unknown number," I hold the burner up for Bella to see it. Then I answer the call.

"Yes?"

"Jackson Quick, you are full of surprises." The caller laughs a familiar laugh. "Was it SEMTEX? A plastic explosive? How did you trigger it, good man?"

Sir Spencer's alive.

"You thought I was dead too?" He laughs again. "Oh, please. I didn't get in that car. I knew something was wrong with those iPods. If I know you, and sometimes I question if I do, your intractable moral compass would never point you in the direction of betraying your convictions."

"If you knew, then why did you let me leave? Why didn't you fight?"

"Oh Jackson," he sighs, "if there's one thing I've learned it's when to cut ones losses."

"Where are you?"

"On my way to Washington D.C.," he answers. "I have a driver taking me to the airport. I have a meeting regarding some disagreements I have with the current administration. President Dexter Foreman is leading us down the wrong path, don't you think?"

"You know Blogis is dead."

"I assumed," he says. "Corkscrew too. She had the other iPad. I told her to run diagnostics on it for me."

"You knew they were rigged to explode?"

"No, I knew something was wrong, though. It's a shame about poor Liho. He did love your mother and, in his own sick way, had a soft spot for you."

"Sure."

"That said, good man, I wish you the best of luck."

"So what's next?" I ask. "What do you want from me?"

"That's up to you, Jackson. As I mentioned, I know when to move along. If there's no process anymore, there's nothing I can do about it now."

"Seriously?"

"Trust me or don't. I've much bigger fish to fry. New World Order and such."

"So that's it?" I don't buy it.

"That's it," he pauses and then laughs in a way that raises the hair on my neck and produces goose bumps my arms. "Until it's not." And he hangs up.

That's it. *Until it's not.*

EPILOGUE
AFTER IMAGE

"The end is the beginning of all things."
—Jiddu Krishnamurti

The scent of lavender fills our cozy room above the best pizza restaurant on the islands. There are bouquets of the purple flowers dotting our efficiency apartment. A grouping of dried stems hangs from the back of the front door, there's a trio of fresh cut bunches in glass vases on the wood plank coffee table, and a fourth sits on a side table next to our slip-covered love seat. There's not room for a sofa, and we like the lack of space between us on the cool nights that fill eight months of the year.

We are curled up on the loveseat, an alpaca blanket draped over us, and Bella is cheering on the Seahawks. They're beating the 49ers by ten with about five minutes to go.

She grumbles at a Kaepernick third down conversion and I kiss her on the forehead. She rubs my thigh with her hand. This is our life now.

Bella, with her strawberry blonde pixie cut, makes weekly trips to a nearby lavender farm to cut the bouquets herself. She also buys the oils, soaps, and incense they sell at the farm. Those replace the flowers when it's too cold on the island for the flowers to bloom.

San Juan Island is accessible only by ferry and an hour ride from Anacortes or two hours from Seattle.

Nobody here knows our real names. To them, we're Quentin and Frannie Besson, a young married couple who telecommute and stay to ourselves. Both of us have done what we could to make ourselves less recognizable. Aside from drastically different haircuts, or lack of one in my case, I've added twenty pounds of muscle. It's changed my facial structure, making my eyes and mouth appear larger. I've also grown a beard. Bella sometimes refers to me as Grizzly Adams. I joke with her I'm surprised she knows who he was and tell her I prefer the Brawny paper towel guy as a comparison.

The guys at the pizza place know us. The owners of the lavender farm know Bella. They even offered her a part time job. She thought about it but declined.

I occasionally clean charter boats for a company that takes tourists out for whale watching excursions. It keeps me busy, gives me purpose beyond Bella, and helps provide a sense of normalcy.

We've been here for more than two years, slowly building our lives. We're as happy as is possible for two people who survived what we have. There's too much pain underneath the surface for us to be blissful. But it's close. We trust each other. We love each other. We've convinced ourselves that's enough in this Spartan existence of ours. Though we both go a little stir crazy sometimes.

She's been reading Jack Reacher and Mitch Rapp novels by the truckload. We've watched the Bourne Identity at least fifty times. I've tried my hand at writing an action adventure novel. It's not going well.

"You want a calzone?" she asks. "They close in an hour."

"Sure," I scratch my beard and grab my cell phone. I text Willie, the owner of the restaurant downstairs, and tell him I'll be down in a half hour to pick up our usual. He's one of three people on the island who has my number. The charter captain and Bella are the others.

He texts back immediately, telling me it'll be ready. Then he texts again.

somebody is here 2 see u.

I pull the screen closer to my face and reread the short message.

SOMEBODY. IS. HERE. TO. SEE. YOU.

"Calzone will be ready in a minute," I tell Bella, putting the phone on the side table next to the lavender. "Not sure I should get it, though."

"Why?" Her eyes are on the TV. She's probably half listening to me as San Francisco moves inside the Seahawk twenty yard line.

"Never mind," I say and pick up my phone to text Willie.

who is it?
i don't know. said he's looking for quentin. said it's important.
what's he look like?
tall. thin. short hair. dark skin. big smile.
did u tell him u know me?
uh. yeah. why?
no reason. i just don't know who he is.
want me to get a name?
no.
k. calzone going in oven now.
did u tell him where i live? Please say no.
no.
k. be down in a minute.

"Where are you going?" Bella's eyes are still on the television. It's 4th and five from the seven yard line. San Francisco's going for it. "The game's not over!"

She jumps up when Seattle stuffs a naked bootleg short of the first down. "Yes!" she points at the screen and pumps her fist. She's become quite a football fan with not a lot else to do.

"Did you see that?" Strands of her bangs fall across her eyes. I still can't get used to her blonde hair or the severity of the cut. She looks great. But sometimes she doesn't seem like Bella.

"Yes, But I gotta go to the bathroom before I get the food."

"Okay?!?" She looks at me as though I've got a third eye, then plops back down on the loveseat. She pulls the blanket over her legs. "I'll be waiting right here for you, sexy Q."

Sexy Q. Her endearing new nickname for me. Or *Grizzly Adams.*

I fake a laugh and walk to the bathroom as nonchalantly as possible. I close and lock the door behind me. Aside from the closet and the space behind the pony wall that separates our double bed from the rest of the apartment, the bathroom is the most private place in our apartment.

I get on my knees and run my hands along the edge of the wall behind the toilet until I feel a ridge. I dig my fingers behind the ridge and tug, revealing an opening for plumbing access. Just inside is a blue lock box. Somehow, despite all our misadventures, I managed to hold on to my sole belonging from childhood.

Elbow deep, I blindly grab for a large plastic bag and drag it through the opening and onto the bathroom floor.

In the clear, gallon-sized bag is my six-shooter and a box of shotshell. Aside from the double barrel shotgun Bella keeps under her side of the bed, this is the only weapon we have. It's a grim but needed reminder of our past lives. They are lives, apparently, we won't ever be able to leave behind.

I replace the plumbing access after stuffing the box and plastic bag into the space, and tuck the revolver into the of my back, hiding it under my plain gray sweatshirt. Bella's watching the post-game interview with the Seahawk's coach when I tell her goodbye and jaunt down the stairwell to the street and the restaurant below.

The pizza place is nearly empty, aside from a fisherman I recognize. I walk to the counter and stand next to the register, waiting for Willie to emerge from the kitchen with the best pepperoni and black olive calzone this side of Italy.

Instead, there's a tap on my shoulder. I start to turn, my right hand moving to the revolver, and a man says below his breath, just behind my ear, "Don't reach for the piece in your waistband. It's not necessary."

I stop and slowly spin to see a familiar face. I've never met the man, and I don't remember his name. But I've seen him before. The ease of his smile is unforgettable.

"I'm Bernard Francis," he says, extending his hand. "I've been looking for you for two years now."

"I didn't want to be found," I don't take his hand. "Willie!" I turn and call into the kitchen. Our large calzone is sitting atop the pizza oven. It's got *Quentin* scribbled on the side of the box.

"Can we talk for a minute?" he slips his hands into his khaki pockets. He's wearing a black golf windbreaker over a high, white turtleneck. "I came a long way to meet you." It's still not registering who he is.

"What do you want?" I'm craning to find Willie. He's not answering. "What did you do with Willie?"

"I didn't do anything with Willie," he says, hands still in his pocket. "If you're talking about the owner, he's in the bathroom."

As if on cue and over the man's shoulder, Willie emerges from the unisex bathroom. He sees me and waves, then points to the visitor and mouths, "That's him!" just as he turns around.

"So you know I've been looking for you, then?" he asks, turning back to look me in the eyes.

"Maybe," I say, "but it doesn't change anything. I'm not interested in what you're selling."

"Five minutes," he pleads. "Then I'll leave you alone."

Willie passes us and snakes behind the counter to grab the calzone. He walks it to the register and sets it down. "No charge today, buddy," he says. "It's on me."

I thank Willie, pick up the box, and turn to walk out. The visitor is still standing by the register when I turn around to butt push the door open. His hands in his pockets he doesn't say anything until the nanosecond before the door closes. I'm already on the sidewalk when he calls out.

"What about Bella?"

Damn it!

Securing the calzone with one hand, I reopen the door and march back into the restaurant. Willie must sense my irritation. He moves swiftly into the kitchen, disappearing like a barkeep in a western right before the shootout.

"What about Bella?" I ask, knowing that pretending I don't know what he's talking about will only waste my time.

"I have a proposition for the two of you," he says. "Five minutes." His smile spreads across his face again and it hits me.

"I know you," I wag my finger at him and walk toward him with less trepidation. "You're the former FBI guy. I saw you on cable."

He presses his lips together and nods. "That was me."

"You defended me," I remember. "I saw that."

"I just read between the lines," he says, guiding me toward a booth. "It never made sense to me that you were randomly violent."

"I am violent," I slide the calzone box onto the table and sit down across from him.

"Not randomly," he shakes his head. "You were always concerned with self-preservation above all else. That was just my gut feeling."

"So what do you want?" The calzone's going to get cold.

"My colleagues and I believe you and Bella would make outstanding assets," he pulls a card from his breast pocket and lays it on top of the box. "Outstanding."

"I've been down this road before," I wave him off. "No offense…"

"Bernard Francis."

"No offense Mr. Francis, but we're happy and safe hiding out here on the island," I explain.

"Is that why you have a gun in the small of your back?" his smile returns.

"I'm from Texas," I remind him. "I have a gun."

"Look," he says, "I'm not going to go with the hard sell here. I know you've been through more than most. You're just a regular guy with some extraordinary abilities."

"I have extraordinary luck."

"Whatever it is," he lowers his voice, "you're sitting here."

"It's luck," I assure him.

"I'll leave it as this, Jackson," he's speaking in a hushed tone as he leans in, no doubt smelling the goodness of the calzone. "We do a lot of work that's off the books. We do the things the feds cannot or will not do. We're good. We're effective. We're everywhere. We are the Halliburton of black ops."

"I thought Halliburton was the Halliburton of black ops," I chuckle.

"Just think about it," he says and pushes himself out of the booth. "There's no deadline. You're always welcome."

"Okay."

"I've already wiped clean your considerably dirty slate," he says. "Same for Bella. We can start fresh with new identities, ones far better than what your friend Wolodymyr can concoct." He stands and offers me his hand. This time I take it.

Bernard Francis nods his head, smiles one more toothy grin, and turns to leave. He pushes his way through the door, turns right and disappears. My guess is he'll catch the next ferry off of the island.

I pull the card from the table and read it.

BERNARD FRANCIS, LEAD ANALYST
WIGNOCK HOMELAND INTELLIGENCE GROUP
BF@WHIG.ORG

The card stock is super thick and I rub my thumb over the raised letters of his name. There's no phone number and no address, only the email address. The backside of the card is blank. I stuff it in my pocket and pick up the calzone box.

"It's clear!" I yell to Willie and head for the door. "Nobody died."

The climb up the stairs to the apartment is agonizing, as much because I'm suddenly starving as it is because I'm not sure what to say to Bella.

That fear evaporates when I reach the door to our apartment. She's standing in the doorway, leaning against it, her arms are folded across her chest. She knows something.

"So when were you going to tell me?" she smirks, blocking me from entering the apartment.

"Tell you what?" I play dumb and try to hand her the box. She doesn't take it.

"The gun is missing from the bathroom," she says. "And it took you way too long to bring back dinner."

"Okay."

"That guy leaving Willie's," she motions to the street below with her chin. "What did he want?"

I reach into my pocket and pull the card. She takes it, flips it over, and reads it.

"He offering us a job?" She walks into the apartment, reclaiming her spot on the love seat. There is a pair of wine glasses, half full of a seasonal red, sitting on the coffee table. Next to them are a stack of paper napkins and a couple of plates.

"Yes," I carefully set the box next to the plates. "He thinks we're bored and talented."

"We are."

I open the box and the aroma of the calzone momentarily overpowers the lavender. Ripping it in half, I plop a huge piece onto a plate. I have to pull at the cheese rope connecting her plate to the box.

"What's the job?" She reaches for her wine and takes a sip.

"I don't know," I say, still processing her admission of boredom.

"When do we have to let him know? What's the deadline?"

"There isn't one."

"Hmm." She picks the plate up with one hand and carefully takes a bite of calzone.

"So you're bored?" I ask.

"I'm watching football, Jackson," she says. "I'm obsessed with lavender. What do you think?"

"You're bored."

"You are too. Don't get me wrong," she clarifies, wiping her mouth with a napkin. "I'm happy. I love you. We're good. But don't you miss the action?"

"You mean death around every corner?"

"Not exactly. But yes. I couldn't wait to live a normal life with you. Now, a normal life with you is the one in which we're running for our lives. We're righting wrongs."

"Breaking into secret labs and blowing apart iconic architectural achievements?"

"Exactly!" She takes another bite of calzone.

I pick up my slice and inhale the smell of the mozzarella and buttered crust. Before I take a bite, I reach around to the small of my back and pull out the revolver, laying it flat on the table.

The absurdity of our lives has never been more evident. We're a pair of addicts, codependent and in love. We need the rush as much as we need each other. There's no other answer. No choice. At some point we'll need a fix. Not yet. But it's coming.

ACKNOWLEDGMENTS

There's no acknowledgment suitable for the support, love, and guidance my wife, Courtney, gives me in writing and in our life together. Without her, these stories wouldn't exist. So if you love them, you love her. If you don't like them, blame her.

Our children, Samantha and Luke, are equally inspirational in the hopeful way in which they view the world. They make me confident our future is in good hands.

Thank you to Michael Wilson and Anthony Ziccardi for their confidence in my work. Their team at Post Hill Press does a fantastic job of getting books into the hands of readers.

Felicia A. Sullivan, editor-in-chief, I am grateful you take the time to wade through my gobbledygook, both literally and figuratively, to grind and polish my mess into a cohesive, fast-paced narrative.

Ryan Truso, your cover designs do a stellar job of conveying the story without words. Thank you.

My fearless team of beta readers who tell me what's wrong and what's right with the story in its earliest phases, is beyond comparison. Gina Graff, Tim Heller, Mike Harnage, Steven Konkoly, and Curt Sullivant, I appreciate your critical eyes and willingness to be brutally honest. Additional thanks to Curt for his aviation expertise and to Mike for his knowledge of weaponry.

Thanks to the fellow authors who've been kind enough to help promote my work as they work on their own; Steven Konkoly, Murray

McDonald, Clayton Anderson, Bobby Akart, A.R. Shaw, Ian Graham, and Russell Blake.

And to my parents, Sanders and Jeanne Abrahams, my sister Penny Rogers, brother Steven Abrahams, my in-laws Don and Linda Eaker, thanks for your daily (bordering on Spammish) promotion of my work. I love all of you.

Finally, thanks to the readers who buy these stories and then take the time to write me and tell me what they think. It's my favorite part of this...other than typing THE END.

EXCERPT FROM *SEDITION*

For a man known to make noise literally and figuratively, Dexter Foreman's death was remarkably silent.

He was alone in his office.

Foreman liked to have one half hour of office solitude each morning to read the paper and drink a cup of fully caffeinated coffee. He often joked coffee was a drink that, without caffeine, served no godly purpose.

It wasn't just the sense of quiet, the newsprint, and the Arabica he enjoyed in his office. A student of architecture, Foreman loved the neoclassical style of the room; the two-foot rise of its domed ceiling, the niches inset into the curved walls. He admired the Eighteenth Century sentiment.

He and his wife had chosen to honor the office's first occupant with green accents throughout. The subtle pea green of the rug complemented the alternating white pine and walnut flooring.

The matching curtains and valances on the windows were muted with cream sheers. It was colorful but tasteful. Historians loved the homage to an earlier time. Despite the office being more ceremonial than practical, Foreman loved his time there.

He was reading *The New York Times,* a below-the-fold article about his efforts to enhance Public Law 107-56, an act initially designed to "provide appropriate tools required to intercept and obstruct terrorism". He'd not gotten past reporter Helene Cooper's byline.

The moment the artery blew within his head, he felt a sharp lightning bolt of pain as the blood exploded into his brain.

The last image he saw was the portrait of George Washington hanging in its gilded frame above the white marble fireplace across from his desk on the north side of the room.

He lost focus. The portrait dissolved to black. His eyes fixed.

His face dropped onto the thick English oak, cracking the bridge of his nose. Blood pooled resolutely around his head, sticking to the gel in his styled salt and pepper hair. It leeched onto the corner of the *Times*.

Had it not been for a planned meeting in his office just three minutes later, his body might have gone unnoticed for a half hour. But because of the meeting, his senior aide knocked on the northwest door of the office just forty five seconds after the vessel popped.

That aide knocked twice, as was the custom with Foreman, and then opened the thick door from the hallway outside. The young man's head was down as he entered the room. He lifted it to meet Foreman's eyes with his. But instead of the expected nod from his boss, he saw him slumped on the desk across the room.

His mind flooded with confusion and panic. At first he wasn't certain he was processing the scene correctly. There was a bright, diffused light from the triplet of south facing windows directly behind the desk. It backlit Foreman's body and made it difficult for the aide to focus. And what the aide saw before him appeared surreal: a cup of coffee, a newspaper, and an unconscious, bleeding Dexter Foreman.

He hurried to the desk, lifted his wrist to his mouth, and spoke hurriedly.

"Bandbox respond. Boxer is down. Boxer is down."

Two other doors swung open into the office from the rose garden outside and from an adjacent smaller room. Men in dark suits rushed to the desk, their fingers on the DAK triggers of their drawn .357 Sig Sauer P229 side arms.

"Sir?" The aide touched Foreman's shoulder, not expecting a response.

Regardless, he repeated himself as three more suited, armed men ran into the office. This was not the meeting on the schedule.

"Mr. President?" The aide's voice was shaky. He swallowed hard past the thick lump at the top of his throat, focusing on the empty distant gaze in Foreman's eyes. His own welled.

Steam rose from the cup of coffee to Dexter Foreman's right. It was inches from his hand, untouched and black.

The president was dead.

ABOUT THE AUTHOR

Tom is a veteran television journalist and author who has spent the last 20-plus years covering the biggest stories of our time.

He's interviewed Presidents, cabinet members, and leaders in congress. He's reported live from the White House and Capitol Hill, Chernobyl, The Canadian Badlands, the barrios of Mexico City, Central America, and the Amazon Jungle.

Tom's covered five national political conventions. He has flown with presidential candidates, gone backstage at their rallies, and broken stories about them on television and online.

He was at the Pentagon while smoke still rose in the hours after 9/11 and was in the room when Secretary Colin Powell made his case to the U.N. Security Council for war against Iraq.

Tom lives in the Houston suburbs with his wife, Courtney, and their two children.